The Confession of Dieter Berenson

by

Nicholas Leigh

Cover by Charlie Tetlow

First published 2015

Published by Liborwich Publishing

Contact us at:

liborwichpublishing@gmail.com

Dedicated to
Bambos Charalambous, Nana Prempeh,
Sarah Brent and Eleanor Best

And in memory of
Anne and Manny Bloom, and
Sally and Jimmy Leigh

London

Chapter 1

Steam rose from the coffee. He noticed how good the china was.

'Milk?'

He nodded. A small trail of near-cream was poured into his cup. Scott Roth wondered why on earth he was being treated so well by a lawyer he'd never met at a firm he'd never heard of. Following the call, he'd decided he had no reason not to come. Now he was here, though, he wished he'd stayed away. A scarecrow in his clothes, ill at ease, he felt his age and then some, forty years a stone in his shoe. His eyes drifted over to the endless panes of glass surrounding them, hardly a wall to be seen even though they were on the seventh floor of a fancy building in a fancy part of London. Other lawyers were visible, working on matters of a no doubt equally confidential nature, suits and papers and crystal-clear light. He looked at the man preparing him a drink in an office of success.

He shouldn't have come.

The lawyer said, handing him the coffee, sitting on the other side of the desk. 'It's taken longer to track you down than I'd have liked.'

'If I'd known you were trying to find me,' Roth replied, 'I would have helped you look.'

'I'm sorry I couldn't tell you more on the phone.'

'Don't you mean "anything"?'

Brittle, and they'd only just met. The lawyer, in his mid-fifties, a scalp as smooth as silk. Roth, the long-term inhabitant of desperate places, unkempt where the lawyer was smart; conscious of having gone feral – and embarrassed about that fact. Both weary for different reasons, not at their best; at least they each recognised it in the other, and tried hard to accommodate the strain as best they could.

'Do you remember Dieter Berenson?' the lawyer asked.

'Of course.'

'I'm sorry to be the one who tells you this. He died five days ago.'

A look of dismay passed across Roth's face. *How could Dieter be dead?* A man destined to outlive the next five generations, surely. Gone: that priceless grin when he'd got his way at eye-watering cost to his competitor; modest until that moment, when you realised a fraction too late to save yourself that you were out of your depth dealing with this guy. The moment he'd first seen him? During a meeting, while Roth was working for someone else. Shortly afterwards, a call on his mobile: Dieter offered him a job right there on the phone. 'You don't want to interview me?' Roth had asked. 'I know all I need already,' Berenson had replied. That, along with a pay rise of fifty per cent, was how Scott Roth came to work for Dieter. A man of wealth, taste, judgement and power. *How could he be dead?*

'You were fond of him?' the lawyer asked.

'I'm – he was . . . good to me. I haven't seen him for ten years. The smartest man I ever met. That's . . . What happened?'

'His housekeeper found him dead in his study when she brought in his breakfast. He'd died during the night, at his desk, still at work.'

'Alone?'

'Yes.'

'I'm . . . I can't – Poor Dieter . . .'

'He was a man of secrets.'

'I know about his sideline. But I only worked with him for eight months.'

'You were an important part of his business.'

'Not at all, just a lowly functionary in his team.'

The lawyer fell silent. Dark circles ran round his eyes, from which fell a gaze of immense unhappiness. No traces of family on his desk, no hints of a personality – yet he was suffering too. *So what,* thought Roth. Such matters were no longer his business. He looked around the room, at a wall of boxes running along the edge of the office. Scrawled on the side was a hieroglyph of bad handwriting. He wondered what lay within, if they were part of one case, a moss of paper that would grow until it filled the glass office, an ecosystem strewn with the debris of a narrow-focused life. And the lawyer himself, fighting all kinds of deadlines in his mind, his *soul*, lost among the paper, missing in action.

'Do you have any idea why you're here?' he asked.

'No,' Roth replied. 'Should I?'

'You don't like answering questions.'

'I don't like getting the kind of call I got from you.'

'Dieter Berenson was my friend as well as my client. His death is upsetting to say the least.'

'I'm sorry to hear that,' Roth said, with a tone that still said he wondered what on earth any of this had to do with him.

'Berenson liked you.'

'We got on fine.'

A piercing gaze. 'You travelled around the world with him?'

'Pretty much.'

'In the limo? On the plane?'

Roth replied, 'I went wherever he wanted me to go, whenever he wanted me to go, by what means he wanted me to take. I travelled with him virtually all the time anyway, so what he did, I did. Where he went, I went.'

'You know he became a very rich man.'

'He was rich ten years ago.'

'He was vastly richer when he died.'

Roth felt like he was being judged, without knowing why. Yes, he knew Berenson had millions – but *they* had called *him*.

'You enjoyed working with him?' the lawyer asked.

'The job was fine, the money good, I liked him, yes, but . . . but I still don't understand what any of this—'

'Why did you stop working for him?'

The lawyer's tone was starting to grate, but Roth decided he might as well answer the questions – he had nothing better to do, not today, not this week, not for the rest of his life. 'I left because it wasn't what I wanted, certainly not at that time in my life. I wanted to do something a little . . .' Roth gave a sad little sigh. 'Dieter wasn't happy when I told him, but he made no big deal. There was no reason for him to. I carried his bags, that's all. I was smart and knew my place, I didn't give him the slightest trouble, but any number of people could have done what I did. I'm sure he'd forgotten about me a couple of days after I'd gone.'

The lawyer nodded. 'All right,' he said, and fell silent, descending into obviously painful thought. Meanwhile, the room of glass did little to put Roth at ease. He wanted to remain invisible, yet here he was, in a goldfish bowl, being stared at by nameless bods in the adjacent offices. Did they know his business? If so, they were a step ahead of him. The meeting, requested by the lawyer as a matter of urgency: another non sequitur in his life. No information about its content, just a time and place – and a diktat that he tell no one else on pain of death.

'Okay,' the lawyer said finally, coming back to life (insofar as Roth could tell). He opened a drawer and took from it a large envelope. From inside that came a smaller envelope and a legal document a few pages long. The lawyer laid them next to each other on the desk. Roth saw that the small envelope had his name printed on it.

'I don't propose we go through this,' the lawyer said, indicating the document. 'But I would understand if you wanted to check its contents.'

'What is it?'

'Dieter's will.'

'It looks short.'

'It contains all it needs to; I drafted it.'

'Am I in it?'

'Yes.'

Roth felt a flush of discomfort. 'What does it say?'

'"To Scott Roth, I leave the envelope contained within my safe which is marked with his name."'

The envelope that sat next to the document.

The lawyer said, 'Do you know how many others are referred to in Dieter's will?'

'Hundreds, probably.'

'No one.'

Roth felt his gaze hollow out. He forgot about the people watching him from beyond the glass walls. 'What?'

'No one else is named in Dieter's will. Just you.'

Roth stared at the document.

'He never told me what's in this,' the lawyer said, handing Roth the envelope with his name on it. 'I've booked a room for you to open it, look inside.' But Roth could tell the lawyer was dying to know what it contained. 'I can offer you refreshments, whatever you like. We're well stocked here.'

Without thought or sense, he was about to tear open the envelope. But then he paused, looked to his right through the goldfish bowl's wall, and realised no one could care less about him or his reasons for being here. The other lawyers and clients were consumed by their own concerns, phones attached to their ears, coffee steaming on their desks, papers everywhere. He felt silly, precious and, most of all, invisible. He opened the envelope.

Inside, he found two smaller ones.

'What is this?' he said. 'A Russian doll?'

Even the lawyer looked confused.

Roth opened the first of the smaller envelopes. From inside, he took a key and a business card. '"Mikhail Banking Ltd",' he said, reading the name.

'A private bank,' the lawyer noted. 'In Mayfair, but you wouldn't have a clue if you walked past it. Discreet, to say the least.'

'"Gordon Weston, consultant".' He turned the card over. On the back was a long number, a dozen digits or more. 'Do you have any idea what this is?'

The lawyer took a look. 'Maybe a code for an account.'

Roth put the card and key on the desk and picked up the other envelope. He opened it and chuckled when he saw the contents. 'A hundred pounds,' he reported, smiling at Dieter's twisted sense of humour. 'A valuable legacy indeed.'

The lawyer sat back, fazed, in the salt mines of thought. He looked at Roth, unguarded. 'I don't get it.'

'Neither, it seems, do I.'

'This doesn't make sense. That . . .' He trailed off for a few moments; his brain was running into walls left and right, his face confused. Roth watched his mental contortions until the lawyer realised he was beaten and looked at the pale, hungry man in the chair opposite. 'Do you want my advice?'

'As long as it doesn't cost me a hundred pounds.'

'Go and see Gordon Weston right away.'

Again, why not: *he had nothing better to do.* He'd resented the lawyer's call, as if this stranger knew how unimportant he was, how lacking in value he'd rendered himself, how he'd cut his own life off at the knees. The lawyer called for him at his point of maximum weakness – the apex of his self-inflicted doom. Made to dance for wealthy professionals serving the super-rich, the *high net worthies* whose company and credit so many of the fakes in this world wanted to make. The lawyer had been wholly uninterested in Roth as anything other than Berenson's boy, but what if Weston was the kind of guy who insisted on pointless chat? *What do you do? How's business? How's the wife? Oh, you don't have a wife . . . Or a home of your own . . . Or any money (except for a hundred pounds, hahaha) . . . Or any career prospects . . . Or a career at all . . . Or friends . . . Or family . . . Or . . . Or . . .* Small talk would force Roth to admit that his life was over but for the small detail of starvation, to which he'd been inching ever closer when the call from the lawyer came. He had no idea how the man tracked down his number, but it was timely: any longer and the only way he'd have been able to contact Roth would have been through a medium.

The Mikhail banker tried hard to hide his curiosity. As one would expect in such tasteful and discreet surroundings, Weston was composure personified. So tidy that he looked as if he'd been grown inside his suit, the banker was solicitous, welcoming and sincere from the moment Roth arrived in a cab straight from the lawyer's office (using as little of his hundred-pound windfall as possible – it should have been less but the bank was almost impossible to find). But when Weston saw the long number on the back of the business card and the key, he could no longer contain his zeal. His eyes began to sparkle. 'The account *is* real!' he exclaimed. He was the least stuffy character Roth had met for a long time. Abundant, convivial, youngish, plumpish, animated, clearly the kind of guy who made a good father and a good child, super-bright; Roth wondered if he shouldn't pay attention to the man's excitement after all. 'There's been not a sliver of activity on this account since it was opened,' Weston said. 'We had no idea who its true owner might be. A woman set it up, a secretive lady. She was . . . *intangible*, clearly a proxy. It's not just the Lord who moves in mysterious ways! To this day, we still don't know who the true owner is.' He smiled coyly. 'This sort of thing doesn't happen as often as you think.'

'I don't think about it at all,' Roth replied. 'It belonged to Dieter Berenson.'

The banker's eyes lit up. 'Aha! Aaaaa-ha! Well, that explains a lot! Mr Roth, I'm sure you're dying to inspect the contents of the box. We have a private room where you can open it. And while you're there, can we offer you refreshments – coffee, tea, food? Yes we can: whatever you want!'

And so, Scott Roth sat in a private room in a private bank in the middle of private Mayfair. The pretty female attendant who accompanied him said he could take as long as he needed, before leaving him alone. When the door closed behind her, a sheet of anxiety wrapped itself round his shoulders; the tasteful solemnity of the bank did nothing to assist his mood. The sheen of comfort might have been welcoming to those used to such finery, but he was not, and felt stuck in a fancy prison cell. The last thing he wanted to do was look inside the shallow steel box on the table in front of him, the box Weston had arranged for him to open and inspect, the box settled upon him by the mysterious proxy on behalf of Dieter Berenson. How keen all of these people were to do everything for him, to do anything at all! How sweet the attendant, how brightly she'd smiled, a grin at his reduced state surely, condescension at the mistakes he'd made in his life. But then, if he didn't open the box, he'd be stuck in this airless room for ever. It occurred to him that he could just sit here for a while and tell them all that he'd looked inside, and the box contained only Dieter's toothbrush. But then one had never been able to tell quite what Dieter was up to, and so with this tickle, his old dead boss had piqued his interest enough for him to have to take a look.

He unlocked the box, flipped back the lid in response to those rich fuckers, tilted the container so its contents would slide into his hand.

Plunk plunk! He could feel . . . *two more envelopes.*

He sighed, to no one's notice but his own. *Maybe I should open a stationer's.* He took the envelopes from the box and glared at them with some impatience. Neither had any markings on them.

A hunger pang struck; he was going to be sick. He should have taken the offer of food. *Stupid bloody pride.* Bottles of water sat on the table, standard issue. He opened one and drank from its neck, keeping going until it was done. Ugh, *felt good.* He twisted open the second and downed that too. As soon as he was finished with this private room and private bank he'd use his hundred pounds for a final blowout, a last supper – and speed up the process with a dozen packs of painkillers and a bottle of strongest vodka.

He opened the smaller of the two envelopes. It contained a key similar to the one he'd used to open the box. Strong, precise – serious banking business. The envelope also held within its robust form a sheet of paper on which had been written two numbers in a scrawly, rapid hand. One looked like a telephone number. The other, longer – a code for an account?

What shall I eat when I leave here, he thought.

He opened the larger envelope. Inside: a handwritten letter. Across the top, a scribble he recognised: *'My dear Scottie . . .'*

Only now did he notice a third envelope stuck in the bottom of the private box – it had failed to slide out with the others. He reached in for it, this envelope a lot thicker than the previous pair, significantly heavier too. He tore it open.

A warm numbness passed through his body.

The wad was bound in paper ribbon marked '100 x £50'. He stared at the numbers, thought about calling the pretty attendant, but had no idea what he expected her to say or do. The wad continued to stare at him, proving not to evaporate on closer inspection but remaining present, stark in its attention-seeking, the patterns it drew before his eyes.

The numb faintness was replaced by a surge of excitement. With rapid, clashing fingers he tore open the envelope. Its guts spilled many more wads of cash, all bound in the same fashion. Tumbling on to the table like a welcome rain, each bearing the same binding, each composed of the same weight. He piled them up, a tower of money, let his hand rest atop it; it was firm and strong beneath his palm, flat, crisp and freshly minted. His eyes ran up and down the column, tracing the dimensions, thinking that each wad was more money than he'd seen for years.

Each wad: a hundred £50 notes.

Twelve wads in all.

Sixty thousand pounds!

He burst into tears. A moment ago he was on the brink of disaster. Dieter Berenson had appeared from his past and, just like that, had saved him from utter ruin.

Chapter 2

His misty eyes travelled over the remarkable landscape, the pile of money that was his. He was trembling with shock and delight. In ten years it had never occurred to him to ask Berenson for help – his old boss would have laughed long and hard about how he'd been right, had he even remembered who Roth was. Yet he *had* remembered, and now his old employee, who'd woken this morning with no money and a large hole in his stomach where food should be, had sixty thousand pounds. Berenson's timing had always been impeccable.

He wiped away the tears, picked up the letter and began to read. *'My dear Scottie,'* it said, in Berenson's scraggly but legible handwriting, *'I suspect you must be wondering why all of this mystery. Well, I have something to give you that is of great value. Others want it too; no doubt they're following you already.'*

He thought, *wha—???*

The note continued: *If you are reading this, then you have also found the little consideration I left for you. Use this money; more than that, enjoy it – the Scott Roth I knew was in need of lightening up. Don't be offended! I say it with great fondness. I've met many people in my life, high born, low born, super rich, dirt poor, classy, classless, skinny, fat, ugly and pretty – I've seen it all. And though I may not have shown it, I liked you so much more than everyone else. You followed your path; I respected that. But I have kept an eye on you ever since you left my employ. Nothing sinister – don't get worried! I simply wanted to know where you were, and that you were safe. Is that so bad?*

'What the fuck?' Roth exclaimed to himself.

The dead man continued. *Yes, I kept a tab on you in case I ever needed to get in touch. I had a series of detectives check in on you every now and then. I made sure to tell no one, not even my lawyer – whom you've met by now. He's a little stiff, but they often are. Scottie, you had no idea how disappointed I was when you quit your job. You wanted to carry out your work, which seemed so important to you at the time, but I had high hopes for you with my organisation. I was younger myself then, and annoyed, and prickly. You wanted to go and I didn't want to make you stay. Now I would have done everything to stop you.*

So you must be wondering – what's so secret?! Sadly, the dead cannot be anything but dead, and even I was not so cocky as to assume I'd live for ever. I have no idea how I will have gone, which is a peculiar notion as I sit here and write this. But you know I don't dwell on unprofitable thoughts or matters. In the event of my death, I have only one wish: to make sure my treasure is looked after by someone I trust and who I know is *trust. No one must find it but you, Scottie, so I have made it rather hard to locate. It may take you some time, and you'll have to work out a few things before you can proceed. This little pile of cash will fund you while you search. As I say, use it.* Enjoy *it.*

He looked at the £60,000 sitting on the table in front of him. *A little pile of cash?*

'Do you remember your confession?' Yes, Roth thought – I remember. He continued reading. *In the eight months you worked for me, the tasks I gave you required no more than a diligent, flexible nature and a conscientious work ethic. Despite this, I could see how talented you were. In a world of eaters of time, after five hours of your confession, I knew you were a good good person. And now I am dead, I turn to you. So, take your money, and go from this bank. You have a key and two numbers. I give you no more instructions lest they fall into the wrong hands. My dear Scottie, I know you will not let me down.*

He turned the paper over. There was no more, not even a signature.

He stared at the table in front of him: the cash, the key, the numbers—

He was being followed?

* * *

Weston sat with him, the banker's enthusiasm fostered by this unexpected development. 'Another key . . .' he mused. 'I'd guess it's for another private box. But it's not one of ours.'

'Any idea whose?' Roth asked.

'Not a clue. I mean, how many locks are there in the world?'

A dizzying amount.

'Anyway, welcome to the fold!' Weston said, passing him a series of items. 'Debit card, credit card, online password . . . I've approved a fifteen-thousand-pound limit for – well, whatever takes your fancy.'

'Thanks.'

'My pleasure! It's great to be in business with you.'

'We're in business?'

'We certainly are, with sixty thousand pounds percolating away!' Weston grinned. 'So what are you going to do now you have a nice nest egg?'

'I . . . unh . . . Actually, I have no idea.'

'Well, don't forget about us. Call any time, from any place in the world, and we'll assist you in your banking needs, your local needs – hey, call us if you just want to know how to spend it!'

Mikhail Banking sat on a road in a part of Mayfair Roth was convinced was not on the map – an area of London uncharted so as to provide opaque services for those with money they wanted to keep quiet. The only ambient sound was the noise of a car. A low-slung Audi with blacked-out windows seemed to slow as he came out of the bank, then rolled away into the maze of London's streets. He watched it go, its engine noise receding until he could hear only the breeze.

He stood, sixty thousand pounds the richer, tasked with the search for his old dead boss's hidden treasure, for which he had no clue where to start. All of this left him thinking that Weston had asked the spot-on question: what on earth was he going to do now?

At the very least, he knew for sure that he was *not* going back to the grotesque room he'd been renting in a shared house in south London. The cracks in the walls, the damp across the ceiling . . . The other down-and-outs who lived there were lost causes all, though he'd known that when he had moved in a couple of months ago, seeking shelter of his own after the Bradley Incident. He settled there to regroup, lay low, reconsider – at which point his meagre job had been taken from him, leaving him with no money, no sympathy and a body still in need of feeding (his ego had long since given up the ghost). In pursuit of his grand plan, Roth had learned over the years to pay a chunk of rent a few months in advance. On this occasion, the tactic had proved invaluable, for at least he had a roof to shelter beneath in the weeks after he'd been cleaned out by his last two projects. Over this unhappy period of time, he'd come to know every inch of disrepair in that house, with plenty of hours to study all of the corners of the property in which he was convinced he'd starve to death, unnoticed. To go back to that dump with sixty thousand pounds, surrounding himself again with the hateful and the venal? *A very bad idea.*

So that's what he should *not* do, but what he *should* do remained unclear. He was close to Oxford Street, Bond Street; he could have a blowout of epic proportions, flush the painful decade from his system, send a message to himself that things *had* changed. But, walking along the morning street, he had to ask himself if this was really the case. He'd thought so when he moved into his latest house share – and then had the misfortune of 'meeting' Anthea, to the extent that someone such as she 'met' someone such as he.

This miserable woman had been sitting in the kitchen of his latest grim accommodation, his supposed sanctuary, late one night, clutching papers. Fragile face, shoulders curving in on themselves, the distant stare of a once-pretty girl who no longer had any direction in which to look. Light blonde hair as stressed as the rest of her, clothes that seemed to make her vanish. She heard him, looked up. Their eyes met and, in that moment, she began to cry. He didn't know her; for once, he'd been trying to ignore his housemates, to the extent of no longer even knowing when one moved in or out – but the bad find the good as nature abhors a vacuum. She had wide-open teary eyes, expressing appreciation before any service had been offered; eyes that said it's only a matter of time before that appreciation had a reason for being.

Roth ignored her, set the kettle to boil, prepared a cup of tea. But Anthea continued to cry. And cry. *And cry.* He could resist no more, made another drink and took them both to the table. He placed one in front of her, the tea's warm goodness displayed in its curling steam, and sat down. She smiled at him through the tears. In a large house, people came and went with disheartening regularity, a revolving cast of thousands. His cool, quiet way showed uncommon substance. Anthea took the tea and gave him the papers without a word exchanged. He scanned them. His heart sank. 'Why do you owe so much?' he asked her.

'I took out a loan for three hundred,' she said.

'They want two *thousand*.'

She looked at him with eyes as wide as saucers. 'They'll hurt me if I don't pay.'

He knew that. Just like he knew he was being had. This is what he'd been trying to escape by coming to this house, intending to vanish among their number. He continued to read the papers beneath the gaze of a leaky roof, wallpaper half-hanging over the sinks, trying to make sense of the mess she'd got herself into, trying to find a moment to slip away.

'Perhaps you could talk to them?' she asked. 'They don't treat men the same way.'

'I don't know about—'

'Please,' she begged. 'I don't have anyone to turn to.'

The extent to which he did *not* want to have this conversation could not be quantified. And yet she was dialling the number, handing him the plasticky mobile phone. The next thing he knew he was talking to a hardcore lowlife.

'She fuckin' owes us a fortune,' the heavy heavy said. 'She's gotta pay according to the terms.'

'But she's in dire straits,' Roth had replied.

'She's a fuckin' waste of space. No one forced her to do shit. She knew what she was doin' and now she's trying to wriggle out of paying what she owes, by getting you involved. She's a fuckin' liar. Lucky we haven't broken her legs. *Yet.*'

'But you have to give her a chance.'

'Why?'

'Listen, I'm—'

'What the fuck *you* wastin' your time for? You got nothin' better to do than piss around helping this piece of shit? You're a fuckin' mug, my friend.'

'You don't need to be so rude, okay? It doesn't help that you're charging such ridiculous interest.'

'Listen, prick: no one forced her to borrow the money. She took it knowing the rate. And she took it knowing she couldn't pay it back, or else she was gonna get some fuckin' fool to pick up her tab. Is that what you are?'

Roth ignored the aggression. 'What'll it take to clear the debt?'

'She pays us what she fuckin' owes.'

Roth looked at Andrea – who could hear everything the loan shark was saying. She shook her head vigorously.

'To clear this debt?' Roth said. 'A debt that's only come about because of these awful rates of interest? So what if you're right, and I am the fool who'll pick up the tab? I'll ask you again: what'll it take to clear the debt?'

'What she fuckin' owes.'

The negotiations continued in the same, grinding vein for an hour. Despite their hard-nosed stance, the loan sharks eventually recognised that, with this moronic Good Samaritan on the scene, they may get at least some of their money back. So, for twelve hundred, Anthea's loan of three hundred was settled. Roth thought she'd explode with joy. He made the transfer online, cleaning out the last of his savings. She promised to pay him back within six months, every last penny. No one had ever treated her with such kindness, she cried, he must be the nicest guy in the world, she'd go back to work, cleaning, whatever it took to repay. She was so effusive Roth wondered if he'd been too hasty in giving up his grand project, that perhaps he shouldn't have been so disillusioned by the Bradley Incident and all that came before.

The next morning, he woke to learn that Anthea had moved out of the house without saying a word. No contact details, no forwarding address. That was the last he saw of her or his twelve hundred.

Moron. He was furious at himself for getting duped yet again. Rehab was supposed to follow three simple steps: one, find somewhere new to live; two, stay down and save up; three – *don't offer to help anyone,* the last being the easiest: it only required that he keep his mouth shut and that, should anyone flutter their eyes, or cough sadly, or whimper the extent of their troubles, he say nothing. *What was so hard about that?* It wasn't even like he enjoyed it any more. Looking back across his shattered decade, he wasn't sure he ever had.

He wondered where Anthea was now, with his chit for twelve hundred. Long gone, moved on, her conscience trouble-free. Bradley? Hopefully at the bottom of a staircase in a heap, one leg pointing east, the other west, his skull a pizza on the floor. The others too. They probably remembered Roth as much as they recalled their last tub of bathwater (for those who bothered to bathe). What an amazing legacy for ten years of painstaking, ruinous work.

The sound of a car accelerating.

He looked in its direction, anxious. When he saw a taxi, he calmed, thought again those magic words:

SIXTY THOUSAND POUNDS!!!!

Anthea, Bradley and the hundreds like them dissolved in the wash. Saved by his dead saviour! How could he be anything but thrilled?! He pinched himself, for symbolic as well as actual reasons. In the distance, he saw the Dorchester. *All right, Dieter, you really want me to start enjoying myself . . . ?!*

* * *

He booked in to the grand hotel. A valet guided him to his room; they walked along halls that contrasted vividly with the feral estate he'd crossed this morning on the way to see the lawyer. Carpet underfoot rather than vomit; tender voices instead of shrill neighbours, the leeching, the playing upon his sympathy; the sudden appearance of faces lest they arrive too late and the generous man has nothing left to give. And now it was a weekday afternoon and he was sitting in his own room in the Dorchester.

Super-plush bedclothes, a glorious view across Hyde Park, tea and coffee making facilities appropriate for royalty, a bathroom full of unctions and towels fluffy enough to soak up a week; not a shade of damp, no cracks whatsoever, just style, class, peace. And a valuable intangible: it hadn't struck him in the past, but he could see why famous people stayed in expensive hotels: it sure was nice to hide from the world when suddenly you felt at your most visible.

Chapter 3

He woke in the middle of the night, a surge of memories, the last six months the worst of his life. Faces of ingratitude, of *hatred* for what he was trying to achieve. His help came with no trace of an obligation upon those complaining that no one ever tried to help them, the world so harsh and unfair. These same people sneered at him when he moved into a new house and said *I am that help*.

He lay back, still in food deficit despite his feast the night before. He'd fallen upon dinner in the Dorchester's restaurant with what he hoped would be the last of his desperation for a while. Near-starvation was almost worth it for the resurrecting joy of consumption. His body was then caressed by the sheets, the mattress, his head by the pillow. He thought of the umpteen troubled beds he'd slept in over the years. A lumpy mattress. A rotten underlay. A toxic pillow. *All gone!* In their place, thanks to Dieter, a chamber fit for a king. He hadn't slept so well in a decade, could sleep a decade more. The closeness of oblivion averted; the money a chance to escape. Sixty thousand wouldn't last for ever – but it certainly did enable him to start again.

He put a soft light on, waking the air but not by much; got out of bed. The sheets reached for him, called him back, but he needed to eat, to fill the holes where food should be, all the way down in his legs. He surveyed the choices on the room service menu. After tilting back and forth, he ordered a burger and a pot of tea. With sustenance on its way, he wandered over to the window, where he gazed across Hyde Park, morning too far away to freshen the dark sky.

In the middle of the night, wide awake, come the thoughts.

The boss had been generous with his time as well as his money. Roth had been Berenson's assistant – his *gofer*. A fancy version, for sure, accompanying the big man wherever he went, travelling worldwide, but a bag-carrier nonetheless. The demands of the job matched his nature well. Roth was polite, focused, meticulous. Dieter: tetchy under stress, but dazzling, brilliant, a worldly entrepreneur with fine tastes and sophisticated opinions. Roth's job was the kind that led the right person to the right places. When he quit, it was not to improve his prospects but to resolve issues that had emerged during the confession Berenson had forced him to make. Oh, how they did not laugh at the irony . . .

A knock at the door – his food.

Burger satisfaction sent a warm glow through his body. Tea chased it down. He returned to his vantage point by the window, stared at the street below. Park Lane headed south to Hyde Park Corner, north to Marble Arch. London would spring to life again soon and so, it seemed, would he, as a man of means.

He reread the letter from Berenson, and arrived at the same conclusion as he had the first time: Yes, Dieter, but what do you want me to *do*?

He put it on the desk and curled back into the blissfully comfortable bed. Before he closed his eyes, he was asleep.

He woke after eight, delighted to find that he was still in the Dorchester, that it hadn't been a dream and that he wasn't back in his poky room in the dismal house share with the smack head on one side screaming at the TV and the ex-con on the other side screaming at his girlfriend. He wouldn't have to wait ages for the bathroom (only to find it disgusting) nor the kitchen's one pan or microwave (caked in dregs). He wouldn't have to suffer quiet intimidation from serial oafs, or worry that he was going to have his head kicked in, or his clothes stolen, or his food taken. The world around him was no longer cancer-grey, insulted, infused with a despair no one did anything to change. He wouldn't have to wonder what that substance in the toilet might be, or whether he'd caught fleas from sleeping in the bed, or if he could do anything about the smell in the fridge and food decaying in the cupboards. He wouldn't have to dumb down his speech to get through to his housemates while sitting among them watching abysmal TV. And if it went wrong, he wouldn't have to talk his way out of an argument or explain why his attempts at trying to help shouldn't be considered rude, intrusive, condescending . . .

The double whammy: good old Bradley cleaned out his cash; Anthea drained the last of his reserves. He could have weathered even this financial vortex had he not then had his job yanked away by his zombified ex-boss, as large a waste of space as anyone he'd ever met. He'd seen enough down-and-outs to know what awaited him when his paid-up rental period came to an end. The days to eviction had passed with frightening speed and debilitating slowness. He couldn't tell if he'd been stupid or naive and, thanks to his final two projects, he had no funds to divert these thoughts. He was getting hungrier and hungrier . . . And then his phone rang and it was the lawyer.

The voice, prodding from the edges of experience, so pleased to be speaking with Scott Roth at last. A call he'd taken while staring at the stains on his ceiling, thinking what a colossal failure his last ten years had been and wondering how on earth he was going to feed himself. This last question was no longer hypothetical, but a crucial, impending issue, for he was starting to feel the cramps of a severely constricted diet, the elemental panic of a body suspecting it was not going to get what it desperately needed. Maybe he wouldn't survive, for there was no one to help him; again, irony of ironies – *and then the call from the lawyer saved his life.*

It was time to get up, though he didn't know what for – other than a glorious Dorchester breakfast. The unblemished carpet welcomed his feet as he crossed the room from the luxurious bed to the dazzling en suite. He stepped into a shower Caesar might have enjoyed following a parade, the water so hot as to be decadent. The last three months – the last ten years – washed from his weary skin; he looked into the plughole and saw dribbling away the insults, the abuse, the cynical use of the victim mentality he'd endured for so long.

He took breakfast with unaccustomed grandeur, treated by the hotel staff with deference and respect – such alien notions! He couldn't remember the last time he'd eaten so pleasurably. An exquisite start to the day, and then his plates were cleared and he had a key that led to a treasure chest somewhere in the world – with no idea where to start looking.

Berenson had given him just one clue: the phone number written on the sheet of paper enclosed with the key. He sat in his room and punched in the numerous digits. His heart started to beat fast, a surge of excitement – a tone! Four rings became eight, eight sixteen – and then the line cut dead.

He sat for a moment, perplexed. He tried the number again; it connected – rang – rang-a-rang-a-rang – for sixteen tones and then cut out once more. He frowned. Looked at the clock – nine in the morning London time. Too early perhaps? He'd try again later.

On Oxford Street, swathes of people made a mockery of Berenson's warning that he was already being followed. Good luck to whoever they may be! He walked into Selfridges, the golden light, the infinite array. In menswear, the labels, the styles . . . How many trends he'd missed! How long since he'd bought himself clothes! After mooching, he stopped for a well-earned coffee and to consider what to purchase from the range of options. Even with disinclined eyes he'd racked up a sum of possibilities; denying himself much, he still spent more on clothes than he had in the last six years combined. And books and music and devices on which to read books and listen to music. How tasty the coffee when it washes down consumption! Giddy at the till! But sixty thousand wouldn't last long if he didn't set himself parameters. After this welcome splurge, he decided to avoid buying unnecessary *stuff*. Instead, for the first time in his life, he'd live well.

Although, to be honest, that simply meant not having to go back to a shared house, full of hostile, hateful strangers.

He returned to his Dorchester room for a late lunch, flushed with the delight of wanton spending, his own Christmas Day: he certainly enjoyed *that*. He put his trophies in a corner of the room and leapt on the bed in delight. He wanted to shower every few hours, at first just because it was so amazing and the water so hot, the bathing facilities so grand and the free soaps and shampoos and gels so enticing; but as he watched the water vanish down the plughole, he realised that he also still had more shite to clean from his skin, frustration ingrained, innumerable hard knocks and bruises to bring out; dead matter to scrub away, grit beneath his fingernails from hanging on in bad situations; the soreness of his back from all the times he'd been stabbed by those he was trying to help; he'd need to shower until he'd grown a new cover with no memory of the past.

In a vast towel, his toes curling in and out of the carpet, a newborn baby in a tub chair, listening to the silence, letting his mind wander – to places he'd rather it not go he flicked through the TV channels to find a gripping show or film, but everything was trite; he looked through the room service menu until he knew the listing inside out and no longer had an appetite; he couldn't decide which of his books to start reading, which of his records to start listening to.

He tried the number again. The dial tone chimed. And chimed. And kept on chiming until it disconnected after the sixteenth ring. He dialled once more. As he listened, he watched the clock. It was nearly three in the afternoon London time. Anywhere in the world, *somewhere* in the world, the receiver was bleating. Yet the line cut out yet again. He put the phone down, sat on the bed, trying to figure out what this clue-not-a-clue might mean. The Dieter Berenson he remembered loved a laugh but had no fondness for practical jokes. Does a man change in such a way over ten years? That he should claim to be a fan and yet send Roth on a wild goose chase with no means of navigating the route? He'd try again at midnight.

He stepped out of the hotel, to find a smart place for dinner. He walked along Park Lane before snaking through the backstreets of

Mayfair, a huge smile growing on his face every time he thought of Berenson's gift. He wanted to jump on a plane right now and go somewhere he'd never been. He didn't even need to pack, so meagre in number were the items of his life. His mind flooded with possibilities – the Rio carnival, the souks of Marrakesh, hiking the Inca Trail, reading the *New Yorker* in Greenwich Village, eating in patisseries in Vienna, taking a train to Moscow, living cheaply, nothing to keep him in this godforsaken—

A low-slung Audi with blacked-out windows drove past.

He took off like a startled horse, ran along streets filled with tourists and the rich. Fear made him feel ill as he dashed. He couldn't see the car ahead of him; daren't look over his shoulder in case it had circled round and was close behind. He emerged by the Royal Academy of Art, stumbling into a throng of people. Stuttering to a halt, sweating, his eyes scanned along Piccadilly, but there was no sign of the Audi or any other pursuer, just the bustling normality of a large London thoroughfare.

He'd seen a car, yes – in a city full of them he may well see a car . . . His breathing calmed, he felt stupid at being so frightened; there was nothing at all to be scared of, *you need to get a grip, Fortune has smiled on you at last. Don't be such an idiot: Berenson has told you to enjoy it, so enjoy it.*

He walked on to Hatchards and Fortnum and Mason; through Piccadilly Circus and Leicester Square to Covent Garden, by which time he'd forgotten all about low-slung Audis. Instead, his mind had filled with thoughts of Dieter. His old boss *did* have a fondness for food that might have clogged his pipes, along with the stress of his lifestyle. Fifty-seven years old but, it had to be said, if Berenson had had Roth followed all these years, he was significantly weirder than he'd thought. Dieter was a man of secrets, his own and others'. Confessor to the world, or so he liked to think; there was no one's innermost darkness he didn't want to hear about. But perhaps it had backfired. Perhaps someone had told him something so shocking that it had pushed him over the edge, his heart unable to cope. He consumed the secrets of others as he consumed his food. They became digested, broken down, absorbed. Behind secrets there stands damage, people with long memories and hostile intent. That, if nothing else, was bad for the health.

'Get 'em before they get you,' Berenson had liked to say. *'I don't mean in a homicidal way, I mean the kind of folk you're gonna come across will take all they can and will chuck you away when they're done, but only if you let 'em. So, the answer is: don't let 'em!'*

Such comments rolled off Roth's back and into the slipstream.

'You have to assume every face smiling at you has a reason for doing so,' Berenson had said on another occasion. *'Models and hunks can get smiled at. For the rest of us, a smile is a potential lie – you must be a detective, Scottie. You must find out why the smile is there before you trust it.'*

After dinner, he went to a bar, though he didn't know why – he'd never cared for them. Beautiful women in every direction, but an invisible barrier separated them all from his longing eyes. He could feel his lust take its jacket and head on back to the hotel, where it would wait for him to return alone. He made do with the commercial affection of the barmaid.

'Nice shirt,' she said.

'Recent shopping trip,' he replied. 'I wanted to go crazy, but I only went half-mad.'

'It suits you.'

'Thanks.'

'Pleasure.'

'It's not busy tonight,' he said.

'No,' she replied. 'Do you live around here?'

'Not really.'

'Making a day of it?'

'Making two. Maybe a few more.'

'You like art?'

'Very much.'

'There's a great exhibition at the Tate. I'd recommend it,' the barmaid said. 'If you have time.'

'Thanks for the tip.'

'No problem. Stunning show. I'd go again.'

'Maybe I'll see you there.'

Another customer called, she moved on, floated away, a snub as obvious as it was pitiful. But then whatever Berenson might have to say, Roth knew the truth: he didn't deserve to be happy.

Chapter 4

In the cab back to the Dorchester he realised that, absent of any clues, there was only one way to find the box this key fitted: he'd have to look for it, bank by bank. And to do *that*, he'd have to get a list of all of the private banks in London and visit each one.

Ugh!

In this painstaking task he was ably assisted by Gordon Weston, who didn't even flinch when Roth called him on his mobile at 11pm to ask if he could provide such a list. He doubted that Weston was impressed by the money he'd deposited with Mikhail Banking so far; rather, he suspected the man believed that anyone associated with Dieter Berenson would prove far more lucrative in the future. Good – he could use all the help he could get.

The list arrived shortly before 1am; he opened his room door to see a waiter standing there with an envelope couriered by one of Weston's overworked bods. The list of private banks in London was forty sheets long. He let out a weary sigh and decided to look at it tomorrow, hit fifty or sixty a day, area by area, street by street. He was relieved to have hit upon a method for conducting this quest.

He settled by the window, looked out across the city. Having not thought about his old boss for a decade, now he couldn't stop. Berenson had been an expert in the human psyche, and the parts that became psycho. *Especially* those parts. No quirk too strange, no foible too disgusting, no deviancy too sickening, no crime too indigestible. The go-to guy for the very very bad. Hearing those confessions must have been like reading hundreds of medical case studies: doctors knew what to do because other doctors had faced similar situations in the past and reported on what had happened and how they'd dealt with it, successfully or otherwise. Berenson must have heard so many people try life in so many different ways; a precedent for all conceivable cases, including the most extreme. As for Roth, this callow, jejune boy could not be dissuaded from a path that would lead him to the same dead end Berenson had heard many others speak of in such heartbroken tones. *They will lie to you, Scottie. These fuckers will get away with whatever they can, and they won't lose a moment's sleep! And at the end of it all, you'll be the one who's destitute, broken and dispirited, not them.*

Close to midnight, he tried the long, strange number once more. It connected, rang, cut out on the sixteenth chime. He tried again. *Nothing.* He put the phone down, wondered why, of all the data Berenson could have left him, he'd chosen a number with no apparent reason for being. Perversity piled upon weirdness – did Berenson even want his treasure to be found?

He hadn't a shard of sleep in him: his body clock had no idea of the time, not least because of all those showers he kept on taking. His skin was buff, close to tipping into redness and soreness. He must stop lest he cleanse himself to death, regardless of whether he was making up for ten years of cold showers, no showers or showers spent trying to avoid the crud left by others. He thought about the barmaid and her rebuff, of the three or four other women he'd seen during the day, any of whom he'd have married in a flash had they given him the chance to ask. One looked as if she'd stepped out of his fantasies: cool, smart, sleek. She was walking towards him on Piccadilly – and then she was gone. He'd seen her for no more than five seconds, hadn't looked at her, spoken to her, hadn't breathed as she'd walked past, and yet she'd rejected him totally, for he knew beyond a shadow of a doubt that she was not now thinking of him, as he was thinking of her.

'There's a reason why they call me the Confessor.'

Roth had heard about the confessor thing soon after he'd joined the company, but he'd never expected to experience it himself. At first he thought it was a test of his loyalty or resolve, and was determined not to play serf or flatter his new boss's vanity. He'd been working for Berenson for just six weeks when the boss uttered those fateful, egomaniac words, but Roth didn't reply – he was no kiss-ass, his parents hadn't brought him up like that.

The maker of the statement was not deterred; he was a relentless figure in all aspects of his life. Roth had worked for other wealthy people. They often mistook their luck for wisdom, the success it brought them inevitable; they assumed a grandeur with no reason. Even Berenson, the best of the bunch, had his Sun King moments. The low light, now, placed him in silhouette. 'People tell me things,' the boss's silhouette said. 'Things they wouldn't tell anyone else, their family, their spouse, their children, their shrink . . .' He leant forward. His face came back into view. 'They tell me the things they can't even tell themselves.'

'Lucky you,' Roth had replied.

'I can always tell when someone wants to get something off their chest. Something they've been carrying around in their gut and their soul for years, still there, festering, only growing worse. A cancer of the spirit that will never go away by itself. There's something you want to tell me, isn't there?'

'No,' Roth said bluntly. 'There is *not*.'

'You don't need to be coy. You don't need to be afraid. I can tell how much you want to set this secret free, this nag inside you . . .'

Roth blinked a little. His head tipped.

'You can tell me,' Berenson persisted. 'Yes, you can. I've heard it all, so whatever you think it is that may shock me, I can assure you it won't.' He was utterly calm. Thoroughly warm and welcoming.

'I don't have anything—'

The boss held up his palms; he'd brook no resistance.

Roth looked at him, passive-faced but with anxiety piling up behind the mask. Yes, there *was* an ease about speaking to him, as if Berenson was pulling up the blind on a magic window, and whatever you said would get carried away by the breeze until it was trouble no more. And perhaps there would be relief in telling him what he'd told no one else, what he'd carried in his belly as if it were a tumour that could never be cut away. But the man was still his boss, his *employer*; even if he had divined that his newest staff member had a terrible secret, a display of deviancy that marked him, was confirming this to be true the best way to advance up the career ladder?

The boss sat there, waiting for his fresh employee to fight past his reservations, as the self-confessed 'Confessor' was evidently used to people doing.

'I killed someone,' said Scott Roth eventually.

Berenson's eyes didn't flicker. He remained inactive, without comment. It seemed to Roth that the restaurant expanded to allow him room to elucidate. He was shocked by the release of words, words he had thought could never come out of his mouth. But there they were; they had chosen of their own free will to leap from his soul of secrets, and were lying on the floor in front of his boss. Berenson continued to look at him with that same welcoming calm, that magic window still wide open, a sense of inevitability about the process.

'It was late one evening,' Roth started. 'I was on my way home. Just an . . . an ordinary night. I didn't notice but I was walking past a wall. I didn't see him, didn't hear him, but a robber jumped out at me. He had a knife, didn't ask for my wallet, pulled at my coat and tried to push me to the ground. I punched out a couple of times. One caught him on the jaw. He wasn't expecting it, he looked . . . dazed. He went down, his head hit the floor – one of those sickening crunches. *And he did not move*. Lying there like he'd *never* moved. I watched him for a few moments. And then I realised he wasn't breathing. He was . . . *young*. I hadn't noticed how young when I hit him. I called an ambulance, the police came. I told them what had happened, they said it was self-defence. They knew this kid from robberies, burglary, aggravated with knives. A couple of witnesses saw it too, the police checked them out. They said this kid jumped at me from nowhere, had a knife, I hit him, he fell down and didn't get up again. And that was that. A teenage boy dead because of me.'

Berenson might also have seemed stone dead were it not for his silent breathing and watchful face, at which Roth looked and then glanced away.

'So that's it,' Roth said, staring hard at the floor. 'Make of it what you will.'

'Did you mean to do it?' the confessor asked.

'No.'

'Were you frightened?'

'Yes.'

'When he jumped out at you, what did you think?'

'All I could see was the knife. All I could think was . . . that I didn't want to die.'

'How long ago did it happen?'

'Four years.'

'So you were . . .'

'Twenty-six.'

'With plenty of time stocked up and still to come.'

'Yes, but I robbed him of *his* time, Dieter, fifty or sixty years. And no one made me pay for *that*.'

'It was self-defence. According to society, you have absolutely nothing to pay.'

'But how often is society wrong?'

'Frequently. But not this time.'

'If I hadn't punched him—'

'If he hadn't attacked you.'

'If I hadn't walked that way—'

'If he hadn't drawn a knife.'

Roth fell silent.

Berenson said, 'So you killed a person, this – boy. You took away all the time he had left – though he'd tried to do you the worst possible harm. And though it was not your fault, you carry a sense that you've done a terrible wrong.'

'I *did* do a terrible wrong, I ended his life.'

'Do you accept that you had to defend yourself?'

'Yes.'

'And in doing so you punched him, nothing more?'

'That's all it took.'

'But you didn't *mean* to kill him.'

'I wanted him to stop.'

'You were glad when he fell to the floor?'

'Yes.'

'You were no longer about to die.'

'That's right.'

'So why didn't you pop a champagne cork? Jesus, Scottie, I've heard more troubling confessions from a toaster.'

'He looked pathetic. And the knife harmless. Flat at the kerb. I couldn't believe I'd been so scared of it a moment earlier. How could I have *killed* him over that piece of metal?'

'You went from walking along to thinking that you're about to die to looking at a dead teen on the floor in the space of fifteen seconds?'

'Something like that.'

'You were frightened for your life! You defended yourself! *Good for you* is what anyone with sense would say! You've been carrying this around like a rock the size of a truck for *four years*? Why do you empathise so much with the person who attacked you, who might have killed you? What if he *had* stabbed you, what if you had been the one whose head had hit the pavement and you'd never got up? *You'd* have been the one to lose all of that time.'

After a silence, Roth said, 'No one's ever used that word before.'

'What word?'

'"Empathise".'

'There's another word I could use,' Berenson exclaimed. '"Schmuck"! He had a knife, Scottie! You could have been dead that moment! And you empathise with this thug and what happened so much that in the time you've worked for me, I haven't seen you laugh or smile once!'

'I didn't want to hurt him.'

'He made you do it.'

'I didn't have to.'

'You didn't *mean* to.'

'He was a child.'

'Children kill, Scottie. And you're no less dead if they do.'

'I was the grown-up.'

'He was old enough.'

'Seventeen?!'

'That's old enough.'

Roth fell silent.

'You've committed no crime,' Berenson said. 'But in this prison of your own making, how long is this sentence that you've bestowed upon yourself?'

He didn't need to respond – the answer was obvious. The quiet corner booth of the restaurant they were sitting in kept them secluded from the rest of the world. Roth could have done with an interruption. He was feeling naked, unclothed by someone he hadn't permitted to carry out such intimate acts. Berenson could see his patient was closing down.

'Well,' the boss said. 'That's a start. But if you think I'm done with this, schmucko, you've got another thing coming!'

Berenson's voice from that long-gone, painful afternoon faded. Roth glanced at the clock; it was twenty past two in the morning. He was still in his luxurious room at the Dorchester.

He stood up, walked around a little to shake the recollection from his bones. London was at rest, but his mind was not.

He sat down by the bedside table and tried the mysterious phone number again.

The connection . . .

The rings . . .

The cut-off.

He sighed, stood and walked across the room. He poured some water and drank it all in one go. He refilled the glass and settled by the window once more. He saw the city again, but now his old boss loomed large over the landscape.

Yes, Berenson was a strange fish, and – despite what he might have said in his letter – had been angry and brusque when Roth gave in his notice, six months after his confession. 'So I suppose this is my fault,' the boss had growled, as he sat back in his chair with a look of grave disappointment bordering on frustrated fury. He was shocked, yes – it hadn't occurred to him that Roth had thoughts of moving on. He crunched his employee's reasoning, came to the obvious conclusion. 'I put the idea in your head, didn't I, the one you've been looking for all this time. Well, I can be too smart for my own good; that much I know – I didn't need to learn it from you. I can't imagine why on earth you'd want to leave my organisation to do *this*.' He was starting to glow red with temper, could hold it no more. 'You're a fucking lunatic if you think any good will come of it. Who's the confessor, Scottie? Who knows the world better than I? No one, not even you. So you think that this is how you solve your big problem, your misplaced anxiety about that fucking teen? But let me tell ya, buddy, you're only going to make it worse for yourself. You think the outside world will give a shit about you, that they'll appreciate it? You're gonna find what you've avoided so far: the problem is not with you, it's with *them*. Scottie, for fuck's sake, this is just . . . you're making me so angry with your fucking stupidity! How can you do this to yourself? How can you take a glittering career and shove it up your rear end in such a careless way? You're nuts!' A wholly unexpected tirade, by the end of which Berenson was flushed and fuming. 'I can't stop you from quitting your job,' he said, calming a little after a few breaths of much-needed air. 'Just don't forget about me, okay?'

'Okay,' Roth had replied, and then promptly forgot about him. Not through malice (or even shock at Dieter's outburst) but simply because he was too busy for the next ten years. Yes, it was true: his decade-long scheme did have its roots in his confession that day, when at last he'd told someone he'd killed a man, a *child*. He reflected on that horrible incident after his confession in a way he'd never done before, as if Berenson's magic window had cast a light upon it that brought Roth to the simplest of solutions. The only way to make amends was to go out and do some good, in a way no one had ever tried before, at least as far as Roth knew: find people in need of a lift – and give it to them. Whisper the right words into the right ears at the right time. Offer encouragement that no one else had offered. Dive into psychological waters others had chosen not to swim in. Give to those familiar only with people taking. Smile at those who knew only the rough end of the lash. Finding the deprived, the beaten, the discarded was simple; they were everywhere. Make them feel better and you'd feel better too. Inspire others and you'd be inspired. Help one person and they'd help five more. *Start a movement.* It only needed someone to set the ball rolling, to make others aware that you *could* improve things yourself, you *could* have a direct impact on the world around you whatever the pessimists (like Berenson) might say. Roth was not a model or a movie star; he wouldn't seek reasons for the smiles he'd receive, or determine whether they were lies or not. He'd give the needy, the desperate and the impoverished what they'd never been given before: the benefit of the doubt. He wouldn't make them beg, destroying whatever hair's-breadth of pride they'd managed to retain after a lifetime of humiliation. He wouldn't treat them as they'd always been treated so far: ignored, rejected, forced to explain how their smiles were not beseeching mercy, or money. He'd know they were smiling because at last someone had shown them a little sympathy.

And now, as he sat in the Dorchester room paid for by the boss he'd walked out on, he could hear Berenson's voice ringing in his head. *Schmucko! I told you not to waste your time!* Yes, thought Roth, you gave me all the answers, and now I can see – now I can *admit* – that you were right. So many smiles I should have turned from. So many liars, so many thieves. So much wasted sympathy.

He tried the mysterious phone number again, but no one picked up at the other end of the line. The experiment was complete: he'd made attempts across all hours of the day and no one had answered any of them. The only clue he'd been given was a dud. Berenson may have preserved the secrecy of his treasure a little too well.

Chapter 5

It was time to downscale. Over his final Dorchester breakfast, map and pen in one hand, toast, jam and coffee in the other, he marked banks on the list provided by Gordon Weston, putting an asterisk next to the ones he wanted to visit in clusters close by. He finished his third cup of coffee and third round of toast. It was clear he had a lot of walking to do.

Roth moved his quest to the Hotel Salon, a sleek little bolt-hole much cheaper than his Dorchester spread. He was pleased to see that he'd been given a well-cared-for room with a comfortable, discreet finish, on the sixth floor. It felt as if it had seen many residents on their own great voyage through life. Perhaps a musician getting gigs in London before hitting the big time, or a young woman in town to interview for jobs and meet friends. Hotel rooms hid so many secrets of their own that they had no trouble keeping those of others. Yes, he'd be happy here for the next few weeks.

It was 11am. The time had come; unpacking could wait. He took his now-annotated list of banks from his bag and the key, which he kept in the envelope it came in. He was actually setting out on the quest Berenson had laid upon him. And he felt nervous! He told himself to stop being so silly, get moving! He left the hotel with a steady purposefulness.

Outside, the sun was shining and the birds singing, but that couldn't hide the fact that he had no idea what he was seeking, what he may find or how long it may take. As he headed towards the first bank on his list, the reality became increasingly acute: he only had a starting point because he'd concocted a plan to hide the fact that he had no plan. Yes, the comfy hotel room, yes, the sixty thousand pounds, yes, the saving from oblivion; but if he reflected upon how vague his current situation was, he'd abandon the task, thinking it impossible. He tried to put such thoughts from his head.

He arrived at the bank, chosen due to its closeness to the Hotel Salon: a façade of marble, frosted windows, a tiny brass plate by the door that breathed the name of the institution rather than announced it. The private bank seemed to want to hide itself from its clients as well as unwanted passers-by. Roth checked his list. This was indeed the right address. He glanced around the quiet street and saw nothing amiss. Still deeply unsure, he went inside.

The lobby was smaller than he'd expected, more like a private members' club than a bank. Fine art covered the walls, the hush authentic, the money in a light sleep that the smallest chime may disturb. The oppressive atmosphere knew Roth shouldn't be here, tried to force him back out of the doors he'd just walked through with apt uncertainty. Two well-dressed people sat at the reception, a man and a woman, both with poise that would be at home on a catwalk. They looked up: industrious in their composure, unfailingly polite, their expressions blank.

'Good morning, sir,' the man said. 'How can we help?'

Roth had focused so much on where he was going that he hadn't thought what to say once he'd arrived. He was suddenly stricken by the oddness of the words to explain his request; so much so that they stayed right where they were, inside his mouth. In their absence, the gazes coming back at him from the man and woman put him off even more; he was keeping them from their business and they were not impressed. 'I have a key,' he said, his awkwardness growing. 'I need to find out if it's one of yours.'

A courier glanced over, picking up that something odd was happening in the otherwise dead atmosphere.

The woman said, still polite, 'Let's take a look.'

Roth handed them the key. The man and woman didn't take long to carry out their analysis – there was little to see. The key was small, surprisingly heavy, made of strong stuff, had no markings on its handle, was flat and smooth, unadorned with scratches, its teeth shiny and robust. This was no front door key, no car key, no key of constant use. This was a key of breeding, of class, of wealth. It was a key that claimed it should be in this kind of atmosphere by birthright. After a few moments, the two bankers looked at Roth. The man said, 'Sorry, but this is not one of ours.'

He knew his luck couldn't be so good as to hit the jackpot straight away. 'But it is a key to a private box?'

'Quite possibly.'

'I know it's an odd thing to ask, but do you know which bank may have keys like this? Where I should go to find the box it fits?'

There was a marginal widening of their eyes; the woman said, 'I'm afraid not.'

'Something that you may have seen at other banks, or noticed when talking to colleagues?'

'No,' the man confirmed. Roth could feel that he was becoming a nuisance. They said nothing to make him uncomfortable, but the tone was heavily skewering towards wanting him to leave.

'Okay.' He nodded. 'Well, thanks anyway.'

He could feel the stares on his back as he walked out.

That didn't go that well, he mused as he strode on to his next destination. He'd barely made a dent in the day but the day had already made a dent in him.

A bright morning, the quiet location, the hum of the occasional car that passed. He stared in at the drivers – when he could see inside, that is: some had tinted windows. Their inhabitants took no interest in him, gliding on as if he was not there. For a moment, he was not so sure that he was.

He arrived at the next bank, passed through its prim, discrete entrance to be met by more immaculate, super-polite representatives, the same combination of bafflement and disbelief – and the same negative response.

A few minutes later, he stood outside bank number three with his key and third straight 'no' and his list of banks, feeling *insane*. These poker-faced buggers were finding his questions baffling, or amusing, or insulting, or all three; Roth could hardly disagree with them. It had taken only fifteen minutes to reach this point, but unless he could come up with a better plan, he had to keep on trying, however heavy his embarrassment may get.

Walking into bank number four, he could barely get the questions out. It was design-hotel stylish and he knew as soon as he walked in that this was not the place, that his key was too old-fashioned for such a hipster venue. Still, the bankers took pity on a man either disturbed or easily led. Their answer was, of course, in the negative.

He stood on the pavement, scanning his list. It was already starting to show signs of wear, of markings he'd made and smudges. The day had been dry, so he didn't have to wrangle with rain turning it into papier mâché. Even so, the names of the banks blurred into one another, inscrutable, revealing nothing about what lay behind them and how much money there may be. He squinted to bring life back to his eyes, but the more he stared at the paper, the more the banks' names seemed to run away from him.

Three more fruitless banks and it was a race to see which would come first: lunch or his psychological crushing. He got in another couple of humiliations before he felt he could justify stopping for food. Munching on an uninspired sandwich, drinking a forlorn cup of tea, he flicked through his list. It grew no shorter nor more user-friendly. His notes were yelps of scorn – Berenson could have given him sixty *million* pounds; there was just no way of knowing where to look.

His questions sounded sillier with each bank he visited. *Does this key fit one of your boxes? No. BANG! Do you know which bank I should go to? No. BANG!*

'Are you really asking us that?' one banker had said to him, Alpha Male rage in his eyes. 'Do you think we have time to waste on something like this?'

'Well . . .' Roth had replied, going red with embarrassment.

'I have never heard anything so ridiculous in my life. No, this key is not one of ours. Now fuck off, and don't ever come back.'

The burning sensation in his cheeks did not subside until he was standing by the door of the next bank on the list. He composed himself and, steeled for further humiliation, went on through.

This new banker inspected the key in a calmer, friendlier way, for which Roth was eternally grateful. Nevertheless, the answer was still no, and the rest of the afternoon proved as wasted as the morning.

He returned to the Hotel Salon shortly after 5pm. The banks had closed – at least to randoms such as he. He felt weary and dumb: twenty-three visited and no advances made. He could sigh his despair out loud and no one in London would hear.

It was a lesson. It had to be. Berenson was trying to teach him something, from beyond the grave. *Like what a fool he was.* And by teaching him, he meant *rubbing it in*. The boss had a deviant streak. When Berenson had liked to relax and let loose, he could be savage. Roth rarely saw him drink and never seen him do anything worse than that, but he'd always found it frighteningly easy to picture his old boss wearing a rubber mask while a dominatrix raised him into position via a metal-chain contraption to be ruthlessly, expensively abused. Berenson was a black hole without an event horizon, sucking in all those confessions and letting nothing escape again. *'There is no end to the perversions on this planet,'* the boss had once said to him, less than at his best, heartsick following a 'meeting' with one of his 'clients'. *'Believe me,'* he said, before Roth had a chance to say he didn't want to know, *'You don't want to know.'*

Only a man of secrets could have started a treasure hunt with a clue that led nowhere. Looking back, Roth realised that he knew nothing about Berenson, the man with whom he'd spent eight months of almost 24/7 days.

'Do you know what the greatest pleasure in the world is?' Berenson had said to him a month before Roth gave in his notice. They were sitting at a table in a plush restaurant, waiting for others to join them for a dinner meeting. The boss wanted Roth there – as far as he could tell – to make up the numbers. The matter was so confidential, Berenson had told the other attendees that only the key decision-maker of their respective organisations could come. So each of the diners turned up alone. Roth recalled their faces as they realised they were outnumbered by the home team, two against one against one against one. He also remembered the extent of the humiliation Berenson had visited upon them. When the 'guests' had left, their egos shattered and their balance sheets assaulted, Berenson and Roth finished off the cognac the boss had boastfully ordered, kings in an impoverished land. 'Well, Scottie?' he asked, demanding an answer.

'No,' he replied, playing along for the sake of his employer's joy. 'I don't know what the greatest pleasure in the world is.'

'Nor do I.'

Roth raised his eyebrows – he wasn't expecting *that*.

'Sometimes,' Berenson continued, 'I don't think there's pleasure to be had in *anything*.' He sipped more cognac, liquid on his tongue, his eyes rolling back in his head, delighting in the alcohol.

'Well, Dieter, you could have fooled me.'

'No, Scottie, I don't think I could.'

'You fooled *them*.'

'Unlike you, they were fools already.'

Roth lowered his head: a compliment!

Berenson looked at him, at his embarrassment. 'You know, you mustn't be so fucking *modest* all the time. This is not a world designed for the glorification of the humble. It's true, yes: modesty is becoming, but you take it too far. Be *immodest*, that's the Scott Roth I'd like to see! The one who says, "This is not good enough!" or "I can do that better than you!" or "How dare you serve me this shit!" Believe me, it's good for the soul.'

'I can't help it, that's not the way I am.'

'So let it be the way you are! Let's see some Scott Roth prickliness!'

His boss was laughing now.

'Like I stuck it to them tonight! I was awful! I bet they wanted to put cyanide in my coffee! And I love it! Because they deserved it. They think I don't have a clue, but I knew they'd all got together beforehand with the sole intention of sticking it to me. Thought they'd be smart and short-circuit my attempt to short-circuit them. But I have my sources, and I gave it right back, Scottie, didn't I! I gave it right back to them and then some!'

'Yes, Dieter, you certainly did.'

'*I got them*,' he said, his face full of untrammelled delight. 'I got them all! They came thinking they'd be able to resist, but I picked them off one by one. Fools! They deserved to be taken for every penny! Which, by the way, is exactly what is going to happen!'

'I think you do know what the greatest pleasure is, Dieter: everything in the world at once.'

Berenson was tickled, a titan reclining. 'Without exclusion ... or limitation—'

'And without the weight of those confessions.'

'No! Believe it or not, Scottie, I couldn't get by without hearing the confessions. However deranged, morbid, sickening . . . Yes, amen to the dark side of our world! It's all the other shit that makes me feel like I'm losing my marbles.'

Now Roth felt like he was losing his marbles too, thanks to his old boss. Based on today's pace, it would take him ages to go through all of the banks on the list. His mind craved distraction. He chose to dine in a comfy restaurant near his hotel, and settled in to people-watch a couple at a table nearby, their well-adjusted happiness, their unity; he wondered what children they may have. Good-looking kids, brought up on good vibes. He heard the ticking of his own genes – it wasn't just women who feared the biological clock. He didn't want to be an old dad, yet that's what he was on target to be, if any kind of dad at all. Another assumption of his youth: that one day he'd turn one way to see his wife, the other to see his kids. Yet now when he looked in both directions, all he saw was the pavement. This is not how it was supposed to be.

He tried to engage the waitress in conversation, but she had little to say. Eventually he gave up, annoyed with himself – it was no sign of maturity to fall so easily for the hospitality. The restaurant was loud, unfriendly – it had looked so different from outside. His spirit longed for some company, his body for release.

The streets were busy as he walked back to the hotel. His head empty, the food still fizzing on his tongue. There'd be no bars tonight, no more series of unreturned looks. He caught snippets of people's conversation as they passed, a pointless commentary that made no sense when run together.

In the chic warmth of his bijou room at the Hotel Salon, he listened to the radio while sipping on the late-night tea he'd already grown accustomed to. He couldn't be bothered trying that pointless number again: after twenty times of sixteen chimes and cut-out, a twenty-first would make no difference. Sunk on the sofa, he doubted he'd be able to rise from his seat to make the journey to the bathroom and then to bed.

After a sour night, he started to feel a little more relaxed. If luxury was no more than a cosy place to sit, a sparkling book to read and some great music to listen to, he could go a long way on sixty grand after all. He lay back, stretching on the long couch, bones cracking, the stillness of peace. The music faded. He started to fall asleep.

There flashed into his mind a bank he'd gone to with Berenson, in Paris, a mighty and unmistakeable landmark nearby.

He woke with a start, and realised that he knew exactly where he should go to find the box that key fit.

Paris

Chapter 6

He browsed in Foyles at St Pancras station, then made his way to the departure gate. His mind drifted as he progressed through check-in and security, looking forward to a relaxing journey on the Eurostar. He'd tickled himself with the notion of First Class but decided to stick with good old Standard passage for now.

The long train sat on the platform, a spear of time. He boarded his coach and shuffled to his seat: window, facing forward.

So, at last: his first piece of good luck since this strange mission began. In his sudden flashback, he'd remembered standing in a bank with his old boss – but not the name of that bank. That was the bad news. The good news was that he recalled one detail with absolute certainty: Berenson had pointed to the Louvre nearby, just before they'd gone inside.

First thing this morning, Roth had called his new friend, the happy-to-suffer Gordon Weston, and asked the banker to email him a list of all the banks in Paris that fell within a half mile radius of the Louvre. Weston assured Roth that he'd get the list to him as soon as possible. So for now, there was nothing more to do than lie back and enjoy the trip. When he reached Paris, his search would continue. He began to read, Paul Auster's *The Book of Illusions*. He was quickly consumed by the book, fell deep into it.

He looked up. A woman, mid-twenties, boho, attractive, was placing her beaten-up rucksack in the overhead storage. She took a book from its innards and crumpled into the seat opposite him, so close their knees almost touched. Their eyes held briefly. Then she opened her book, *Germinal* by Zola, and started to read. Roth watched her for a few moments; he hadn't realised at first glance quite how pretty she was. An amazing face, huge brown eyes, dark hair, funky dress and slim. Outside, the platform began to move. He returned to *The Book of Illusions*. The two read in silence as England slid by, soon to be replaced by France.

Her presence – her proximity. He closed his book, placed it on his lap, let his head fall back against his seat and stared out of the window. *We're travelling in a time machine,* he thought, as he gazed at the rapid-speeding countryside. *How can it take only two hours to get to Paris?*

'Pretty amazing,' someone said. He turned in the direction of the voice. With a thrill of delight he realised it belonged to the woman sitting opposite him. She'd also placed her book in her lap, taken a pause to admire the view. She smiled at him. 'Business or pleasure?'

'Business, unfortunately. And you?'

'I'm staying with a friend. I've been travelling around the northern hemisphere for the last six months and it's time to get on with my life. I studied fashion, I'd love to get a job in Paris some day, so I'm going to have a look around, to find out if there's a chance of . . . but – ah, we'll see. Have you been before?'

'Not for many years,' he replied.

'It's my first time; I'm so excited!'

'It's a lovely place.'

'City of romance!'

He nodded, smiling.

She looked at him with open excitement.

She was *stunning*.

'What are you reading?' she asked.

He held up the book.

'Is it good?'

'Extremely.'

'Probably more fun than this,' she replied, indicating *Germinal*. 'I wanted something to get me in the mood for France. I didn't realise that mood was going to be miserable and revolutionary.'

'Perhaps you should have watched *Amélie* instead.'

'Perhaps we should have had this conversation sooner.' She laughed. 'I'm Mia. Mia Fletcher.'

'Scott Roth,' he replied. 'Nice to meet you, Mia Mia Fletcher.'

'Hahaha, yes! Bond, James Bond!'

'So good they named you twice.'

'Well, I don't know about that.'

He was going to compliment her further but she was *really* gazing at him. 'Would you – like some tea?' he asked, flustered. 'I was just about to go and . . . and get myself a drink from the restaurant car.'

'Coffee would be *great*.'

'I'll be back shortly.'

'You better.'

He smiled at her, low-key – inside, he whooped for joy! He stood and started towards the door. En route to the restaurant, two coaches away, he had a conflab with himself and decided that, yes, he really did like this woman and, as they had more than an hour to go before they reached their destination, he must chat with her, engage her, and – well, who knew what might happen?!

He returned to his seat ten minutes later, beverages in hand.

'Thanks,' Mia said, taking her coffee.

He sat in his chair, scooped the top off his cup and began to sip.

'How long are you in Paris for?' she asked.

'I'm not sure.'

'Oh?' she replied. 'Enigmatic!'

'There's a couple of things I need to do,' he replied, not wanting to go into too much bonkers detail just yet. 'A few days, fingers crossed, and then I'll be on my way – I don't want to be in Paris any longer than I have to.'

She continued to look at him for a few moments without saying anything. Then she turned and stared out the window, at the countryside. A few moments passed. He could feel the heat cooling. Should he have said that he was going to be in Paris for longer so that they might have the chance to spend time together in the official Most Romantic City in the World? Had he said that nothing but his business would keep him here? *Had he just blown her out???* Ahhh, he could shoot himself! *Do something,* he screamed inside, *do something!* – but he was panicking, and nothing came out of his mouth.

A couple of moments later, Mia took up her book again and continued to read.

Shit!

They passed through the Channel Tunnel and were *en France,* racing through the countryside; earlier so impressed by the time-travelling Eurostar, now he wished they were trundling along dusty backroads in an old-fashioned coach that took ten hours to cover the same ground. Mia's nose was in *Germinal,* an expression of discomfort on her face, the cause impossible to say: the book? Him? The challenges awaiting her in Paris?

'What's your plan when we get there?' he asked, forcing the words out of his mouth, albeit with immense, hazardous effort.

She looked up at him. He couldn't tell if she was pleased about the resumption or not. She said: 'My friend Becky is coming to pick me up from the station.'

'Ah, interesting. And what does she do?'

'She's an architect,' Mia replied, warming up again. 'She recently qualified at one of the coolest practices in Paris.'

'Wow!' he replied, gamely. 'How did you meet?'

'She's a little older than me; through a mutual friend at a party. You know how you get talking, and we hit it off. When she moved to Paris she said I should come. I wasn't so sure at the time, but after all of this travelling . . .'

'I'm hoping to adventure myself, before long.'

Mia's excitement bubbled all over again. 'Ahhhhh, it will be so good if I can get a job in Paris! I grew up in suburbia – living and working as a designer in one of the great centres of fashion was as much of a delusion for me as planting an oak tree on the moon.'

He nodded sympathetically.

'So you have to take what they give, right?' She was animated now. 'Working in a supermarket or stuck in a corner of a clothes shop or an office or any of that shit. You don't get the chance to do what you really want!'

'Well,' he said, '*That* can be a double-edged sword.'

'The voice of experience?'

'I wasted a huge amount of time doing what I thought I should. It turned out I was wrong.'

'And what was that?'

'Helping people.'

'Hmmm . . . ' She nodded. 'I can see how that may not work out.'

She laughed; he did too. Her brown eyes dazzled as she gazed at him with the kind of desire he'd longed to see flashed in his direction for so long, the look that singled him out from all others and said, *I want you right now!* Pouring from her: a torrent of fancy and affection, which he found so wonderful and happy-making he thanked the Lord that he had decided to buy a seat in Standard. To Mia, perhaps he had said the right thing after all.

The Eurostar slid in to Paris Gare du Nord. He felt the sting of imminent separation. They'd continued to chat for the rest of the way, but neither had tried to find out if the other was interested in carrying on this tête-à-tête in a cool café or bistro. Once again, he found himself in the age-old dilemma: even if she was interested *and* available, she was waiting for him to ask, while the prospect of asking was never less than fraught. But the train had stopped, they were collecting their luggage – it was now or never.

'Umm . . . tonight?' he said.

She looked at him. 'What about it?'

'I . . . can't recall the French—'

'*Le dinner*?' she said.

'*Oui oui*!'

'Ah, *non*,' she replied. 'I have to catch up with Becky tonight.'

'Ah *non* . . .'

'She's putting me up, no charge – it's the least I can do.'

'Ah . . . *oui*.'

'*Le tomorrow*?' Mia said.

Roth beamed. '*Oui oui*!'

'*Oui oui, bon*!'

'*Bon beaucoup*,' he said, and they both began to laugh, equally palpably relieved.

They clambered down from the train, she with her rucksack, he with his wheelie case full of recent buys. They walked along the platform. 'Where are you staying?' she asked.

'I don't know, I haven't booked anywhere yet.'

'A true adventurer: yes, just like me! Give me your email.'

They stopped. She took out a pen and a battered, beat-up notepad, tore off a page and handed it to him. He wrote down his email address and handed it back to her. She said, 'I'll be in touch; we'll go for dinner tomorrow night.'

He was *thrilled*.

They walked on into the faded glory of the station atrium. Mia started waving her arms like a madwoman and went running off. Roth followed her gaze and saw another woman – slightly older – waving back. By the time he caught up, Mia was deep in delighted conversation with who he assumed must be Becky, newly qualified architect and temporary landlady to a most welcome lodger. It took them a few moments to register his arrival. Mia introduced them to one another.

'So you kept this chatterbox company all the way from London?' Becky asked.

'My pleasure,' he replied.

'Can I give you a lift?'

'He hasn't got a hotel yet,' Mia said before Roth could, which made them all laugh.

'I'm fine,' he replied. 'But thanks.'

'Okay,' Becky said to Mia. 'We've got a *lot* of catching up to do!'

'Yes, we do!' she replied, before turning to Roth to give him an all-encompassing hug. 'Keep an eye on your email, sweetie.'

'I will!' he said, hugging back.

She gave him a kiss on the cheek and then vanished into conversation with her reunited friend. Roth watched them disappear into the crowd. When they were gone, he felt elated: he was in Paris with a date! He assured himself that it *was* a date, even though Mia seemed so casual about the whole thing. Still, he allowed himself the warm glow that comes from being wanted – he couldn't remember the last time he'd felt so good. He wandered out of the station into the city of lights, the city of love, yes: the Most Romantic City in the World.

Chapter 7

After a slightly spacey walk through the Parisian streets, he found the pretty, inexpensive Hotel Foucault, tucked away in the third arrondissement. He checked (a) into the hotel and (b) his email. Not only had Gordon Weston sent him the list of banks local to the Louvre but Mia had already sent him a message saying, *This is me! Let me know when and where for our date tomorrow! M.*

A surge of excitement! So much so that he almost forgot to ask the hotel receptionist to print the list Weston had sent. They waited for several minutes as another pile of bank contact details chugged out of the machine.

His third hotel room in not many more days. Like the Hotel Salon, this one's bijou walls spoke of literary treats and stolen adventures, of deep thoughts and nights of passion. He could imagine a delightful dinner with Mia, their return to this jewel of a chamber, both standing by this very window, looking out across the rustic street, his arm reaching behind her, she moving in to his torso, their eyes closing and the effervescent fizz of a kiss.

He scanned the list. None of the banks' names rang any bells from his time here with Berenson ten years ago. Irritating, yes, but the outcome decreed by the odds: he was back to scouring through dozens of private institutions one by one.

He set out for a walk, keen to explore before the trudge of business started the next day. Buff in his new clothes, he glanced into a café across the road from his hotel, imagined artists sitting in its mythic space, sketching, writing, thinking, being French, discussing the great ideas of the day, the latest movements in art, the newest advances in philosophy, perfect for a *très bon* post-party breakfast!

He strolled on, walking through the lush atmosphere. The city hadn't seemed to change in ten years. Parts were deeply familiar, a flicker here, a head turn there. He gazed along a street that seemed to echo of the past. Roth had seen too much of the uglier side of London in recent times; how nice it was to be laying his feet over such eloquent fresh territory. Seduced by the architecture, the fine trees, the passers-by; a Mondrian exhibition heavily promoted by posters and vast prints – perhaps he'd have the chance to go there with Mia?

He came across Café Mauve, where he decided to settle for the evening after his pleasant, circuitous stroll. Delicious food mingled with spells of reading his book and reading people – locals and tourists in varying states of seduction. Waiting for his dessert, he wrote to Mia, saying he'd found the perfect place for their date tomorrow night, how about 8pm? He sent the email with a flourish of excitement and settled back into his observer's nest, letting the blithe, sunny atmosphere dance around him.

He must have been starting to enjoy himself, for this evening's memories of Dieter tickled him. The confessor would surely have enjoyed the intrigue of the couple sitting two tables along, and the ungainly way in which the man was trying to woo the woman. She seemed uninterested, or playing a longer game. Perhaps they were here solely *for* the game. Berenson would have been desperate to discover what each was hiding from the other – in his concept of the world, people were always hiding facts and truth and news. He would have ruminated upon what each sought from this liaison. In particular, he adored assessing who would seal the deal in their favour. Just as there were always secrets, the boss insisted there was always a deal to be made. The dude on the table two along may want to give his lady companion a fine life, and she may wish to do the same for him – but neither would be here if they didn't also believe that they would benefit personally.

Dieter had once told Roth that a consistent theme in many of the confessions he heard was how his subjects felt that, like Roth, they were tied to bad acts they'd committed in the past. They may not be that person any more, but the deeds nagged too much for them to escape their former self. Or they may even be a worse version nowadays, confessing to clear enough mental space simply so that they could commit yet fouler deeds.

Perhaps this couple hoped their relationship would free them from their pasts, make them new again so that they could move on without having to address their historic agonies or, even worse, *confess* to the depths of those histories that had brought them to this point. *On the other hand, they may just want to get their leg over.* At this last possibility, the boss would hoot – you could never discount *that* as a motive for anything. He had a good laugh, Berenson . . . It was still so strange to think he was dead.

With his coffee came a sense that he'd love Dieter to be here with him now: they could chat about that couple rather than him constructing conversations in his mind. After a decade chained to the gloom, he wanted to enjoy himself, as his old benefactor had encouraged. But his boss had confused himself on a character detail: for Roth, enjoying himself was not the point. *Enjoying himself* would have detracted from his scheme, which required zero flippancy, extravagance or deviation. Berenson knew how conscientious Roth was, how determined he could be when set upon a course, and how allergic to fun that made him. Perhaps how allergic to fun he'd always been. Yes, Roth had been a serious fellow from an early age; that's how he was built: you can't trump your make-up, and certainly not when you know at last what you're supposed to do with your life.

After he quit his job, Roth had hoped to use the few contacts he'd made thus far to get businesspeople to pony up the money essential to his plan. Those in need – the people he wanted to help – would laugh in his face if he offered kind words without any cash to back them up. The more funds he could raise, the more people he could help, the more good he could do, the larger the touch paper he could light. He hadn't asked Berenson for a penny – that was too close to home, and his old boss would have been offended by the request on account of how he felt about the whole idea to begin with. But Roth did ask him to tell others about the project, which itself was met with a stony face. Whether or not Berenson had ever asked any of his super-rich contacts to fund his old employee's crazy scheme, Roth never knew. However, sponsors were noticeable by their absence. Berenson had been a persuasive man, so it was clear that he almost certainly hadn't bothered. Of the people Roth himself tried to chat up, they'd said it was an interesting proposition, but they'd have to pass it through their corporate sponsorship channels. Promises were few but pledges encouraging. He'd continued anyway; contributors would catch up. In the end, he didn't manage to raise a groat from outside sources. None of the possibles became actuals, no private channel was successfully navigated, no corporate dime made it to the neglected. Roth had to fund the scheme himself. This unhappy turn of events required him to spend much of the time he'd otherwise be using to help run-down people in run-down places to improve their run-down lives working in jobs that were nowadays beneath him. There were few roles that allowed him to take the time he needed to do the work essential for getting to the roots of people's lives. His CV took a nosedive as he tried to balance his time between making money and making a difference. Soon, not only was he among the poverty-stricken physically, he was among them financially as well. He worked hard to have any kind of money coming in. Like micro-banks, it took little to make a difference if the person you were trying to help had nothing to begin with. But the struggle was constant, and increasingly hard.

How different this new existence was. When the famed confessor had plucked him from his previous job, Roth was ensconced in a cosy flat, working his way to ever better wealth and prospects. It had taken him a while to get this far, but he was unwavering and bright, a valued assistant to bosses (albeit in a role he was never much enamoured of). His employers found him ever more useful. For years he'd accumulated the sheen of comfort: an escalating income, a nice home, a large amount of business sense and, that most treasured of things in the modern world, a future.

How easy it had been to discard all that stuff.

Of course it is, Berenson would have said, staring him straight in the eyes; *you're running away, my boy – and we all know from what.*

In the classy, comfy Café Mauve, a warming glass of wine a boon to his memory, which ebbed further out of the concrete bunker it had retreated into for the past ten years. In the mild haze of the Beaujolais, more of the past bubbled to the surface, things he hadn't thought about for years.

For his first 'project', Roth had chosen a rented room in a shared house in a plague location with ne'er-do-well inhabitants. Following the experience of having travelled zillionaire class with Berenson for eight months, privilege still ringing in his ears, he was suddenly living with three men whom life had passed by. The paint peeled off the wallpaper, and the wallpaper peeled off the walls. The guttering leaked and the damp gained ground, the cooker dirty, the rent cheap. For two of these men, their conditions were no better than the property in which it seemed they were condemned to live, set to decay mode, the breeze wearing them away, the hopes and dreams they once had as nasty a memory as the numerous bad turns done them by others. The prospect of marriage and children diminished with every month for these couple of wastrels – to be honest, it had long since gone, and there was no use pretending otherwise. They had nothing to show for their years but the reservoir of bitterness in which they swam, drank and shat. But the third man – a twenty-something called Ralph – was as razor-sharp as he'd been neglected. Roth could tell the moment he laid eyes upon him that this was exactly the kind of person he'd given up his job to go out into the world to help. So much untapped potential. Though Ralph gave the impression of being lost, Roth was sure he was in fact desperate to be found, waiting around for someone to do the heavy lifting needed to locate this needle in the centre of the haystack. He wondered how the man had stumbled from the path so early in life – he couldn't have been older than twenty-three. But Roth had been fortunate in his own saviours, the two people who'd appeared from nowhere at the start of his life and plucked him from the pile of parentless babies. How easy it would have been for him to end up in one of these dosshouses begging for someone else to come and help *him,* had things been other than they were.

In this frayed, blue house, he listened to tales told by each of the three men about how life had dealt them awful hands time and again. To stories of petty hatreds, bitter twists and hard-heartedness. How no one had ever thought of *them* or gave *them* a hand up. How all opportunity had been denied them, steered towards those who simply did not deserve it. One would start and trigger the others, the negativity spiralling determinedly downwards, and then, at a certain point, out would come a bottle of cheapest vodka, and the night would be lost thereafter. Roth would try to intercept their better natures before alcohol amplified their collective bitterness. At times he felt like their confessor, only they were not revealing their secrets to lighten the load of their tormented souls. They told the same tales over and over again, to each other, to themselves, to anyone who hadn't heard them before and was not fast enough to get away. They longed for unknowing audience members, for fresh sources of forced sympathy. The newcomer soaked up their self-pity as Berenson consumed the confessions of the rich and powerful (and which may ultimately have consumed him). Yet this was the start of his campaign to make the world a better home for the human race. For the first time in his life, he felt in the right place to do the work that was coming so naturally to him that he wondered why he'd needed a confession to show him what made his heart sing in the first place.

His method was simple: he was going to provide people with the secrets to success no one else had ever shared with them before. All of the tricks he'd learned in life and business, up close to people like Berenson: how to better yourself, tap into your potential and escape the leg weights of a deprived start. In the rotten house with Ralph and their two other beaten-down housemates, he met every moan with a solution, every loss with a means by which to convert that failure into a shining victory. Epic conversations about how hard their lives had been? He put forward a range of alternatives with the interest and care they claimed had been denied them. Roth would talk with them for hours until they were exhausted, while he felt like he'd only just got started. He'd see the strain on their faces as their miseries were challenged in the least aggressive way, the effort as they'd start to push back against his sweet reason. Quickly he realised the extent to which their miseries were beloved, their squalor revelled in. He was not here to judge. He was here to help them all if he could. And he tried, a zealot for his cause, enlivened by the pursuit – never in life had he felt as bold as he did now.

As the weeks passed, he grew sure that only Ralph had the potential to escape this moribund life. Their other two inmates were already de-fanged, demotivated by life, past the point of no return. And yet the more Roth knew Ralph, the more he came to dislike him. The young man poured with ferocious, disgusting vitriol, precise in target, fierce in expression – impressive had it not been so vile. Ralph was a racist, a xenophobe, a sexist, a Luddite ready to rip anyone's head off should they have the stupidity to challenge his views. He'd lived a life of torment, if you took his claims at face value. Roth tried to listen patiently and respond with engaged argument about why those Ralph thought were keeping him down were not. They'd talk beyond the politics and go as far into his background as the young, damaged man would let him. And then Roth would smash hard against something disgusting, despicable, and feel the sting of disappointment. A peculiar boy, grown toxic from numerous punishings, able to take diametric leaps of points of view without reference to an opinion held just a few moments earlier. The more appealing side of his nature was also the most guarded; a flash and it wouldn't be seen again for days. Roth took all manner of verbal beatings in order to salve this man's spirit. And then finally Ralph started speaking to Roth the way Roth felt he'd spoken to Berenson on the day of his long confession. *A breakthrough*. The most rewarding sensation of his life.

Progress in one area generated tension in another. Their housemates were increasingly jealous of Roth's interest in the kid and the promise it appeared to contain. They could smell opportunities heading Ralph's way but not theirs. Who the hell *was* this do-gooder, anyway, what did he *really* want? You couldn't trust people, least of all those with nothing to gain. For every slice of encouragement Roth gave Ralph, their two housemates insulted him, belittled him, reminded him of gruesome echoes of his past he'd been careless enough to reveal in vulnerable moments. Ralph had issues, to say the least, which is why he'd ended up in this rotten house share to begin with. The young guy became increasingly hostile, contradictory, short-tempered, damaged, immature. Roth displayed a level of patience even he found remarkable, and he was *used* to waiting on the whims of others: trying to bring Ralph back from one of his rages was tiring and scary. He knew he could move out at any time, find other, more amenable surroundings. Yet if he decided this environment was too nasty and flitted elsewhere, he'd achieve nothing. He wanted to leave a trail of improvement, not discontent. So he stayed, and persisted. He'd do whatever it took, however resilient, however resolute he had to be.

He walked into the kitchen one morning to learn that Ralph had moved out in the middle of the night. No forwarding address, no mobile phone number, no email. Weeks of painstaking work had just vanished into thin air.

His alarm rang at 7am. He checked his email.

No response from Mia.

The glow from the wine and the voyeuristic pleasures of Café Mauve had faded with morning. He ate breakfast in the minuscule dining room at the Hotel Foucault. The vertigo of abandonment was flushing through him. Hope fought with fear: scenarios ran through his mind. She must have stayed up late last night, yammering away with Becky; they were both so excited to see each other, right? To be in Paris, escaping the gravitational force of their backgrounds. They must have spoken about every damn thing they'd missed in their time apart until they'd crashed at four in the morning, hence why Mia hadn't checked her email in the time since he'd sent her the message.

Even now, she was probably snoozing away in the guest room of Becky's no doubt grand apartment. So he wasn't being a complete fool to think she *would* get in touch with him. There was simply no reason for him to expect her to have replied so quickly.

He checked his email again.

Nothing.

All was lost! He couldn't help wondering if he was being a fool, overwhelmed by the moment, the romance of the journey, stupid to think such a young and beautiful woman would be interested in spending any more than forced time on a train with him. That there'd be any more than the brushing of fingers as he handed her the coffee won from the beverage carriage of the Eurostar. Yes, a fool, and increasingly – as the time ticked by – a fool older than he used to be.

He stood in the shadow of the Louvre. The grand walls, the carving, the view of the Seine . . . How appealing the thought of travelling around the world visiting buildings of wonder and beauty – the sheer scale of the palace combined with its beauty burned itself on the retina. No wonder he recalled it from his trip here with Berenson.

'*Parlez-vous Anglais*?' he said to his first unwitting banker, in his first unwitting French bank, with as much accent as he could manage.

'Yes sir,' the man replied in clear, clean English.

'This is going to sound unusual,' Roth began, 'But I have a key to a box held by a bank.'

'So far, *monsieur*, that sounds quite usual.'

'Problem is, I don't know which box or . . . which bank.'

Quoi? the man's expression said.

'Can I show you and you tell me if it's one of yours?'

The smart, startled banker nodded slowly in disbelief. Roth passed the key over to him for inspection. The Frenchman looked at it with outsized concern. A few moments later, he shook his head. *'Non monsieur,* this is not one of ours.'

Roth nodded. It was inevitable that he'd be disappointed first time out. 'Do you know whose it might be?'

'Non.'

'Okay,' Roth replied, taking back the key. 'Well, *merci beaucoup.'*

'You are welcome,' the banker replied, his disdain intense.

And so started another day in the peculiar life of Scott Roth. He moved from bank to bank, asking the same questions, getting the same humiliating response. He saw more eyebrows rise than he thought were contained in the whole of Paris. He edited them together as a comedy sketch in his mind, rise after rise after rise to a soundtrack of jaunty music. He checked his email repeatedly; still nothing from Mia. The day stretched on, until it was clear to him that she had no intention of replying.

Lunch came as a salvation. He ate fast, knocked back some piquant coffee and wavered into the afternoon. But his toil only produced more turned-up noses, more raised eyebrows. The process was bad enough back home – here he felt like a silly little-Englander stumbling around.

'Monsieur,' a lady said, another smart, youthful, well-dressed banker: 'This key is not one of ours, but I used to work in *le Banque de Louis Quatorze,* and it looks exactly like the ones they use.'

Roth stared at her, the words fluttering into his ears as if upon angel wings. The banker looked back at him with an honest, open face, as if she were doing no more than passing on a handy piece of data rather than providing him with the first piece of good news he'd had for an age. He could have kissed her. 'Thank you so much!' he exclaimed with delight.

'No problemo,' she said, with a strong French accent and perky grin.

He checked his list – the *Banque de Louis Quatorze* wasn't even on it.

* * *

As he approached the benighted institution, he realised the Louvre was further away than he'd remembered: more than half a mile. He took out his phone and checked his email.

A message from Mia!

His heart leapt again – what planet had suddenly slid into alignment in the heavens above? He pressed 'open' so hard he almost broke his screen.

'*hey*', the email said, '*cafe mauve sounds great! See you there at 8. Mia*'

'*Magnifique*!' he roared with delight.

A wave of joy carried him into the *Banque de Louis Quatorze.* He introduced himself to the bespoke front-deskers (they were all so well turned out!). The man and woman studied the key with blank expressions. The latter looked at Roth with the same exactitude she'd used on the key.

Waiting for them to finish their inspection, he glanced around. This bank had zero personality. The silent hum of vast wealth spoke of faceless cliffs of money that served neither the greater good nor even those to whom it belonged; money creating money, for the sole purpose of creating more money, only to be invested back into ever more money, and never to be spent on a human.

The front-desker shook his head. 'This is not one of ours.'

Roth stared at him for a few moments. '*What?* But I was told —'

'*Monsieur, non.*'

'But—'

'*Non.*'

Roth couldn't bring himself to leave. 'But I was expressly told that you use these keys.'

'*Monsieur*: used to.'

'How long ago?'

'Many years.'

'But I was *told*—'

'We have no such keys here any more,' the woman said, with such strictness that it was clear they wanted to waste no more time on him.

Roth wanted to protest but had no cause, only a stranger's hunch, and you can't take that to the European Court of Justice. The Frenchman held out the key. He took it, as crestfallen as he'd arrived overjoyed. He wandered out of the bank, ready to jump into the Seine.

He lay on his bed at the Hotel Foucault, disappointment washing through his body. Only the prospect of his date with Mia prevented him from taking the next plane to the hottest beach, getting as far away from it all as possible. But even she might stand him up, for he'd noted, with dismay, that she'd not put a little kiss after her name.

He jumped off the bed and walked over to the window, cursing the man who'd placed him in this awful situation. *'Enjoy yourself, enjoy yourself,'* he growled to no one but the walls. *'How can I enjoy it, Dieter? Why didn't* you *bloody enjoy* yourself *instead of telling everyone else what to do?'* Berenson had had plenty of money when Roth worked for him; later it turned out that he had a whole lot more. But the man had died in the middle of the night working at his desk at home, alone, found in the morning by a member of staff. Sad and, in the final analysis, pathetic. This titan with no one in the world to care for him, or to miss him now he was gone – except for his lawyer. Pffff, what kind of a legacy is that? Berenson was always in his element when telling other people what to do – but the facade had crumbled in his absence. His old boss had loved to be in on the biggest secrets, the hottest knowledge . . . Well, nothing strange about that, many people were possessed of the same egocentric cravings. Dieter loved to make it known that he knew and no one else did. Now he came to think of it, he had been a rather unpleasant man. Perhaps that was why so many other unpleasant people felt so comfortable telling him about their worst offences against the human spirit. Not that Berenson would ever talk of the horrors revealed to him. He didn't need to: the routine remained the same, and those around him could recognise the variations in his behaviour following each confession, and what they may mean.

It always began with an afternoon at a very expensive restaurant with booths of exclusivity. Any kind of lurid behaviour might take place there – sex, drugs and possibly rock'n'roll – with the management ensuring that no one would ever know. Such location set the confessee at ease. Berenson would order a light lunch for them both, so as not to exhaust them with digestion. A little alcohol to loosen the lips, but not so much as to dull the senses or reverse the flow of truth. At the end of the confession – which lasted as long as it had to – Berenson would call for cabs and both parties would return to their lives. One would feel lighter-hearted, the other polluted with second-hand toxins. When the boss returned to the office after one of his lunches, Berenson's staff knew not to ask questions, nor to comment on his low spirits. But one day, Roth was sitting at his desk when an ashen Berenson passed by and said to him, 'Come with me.'

A surprise: was the man about to spill?

Into the honcho's office they went. Dieter gestured for Roth to close the door behind him, which he did.

Berenson dropped onto his chair, looking ill. 'I have just heard something *very* depressing.'

Roth sat, uncertain whether he was supposed to comment. He had no idea what Berenson might want him to say, so he remained silent.

Finally the boss gasped, 'How can there be so many deviants out there? I can't have a cup of coffee without hearing about acts so disgusting by folks so base that . . . it's not even how these fuckers sleep at night but . . . how do they even think of this shit in the first place? Christ, Scottie, it's repulsive. Do I have to listen to this for the good of mankind for the rest of my life? There are times when it ... it gets so awful—'

He stopped talking, so depleted that Roth felt like he should provide some kind of response, the content immaterial as long as words came out of his mouth. 'Well, there's a lot of people out there who never get help. Who society just—'

'Fucks?'

'Squanders, is what I was going to say.'

'No.' Berenson shook his head. 'This planet is *fucked*. It's awash with the most hideous, foul, disgusting, lying, evil perverts . . . They make me sick! These awful, malevolent— I have to sit there with a straight face while some so-called pillar of the community with his profile in the national press tells me he fucks babies on regular occasions. What am I supposed to do with *that*?'

'You really want me to answer?'

'Yes, I do! You're precisely the person I want to answer, yes, you, Scott Roth! Tell me what I'm supposed to do with these fuckers.'

'I . . . I don't feel qualified to pass judgement on others.'

'I don't need your qualification, just tell me what you think!'

'Dieter, there's a lot of people who get a raw deal—'

'*I'm not talking about them!* I need you to tell me how I deal with the ones who are doing all the *fucking*.'

'I don't know about those kind of people.'

'Well you've worked with *me* for long enough.'

Roth wasn't sure where his boss was going with this. He fell into the safety of silence.

Berenson sighed long and hard. 'I need to hear the view of someone who is *not* a polluted vessel, Scottie. And before you go on about that kid who died, you know what I think about *that*. I am begging you! Don't make me beg, Roth! Be kind to me, because I'm lost and I need you to be good enough to save my soul! I don't want to think this world is already a waste, I don't want to think that the bad guys have taken over and everyone else breathes only to provide these gross fuckers with a pyramid to sit atop. I want to believe in this world so much: I am that bleeding heart! Is this what it's like for priests? How can their good nature survive such cynicism? How can they keep doing their jobs? I've heard three confessions this month, and each one has made me sick!'

'So stop!'

'That's not the answer! Who will they confess to if not me? Without my intervention they'll bend even more out of shape, and Christ alone knows what they'll do then. The Marquis de Sade would blush! I'm not a prude, you know that, but when I hear these tales of deviancy over and over and over again from all of these different people – I wonder if they've *all* read *The Pervert's Handbook*. Men and women who run companies, influence investments worth billions of dollars, employ hundreds of thousands of people – it's disgusting, Scottie. It's evil!' He sat back in his chair, drained. 'I'm forty-seven years old. I have more money than I'll ever need, but I can't stop. Even if I try, they won't let me. They seek me out, and don't take no for an answer, keep on raising their offers until it offends me not to take so much money for such little work. And they know I'll keep their secrets. They know I won't let on about their despicable natures, I'll advise them well and they can use my words as exoneration. And that's the worst thing: they leave with a fucking *smile* on their faces, because I've made it okay for them. I've listened to their hideous confession and the world hasn't come to an end. They dance away, renewed. And I sit there with such . . . They have no idea how much I want to smash their faces in with . . . with . . . *with a fucking fire extinguisher*.' He fell silent, his expression hollowed out.

There was a long pause. The sky, in its innocence, passed by the window, its conscience clear.

Roth said, 'Are you done?'

Berenson looked at him. '*Et tu*, Scottie? *Et tu*?'

The assistant replied, 'We need to talk about the Milan trip.'

The boss sighed. 'That we do, my friend. That we do.'

He reached Café Mauve at twenty to eight. He'd walked from his hotel heaving with disappointment at the day's dashed hopes. The pain he felt at the front-deskers of the *Banque de Louis Quatorze* telling him that they did not carry such keys as his, that the box he was looking for wasn't there after all . . . Back to square one: hunting through his list, bank by bank, humiliating response by humiliating response. Wondering if he was going nuts, thinking of his old boss, the self-appointed confessor, looking down at him from above and laughing his head off as his hapless wastrel trudged around Paris.

And now he stood outside the café, his date nowhere to be seen. Sleek couples, chic and full of life, walked past, observed by Roth and his detached, morose expression. He had to buck up if he wanted to show Mia a good time, but as the minutes ticked by, his gloom grew a second head. The bonhomie in Café Mauve seemed to expand the more couples he saw go in. He was still standing by the door, a sucker, when eight o'clock came but Mia had not. A quarter past, twenty past . . . Wearing new clothes, he felt overdressed and underwhelming. Alone in the most romantic city in the world – which seemed to be participating in a conspiracy against him – what on earth was he doing, he wondered, holding on for a woman who was patently *not* going to show up?

Chapter 8

He collapsed onto his side of the bed, exhausted. His body pulsed with the aftereffects of orgasm; Mia traced him as she settled, reached out, a palm on his chest, she too coming down from a high of her own. Their animal sounds, a few moments earlier wild as their lovemaking reached a frenzy, were silent. They had tasted in each other a hunger, energised by the sparks, and now, past their panting, he could hear the night, bereft of lust. He gazed at her. And, in her expression, saw joy and relief. They need not congratulate each other or give thanks to the great beyond; those graces were visible already. She smiled at him, unleashed a corner of her beauty that he hadn't yet seen. And then, carefree and worn out, she closed her eyes, murmured a soft *g'night* and fell asleep.

Just like that, she was gone! He watched her for a while, marvelling at her beauty, and the ease with which she'd just conked out. And then he too lay back, happy and empty. After the day's disenchantments, an amazing night. Mia had finally turned up at Café Mauve past eight thirty, full of apologies for being late. She looked *fantastic*. And then they sat like every other funky couple in the sequestered cool, drinking coffee and nibbling on crudités; they'd eaten a tasty dinner with quite a bit of wine; walked back to his hotel, wobbling like a couple of bowling pins thanks to alcohol light-headedness, after which had followed the passion. He chuckled: *okay, Dieter, now I'm starting to enjoy myself!* He closed his eyes and, in a short moment, he too was asleep.

He woke, *could hear someone in the room.*

A rush of anxiety: they were being robbed. A figure in the darkness, at the edge of his awareness. The intruder: trying to be silent but failing. Roth remained still, sucking in his breath to stay invisible in the soundscape. But despite best efforts on both sides, every now and then, from intruder and guest there came a wheeze, a murmur.

Slowly he turned on to his back as if he were moving in his sleep. He tilted his head enough to see the interloper's silhouette. The thief was looking through the drawers of his desk. Deft, moving quickly, slim shoulders. Focused, urgent – businesslike. Roth was trembling at the shock of the invasion, the unexpected closeness to his scene of greatest love. He wanted to close his eyes and go back to sleep, but the figure persisted in pulling open drawers as quietly as possible, searching through them and then moving on to the next – this was *happening*. He stared at the silhouette, his mind a blank, knowing he had to do something but with no idea what that might be.

The figure suddenly went rushing from the room – spooked by a sense of someone else awake?

Roth jumped from the bed and hid by the door frame that led into the hall. He couldn't hear the opening or closing of the front door.

The intruder was still in the room.

A long sheet of terror curled itself around him. Here for the key, of course – but did the thief have a weapon? He was naked, unarmed, utterly defenceless. He looked at Mia asleep, half-wrapped in a bed sheet. In the opposite direction, at the other end of the hall less than ten feet away, the person who'd broken into their room, who was waiting by the door, poised . . . to do what?

Roth cursed Berenson: *couldn't you have left a gun in that fucking box?*

He could hear the intruder make their way back along the hall.

He almost stopped breathing. The sound of the footsteps getting closer, the conclusion reached: the only way to escape was to quieten Roth and Mia for ever.

His heart was beating at the pace of a stampede.

He heard a click, could see a faded shaft of light.

Then came the thud of a door.

The intruder had fled.

He let out a breath of life-giving proportions, stood for a moment, knowing that he had to check the hall. Dieter had said there would be others, and he was seeing the shadows of low-slung Audis in the distance. It hadn't occurred to him that the Audis might start driving into his bedroom.

He reached for the nearest lamp and flicked on the switch. The bedroom became light; he dimmed it. The desk drawer was open. He pressed it shut. Thank the Lord the intruder hadn't ventured inside his wheelie case, which lay in a corner of the room. He sighed in heavy relief when his eyes fell upon the sought-after key, still where he'd left it in the pocket on the inside of the lid. A warning indeed: he was going to have to beef up his security.

He looked into the hall, protecting himself with the door frame, just in case. A glow from the bedroom dissipated before it reached the far end. He could see no dark mass lurking, no human silhouette with gun cocked, ready to blow his brains out and steal Berenson's treasure, no old school trickery of opening and closing the door but still being in the room.

He walked into the darkness, switched on the light in the bathroom; illumination flooded the hall. He looked at the lock.

It had not been forced.

He switched off the light, stood cold and naked by the bathroom, thinking. Slowly, he walked back into the bedroom.

He looked at his bed.

At Mia snoozing softly.

His stomach began to churn with dismay.

The café across the road from the Hotel Foucault, the venue Roth had imbued with the notion of myth when he'd spied it on his first venture out, served indeed a glorious *petit dejeuner*. He sat across the table from Mia as the modern *pants au fancy* brought themselves back from a heavy night's sleep. Around them, the din and sunlight of morning, of chat and flirting, of Parisian life. Mia ravishingly boho, buzzed on good vibes and coffee. She'd emerged from her sleep as refreshed as Roth was not, a model woken up in a cover shoot. Full of beans, a flinging together of clothes, she was thrilled to be sitting across the table from him. All of which underscored the colossal conflict he was feeling inside.

'What shall we do today?' she said, full of abundance as she layered thick marmalade onto her toast. 'How about something *really* special?! We could go to the D'Orsay, or the top of the Eiffel Tower, or – I know! – we could take one of those romantic boat rides along the Seine! Yes, let's do that! They're cheesy but they look such fun!'

'Don't you have stuff you need to do?' Roth asked.

'No way, no sir: all I have to do is live!'

'I mean, you must – you're looking for work?' He was trying to keep the creep of suspicion from his voice.

'I've got time for that,' she replied. 'I just want to be with you. *This* is living. A cool, pretty place to eat, a picturesque backstreet in the middle of Paris . . . And I'm here with *you*, darling. What more could I possibly want?'

'But seriously, I mean . . . what happened to fashion?'

'Fashion and me had a good day yesterday,' she replied, grinning. 'And then you and I had a *great* night! And I am not ready for it to end. Let's make a day of today! Let's you and I go out and *live*.'

'I have stuff I need to do,' he replied, testiness inflecting his voice. 'I'll – I'll be distracted by your beauty, I won't get anything done.'

She hit him with the sweetest, beamiest face. 'Oh, well! You do what you have to do! I'll go and have fun for us both. Where do you want to meet tonight?'

He hadn't thought that far ahead. And then, a strange product of anger, instinct and want, he knew exactly where he should propose: 'Why don't I pick you up at Becky's place?'

'Perfect!' she replied. 'I'll send you the address!'

Joyful joy of joys! Of course Mia wasn't involved in the break-in last night! Impossible, absurd, and here was the proof! It took only a moment of clarification, and now he could enjoy it anew! For if Mia *had* been involved in the attempted robbery of his hotel room, there could be no 'Becky's apartment'. For they'd be based out of a mission control HQ Roth could never be allowed to visit, however hard he pushed. Yet Mia hadn't even blinked when he asked to pick her up at Becky's place, so it had to exist, it couldn't just be some place where they planned all kinds of nefarious acts! And now his heart was singing again, songs of joy! For he could feel himself falling in love with the *Germinal*-reading beauty. Yes, and deep. He crackled with excitement when she was close, and couldn't bear to be separated from her. The long hours when they were apart, the delight of seeing her when they were reunited; gosh, all of that stupid stuff was flushing through him as if he were fourteen years old. Yes, love. Its sudden, unexpected arrival from the unknown quarters of nowhere, at a juncture that he couldn't decide was opportune or detracting – he had strange work to do and a vast world in which it had to be done. And now there was love! The stun of deep attraction, the deciding vote cast by the heart. He'd only known her for the shortest time, but he was already grinning at the moon. Opportune or not, he knew how he felt. There was absolutely nothing he could do about it.

His questions were growing slick with practice; less abashed at asking stuffy front-deskers of esteemed institutions to inspect the key he gave them; less perturbed by watching their faces as they simultaneously couldn't believe what they'd been asked to do and yet did it. Roth was helped by the fact that the range of responses was starting to grow. Some wanted to provide this peculiar questioner with good news, others for him to get the hell away and take his dumb key with him. Even so, regardless of their motives, the result was always the same: Roth left each bank without success. Paris was not the cheapest of cities, and if he was dating while here, the money would go even quicker. The sixty thousand was now fifty-three thousand, and would soon be fifty-one and ever-diminishing. There were only so many banks he'd be able to visit before his money or his time on this planet Earth ran out.

He stopped for lunch at a luminous café. So evocative, you only had to order black coffee to feel like a Left Bank radical wondering where to chuck your next figurative and/or literal Molotov. He let his mind wander, and was instantly thinking again about his night with Mia. *Concentrate!*

He racked his brains trying to recall outside which institution he'd been standing when he'd formed the memory of Berenson in the foreground and the Louvre dominating the background. He could feel himself layering images upon fragments that may or may not have been remembered correctly in the first place, ebbing further and further away from the facts.

He gave up, checked his email.

'Hey you,' an incoming message said. *'Been thinking about last night all morning. Can't wait to see you again! Mia xx'*

More joyful joyness! More wonderful wonderfulness! Humongous dollops of superduperness!

But what happiness does that boy have, fourteen years dead? He'd be thirty-one now, had you not felled him. Maybe he'd have had a family of his own, having wised up and forsaken his criminal endeavours. Even if he'd wound up in jail for five years, he could have grown remorseful and vowed to mend his ways, studied hard, discovered literature, learned a trade and emerged from prison a new man. At the least, he'd still be breathing – but he is not, and never will be, and for that reason alone, you cannot let yourself fall for this woman, however much in love you feel.

He read the email over and over again, the stretching, the strain of his emotions amplified by those two glorious kisses. But history was always right (another of Berenson's stupid sayings): you could never pretend the past was not with you at all times. Right now, the shark of his past was circling him. *You have no right to be happy, certainly not with someone like her.* With superhuman effort, he put all thought of Mia from his mind and continued to work.

The afternoon progressed in the same vein as the morning: *non après non après non*. The good news: he was speeding up. The bad news: to no great purpose whatsoever.

He returned to the Hotel Foucault at five, the banks closed, his efforts unrewarded, his pride worn down by the day. He lay on the bed, reading *The Book of Illusions*. The ambient sounds of Pareeeeee provided a pleasant lilt, taking a strain off feet that had pounded *rue* all day. He looked up from his book at the time. It was before seven; a pre-dinner cup of tea was in order.

He called reception to make his request, was about to put down the phone when, on a whim, he dialled the mysterious number again. He knew it by heart by now, and his fingers leapt across the keys free of mindful direction. The phone half at his ear, he heard the rings ping by one by one.

'PLEASE COME, YOU MUST HURRY, I'M SO SCARED HERE ON MY OWN.'

He jumped in shock, but before he could speak, the line died and the voice was gone.

'Hello?' he said into the phone. 'Hello? *Hello?*' He clicked the hook, but no one was there. He dialled again. The tone led to the sixteen rings and then the cutting-out he had heard on dozens of previous occasions.

There was a knock at the door. He leapt like a cat. And then he remembered: *room service*.

The voice. A girl. *Terrified*.

He drank his tea, shell-shocked by her tone as well as her message. Perhaps he'd pressed a wrong digit? The number was so long, he could try any number of variations and never work out if he'd made a mistake to get through that one time. But the sound, the *fear* . . . The voice a beat from another world. He tried the number again, to make sure he hadn't blundered when dialling. There was no reconnect, just the same sixteen chimes, the same dead end.

He sat and thought, *the fright in the voice* . . . The normality of the hotel room soaked up the weirdness. A bleak sensation passed over him, the tingling of unwanted recollection: the nadir of life in a decade of dosshouses, an occasion last year when he'd heard voices that were not real. He was suffering badly for his good nature by that point, emotionally and spiritually worn down by the constant negativity he kept on finding when all he wanted to do was help. And then, one night, after a particularly heavy disappointment that had simply floored him, he was beset for an evening by voices that were not only figments of his imagination but just would not shut up. There was simply no getting away from them, or pretending that he'd misheard a conversation taking place elsewhere. All night these voices yammered away, though he was alone in his room. The only occasion when he'd felt madness come close, and not in a spacey, self-aggrandising way, but in a genuinely unavoidable episode of temporary insanity. The voices spoke for more than two hours, and then abated like the echoes of people who had just left the room. Roth had never told anyone about this, only partly because he'd never had anyone to tell.

He tried to push the recollection from his head, but the brain was a peculiar organ, and echoed in disloyal, unhelpful ways. Imagined or not, he could picture the girl's face, full of fear, somewhere far away –

but where? As he was finding out bank by bank, even the real world was so much bigger than it seemed, let alone the infinity of imagination. Her image began to fade from view, eaten by the passing seconds, smothered by thoughts of the last time he'd heard voices in his head, an occasion he'd hoped never to repeat. A shadow across a cloud vanishing in the rain; a face that may not exist, yet the fright in the voice was real enough. He couldn't ignore it. He had to try the number again.

First time. Rang out.

Second. Rang out.

Call number three. Rang out.

Call four. Rang out.

Call five. *Rang out.*

He was trembling as he put down the phone. The hotel room had taken on a hue of dismay. He sat in the silence, sipped his tea and thought of Mia. Instantly, he started to feel better.

She called him ten minutes before he was due to leave for her apartment. Becky, she explained, had offered to give her a lift to the restaurant, which was close to Roth's hotel. Naturally then, it was silly that he should get a cab *all the way* over to Becky's place and then go *all the way back* into central Paris. It made *far more sense* for Becky to bring Mia over. 'So that's what we'll do! See you soon darling. I'll look so amazing you won't even want to go out for dinner!'

The phone went down, and before he'd even had the chance to protest, he was no longer picking up Mia from Becky's apartment but meeting her at the restaurant, where she'd be dropped off by her bestest friend. She hadn't let him say a word, had crowded out the conversation with words start to end. In this way she had managed to avoid even giving him Becky's address.

* * *

'You should have come with me to the Louvre,' she said, sitting opposite him at their table in the boutique restaurant. 'It was *amazing*.'

'Maybe ... in a few days,' he replied, deeply uncomfortable all over again.

'The Impressionist masters—'

'When my work is done.'

She smiled at him, looked at the wine list. 'Shall we have a red?'

He nodded, despite his squall of misgivings. He was so delighted to see her again, to be back in her company; proximate to her beauty, her superstar grin: *agonising*. Her brown eyes were full of pleasure at the sight of him. For whatever reasons he may want to resist, or feel that he shouldn't be allowed to receive such love, it was impossible for him to defy her grip on his emotions. He was damn sure he didn't *want* to resist. As for the rest of it . . .?

The wine came – a sumptuous red, a true cockles-warmer. Mia was on full-glow superbness, crackling with effervescence. She couldn't keep her hands off him, threw love bombs that wore him down. After a few glasses of wine and the running of her legs up against his in the restaurant, he couldn't have cared less whether or not she had been involved in last night's break-in and gave into her utterly. They made whoopee again that night – *at his hotel*. As she pulsed beneath him, a hazard of delight, he knew beyond doubt that he loved her – *and that she was up to her neck in this business*. She played her cards so close to her chest that he could barely see the edges, but his spider senses continued to flicker like mad.

They fell against the bed. Mia was soon asleep again, and he wide awake. He'd already planned what he was going to do to spoil the intruder's second attempt to steal the key, should he or she (Becky?) return to get what they'd been disturbed from finding the night before. Roth slid out of bed and walked to the front door. Carefully, he poured a bottle of shower gel across the floor. Anyone coming in without his knowledge would slide over and smash into the ground, cracking bones or at least making a ruckus that would send them rushing off.

As an additional measure, he took some tape he'd bought earlier in the day for this very purpose and, feeling unusually like James Bond, fixed a sliver of adhesive across the join between the door and its frame. If Mia managed to clean away the shower gel and unlock the door while he was asleep, he'd still know that someone had come into the room if the tape had moved.

He returned to bed and angled himself against the pillows. He put his alarm on early enough that he could get up and clean away the shower gel before Mia awoke. As a further precaution, he left an ash tray on the bedside table with which to fight aggression, though the thought left him sick with anxiety.

Slow minutes passed, each bringing him another drift closer to sleep. He used all kinds of mental forks-in-the-legs to stay awake. He squeezed his thighs and moved out of every comfortable position into which his body crept. His dry eyes flicked between Mia and the doorway. He thought about the ash tray, if it was in his hand, what he might have to do with it . . .

He was awoken by his alarm, beside the still-snoozing Mia. It was past seven o'clock in the morning, a sliver of bright light passing between the tiny crack in the curtains. Roth felt a surge of anxiety: *the key!* He jumped out of bed and ran to the hall, where he saw neither a pile of tripped intruder nor the door-frame tape disturbed. The shower gel had congealed into a shiny layer across the floor, smooth for lack of disruption overnight.

He came back into the bedroom and inspected the safe, the last of his security checks. The key was still where it should be.

Roth looked at the woman in his bed. Mia was swaddled in the duvet, dead to the world. There'd been no new break-in, no key theft, no missing girlfriend. Now he didn't have a clue what to think.

Chapter 9

'*Oui monsieur,*' the banker said. 'I have seen a key like this.'

Roth was thrilled. 'It's one of yours?'

'Non, monsieur,' she replied. 'It is for *le Banque de Louis Quatorze.'*

He frowned. 'Are you – are you sure about that?'

'Certainement. I used to work there until six months ago. I saw keys like this all the time.'

Roth stood outside the *Banque de Louis Quatorze* – again. He was down to the last few banks within close enough range of the Louvre to match his memory of his time here with Berenson. He was soon about to run out of institutions, and had had no idea where else he should look. Still, he hesitated. Would the friends he'd made on his first visit here be pleased to see him a second time? He might have to force his way past the front desk. No, there'd be no bullying, no blunt instruments, no aggressive acts of any kind. He'd be charming, have them eating out of his hands. He took a deep breath and walked in.

The same two members of staff were poised at the front desk. Dark expressions passed across their faces as soon as they saw him. They stopped what they were doing.

'Hello,' said Roth, with the creamiest gaze he could muster. 'Now: I have this key, and I was wondering if you could—'

'Monsieur,' the man said, before he could say any more. 'Let us go to a quieter room.'

The door closed. It was just the three of them. 'Forgive us,' the Frenchman said. *'Je suis* Francois – and this is my associate Sophie.'

'Bonjour monsieur,' she said, as if it were the first time they'd met.

'Hello,' said Roth cautiously.

'So,' Francois continued. 'You saw through us.'

'It was our instructions,' Sophie said, equally embarrassed, 'Should a man come here with the key you brought, to say that we did not have this account.'

They watched Roth with patient dismay; unique circumstances meant a unique response – and quite possibly a dangerous one.

'If the account *is* here,' Roth asked, 'Can I have the box?'

Francois and Sophie exchanged a look he was becoming quite familiar with.

'It is not quite so easy as that,' she replied. 'Do you have an account number?'

'No.'

'You have anything we could at least consider?'

Roth felt the onset of another brick wall. And then a thought occurred to him. He took a pad and paper from a nearby table and wrote down the mysterious phone number, which he had by now rung dozens of times and which may or may not have connected that one time. In his head he heard the chime of the girl's voice – and the fear that she may be imaginary. He pushed such thoughts from his mind and handed the piece of paper with the number on it to the bankers.

Francois looked at it and said, 'No *monsieur*, this is not right.'

Roth was fazed and relieved at the same time.

And then he remembered the second long number on the sheet of paper that came from the box at Mikhail Banking. 'Hold on.' He'd kept the leaf along with the key in the envelope they came in, which was starting to look threadbare. It had maintained its structural integrity, despite the constant removal of the key. He took out the sheet of paper and handed it to Francois and Sophie. 'Is *this* it?'

The bankers inspected the number for what seemed like an age.

Francois said, 'I will get the box,' and left the room.

Roth was left alone with an awkward Sophie.

'Should I be worried?' he asked.

'I could not say.'

'Is there anything you could say?'

'*Oui monsieur*. I would recommend that you go to the Picasso exhibition at the D'Orsay.'

The door opened. Francois came in with a small steel box, which he placed on the table.

Roth's whole world had narrowed down to this minuscule container. He stared at it in mild disbelief; he'd been sure he would never find it. Were he on his own, he might have thought he was hallucinating. But Sophie and Francois gazed at it too, all three of them possessed by the sight.

Roth took the key from his pocket and pressed it deep into the lock. He paused for a moment, then twisted.

A click.

It opened.

He gave a gasp, the echo of weeks. He leant forward – then stopped, looked at Sophie and Francois, who were staring at the box with unprofessional interest. They caught Roth's expression and realised it was time for them to leave.

'We will be outside, *monsieur*,' Sophie said, with more disappointment than she intended to show. 'If you . . . need anything.'

'Thanks,' he said. 'I'll keep that in mind.'

He was alone again, and wondered what hell was about to break loose. He lifted the lid, picked up the box and tilted it.

Three envelopes slid into the open end. Two small and one large, A4, slim. He took them out and laid them on the table in front of him.

The A4 envelope and one of the smaller two had his name typed on them. The third was blank but for another crazy series of digits.

He opened this envelope first and found inside it another key, as anonymous as the one he'd spent the best part of two weeks trying to find a lock for. It was roughly the same size; he could only assume it served the same purpose: another private box to hunt. '*Great . . .*'

He picked up the second small envelope, found inside it another letter written in Berenson's familiar scribble.

So you remembered our time in Paris! I knew I was right to turn to you in my time of need! Scottie, you truly are my angel. I hope you're keeping your eyes open for those in pursuit; they're dangerous bastards. I never had any doubt that you were strong and smart enough to get the better of them. There's a little something extra here, to apologise for dragging you around.

Now, some information. My fear has been such that I couldn't write down your instructions. I had to leave the clues in your mind, and trust you to use your memories of our time together to work out where I wanted you to go. The fact that you're reading this shows how right I was to rely on you. Your progress delights and impresses me beyond words. Even I, your biggest fan.

Roth sighed – so that's the game, huh?

Nice idea, don't you think?! It's perfect! You were always able to read my mind – I prized that greatly. But you must remain forever on guard. You're engaged with the scum of the earth, for whom no trick is too disgusting, no means too despicable. They'll throw all kinds of things at you: threaten you with your worst fears and send beautiful women to trap you – if they can break your heart to get what they want, so much the better. But they don't know you like I do. They don't know that you're such a force of good, that you have grit as well as soul. Carry on the great work, and stay ever vigilant, my angel.

Roth shook his head, folded the letter back into the envelope and put it down on the table. What is it with these rich bastards, that they think of no one but themselves? How could Berenson turn to *him*, of all people – when he knew he'd dedicated his life to helping the mistreated? Even the zillionaire hardest done by had no right to call on his time.

Supremely irritated, Roth picked up the A4 package and tore off the seal. He reached inside and felt nothing but a sheet of thick paper, which he took from the envelope and looked at in disgust. A technical financial document of some kind.

Bearer Bond

In the sum of

One million euros

He stared; his eyes ran over the words until he was sure he was seeing what he thought he had. He'd worked with Berenson for long enough to know a bearer bond entitled whoever possessed it to the amount stated on its front. He – Scott Roth, of Finger Dick, Northumberland – was the bearer of this bond. He'd changed sterling to euros at St Pancras so he knew the exchange rate. Starting to perspire, he made the calculation amid palpitations, this *little something extra*. He reached the same figure again and again.

Berenson had just given him eight hundred thousand pounds.

Again: the numbness, the shock, the *wealth*.

A little something extra in this box.

He was stuck, couldn't move. The bearer bond.

Eight hundred grand lay there on the table.

It seemed like a joke. But the words, the words, *the words*.

Bearer Bond.

In the sum of.

One million euros.

Sixty grand allowed him to prise himself loose from a lost decade. Eight hundred was a whole new life, the freedom that came from having wealth. It was retirement money to a man like him, who'd been living on no more than fifteen grand a year. And there were other possibilities too: *think of all of the people you could help now!*

Well, let's not get carried away . . . But it *was* too much. How was he supposed to make sense of that kind of money? Dieter knew he wouldn't have the faintest idea how to— He knocked off one of the zeroes, and *now* felt a surge of excitement. Eighty grand was so much easier to understand.

He saw a phone, could think of only one person to call.

'Good Lord!' Weston exclaimed. 'Lucky you! I wish that kind of thing would happen to me!'

'But what should I *do* with it?'

'Cash it!'

'Where?'

'Why, the *Banque de Louis Quatorze,* of course! Speak with the manager, give them the details of your Mikhail Banking account. There'll be a charge but you're a rich man now! You'll have eight hundred thousand pounds ready to roll in forty-eight hours at most!'

'You'll call me when the deposit is made?'

'I'll dress up in a tutu if you like.' Roth didn't laugh. 'Can I give you some advice,' the banker said, 'From one who sees rich people day in, day out, year after year?'

'Please.'

'Enjoy it.'

Now Roth laughed, a stifled chuckle. But he could already sense a change in his cells and wasn't at all sure he liked how that felt.

Chapter 10

He had another key: his search was on once more. *Where next?* But at least now he knew he wasn't on a wild goose chase. He checked with Sophie and Francois – the new key was not one of theirs; Berenson wouldn't have been so incautious – and made it so easy – as to have placed two boxes in the same bank.

He searched through memories of the places he'd been to with Berenson: New York, Berlin, Geneva, the Cayman Islands, Buenos Aires, Tokyo, Amsterdam, Sydney, Wellington, Dubai . . . Each of these destinations was home to hundreds of banks, with thousands more nearby. Berenson's business was funded by all kinds of consortia: Roth recalled him moaning about how he only seemed to spend time with bankers. They also formed a large part of his confessions practice: their kinks, foibles and deviancies represented the spectrum of secret, abhorrent behaviour. Where you found people, you found savings, loans and houses of finance. You also found perversion. But this time he had no Louvre-sized landmark looming in his recall to help narrow the parameters.

He closed his eyes, felt his body ache. He realised there was nothing he wanted in this world now more than Mia.

'Picasso at the D'Orsay was *amazing,*' she said, smiling.

He couldn't keep his mind and body in alignment. They were eating in yet another Parisian bistro. She regaled him of the wonders of her day – the more he heard, the greater became his regret at not tagging along. He hadn't told her he was practically a millionaire. His body was aflame with attraction; he was enchanted by her enthusiasm, her optimism, her sheer good cheer.

A hell of an actress.

He wasn't even sure why he'd made this dinner date; he'd known how tough it would be. In his lovelorn state, every light chuckle she made, every turn of her head, every subtle wisp of her hair would further drive his craving, his lust, the hunger in his balls. No man had listened to an account of a day at an art gallery with more longing than he right now. What impact would it have if he told Mia that he'd found the first box on the treasure hunt, and now had so much money that he'd had to divide it by ten to grasp it in real terms? Her gaze was fierce upon him, awash with a fire that would rip him to shreds if she could have her way with him. Berenson had placed this quest in the hands of a man he deemed utterly sensible, yet Roth felt like he was losing his marbles. This woman; he should get up and walk out on her, for she was the enemy – *yet he couldn't move.* The bistro seemed to be a part of the conspiracy. The candles flickered between them, her hands held his, the indelible nature of such a moment as . . .

Downtown.

Near Wall Street.

Walking through the Financial District, going from bank to bank, Berenson marching like a general and his army all in one. Me struggling to keep up, tight deadlines, pointless making the trip by cab.

A glow passed through his body that had nothing to do with Mia. Her mouth moved but he could no longer hear her voice. For a good fifteen seconds he could sense nothing but that memory.

'Maybe we can go there together,' she said.

His thinking flipped from background to foreground, from a decade ago to the present. He looked at her, suddenly alarmed – *can she read my thoughts?*

'The exhibition,' she said. 'I'd love to see it again. Maybe tomorrow?'

'Sure,' he replied. But now he could only think, *New York.*

His heart was beating hard, and not just because they were engaged in kissing appropriate to the nation they were in. A ten-minute bust-up had taken place at the end of dinner, after which Mia had agreed that they *would* go back to Becky's apartment instead of his hotel. Only a change yet again was afoot.

'Come on,' she whispered. 'Let's go to yours, we can make *so* much more *noise* without Becky in the next room.'

He quietened her mouth with a kiss, felt her succumb to his lips. She breathed how much she loved him, the dissonance consumed by his lust. Her hand moved to his groin. He fizzed with excitement; the pressure risked blowing out his frontal lobe. Mia started to rub. 'We can do whatever you want at your hotel . . . stuff you've never done with anyone else . . .'

'How much longer til we get there?' Roth yelped at the driver.

'Deux minutes.'

The lights of central Paris gave way to residential streets. Roth gasped, 'It's silly to go back to mine now.'

'What about Becky?'

'We'll be quiet.'

'When are we quiet?!'

'Tonight we'll be quiet.'

She pulled back from the kiss, the removal of her lips, a change of tone. She glared at him. 'You're serious.'

'About being quiet?'

'What's so important about my flat?' Mia asked, her eyes flashing with an escalating anger.

'I want see your world,' Roth said, his heart pounding.

'It's *not* my world,' she replied, 'Just somewhere I'm crashing for a few months.'

'So what's the big deal?'

'Yeah: what *is* the big deal?'

'I thought it would be romantic.'

'Well it's fucking annoying, is what it is!'

He gawped at her stupidly.

She stared back at him for what seemed like years.

The cab stopped outside a quiet, shabby building. Roth and Mia stepped out and he paid the driver.

He looked at the building. 'This is it?'

She nodded, scowling.

A sullen pause. They walked to the front door. She fumbled for her keys. He looked along the street. There was no one around. She unlocked the door. They went inside.

A narrow flight of stairs. At the top, a door. Mia looked at him in the dark. Whatever was going through her mind, she decided not to say; instead, with reluctance, she unlocked it and pushed it open.

His heart began to beat like a train.

With a glance, he consumed the vista: a smallish lounge, sofas and cushions; a TV, an open kitchen with washing-up to do; a table to one side, empty wine glass on the floor, Becky on the sofa in a T-shirt and jeans watching TV, a tub of ice cream in her lap. A hurricane had passed through these walls but the clean-up had yet to take place; an apartment lived in – perhaps too well.

'Oh!' Becky said, surprised. 'I didn't think you'd be back tonight.'

Mia was fuming. 'Yeah, me neither.' She shook her head in fury, walking towards the hall leading off the lounge.

Becky's eyes fell on Roth, who stood for a moment, awkward, confused. Mia vanished through a door; it slammed behind her with a noisy thud. Roth tried to smile at Becky before turning and walking after Mia.

And so, in the bedroom, a place he had been sure did not exist, Mia's clothes were strewn all over the place, *Germinal* sat on the rickety bedside table, toiletries here and there, carrier bags with rolled-up Picasso prints . . .

'Well,' she said, furious. 'Here we are.'

'Yes,' he replied, embarrassed . 'Here we are.'

'You didn't believe me, did you?'

He blushed. 'It's been a – a strange time for me.'

'Can't you see what a fucking mess it is?! Becky's a slob. Just because she's got this super-hot, super-pressurised job in architecture doesn't mean she can use a mop. Now you see why I didn't want to bring you back? This is so embarrassing! Why the *fuck* did you think I was lying?'

'I . . . unh . . .' There was a pause; longer than he'd have liked.

'I was in such a good mood before but now I'm so angry with you! You just didn't listen to me, typical fucking man! The only thing that matters is what's going on inside your head! What about my head?! What about how I was feeling, coming back here when I told you I didn't want to!'

'Mia—'

'No, Scott, don't do that! I want to fucking *punch* you.'

She was glaring at him with such furious anger that, he thought, a sock from her would lay him out for a week. They made this assessment at the same time; the thought clearly amused them both. Mia's temper calmed. The two stood in the room, looking at each other, wondering how they'd got to this place in space and time.

She walked over to him, took him by the hand, led him a metre to the bed. They fell next to each other, and, with the noise reduction button switched on, made secretive, passionate love, far away from the ears of her flatmate, and the rest of the world.

She fell asleep first again – *quelle cheek!*

He looked at her, naked next to him, conscience free as the air. He gazed around at the room, the walls bare, no posters pinned up. He watched the woman ensconced in slumber, a vibrant creature, alive to the possibilities of the world.

He got up and settled by the window. There was no exterior view, just the back of the opposite building. Poetic in a down-at-heel way, yet so different from the sights he was used to nowadays, from the windows of the Dorchester, the Hotels Foucault and Salon. He relived the night, the preceding three days, packed with more excitement than the past decade. She'd given him the truth of her domain; she was Becky's lodger . . .

He sat there until the sun broke through, at which point he collected his clothes, put on his underwear, shirt and trousers.

Mia started to move. He froze, two-thirds dressed.

She settled back into her doze.

On went his shoes, his coat.

He took a last look as he walked towards the door. Mia was nuzzled deep within the bedclothes, thinking he was next to her. Roth turned his head and listened. When he was sure Becky wasn't lurking nearby, he poked his head into the hall. *Clear*. He walked out of the bedroom, along the hall and – after another cautious pause – into the silent lounge.

A few moments later, he was in the street outside, the shabby, run-down Parisian suburb, scanning the horizon for a cab. He walked for a while until he found one. An hour later he checked out of the Hotel Foucault and was on his way to the airport, where he caught the first available flight to New York.

New York

Chapter 11

'Wine, sir?' the cabin attendant asked.

He shook his head, turned back to the window. He stared at the endless day as they flew in tandem with the sun. He couldn't get comfortable, kept on thinking about Mia's reaction when she woke to find he'd gone.

Her interest in him was too quick, too easy, too all-encompassing – his luck wasn't that good, so there had to be another reason for her interest, and there could be only one: the pursuit of Berenson's treasure. She *must* have let the intruder into his room; there was no other way that person could have got in so easily. The discovery by Roth of the attempted robbery as it took place, spooking the intruder, meant there could be no return the following night; another way of obtaining the key would have to be found. More direct? More dangerous? Who knew? But for as long as he stayed with Mia, they'd be aware of his location at all times. A hell of a risk to take.

'Actually,' he said, to the cabin attendant, 'I think I   I will have a glass, thanks.'

And how. He knocked back a bottle of red. It made him feel no less strung out, no less guilty about his disappearing act. He could drink the plane dry and still be in the grip of this pain, this echo, this self-defeating guilt.

At JFK, squirming from an airplane hangover, he turned on his phone. Among the texts, a message from Gordon Weston that he should call as soon as possible.

'Scott!' the Mikhail banker said.

'Yeah . . .' he murmured, standing by the baggage reclaim, rubbing his eyes and wondering why Weston sounded so jovial.

'So we just got a credit to your account,' the banker said. 'It's gonna put a smile on your face if nothing else has. You've had to stand a few charges, but I have great pleasure in telling you you're richer by £807,249.19.'

Hearing the number relayed in such precise terms brought him out in a flush of anxiety. 'That's . . .' he said, staring at the cases riding around the carousel, none of which looked like his. 'That's—'

'So what's the plan?' he heard Weston say. 'A couple of weeks somewhere like Maui?'

'I . . . I just arrived in New York.'

'Well, *someone's* getting on with enjoying themselves at last!'

'No, it's . . . I need to ask you—'

'Oh Lord, not another one of your lists.'

'I'm afraid so.'

Weston sighed theatrically. 'Of course, of course, but there's a lot of private banks in New York. It might take a while to compile.'

'I'll see the sights.'

'Have you anywhere to stay?'

'No, and I'm not in the frame of mind to wander.'

'There's a lovely place by Union Square called Hotel Rumours. Very comfortable, *very* discreet.'

'Perfect.'

'Scott, you sound tired.'

'Late night, early start, no sleep on the plane—'

'And plenty of wine, eh?' Weston started to laugh.

'Maybe . . .'

'Let me know when you're back in London. There's a restaurant near the bank I think you'd love.'

'Sounds great.'

'Don't knock yourself out, my friend. Speak to you soon!'

They rang off. Roth let his new reality wash over him. The unsolicited benefits of wealth – great hotels and restaurants, excellent service and bonhomie – were already flowing his way, and he'd only been rich for five minutes. He gritted his teeth, opened his email and waited. The usual confluence of subscriptions and alerts came flooding in, but nothing at all from Mia.

Downtown and plugged in, Hotel Rumours became the next addition to his list of venues tried and tested. He slid his case into the corner of the room, knew that if he lay down he'd fall asleep instantly. The hotel's vibe filled him with a churning feeling of hip, as if he could go to a nightclub and find Woody Allen in the midst of performing stand-up, a concert with Dylan about to go electric or a street corner with Marty Scorsese and Bobby De Niro hanging about, talking and dreaming of film.

He fell on to the bed and was asleep in seconds.

Her screaming cut through the jet-lag.

In the dark, curtains open, moonlight shining through, his forehead burning, anxious, *helpless*, her voice curdled, in need of help and *he hadn't answered*. He was rootless, torn free from all he'd known these past forty years by that voice, penetrating all the way down, saying *nothing else matters but that you come to me now, and hurry like never before.* But to which corner of the planet should he rush to calm a figment of his overtaxed imagination?

'*Christ* . . .' he sighed, mopping his face with a corner of the duvet cover. He looked at the clock: 2am. Wide awake, he got up, sat on the edge of the bed, picked up the phone and dialled the mysterious number. It connected. The tones chimed. The line cut out after sixteen rings. He tried again: the same. Nothing, but still he felt the sense of dread in her voice.

You're hearing things, he told himself; *and now you're dreaming about what you've heard when you've been hearing things.*

He was the diametric opposite of mad, everyone said so, but he'd been under such pressure lately, had to deal with so much rubbish . . . He tried to let his mind rest but kept on hearing that child's voice, or was it truly just a part of his imagination? Increasingly hard to tell.

He put the phone down, remembered that he hadn't unpacked. He opened his case and left it by the chest of drawers: *there,* he thought, *unpacked*. He grabbed the key from the Paris box and set out into the New York night.

At Union Square, a full moon, a light affray of passers-by: even his money couldn't find him here. Warm air, no time: deep in the night of a place at which you've just arrived, the definition of lost. Was it possible to recover wasted days, weeks, years? *Where can a rich man get a burger at this time?*

A shadow hustled towards him. 'Hey buddy, you got a dime?'

Through grit and night, Roth could see clever eyes. 'I got euros.'

The tramp replied, 'You can give it to me in fuckin' bearer bonds if you want.'

Roth laughed, reached into his pocket and took out all of his leftover cash from Paris: more than a hundred euros. 'Don't get stiffed on the exchange rate.'

The tramp swivelled off into the night, pleased as punch. Roth watched him before walking on to find a cashpoint, dollars and a midnight burger.

As he walked, he realised how little he recalled of Manhattan from his trips here with Berenson a decade earlier. He wondered now where his head was back then. He'd been so much younger, though hadn't felt it at the time. He walked on through Greenwich Village, the Financial District, Midtown . . . Memories of Dieter flooded back to him on this tinted day-for-night.

'They come to me with their darkest secrets,' his old boss had explained to him one late afternoon. 'But what they really want is for someone to tell them the truth about the kind of person they are. They know it, Scottie – at least many of them do. Some don't, so when I lead them by the hand to the grand illumination, it's *shocking*. I've seen big men, giants of business worth hundreds of millions of dollars, sit in the chair opposite me and *sob* because, for the first time in their life, someone has shown them what they really are. Some have run from the truth for years, and suddenly grasp the essence of their nature. Nothing comes as such a shock when it's spelled out. There's a consistency, Scottie. I'm not saying that all bad people are alike, but a *lot* of my clients discover the same shitty thing about themselves when they confess their wicked acts to me. I can feel the strain in my heart, like a herd of horses rushing across my chest. I've had to tell this truth to so many of them. Because I can see what they are – and few other people can. I don't know why, but there we are: I can just tell. And it's my role as their confessor to inform them of this hideous fact. They want the truth – and they get it. I have my doubts about whether or not they're capable of doing anything with it once they know; I suspect not. But I never see them again, for confession at least. Once is enough. Maybe I'm too good. Or the truth hurts too much.'

'What if they don't agree with your version?' Roth had asked.

Berenson's eyes opened wide: *you suggest I might be wrong?*

Roth continued bravely. 'You listen to them for an hour, or two, or five, and then tell them about themselves, as if they're strangers to the person looking back in the mirror, though they may be forty or sixty years old?! I'm just saying—'

'You're being a provocateur, which is *most* unlike you.'

'I'm just pointing out—'

'That – my dear boy – is why they pay me the big bucks.'

And *that* was the end of the conversation. Even so, Roth knew that whatever went on between Berenson and his 'clients', the truth could only be what they were prepared to admit, acknowledge, avow. They were paying him for his advice and, like all clients, were free to disregard that advice if they so chose. They were more than capable of buying other truths elsewhere.

He was getting sleepy again: there was more New York City to New York City than he remembered. He found his way to the Hotel Rumours as the sun began to rise. He wandered through the corridors to his room, where he fell into a disjointed sleep.

He woke around midday, fumbled with his phone, checked his email: no list from Weston, no word from Mia. His shoulders were raw with tension. Perhaps he should use a portion of his new, vast wealth getting a massage. He picked up a recommendation from reception. He also arranged a safe this time, to make sure that any would-be intruders couldn't just flip open his wheelie case and find the key inside. As per the unwritten rule, the safe was located in the bottom of the wardrobe. So sorted, he headed out.

He walked the streets for an hour, his ears and mind filling with the city buzz. He passed high-end shops with high-end product in the windows; it was impossible not to catch a glance of some of the numbers. It remained shocking to him that he could now walk into these stores and buy himself a super-expensive watch, a super-fast car, a *property*. He didn't deserve the money Berenson had given him, yet he was perched in a café, a man with a million in Manhattan, with nothing to do but wait for a list of banks that may take days to compile. The coffee, an internal hug, the blood vessels opening up, trying to think his way through this new, peculiar forest of being monied. Was he was supposed to behave in a certain way? Was he supposed to start behaving like Berenson?

Back at the hotel, he sat on his bed, phone number in hand to make sure he was getting it right. He dialled, waited; the line cut out after sixteen rings. He dialled again. Waited. Sixteen rings. Cut out, dialled a third time, a fourth, a tenth, a nineteenth, a twenty-third. He rang and rang for an hour. All the while the tone whined, never connecting, bringing him back the voice of the girl. Finally he gave up.

He stared out of the window across downtown Manhattan, feeling his confidence wane. The city seemed so much bigger than the lock he sought. Eight hundred grand would become a burden to him the way his many millions had become a drain upon his sponsor's soul. He didn't want it – and nor had Berenson, if his old boss had been honest. But Dieter was so competitive that he couldn't help but make as much money as possible and keep on going long after he had enough to last umpteen lavish lifetimes.

'Tell me about … your family,' the boss had asked, during Roth's confession.

Roth was silent. Was this a test, a game? A right and a wrong answer, the truth too truthful? 'I was adopted,' he said finally.

Berenson did not respond.

'I never met the people who gave me the so-called great gift of life,' Roth continued. 'Yes, I was adopted when I was four years old. What came before is, thankfully, a total blank.'

Berenson smiled, shook his head. 'Your misanthropy is a pretence; I can see right through it. So you never learned the identity of your biological parents?'

Roth shook his head.

'Why not?'

'What was the point? They didn't want me. And my real parents were just terrific.'

'The people who adopted you?'

'Yes.'

'But didn't you want to know where you came from? Didn't you have that famed sense of longing to find out *what you really were*?'

'I am what I do from day to day. Who is more than that?'

'And what *do* you do, from day to day?'

'As well as I can.'

Berenson smiled; a decent answer. 'So you loved your parents?'

'Very much.'

'And how about a family of your own?'

'I don't have one.'

'Do you want one?'

'Yes,' said Roth, after a pause.

'That took a while,' the boss noted.

'It's not a simple question.'

'No?'

'No.'

'Why not?'

'I don't – It's how I . . .' Roth trailed off, unable to finish the sentence.

'I know what the answer is,' Berenson announced grandly.

Roth's expression said, *go on then*.

'Because you don't think you deserve one.'

Now it was Roth's turn not to respond.

'So you're going to deny yourself a family for the rest of your life,' Berenson continued. 'Because of an incident that took ten seconds and in which you did nothing wrong? In which you committed no crime.'

'I don't want to talk about it.'

'Then you don't get how this works.'

'Then we can stop right now.'

Berenson was cool, didn't react. He let a few moments go by. 'Have you ever come close?'

'To what?'

'To having a wife and children?'

'No.'

'Why not?'

'I always worked too hard.'

'Is that ever a good answer?'

'Good enough for you.'

'You assume I haven't had my chances.'

Roth drew back into his cave.

'So no family,' the boss said. 'And you don't want one.'

'I do. But not for the sake of having one.'

'Wise, but foolish – in the longer term, because ... none of us are getting any younger.'

'I wouldn't want to resent them.'

'But you know what they say about the baby and the bathwater?'

Again, Roth chose not to answer.

'Scottie, you're a man of few words. I respect that. You're worth listening to when something does sneak out. Some people say little and still when they speak it wasn't worth waiting for.' Berenson's eyes narrowed. 'You were adopted as a child, and now you've adopted a child of your own.'

'What?'

'It's obvious,' the boss said, 'And we've only been talking about it a short while. *That's* why people come to me with their confessions.'

'You've lost me.'

'This teenage boy, this would-be killer. You adopted him, whether you realised it or not. He was your child right up until the moment you met him. And you feel as if you killed your own kid. You *own* him,' the boss said. 'You can't let him go. You don't know where you came from, and you don't know where he went; you make a perfect pair. But who found whom, Scottie, that's the real question. Who found whom?'

Roth had been ready to volley, his patience at an end. But Berenson had planted in his lap a truth he'd never wanted to grasp: that he *had* taken ownership of that teenage boy when he broke him, and he'd never been able to rid himself of the kid in the time since. That he *had* wanted to rid himself of this child was, he knew, one of the most shameful parts of the whole business.

He went walking again, through the New York night. The city burdened him with the beauty of its women. Plenty to take his mind off Mia: too much.

Past midnight, he received one of the emails he'd been waiting for. Gordon Weston had sent him his latest long list, itemising all of Manhattan's private banks. Once again, they numbered in the many hundreds. Roth had had no idea there was so much money in the world. Small wonder that those who had it wanted to keep it hidden from everyone else. Now the majority of the people on the planet would count him among that lucky lucky group.

The front desk of Hotel Rumours printed the new list for him. He scanned through it, the names anonymous yet the keeper of so many secrets: each account a story of its own, each bank a custodian of tales.

His work had begun again.

Chapter 12

He decided to start with Wall Street and radiate out from there.

The sunny reception at the first institution: a stark contrast to the gloomier welcomings of old Europe. This one was full of banker beans, ripe for the time of the day. 'Yessir! How may we help?'

'I have a key,' Roth said, slightly cowed by the American's good cheer. 'I'm sure it's for a private box. Could it be one of yours?'

The sliding of bonhomie into a distinctly blank look, staring at this strange-requesting limey. 'You don't have any more details than that?'

Roth shook his head.

The front-desker took the key, spent a few moments looking at it. Roth could tell he wasn't engaged in what he was doing. With fake great sadness, the man looked up and said, 'I'm sorry sir, but we don't have any like these.'

Roth nodded; he'd expected no less. 'Do you know who does?'

The man shook his head.

'Well, thanks anyway.'

As he walked off with his key, Roth could feel the front-desker looking for hidden cameras, concerned he might have just been had.

He emerged from his ninth unsuccessful bank of the morning onto a quiet road off Wall Street, thinking about pausing to recharge his batteries. Though he'd grown resistant to the variety of reactions to his odd questions, there was still a toll to be paid by the spirit, a drag that left him jaded as the day drew on.

'Excuse me,' the tall man said, with American politeness, as he put an arm out to block Roth's way. 'How about we go for coffee?'

Roth hadn't seen him approach; he'd loomed in from nowhere. The guy was as sturdy as an Amish barn and looked like a pumped Brad Pitt. There was no way to get past him – nor was he meant to. 'Just a coffee,' he said, with mega-wattage persuasiveness. 'Over there.' He indicated a small café.

Roth mumbled a *no thanks* and tried to walk on, but the man wouldn't let him pass. Roth began to realise he was in trouble. He looked up at the big American, whose effortless charm powered a self-confident grin. Yet there was a coldness, a menace behind the ease.

The man said, 'You won't find what you're looking for by searching every bank in the world.'

Roth's anxiety converted into a steep fear.

'Come with me,' the big American said. 'For a cup of coffee. You must be thirsty, having gone to nine banks already this morning.'

The grin grew a degree. New Yorkers walked past without a clue as to what was going on. Roth glanced at them – they were a thousand miles away, incapable of helping him out. His new friend's bulk was aggressive, possessive; he must spend hours in the gym.

'Do I have a choice?' Roth asked.

'This is the free world, Scottie. You *always* have a choice. And if you choose not to come with me, I'm gonna have to choose whether or not to break your neck or bust your chest with a hammer.'

'Okay,' Roth replied, after a grim pause. 'Let's go have this coffee.'

They sat in a quiet corner of the café. The big American's name was Everett Mulcahy. Charming, cool, smart – he was no longer an aggressor on the street. Now he was an ambassador, a true believer, though unwilling to state in whom.

'We can help you,' Mulcahy said.

'Who can?'

'We can.'

'And you are?'

'The answer to all your problems! Isn't this the piece of news you've been waiting for?' The big American spoke with contagious excitement. 'We know you have the key, that you've been shopping it around to find its home. Neat idea, but the problem remains: you don't know what to do with it.' He smiled at Roth with star wattage hard to resist, an open door to the greatest party you've never been to. So relaxed: *let's have a couple of beers, talk about big things and get high on vibes*. Roth was being seduced, and knowing it wasn't enough to enable him to resist. 'Poor you, that's what I can't help thinking: poor Scott Roth, why's a man like this trying find Dieter Berenson's hidden treasure bank by bank? He must have a pool of patience that's bottomless and, hell, what an amazing swimmer he must be! Will you find what you're looking for that way? Un-unh, not a chance! But good for you, man: this is your lucky day!'

'Maybe I don't need your help.'

'If that's the case, coffee's on me! You can slap me on the back, kiss me on the cheek and tell me to fuck off to the boondocks! I'm impossible to offend. But you *know* you don't have a goddamn clue where you're going, and I'm just this big, handsome guy who's emerged from nowhere offering you the answer to all of your problems. There's a lot of money at the end of this quest. More money than you've ever dreamt of. But you got to find it first!'

'Maybe I'm doing just fine.'

'And maybe you're not! Maybe you're starting to get testy at your old boss for laying this quest on you without a map.'

Roth tried hard not to react, but was having a painful time keeping his face in order. Despite his efforts at showing otherwise, he was intimidated by Mulcahy. Worse: the prospect of a shortcut to the end of the quest was almost too appealing to resist.

The American said, 'It appears to us that you're being so methodical, so logical, so industrious *that you're looking in all the wrong places*. The world is big, my friend, far bigger than you have time for. You're not an old man – for now. But you *do* know how time flies, and how easy it is to waste on shit.'

'Who do you mean by "us"?'

Mulcahy chuckled. 'It's enough to say we can help you. We can be friends in need. There, I said it! We need help. But then so do you.'

'No, I don't.'

'Of course you don't! Which is why you haven't found Berenson's hidden treasure.'

'Maybe I'm wondering how *you'd* know where I should look?'

Mulcahy's eyes sparkled, the longer-for question. 'Because our mutual friend had a plan that was larger than just you. I don't want to make you feel less special, because he must have thought a shit *mountain* of your good self to involve you at all. But do you really think Dieter would trust his estate to the safe keeping of just one man? Did I say we're talking about a huge amount of money?! He spread the responsibility around. Of course, I'm sure he didn't tell you that that was what he was going to do, the sneaky old bastard! That would have made it too dangerous, in case any of his instructions fell into the wrong hands.'

Roth looked at Mulcahy with a cold, blank expression.

'So he *didn't* tell you that part? Well, isn't that like our good old cagey friend!'

'So how do you know about me, if Berenson didn't tell me about you? Not that it matters anyway – I found the first clue without you.'

'Then I'd say you've used up all your luck.'

Roth shook his head. 'You haven't answered my question.'

'It's clear that I know who you are. Just like it's clear I know what you've been up to – and that you're staying at Hotel Rumours.'

Roth felt his guts leave the room.

'And if you *did* happen upon the right place by chance,' the big American continued, 'Or if you *had* worked out where the treasure may be, or if you *did* possess a golden piece of information handed to you by a glorious bystander, maybe even *then* you'd find the people at the banks were still instructed not to confirm that you'd found the right place. Maybe it was all part of a test, to see how dogged and diligent you were, or if the clues fell into the wrong hands, that they wouldn't be able to track down the treasure because they wouldn't know what Dieter expected of them. Scottie, you've got to keep in mind that your old boss was a man of world-class sneakiness. Maybe you think of him, the self-confessed confessor, as if he were a paragon with edge, a good guy not above a little crookery once in a blue moon. You've been in business, you know the type, come across them all the time. If that's the case, you're doing yourself the same disservice Berenson has done you. It's not for me to be a prick, though I am, oh yes I am! There's about a thousand women who could testify to that! No, I don't want to be the prick who tells you what a shit heel your old friend happened to be. I don't want to say quite how venal the grand confessor really was. You worked for him for less than a year, so you saw only a small chunk of a career lasting three decades. This man has put you in a truly shitty position: Scottie, did he even help you after you quit working for him? He could have done you so much good, but he did – *excusez* my *Français* – *fuck all*. He was as selfish as the next rich asshole who couldn't care less for the likes of you. Years, Scottie, years! Years go by and you hear nothing! And then, from beyond the grave: the burden! Of course he was never gonna tell you everything: he doesn't trust even you! Nutcase didn't trust anyone by the time he died. That's why he was alone when it happened, when his days came to an end. But you're good, honest, a true humanitarian. You don't have the same way of thinking he did, so you'll never be able to put your mind into his and work out all the things he hoped you would.' Mulcahy smiled. 'I'm offering you a shortcut, because you need one. You're not going to find Berenson's treasure going about in this half-assed way, which is the best you can do having been given no information whatsoever. I'm offering you the other side of the map. You have the key, and we know where to go. Sounds like we're perfectly placed to help each other. After all, this *is* what Dieter wanted. Unless trudging around banks is something you've really come to enjoy?'

Roth didn't reply. His quavering voice would betray how nervous he felt. And how persuasive Mulcahy had been. The sly smile, the clear light coming in through the café windows, the creepy feeling of people watching.

Mulcahy said, 'I don't expect you to believe me; I'm sure Berenson didn't say anything about us. But he was not a man of trust, whatever else he might have said, whatever impression he tried to leave you with. After all, if he trusted you so much, wouldn't he have just told you where to go?'

No one else was going to help him. Roth wondered how bad the pounding would be if he said no, if he tried to make a break for it? He doubted Mulcahy was here on his own, thanks to the 'us' reference but also because the Brad Pitt-lookalike was too well turned out to be in the field without support. He was not the kind who chased the targets down. He was the kind who administered the beating while others held the captive in place.

There was a dicey silence. But there came again the megawatt grin. 'I can see you need some time to think, buddy,' Mulcahy said. He handed Roth a business card. 'Here's my number. When you're ready to talk, gimme a call.'

Roth locked his bedroom door, rammed one of the super-tasteful chairs against it hard – but still the barricade didn't seem strong enough. He put the TV on top, at which point it started to look a little more resilient. Even so, he was sick at the ease with which the Super Jock could have snapped him in two. Mulcahy was not some goofball. He was a thinking associate. His business card said as much: 'Everett Mulcahy, associate, Exeter Services Inc.'

The key was burning a dark hole through his well-being. He locked it in the safe in his room, glad not to have to look at it for a while. Then he sat in the furthest corner away from the front door, staring at furniture that would hardly improve his chances of keeping out would-be killers.

The question struck him with full force between the eyes: if this new guy had emerged then ... *did Mia have anything to do with the break-in after all?*

A vertiginous sense crawled across his subconscious; he ran through the facts, as rapidly as possible. First, she'd become his lover, which could only give him cause for suspicion; second, her appearance on the Eurostar in the seat across from him was too magical to have been real; third, her keenness to engage in conversation on said Eurostar beggered comprehension; fourth, the fact that she'd responded to his pathetic overtures was curious in the extreme; fifth, she kept turning up to their dates, so she *must* have had an ulterior motive; sixth, she appeared not to have a clue what had happened the night of the break-in, which was obviously a pretence; seventh, she'd resisted taking him back to Becky's apartment though it was unclear why; eighth, her eyes had glimmered with excitement whenever she saw him; ninth, she'd whispered in his ear that she was falling in love with him, which could only have been a lie; tenth, the fact that . . .

The fact that . . .

The fact that—

Oh no oh no oh no oh no OH NO OH NO OH NO.

Berenson's unforgettable gaze: penetrating, one-way – you couldn't see what lay on the other side, what was going on in the depths of that head.

He had asked, with a twinkle: 'So, how *do* you feel when a stranger approaches?'

Roth did not want to reply to this particular loaded question, but was equally aware that, if his confession was to be of any use, he had to explain things to himself as well as to his confessor. And so came the damning admission. 'I feel as if I should help them.'

'Regardless of who they are? You'd help everyone?'

'Only those who need it.'

The piercing eyes were flashing now, a shark about to feast. 'And how can you tell that they really do need it?'

The slippery slope. 'I don't know. A feeling, a look they have.'

'So you don't know for sure . . .?'

'No, it's—'

'Instinct?'

'Yes.'

'You let them play you.'

Bang! There it came. 'No,' said Roth. 'I'm not *that* stupid.'

'No, just a little bit. Do continue!'

'So you can make me feel stupider?'

'Is that the effect the truth has on you?'

'No. It's how *you're* making me feel.'

Berenson smiled. 'So we *are* getting somewhere! I know a confession's gaining traction when the confessee starts to get irritated.'

'And maybe the confessor shouldn't seem like he's enjoying himself so much.'

'*Touché!* So you were telling me how you assist those most successful in making you feel sorry for them.'

Roth did not reply.

'Come on, Scottie, don't be angry! Tell me about this teenager. How did he look when he approached?'

Now he was practically glaring at his boss. 'So this is how you do it? Turn people inside out?'

'Only the ones I'm interested in.'

And why are you so interested in me? he thought but did not say. The man was still his employer: he wanted to hold on to his job, so he shouldn't get too het up.

'You'd help those who'd kill you?' Berenson pressed.

'*Especially* those.'

'So let me get this straight: any stranger who approaches you, be they grey-haired old lady or wild-eyed would-be killer: you feel as if you have to help them?'

Roth said, 'If they need help, yes.'

'Well then,' the boss replied, nodding with unexpected appreciation. 'You really *do* have your work cut out, don't you?'

'Why the fuck are you wasting your fuckin' time on me?' one of his 'projects' said, sitting on the scummy sofa in a bad-feeling hostel, a man who'd spent years on the streets and looked a decade older than he was. His face was scarred and pockmarked from fights and bad karma. He owned a lascivious gaze. It was late in the afternoon. The smell of bad food filtered along the hall from the kitchen. 'You shouldn't be here,' the man said. 'Not with the likes of me!'

'I don't agree with that at all,' Roth had replied.

'*You are not one of us*,' the pug face continued. 'I'm a bad fuckin' man. I robbed people, I mugged people, I held them up with knives. I *used* knives. I cut fuckin' people open without a second thought. People like you!'

'But you were hungry,' Roth said. 'You were out on the street, you didn't have anyone else to turn to.'

'I was on my own.'

'You had your reasons.'

'They were not fuckin' *good* reasons.'

'Society didn't give you a chance.'

The pug face laughed, revealing the moribund condition of the few teeth he had. Roth watched his eyes grow moist with amusement. 'Society had nothing to do with it! I was strong, I could fuckin' work! I knew right from wrong! It was *easier* to be bad, I couldn't have cared fuckin' less! I used an *axe* a few times – made people shit their pants. I mean *people actually shit in their fuckin' pants!* When it was over, they had their lives but they sure didn't have their fuckin' dignity! I never got caught. Cops never fuckin' got me. One day I got myself. I just stopped doing it. I didn't have any fuckin' money so I lived on the streets. Authorities put me in here. Even this shithole is more than I deserve! I was too fuckin' old to turn it down; it was too fuckin' easy to accept! But that's why *I'm* here. Why are *you?*'

'I'm here to help.'

'Pa-hahahahahaha!!!' The old dosser couldn't stop laughing, an expulsion of guttural mass. 'Well, let me save you the fuckin' effort: don't bother! You *know* you shouldn't be here! You got a place, I bet, with some rich fucker who'd love to put you back where you belong. He ain't here, moron! Why *are* you? To help me? I don't need your fuckin' help! This place is too fuckin' good for a scumbag like me. I could live out my days here and die laughing. But this ain't for you, pal. And the sooner you fuckin' work that out, the better!'

'I can encourage you.'

'BAAHAHAHAHAHA!!! Ow, stop it! You're fuckin' killin' me!'

'I can show you that there is a better way—'

'WOOO-HHOO-HWAAAAHAHAHAH!!!'

'Well . . . There *is* a better way.'

'I always *knew* there was a better way! I was just too fuckin' lazy to do it that way, and no one could fuckin' stop me doin' it my way!'

'Please . . .' said Roth, the sting of desperation creeping in – years invested in his project only to end up here.

The pug face looked at him. He held out an open palm, as worn and grey as the rest of him. 'Show me how much you want to help!'

Roth was appalled. But the old dosser stared at him, the palm suspended in the no-man's-land between them, which Roth desperately wanted to cross.

'Come on, I ain't got all fuckin' day, I got meetings to attend!'

This was not how he'd dreamt it would be. But did he want to help or not? It always came down to the same moment, when money assumed its position in the transaction, the assistance wanted always of the financial kind. In the past, Roth had ponied up without having to be asked. But that way bled him of his limited funds very quickly. A few years in, he'd learned to wait until he was asked – and he was always asked, eventually. Now he hated it when it came. But how could he show he meant business any other way? That he hadn't just good words to preach but money where his mouth was? And so, as he had countless times in past years, he reached into his pocket and took out all of the cash he had and dropped it into the man's open palm.

There was a register of disbelief on the old pug's face, the shock of witnessing something new when he thought he'd seen it all. He counted the notes. £45 in total. He looked at Roth, sparkly-eyed. 'You realise I ain't giving it back.'

'I know,' Roth said, feeling a little sick.

The man continued to stare at him, unable to comprehend if he was looking at the kindest or the stupidest man he'd ever met. And then he roared with laughter, an appreciation of the universe far beyond what this strange, do-gooder simpleton would ever grasp, this naïf who hadn't listened to a word he'd said. And Roth sat there listening to it, knowing that he was still taking the punishment he deserved, with much more yet to come.

Now his body ached with another form of stupidity, for Mia was somewhere other than here, driven away by his moronic suspicion, his burned-out insanity. Scott Roth, the man who for ten years had made such a big deal about being so wonderful to others, had treated Mia *shockingly badly*. The young wannabe fashion designer who had nothing whatsoever to do with this business; that was plain now that Mulcahy had appeared. Perhaps it was more of the punishment he deserved, but he felt he'd be torn apart by his longing for her, the way he missed her every damn second of the day. But it was too late, for even if he sent her an email, she would think him utterly bonkers. That is, if she didn't just hate his guts.

Chapter 13

He was a bag of nerves as he jumped into the first cab he saw. From the safety of its innards, he scanned the people on the streets of New York. A chunky dude wearing glasses over here. A whippet of a fellow drinking soda over there. A power-walking woman. Dozens of yellow cabs from any of which the big American may leap with his team of homicidal arm-twisters.

Exposed and vulnerable, Roth made it to the day's first bank unmolested. Swish in style and firm of jaw, the employees of this establishment were moulded from the same movie-star plastic as his pursuer: telegenic surroundings, seductive character actors. For a moment he was frightened that they were in on it too.

'Hello,' the lady at the front desk said. 'How may we be of help?'

Roth glanced at the front door to check that no one had followed him in. He turned back to the woman, who was clearly wondering what he was looking for. 'I have a key,' he said. 'But I have no idea which box it fits.'

'In our bank?'

'In the *world*.'

Once again, that look of utter disbelief.

'Will you take a glance to see if it's one if yours?'

Her face bore serious discomfort as he took out the key and gave it to her for a once-over, a twice-over.

'Not ours,' she said, handing it back.

Expected. Disappointing. 'Any idea whose it might be?'

'No, sir.'

Zero for thousands.

Out on the street, mid-morning Manhattan, the healthy glow, the backbeat of menace: a city of Mulcahys. His eyes searched but he knew that even grand-scale vigilance wouldn't save him: the big American had appeared from nowhere; Roth had no confidence he wouldn't appear as rapidly again, too late to evade. He could barely concentrate on what he was here to do.

He arrived at the front desk of the next bank tense and breathless, alarming the staff with his lack of composure. He asked his deranged questions to the doubtful glory of a negative response. He turned to leave, but this time, as he walked towards the exit, he could feel his heart race, the prospect of going back outside deeply unnerving. All beyond the door was invisible, a threat. He may have to live the rest of his days in this very bank. He looked over his shoulder at the staff, who clearly wanted him to leave as quickly as possible. Gritting his teeth, step by step he forced himself outside onto the pavement, where he was certain that *everyone* was watching him. His head swivelled on his shoulders, an owl checking all directions, in danger of overload. His pulse burst. The whole world wanted his key – and to find Berenson's treasure with or without him.

Three more banks. Three more heart attacks.

He ran into a café, the faces of the other customers stretched as Munchian screams. The walls and ceiling sank a distance away. With a furtive expression, holed up in a corner, he stared at those nearby until he was certain they were not interested in him. His gaze fixed on the door to the outside world, to the domain where his enemies lurked, waiting for him, trying to corrupt the process Berenson had – *surely?* – carefully laid out. The waitress took his order, frowning at his state. She must have noticed how badly his hand was shaking as the coffee cup tapped against his teeth.

'So these people you're trying to help,' the boss had said. 'This endless array of users and takers whose credibility you can tell by their mere scent – how do you propose to help them all? You're a working man, and Christ knows I keep you busy. What about a life of your own, my good, sweet employee? How are you going to keep your own well refreshed?'

'I don't go looking for them –'

'But they find you.'

'It's no big deal—'

'That's no answer to my question! How are you going to maintain your vitality if you spend your free time helping out those who don't deserve it?'

'Who says they don't?'

'I do! Those who need help are not often the ones who ask for it. If you rely on your nose, which smells any old heap of shit and calls it a rose—'

'Now wait a—'

'Listen to me!' Berenson exclaimed. 'They lie, snivel and cry, and when you're sucked dry they won't even remember your face. This is not your confession, Scottie: this is your life!'

And he was right. Almost a decade after he'd embarked upon his grand scheme, Roth felt as jaded as the shabby paintwork of the latest shared house he'd moved into in search of yet more souls to save. He was starting to wonder why. After all these years, he couldn't point to a single success. He'd managed to help no one. Rather, they had helped themselves to whatever they could leach from him. Yet still he'd refused to give up.

Twenty men lived in this latest building, chock-full of Samaritan potential, so run-down it defied logic – an element of will had to be involved, the tenants determined to make their lives as awful as possible by letting their home crumble around them. Scratches along the walls so that every plane looked like a keyed car, the stink of food left to rot in corners untouched. The building had a terminal disease and was losing the will to live: the walls could no longer hold up the roof and they'd be squished beneath it, streams of insects fallen under a heavy stone.

A seventeen-year-old, Bradley, moved into this delightful abode a couple of days after Roth. This kid had spent the last six years in and out of youth offender units and prison. When he first heard about this new arrival, Roth had felt a surge of hope. The profile of his crimes was too similar to that of the boy he'd killed for him not to believe that the cosmos was giving him a chance to make up for his unpunished crime. According to others, Bradley was typical – only worse. Thought he was smarter than the rest; full of wilful energy, strong but vacant, easily led, take him along as the patsy. Others in this house were older, broken, long since wasted – they had little time for him. Spat out of prison, he'd move on shortly, and sooner or later end up back inside. Yes: all in all a perfect second chance.

Roth was cooking a meal in the kitchen. Bradley came in, looking at his phone. He sat down at the table without saying a word. After a few moments, Roth said, 'I'm Scott, it's great to meet you.'

The teen did not reply. Carried on fiddling with his phone.

'When did you get here?' Roth continued. 'I haven't seen you around. I know it's a pretty big place.'

Still no interest.

'Have you eaten? I'm not making much, but you're more than welcome to have some food if you're hungry. I can make more.'

Zilch.

Roth decided to let him be for now and returned to cooking, at which point he felt Bradley look at him. A few moments later, the teen got up and left. Roth ate dinner in silence. Several other residents passed by with nothing to say.

A leper colony with its own substrata; Roth – who'd lived here a week – had made no impression on the other residents yet. Despite years of fruitless delving into the depths of the doomed, he was still so obviously a set apart, a policeman among criminals, prying into business that was no concern of his. To some he was a tourist, down among the needy for his own bizarre reasons, whatever they may be. For others he was an opportunity waiting to be abused.

He sat in his bedroom, reading quietly. The dim light from the lamp strained to reach the corners of the walls. He was surprised by a knock. Even more so when he opened the door and saw Bradley standing there. 'Oh!' Roth said, a bright grin coming to his face. 'I'm so glad you've dropped by! Maybe we could have a chat. You know what these places are like—'

'Yeah, I know what these places are like.' An errant hostility in Bradley's tone, a savage look in his eyes. 'What do you want?'

'Want?'

'What do you want?'

'I – I don't want anything.'

'Right. Yup. Yeah, you don't want anything.'

'No, nothing.'

'So why did you start talking to me?'

'To say hello,' Roth said, realising the teen was not the easiest person to engage with. 'This is not a friendly place. To be honest, it's the worst I've stayed in. And I've lived in some *dives*. All these people here and no one mixes, or talks to each other, or tries to see if they have anything in common. It's made me feel bad enough, being here, and you're a young guy, so I thought you could do with—'

'With what?'

'With a friend.'

Bradley stared at him. He filled the doorway. 'What's a fucker like you doing in a place like this?'

'I'm not a policeman,' Roth said. 'If that's what you mean. Or … or a journalist.'

'But you *are* something.'

'Everybody's something.'

Bradley walked into the room. Closed the door behind him. Leant back against it. The mini-chamber suddenly felt like a prison cell. 'So what are *you*? And what do you want with me?'

'What do I want? Nothing, I don't want anything from you, quite the opposite in fact, I just . . .' But Roth could tell Bradley wasn't listening to him. Rather, he was looking around his room with a piercing gaze. 'I – I'm just a guy who had a bad thing to deal with once and . . . it had an impact on me.'

Bradley looked at him coldly. 'You never been inside.'

'No.'

'You queer?'

'No.'

'So why are you here?'

'I can help you,' Roth said. 'If you want.'

'How?'

'You've just come out of prison.'

'Yeah.'

'For . . .?'

'Robbery.'

'You can do better than that. You're young, strong—'

'Do you wanna fuck me?'

The deep, low thud of intimidation. 'No, I assure you, it's *nothing* like that. I'm trying to help you.'

Bradley twisted the key, locked the door. 'You want to *fuck* me.'

'No, I'm *don't*.'

'That's why you're here. For rent boys.'

'No, it's really not.'

'Yeah, it really is.'

'I want to help you.'

'You want to help me? How did you know where to find me?'

'I mean help people like you.'

'You mean *fuck* people like me.'

'No.'

'You got money?'

'A little, yes.'

'Give it to me. And then you can do what you like.'

Roth stared at him.

'I haven't got all fucking night,' Bradley spat. 'Are we gonna do this, or do you need an invitation from the fucking Queen?'

'You rob because you need money. No one ever said you could be better than that.'

'You want me to suck your cock?'

'The system is tough on people like you.'

'You want to fuck me in my teenage butthole?'

'You don't need to rob any more, that's all I'm saying.'

Bradley started to laugh.

'What's funny?' Roth asked.

'You.'

'How's that?'

'You're really boring.'

His hostility was eating the oxygen in the room. Roth realised he'd made a big mistake with this one. He wanted the snake to leave. 'Listen, you should go.'

'You gonna stake money on me?'

'What?'

'You wanna do some good, is that what you're about?'

A minute earlier, he would have nodded vigorously. But not now. 'What I want is for you to go.'

'You ask me for sex and then expect me to leave?'

'So you're a liar as well as a thief.'

'How much?' Bradley said.

'Never mind.'

'Oh, never mind?'

'I'm tired. I'd appreciate it if you'd leave me alone.'

'Oh, you'd appreciate it, would you?'

'Yes. I *would*.'

'But how can I leave you alone if you don't give me any money?'

'What?'

'How much you got? A hundred? A grand? A hundred grand?'

'I think that you should leave.'

Bradley walked towards him. It took him only a few strides to cross the room. 'YOU GOT CASH?' he screamed in Roth's face.

Roth stumbled back, the noise thunder. 'Why don't you leave?'

'WHY DON'T YOU STOP TRYING TO FUCK TEENAGE BOYS?'

'Get out of my room now. Please.'

Bradley took out a long knife, from where Roth couldn't tell; but suddenly a serrated demon of a blade was being waved close to his face. He tried to move back but hit the wall.

'Now,' Bradley said, leering in, 'If you wanna sponsor me, that's cool. You can sponsor me not to rob any more. A hundred quid for each robbery I'd have done.' He grinned, a toothless scowl. *'Another fucking do-gooder—'*

'What don't you—?'

Bradley punched him so hard Roth went down like a sack of potatoes. In a flicker of consciousness, he saw the edge of the blade catch the naked light bulb. He felt the hateful teen reach for his neck.

He thought, *I'm going to die.*

In that moment, he'd known what it was like to shatter. He'd hit the cold slabs beneath the micro-thin polyester carpet, no softer than the concrete onto which had slammed the teenage boy's skull. He was full of a terror that took no form, that attached to no memories of the past nor grand hopes for the future but to all of the mistakes everyone has ever made. He didn't think of women loved and lost, of unrequited fancies, of friends or family or who his real parents might have been. He didn't think of ambitions never to be fulfilled or moments larger than life. It was all replaced by an amorphous dread that he was about to cease to exist for the rest of time, along with a deep sadness that, despite the best of intentions and the hardest of work, he'd managed to help no one at all.

And then he was coming to.

To have called it a rebirth would have been to misjudge how he felt. Instead, it was a bad punchline to a sick joke. Bradley had gone; his room was no longer ravaged by the sense of immediate harm. He sat up. His cheek hurt like hell, his head throbbed. He put his hand to his neck; he hadn't been slashed across the gullet after all. But the rest of the news was not so good.

His room had been turned upside down, his few possessions thrown around as if by a poltergeist. His cash was gone: Bradley had cleaned him out. He didn't even have to ask the other residents if the boy was still around; he knew the score by now. He was long gone, Roth's money in the disgusting little bastard's pocket, wherever that pocket happened to be now.

Time: always so important to him – *no time to waste,* driven to maximise his limited number of days, trying to help people who didn't want it, not just the savage Bradley but everyone else upon whom he'd lavished precious, unrecoverable time. Users, losers, sick twisted manipulators, bone-idle duplicitous *narcissists*. Feeders on his blood, his hopes, his ambitions for the world. So much smarter than he, they saw him coming, how far they could squeeze him. He was busted, defeated, brought to his knees, everything Berenson said he would be if he took the path he chose rather than that which the confessor said was right, the path that kept him close to his old boss for as long as they both would live.

Chapter 14

'I'm pleased you got in touch,' Mulcahy oozed, his tone suggesting he'd never had any no doubt Roth would.

They were in a diner a few blocks away from Union Square, mid-morning, a sunny day. Mulcahy was already there when Roth turned up, though he had arrived ten minutes early in order to check out the place before the big American arrived, *supposedly*. Kicked off-centre before they'd even started, Roth sat down with the movie star, who remained as charming as he'd been two days earlier.

Mulcahy's food arrived. 'Thank ya darling,' he said to the waitress, before turning his easy charm to the newcomer. 'Scottie! What'll you have for breakfast?'

'I ate at the hotel,' he said, trying to keep his anxiety in check. Berenson might have teased him but Roth wasn't so bad a judge of character as that.

Mulcahy said to the waitress, 'Just coffee for my friend Scott.'

She walked off. The two men looked at each other with fresh acquaintance. Mulcahy smiled a California dream and tucked in to his pancakes. 'Hell of a game to play,' he announced, mid-munch. 'Trying to find the box a key fits with the whole world to choose from.'

'Do you really know where I should look?'

'Wouldn't have said if we didn't.'

'All right then. Where?'

Mulcahy chuckled. 'The direct approach. I like!'

'You know where I should go next?'

'Sure do.'

'How?'

'Because we have the information Dieter didn't give you, because your old boss didn't trust you all the way.'

'You're lying.'

'You wouldn't be here otherwise. You'd be on a desert island sipping your beachside poison. Because he had a shitload of money which by now you'd have got your little mitts on had he told you where it was.'

'And that's what you want? And the people you work for?'

'We have the address of the bank where you *will* find the private box you're looking for. The box that key of yours fits. It's here in New York. But you knew that already.'

Roth did not reply.

Mulcahy smiled, devoured his pancakes. Roth was left to stew. So he was right: the next box *was* in Manhattan. But there were so many banks and so many bankers who may have been told to lie. And now he was being pursued by a man who'd do him harm, who knew his every move, where he was staying . . . He couldn't bear the sense of being chased, of being *hunted*. Maybe if the big American was telling the truth, if Dieter in his deranged wisdom had set up the quest in such a fashion, then it was an opportunity he had to explore, if only to keep the clouds of doubt from his mind.

'So why don't we get that key! Then we can go to the bank and you'll have what Berenson's left for you in twenty minutes!'

'As will you.'

Mulcahy smiled. 'It's not all for you, my friend – don't forget that.'

Roth's mind flickered back to the will. Berenson's lawyer had been clear: Roth was the only named beneficiary. But Mulcahy was right about one thing: his old boss was a man of incomparable sneakiness.

'Twenty minutes from here?' Roth asked.

'From your hotel,' Mulcahy replied.

'Why my hotel?'

'Because you were not dumb enough to bring the key with you when you came to meet me.' Mulcahy gave a cinemascope grin when Roth did not respond. 'You made a shocking decision . . . at not having pancakes – they're beautiful!' Down went his head for the last fill at the trough.

'Everett,' said Roth. 'Where are we going once ... we've collected the key?'

'To the bank that holds the box it fits.'

'And then what?'

'And then I'm done!' the American said, his food finished. 'All right, Scottie, let's go find out what's in this mysterious box!'

With a swell of movement, they were leaving the diner. Mulcahy managed to usher Roth along without seeming to do so, irresistible for being invisible. They were walking through the Financial District, the sun shining, New Yorkers rushing this way and that. Roth was desperate for an alley to appear, along which he could vanish before Mulcahy had the chance to seize him back. There was no shortage of such escape routes in London; he cursed that none appeared to save him now, here, when he needed one the most; he cursed Berenson for making him come to this damned alleyless town. Cars and buses and pedestrians – any surprise he may achieve by darting off would be scuppered by the umpteen obstructions spilling in his way. If Mulcahy wouldn't let him escape, and Roth doubted that he even could, he'd have to take a very different approach.

'So you know New York well?' Roth asked, in a friendlier tone.

'Oh yeah!' the big American exclaimed.

'But you travel all over the world for business?'

'New York is the place I love. Nowhere quite like it!'

'You must've been pleased when your boss told you that the bank was here.'

'What can I say, I guess I'm one of the lucky guys.'

'That's nice. So . . . you couldn't have been working on this business for long. Berenson only died a few weeks ago.'

'Yeah, real shame.'

'But not really – not for your boss.'

'How'd you figure?'

'He seems to have launched into action pretty quickly.'

'You gotta stay up to speed, my friend!'

'Your boss knew Berenson socially?'

'No idea! My boss and your old boss are enigmas of their own!'

'But he's hoping to get a very large amount of money out of this; I mean, your boss—'

'All he wants is what Dieter wanted him to have. There's nothing wrong with that, not in my book.'

'Nor mine.'

'Then it sounds like we're on the same page!'

'But your boss must be expecting millions, maybe lots of millions. Were he and Dieter partners?'

'I don't know what they got up to in their private lives, heh-heh!'

'Ha! But it's a serious question, Everett – because I don't know what the treasure actually is, so if you could illuminate me . . .'

Mulcahy turned to him with a big, understanding grin. 'Scottie, we can talk in circles like airplanes waiting to land all afternoon, but you're not going to get a thing out of me.' He flashed a Monument Valley smile. 'I can't blame you for trying, though! And here we are!'

And there they were, in front of Roth's New York home, Hotel Rumours, the place he'd been feeling so comfortable, as Weston said he would, until he'd discovered that Mulcahy knew of his hideout.

They passed through reception quickly, walked into an open lift.

The doors closed on them. The elevator ascended. Mulcahy's six-foot-three density sucked the air from the chamber; the man could stop a bullet with his teeth and still not stop talking. 'What a nice hotel this is! No wonder you like it!'

They passed several floors; a few more to go.

Roth said, 'I don't like surprises.'

'Did you tell that to Dieter?'

The lift came to a halt, the doors opened. Before Roth could say any more, Mulcahy stepped out into the vestibule. Roth thought about taking the lift back down and running from the hotel, but it didn't matter: Mulcahy's team had surely trailed them and were waiting outside. If he fled, he wouldn't get far.

The lift doors started to close. Roth stepped out, his head banging with stress. Mulcahy looked at him like a best friend.

'You still won't tell me where we're going?' Roth asked.

'In two minutes you'll know.'

'In one minute you'll have the key.'

'Well, aren't we efficient little bees?' Mulcahy laughed. 'Come on, sweet pea, open the door.'

The walls were closing in on him, the ceiling falling on their heads.

'Come on, champ, time's a-wasting!'

'You can do what you like,' Roth said, his voice quavering slightly. 'I'm not gonna give you the key.'

Mulcahy's sunny L.A. expression faltered. 'C'mon, Scott, don't be a dumbell.'

'You're not getting the key.'

'Scottie, look: it's like this. If you don't give me the key, I'm gonna have to fuck you up. By the time I'm done, you'll have no eyes, no balls, no kneecaps . . . You won't ever be a hit with the ladies again, but that won't matter, 'cos you won't be able to see them.'

Mulcahy was far from unhinged. Worse: he was deeply ambitious, and possessed of a task.

Roth walked to his hotel room door, unlocked it with slow, reluctant fingers.

'See, champ, that wasn't so hard!'

The room was cold as he entered. Roth walked in first. Mulcahy closed the door behind them. Once inside – just the two of them, in a silent hotel room – there was nothing to discuss, even less to see. Mulcahy wanted only the key.

'If I give it to you,' Roth said, 'You're going to kill me anyway.'

'We're supposed to work together. That's what Dieter wanted.'

'Then why did you just threaten to beat the shit out of me?'

'Incentivisation.'

Roth stopped in the middle of the lounge. Mulcahy nudged him over to the wardrobe. The big American reached around him to open the doors. There, beneath the lower reaches of recently bought threads, sat the small black safe, solid as the rock beneath the mountain. In its guts, the key.

Mulcahy sighed in relief. 'Open it up, Scottie boy.'

'Who do you work for?' Roth asked.

'The safe.'

'I'm going to be dead the moment I give you the key, so what have you got to lose by telling me?'

Mulcahy put his hands on Roth's shoulders and caressed joints that were stiff with fear. Started pushing him down towards the floor.

'You're going to fuck me up anyway, aren't you?' Roth continued, his heart racing. 'You're going to kill me as I give you this key.'

'Sshhhh,' Mulcahy said. The knees of his captive touched the ground. He let his hands rest loosely on Roth's shoulders. 'You're doing fine, babe.'

Roth's throat seized; he could barely breathe, in dread of what was to come. No one would know until it was too late. The hotel staff would find ruffled bed sheets, towels on the bathroom floor and a dead body in a heap by the wardrobe, his killer long gone. The safe faced him. Mulcahy urged him on like a deranged Little League dad. Tension radiated across his upper torso; he wanted to vomit. The big American knew how to inflict the right kind of pain at the right time. And it would only get worse the longer he delayed keying in the code that would hand over the long-lusted-for key.

Roth stared at the safe. The number, they'd assured him, changed with every resident. 'Unbreakable!' they said. Unless you broke it yourself, of course.

He started to enter the seven digits, could sense Mulcahy's eyes on the pad. A tinge of resistance: he leant forward so Mulcahy couldn't see the numbers, resisting that much at least. Each one brought him closer to doom. The Brad Pitt-alike loosened his grip, held Roth's shoulders almost tenderly.

The fourth digit, the fifth; after the sixth, he paused. He had one more keystroke left of existence. The blood banging in his ears rolled the toll of the end of his life. The safe door would open and down would come the cosh. His brains would spill across the safe and thus the key would be sanctified. There was nothing left to do but do it.

He entered the seventh of seven digits.

The safe clicked open.

Rickard Hay!

His instincts uncoiled all at once. Roth slammed the safe shut, jumped as hard as he could.

'OOOF!'

Mulcahy's arms splayed out as his 'captive' hit him squarely in the chest, dropping back enough to create a space between the slab of a man and the wall for him to flee.

He ran like hell, to the door, which he yanked open and tumbled into the vestibule and darted for the lift. He smashed the call button repeatedly, each second feeling more like a year.

Mulcahy appeared behind him. *'Give me the fucking key!'*

Roth yelled, 'You have no idea where the bank is, do you!'

The big American glowered at him, red with upheaval.

Roth had been filled with the confidence of adrenalin. 'All you've told me are lies! The only place Dieter left that knowledge was in *my* memory! The only person he trusted was me!'

'So what do you want?'

'I *want* you to get the fuck out of my life.'

'Can't do that.'

'But without me, you know nothing! And because you know nothing, you *can't* kill me! You're screwed!'

'Unh-uh, buddy,' Mulcahy said. 'You're going to keep looking for the treasure, and we're going to keep following you. It doesn't matter where you go, Scottie, we *will* be there too. And when you find it, so will we. And the moment you open up that prize . . . well, we won't need to know what's inside your head any longer, will we?'

Mulcahy stared at him with the cold eyes of the hot assassin, the pursuer who will never give up.

The lift door opened, sat there for a moment, its mouth agape.

Mulcahy flashed another of his widescreen smiles, accepting this round was Roth's. He walked past him and into the lift where, cool as absolute zero, he pressed the button for the ground floor. Then he stood with calm aplomb, looking at the man he had been terrorising a few moments ago. As the doors closed on him, Mulcahy chuckled and said, 'See you soon, buddy.'

Roth waited to make sure the lift was descending before he rushed back into his room to pack.

He checked out of the hotel and ran to the cab he'd asked reception to book for him urgently. There, in the broadest of daylight, stood the still-grinning Everett Mulcahy, leaning against a van Roth had seen before, which no doubt contained the rest of his team. It was parked next to the taxi waiting to take Roth to the airport, making him walk within a metre of the big, laughing American. Intimidation tactics, playground style.

In the cab, Roth said, 'JFK, as fast as you can.'

The taxi roared off. Over his shoulder, he could see Mulcahy grow smaller, laughing as he stepped into the van to continue the chase.

Chapter 15

The drone of the plane's engines thickened the atmosphere. Roth tried to relax but couldn't. The cabbie had earned his sizeable tip, driving to the airport too fast for Mulcahy's team to keep up, the van nowhere to be seen as they arrived at JFK. Roth had bought a ticket for the first plane to the Cayman Islands and hid in the corner booth of an eatery, out of view until the last possible moment, at which point he dashed like an Olympian to the gate, arriving just in time to board his plane, scanning the other passengers for would-be pursuers as he walked to his seat. Wheels-up, he'd given Mulcahy the slip, though they'd surely find out where he'd gone. For now, he had a few hours' peace. Good: he needed it.

He fumed at the nature of Berenson's design. A few moments later and Mulcahy might have had the key and Roth could have been taking the one-way flight to heaven or hell. But then perhaps his old boss knew him better than he did himself, for in the moment of his greatest pressure, there flashed into Roth's mind a memory of a trip to the Cayman Islands to meet business partners, including a raft of bankers. Attending that night, a rare thing: a man Berenson trusted, a diverting chap who could get things done. It was this man's name that had flashed through his mind as the safe door opened and Mulcahy had been about to turn him into lox.

A check on Google filled in the details: *Rickard Hay, consultant, Bank Boutique, George Town, Grand Cayman, Cayman Islands.*

He was starting to worry that maybe he did function best under pressure. Good for results, perhaps, but bad for the blood pressure . . .

He wondered if anyone would be waiting to 'greet' him at Arrivals, an ominous fellow in a black suit holding up a card with 'Scott Roth' written on it. But there was no such heavy. He left the airport, asked the cab driver to take him to a *very* good hotel. On the way, he called Hay's office, and only had to mention Berenson's name for the man himself to come to the phone. After a short chat, Hay invited him to meet first thing in the morning. Perfect: Roth would rest the night in a secure hotel, safe from Mulcahy's goons, and add another superb venue to his ever-growing list of plush residences.

* * *

He opened his eyes, the expensive bedclothes an exquisite balm. He stretched, his back bones clicking, his neck sore from strain. The room was full of the glow of morning. Had the earth moved closer to the sun overnight?

He'd woken in a morose mood, feeling especially burdened. *He didn't want any of this.* Didn't want pursuers racing to catch him while he slept. He was not that man: *he was not Dieter Berenson!* He had no claim on a fancy life, to be better than the rest. He wanted to walk through a door of a house he'd lived in for years, to be greeted by the wife he loved and kids who made a racket because they were so pleased to see him, and sit and talk about their day, eat dinner and lie on the sofa to watch TV and have a snooze – and he'd have been on his way to doing this with Mia *if only he'd given her a chance!* Was it possible to sigh yourself to death? If so, Mulcahy would soon have no one left to pursue.

He showered and shaved. The harsh light found every tiny etching in his skin, all of which had grown deeper these last twenty-four hours. The larger lines looked as if a passer-by may fall in and never be seen again. The deepest carpet, the cleanest bathroom, the hottest shower didn't make a difference, for Roth was a hunted man, a running man. A *guilty* man.

He walked to the bedroom and checked his email. Still no word from Mia. Still no reason why there should have been.

Rickard Hay wore Bermuda shorts, a T-shirt – a model of wealth in relief. Small but vivid, a tanned European who'd scrambled to make his life as perfect as it seemed to be, he was far more excited to see Roth than vice versa – what fun to speak to Dieter's friend!

He welcomed the unexpected visitor into his office, which overlooked the harbour. Roth was drawn by the view of paradise beyond the windows, of the locals going about their business and the high-finance immigrants growing bronzed in the sun. Hay chuckled, said he spent no more time here than a few hours per week, his office a place to keep paperclips and shred unwanted documents. His business was seldom done in places of business – he had people for that kind of thing. He laughed an earthy, happy growl. 'I have the office only for the view. Sit!'

They sat, in plush, comfortable chairs that seemed to embrace them as they settled in. Paradise assaulted Roth from all angles.

'I am so glad you came,' Hay said. 'It broke my heart when I heard about Dieter; he has been on my mind ever since. What is it about people dying that makes you want to talk about them?'

'The fact that you no longer can talk *to* them?'

Hay nodded. 'Yes. Wise.'

'You knew him well?'

'There was a time when we lived in each other's pockets. Haha, we were much younger then! Young men, like you are now!'

'I'm not so young,' Roth said.

'Then you must spend some more time here, in the sun, and where tax is so efficient!'

'I've been thinking about Dieter too, these last few weeks. I've had plenty of reason to. He was—'

'A great man!' Hay interjected. 'And totally impossible!'

'Yes!'

'But one of a kind – how could you not want to get involved with him, and whatever scheme he had on the go?'

'Did he ever hear your confession?'

'Ah, his party trick! No, I was far too tame for him. I would have been embarrassed not to come up to his usual standards. Or should I say down!'

'Did he ever tell you what others confessed?'

'Never! He was like a priest, hearing those in need of spiritual salvation; a man of integrity. *Although . . .'* Hay continued, his eyes flashing. 'Now and again he would let slip a detail without naming names. A snapshot of the spice of life – *as other people saw it*. The tip of the iceberg – and that was enough; that was plenty! I didn't want to know any more. I wouldn't have been able to sleep!'

Roth laughed. 'Dieter didn't sleep much anyway.'

'Perhaps if he had, he might have lived longer. I love to sleep! Money makes me relax; other people's problems do not!'

Roth chuckled, at ease with the man already.

There was a knock. The door opened smoothly and in came one of Hay's numerous assistants, carrying a tray of china. He placed the array on the desk with a well-mannered smile and left as silently as he'd arrived.

'A drink?' Hay asked.

Roth nodded, still not used to being waited on. The selection: fit for a hotel. The coffee pulsed with a vibrant aroma, but he preferred to have a drink more calming for his nerves. 'Is that Assam tea?'

'Yes! If that is what you want, that is what you shall have!' Hay prepared the infusions. 'Yes, our good friend would wake practically before he went to bed! Such stamina! Such determination! He could break down walls with his will. I never met anyone like him. I don't expect to again.' He placed the cup of tea in front of Roth and settled into his chair with a hot, black coffee. 'People do not know what genius is, but Dieter was the only one I ever met. A wizard in business – and the greatest reader of human nature the world has ever known. I see these modern pretenders get far more publicity than he ever did. You know what they are compared to him? Shit! That is what they are! The shit of his shit was more talented than they! Our dear departed friend did not care for fame or appearing in public with a dolly bird on each arm at the latest brand new nightclub. He was too great to be bothered with such trivialities.'

'He *was* a secretive man though. Perhaps too secretive.'

'He had much to lose.'

'So I'm led to believe.'

'He was a billionaire, you know. Many times over.'

Now he came to mention it, Roth did not actually know. Allusions had been made to great wealth, but no one had ever used the 'B' word. *Many times over.* He felt a little dizzy and – to his annoyance – quite excited by the thought of what Dieter's treasure might turn out to be.

At the same exact moment, Hay's gaze suddenly lost all of its warmth; a sea-change in persona, a screeching of brakes. 'But that kind of wealth brings its own demons. So I asked myself when I came off the phone to you yesterday – what does this man want?' The small vivid host had transformed into a stone wall, a barricade, a protector, the coldest shark rather than the friendly, appealing laugh.

Roth felt his mouth go dry, a situation upon him yet again. He could see now how this bonny, jovial chap had been able to accumulate hundreds of millions of dollars. He tried to irrigate his tongue with tea. 'It's like I – I said on the phone,' he started to explain. 'Dieter left me a key. I think you may know the – the location of the box it fits.'

Hay's eyes took on a severe gaze. Roth felt his prospects narrow. *Calm down,* he told himself. *Just answer the guy's questions.*

'All I want,' Roth continued, 'Is to do whatever Dieter wanted me to do. He left no instructions, and he's . . . He's sent me on a quest where the clues are in my head. Well, I have a lot of memories, some of which actually took place. I don't know what he wants me to recall, so I haven't got a clue, if I can be that honest, what dormant piece of information inside my brain is supposed to guide me to the end. But you knew Dieter. This is exactly the kind of thing he would do.'

Hay watched him with scorching eyes, scouring eyes, doubtful eyes, *rich man's eyes,* searching for the weakness in one who'd never known money and who didn't have the first idea how the well-heeled function. And then he started to speak, with a grave, bleak voice. 'Two years ago, Dieter called to ask of me a favour. For one such as he, there is no greater currency than that. He had never asked before, but for this man I would have jumped from a plane without a parachute. So I said, tell me what you want, I will do it. And he asked that I keep a box for him in my bank.'

Roth's heart leapt.

'"Is that it?" I replied,' Hay continued. 'After the many good turns he had done me over the years, the friendship, support, the opportunities he had passed my way, this is all I can do for him? I admit, I was disappointed: I wanted to impress him as much as he had always impressed me, although that of course was impossible. But this is what he asked, so I said, *of course I will do it*. He told me he wanted just one key for the box, and should anyone arrive at my bank and present it, I was to put to them a question. And if they answered that question correctly, then and only then were they to be allowed access to the box.'

Hay was watching him with a frozen glare, George Town Harbour a long way away. Roth sighed inwardly. How he wanted to be outside in the sun, walking along the beach, sipping a long, cool drink . . . He tried to see past the mask Hay had plastered over his face, the unfriendly, claustrophobic, cold appearance he was asking his 'guest' to process. It wasn't about the money; it was about the quest. Or was it really about the money in fact?

Hay said: 'Of course, you only get one try.'

Damn you, Dieter! Was it not enough that I remembered the right place to come? Feeling the nag of vertigo, he said, 'Well then. You'd better ask.'

'Why did you think it was so wrong to defend yourself against the robber, when otherwise *you* would have died?'

In the quiet office, Roth could hear Berenson laughing at him from beyond the grave. Huge guffaws as he looked down upon his old friend and pulled-through-a-hedge-backwards ex-employee.

The question asked, the answer awaited – a huge amount of payola tilting on the response.

'Because . . .'

Hay watched him, his eyes warming. Roth realised that, far from being a cold bastard, his host actually wanted him to succeed, so that he could satisfy the only request of his dead friend.

'Because . . .'

And now he could feel himself constrict with fear. He *knew* the answer Berenson wanted him to give – but was that the right one?

Well, he had to say *something*.

'Because I was responsible for his death.'

The host considered the answer for a time and a half.

'No,' Hay said finally. 'That is not right.'

Roth yelped loudly, 'But it *is*.'

A sad expression passed across Hay's face, sad for Roth, sad for Dieter, sad for the man who wanted to complete the favour. 'It is not,' he insisted, the metal shutters coming down, the quest at an end.

'But Rickard—!'

'Dieter left me as his gatekeeper, Scott, to that which lies beyond the doors to his secret life. I am sorry, but your answer is wrong.'

The blood pounded in his head. No doubt Hay only had to press a button to summon bone-crunching thugs to dispatch this oik.

A flicker passed across Hay's face. A thought. Perhaps a remembrance. 'One more go,' he said.

Roth stared at him for a moment.

'For you,' Hay repeated. 'And for Dieter. *One more*.'

And now he was soft, encouraging: a symptom of the dance they were both carrying out on behalf of their surprisingly dearly beloved.

'Okay,' Roth said. *Okay, Dieter, I get it*. 'All right, you bastard. Maybe there was something I always held back, something he always wanted me to say. Yes, I could *see* it was self-defence: the kid started on me and I had no time to do anything else. I wanted to stop that knife sinking into my chest because I didn't want to die. But there *was* more to it. I was *angry*. I was angry that this kid was out there in the first place; he should have been better-looked after by his family or friends. By someone! He shouldn't have been out attacking strangers; how could he have got to that point? Why wasn't anyone looking after him? Why did he have to work it all out for himself and fail because he didn't have guidance from anyone? Fail in the worst possible way: *lose his life*. I was angry because no one went looking for him, no one tried to make sure he was okay, that we live in a world where this kid was deemed no better than shit, so that's how he acted. What if I had been in his place when I was five years old, or ten, or fifteen? He didn't start out as a thief – he was a baby like the rest of us. I didn't start like that either, but I could have gone the same way had I not been so fortunate in the people who adopted me. Maybe he had the makings of a crook, maybe he was born with a liar's gene, but so many people failed him along the way for a thief to emerge from that baby. If *just one person* had taken time out to talk to him, give him a few ideas that may change his world view, his sense of other people – of how he viewed *himself* – perhaps he'd have realised that he *was* worth something, that his life *was* valuable to him, to others . . . But no one took enough care to stop him going around robbing people with knives. He was failed by everyone. And then he was failed by *me*. And of all the people who failed him, I was the worst, Rickard, because *I killed him*. There was me, and then came *death*. I dealt this kid the terminal blow when all I wanted was that he value his own life. Dieter never seemed to grasp how much this cut me up, how desperate I was at having been the complete opposite of what I'd always wanted to be, even if it was just in that moment. I was given so much by people who had no reason to love a stranger's boy. So selfless; my parents were exquisite people. I wanted to be like them, but I was the one who put the knife in, I was the one who killed him. I failed him so badly, I failed my parents so badly, I failed myself: how can it get any worse than that? This rubbish about self-defence – surely I could have defended myself in a way that didn't cost him his life? That's what weighs so heavily on me. Sure, it *was* self-defence, but if my instincts had been better, quicker, *different* then he would *not* be dead. He was a child! But yes, I get it now. I get what Dieter wanted me to say: I *have* served enough time in this jail of my own creation, and I don't want to do so any more.'

Roth stopped talking, caught in the agonies of the past, his eyes wet with tears. The air around them: disturbed, awash. The light of the sea against the coast beyond the window.

Quietly, Hay said, '*That* is the right answer.'

Roth wiped his eyes. '*Fucking Dieter.*'

'I am no one's confessor, Scott, and I am not here to judge. I hope you do not mind. It was an obligation to a much-loved friend who is no longer with us.'

'I understand. He always had to be in charge.'

'Yes, he did!' Hay exclaimed. 'Even now he has us marching to his tune. Ah, how I love him! I miss him. I am so glad you have passed this test – nothing can make me happier today. I will order a taxi to take you to my bank. My staff will help you as much or as little as you need. You will have privacy to inspect the box, but I insist you must come and have lunch with me. What delay will that cause? None at all. You can be on a plane by six this evening, flying wherever in the world you want to go. So yes, you will come, and we will have a feast, and talk about our dear departed friend. Ah, what a happy day this is!'

The cool dark room contrasted with the brightness outside. A quiet, respectful, well-dressed member of Hay's staff brought in the small steel box and placed it on the table in front of him. The man asked if there was anything he would like to eat or drink. His polite response in the negative received, he was left alone.

Roth thought: how many people would love to be in this room? The place Mulcahy had threatened to kill him in order to be? Yet he was the only one here, the only one Berenson had wanted to be here, according to Hay's question. *I knew you were full of shit, Everett Mulcahy.* The leap from the second box to this – the third – had been so much harder than first to second; he wondered how many more leaps there would be before he reached the end of the quest. A part of him did not want to open this box, for who knew what insanity it may lead to? But then, the last one had made him almost a millionaire . . .

He pulled it towards him, took the key from the Parisian bank, inserted, twisted –

Click.

The lid lifted, enough for him to see inside.

He tipped the box. A sliding sound.

Two envelopes came into view. He took them out, could feel that neither contained a key. His eyebrows rose.

He opened the first envelope. It contained a handwritten note from Berenson. He put it aside and opened the second, its innards revealing only an index card on which was typed the following:

Go to Tokyo. Check in to the Hotel Hamishi. Call 6729-0521-44044-9837 and then wait.

No signature, no logo, nothing but the message.

He checked the box again to make sure he hadn't missed anything, but no, there was no key, no cash, no bearer bond, nothing but the card and the next note from his dead tormentor. He sat for a few moments, surprised to feel so crestfallen at having been denied his latest gift. It was little comfort that for once he didn't have to work out where in the hell to go next.

A soft voice, a woman speaking French – no, English with a French accent. They lay on the bed together, she opposite him, light shining in through a window behind – he couldn't quite see her face, but Mia was speaking in a funny Gallic tone, making him laugh, her hair bunched around her head on the pillow, backlit; in Paris, imitating the locals, her accent surprisingly good, the fractured logic of this floating dream: she talked about banks *– he clearly had banks on the brain – two happy people surprised by their happiness, promising each other the world in return for a couple of chances taken.*

He opened his eyes. Warmed by the exquisite light, the slow fade of his reverie, a balm to his soul (bruised), he stretched the confusion of sleep from his shoulders, felt peace in the sighing of his body. He sat in a chair lit by a sunbeam in a hotel suite in the Cayman Islands. And then he fell among the details of his daydream, which faded like a tender reverie, back with Mia in the moment, as she lay on the bed looking at him with innocence in her expression, real affection. With love. And then she was gone.

Rickard Hay had made too much money if he could afford an apartment like this and a cook of his own. Floor-to-ceiling windows in a dining room that opened on to the harbour and the Caribbean Sea. A waiter brought lunch; they ate like potentates. Hay's wife and children were in America; he'd be joining them in a few days. Home alone, he and Roth could talk openly.

Hay said, 'I never thought anyone but Dieter would come for that box – and of course he told me nothing of its contents. But you have made me so happy!'

Roth nodded. 'Glad to help. Rickard: this is a sumptuous feast!'

'It is nothing less than you deserve.'

'I'm not so sure.'

'Do not be so modest. That is your problem, I can see it though we have spent only a little time together. So many bullshitters in the world, Scott: I know – I am one of them! Bullshit bullshit bullshit, everywhere you turn! At night, the powers that be must send vehicles to hose down the streets so that all of the bullshit is cleaned away for people to start again the next. If not, the world would be overrun – by bullshit! Sometimes it feels like it is already. If we could harness bullshit as a means of energy, what need of oil? If no need for oil, what need of war? I hope there are scientists in the world trying to harness bullshit as a form of energy: that way lies world peace!'

Roth laughed, nodding his agreement.

'And we, who live like kings, must search for the truth, or else what is life but one long party?'

'It doesn't sound so bad when you put it like that.'

'That is why Dieter adored his confessions. He was trying to get to the pulse of motivation. Why we are the way we are, why we do what we do. He was conducting a lifelong survey into the depths of the soul – or so he told me one night when he was, for him at least, a bit drunk. His sideline— but they were more than that. He was a collector of tales of the dark side of the world, of the extremes people go to, of what they permit themselves to do and how they justify it. He said to me on more than one occasion: *Rickard, sometimes they confess just to show off*. He was no prude, he had bad habits of his own, but he hated the thought that his confessees were not sorry when he felt they should be. *Then* he would push them hard. You see, they considered him one of their own, so when he shoved them they fell over. They would not have listened that way to a priest.'

'And do you think he reached any conclusions? After hearing all of those confessions?'

'I think he felt our world needed saving even more than you did. The difference is, Dieter wanted to protect what he had from that evil, whereas you – it seems to me – want to stop evil, or at least to try.'

'He was the realist, and I am just . . .'

'Yes, what are you just?'

'Naive,' Roth said, chuckling.

'I do not believe in cynicism,' Hay replied. 'The cynic is no different from the bullshitter. We can be cynics from the age of five. I prefer the optimist: if it is all up for grabs, why let the bad guys get everything?'

'Did Dieter ask you to say that?'

'No! That is my own contribution.'

'The longer he's had me on this hare-brained chase, the more I find I miss him. He was not a man to give up life without a terrific fight. He burned the candle as if he were a menorah. It takes its toll.'

'I am certain he was murdered.'

'What?'

'Despite the hard work, the hours, the stress, I do not believe he died naturally. The death he had? Pfff, he would never in a thousand years have let that happen.'

'But even Dieter was not so powerful as to be able to defeat a fatal heart attack.'

'He was murdered,' Hay said, accepting no argument. 'I am sure.'

'By whom?'

'My friend had many enemies. He knew too much, about too many people. That was the danger of being confessor to the scum of the earth. And a great many people were jealous of his success. He was a very rich man by the end of his life, and with his immaculate taste, you can rest assured he had much worth having.' Hay sighed. 'Maybe I am angry that he is gone, so young. I cannot blame him, so I must blame someone else, no? But Dieter would have wrestled the Grim Reaper to the ground for an extra last minute of life.'

'There's still a long way to thinking it was murder.'

'I spoke to him just a few months ago,' Hay explained. 'Had I known that this would be our last conversation, I would have taken more care to tell him what I am so sad I can no longer say. If it turns out that I am right, that he was murdered, then I have two guys from Marseille who will do what I ask for a good price.' The flash of steel; Hay looked at Roth, smiling pleasantly. 'But let me tell you this: our mutual friend was a man with a plan.'

'Yes. If only I knew what that was.'

Hay poured two glasses of wine and handed one to Roth. 'Let us stop being maudlin, or suspicious – for now at least. A toast! To our dear departed Dieter! Genius, mystery, confessor!'

Roth smiled and clinked his glass against Hay's. 'To Dieter!'

'What a great challenge you are faced with! How typical of our friend to make things so hard for the people he loved!'

'Loved?'

'Of course! You were chosen, my friend – my serious, determined friend – by the finest man of his generation. A man who could have chosen anyone, and he chose you!'

Tokyo

Chapter 16

He hadn't flown so much since he'd last worked for Dieter; he truly was back in his employer's employ, carrying out his mysterious bidding. On another flight, Tokyo-bound this time, he could at least sit and do nothing. Routing through Miami – to throw the bloodhounds off the scent – he was crossing the Atlantic for the second time in two days. But Japan was not his immediate destination.

He was going to Paris first.

The thought of that moment, when Mia woke and realised he was gone, had become his torment. How inexplicable it must have seemed, to find him missing; no trace at all; no note, no text, no email – no call to explain he'd realised Mulcahy's team had been the ones following him, not her. *Nutter, her team!* She and Becky? Ridiculous! He'd conducted himself despicably and now he must apologise, explain his stupidity, beg her forgiveness and ask that she come on this strange voyage with him, and when it was done, marry him, and together they would have kids. Mia could work in fashion or not at all; read books by Zola or not at all; they could love each other and wash away the last fifteen years of his life. For Berenson *was* right, as finally communicated to him through the remote-control means of Rickard Hay: the cosmos wasn't punishing him for a killing that wasn't his fault. Nor did the cosmos want to deny him what every human needs: love, and a future. It had no wish that he squander his energy by sowing infertile land. He'd become so entombed by his pompous, ill-fated good works that he'd become selfish in his selflessness. Berenson had told him this a decade ago, had tried to steer him to happier times way back then. But Roth had rejected his wisdom without a second thought. He'd paid for this hubris with ten years, a prison term for manslaughter. But now – at long last! – he'd grasped what his old boss had wanted him to realise during his confession: that in order to be loved, you first had to make room in your life for people to love you.

He finished his next Paul Auster, *The Music of Chance,* looked up and saw a cabin attendant glance at him. For a few moments, their eyes held; she smiled. He felt an overwhelming urge to propose marriage. If she accepted, he wouldn't have to see Mia, or explain why he'd walked out. He wouldn't have to watch her decide whether or not to beat the shit out of him, cry her eyes out, pour wrath upon his head, call the *gendarmes* to report a madman, have him thrown in prison for crimes against beautiful women or all of the above. He wouldn't have to stand by as she flat out refused to see him, or agreed to a chat only to have the chance to slap him in the chops and kick him in the nuts. How much simpler it would be if Miss Cabin Crew said yes and agreed to marry him. But she couldn't accept if he didn't ask, and as he didn't ask, she served him and moved on to the next passenger. He stared out of the window at the sky passing by. If the plane didn't land, if they circled the world for the rest of his life, setting down the moment after he died, that could work too . . .

He checked in to the Hôtel George V – if you wanted to make a bang, you might as well go nuclear. He could spend his retirement (if it ever came) writing a book about the world's most luxurious hotels. This time, his view was across the Champs Élysées, a remarkable addition to his gallery of vistas. A glittering, vast boulevard, a host of historical moments fearsome and thrilling, a land that could speak for hours without having to say anything.

He could write a book extolling the virtues of that other unerring delight: an extravagant shower. He relaxed in its warmth, feeling philosophical about the morality of water (it must have been something in the Parisian air).

Drying off, his plan was simple: get dressed, jump in a cab, head to Becky's, find Mia, announce his feelings, bring her back to the hotel, ravish her and let himself be ravished, eat, sleep, fly to Tokyo first thing.

A good plan. But would Mia find it as compelling?

There was only one way to find out.

As he had trekked across the Atlantic, he'd read the latest letter from Berenson. Still it made no reference to anyone else being involved in the quest.

'I hope you've kept in mind what I told you about givers and takers,' Dieter had said in this latest missive.

During his confession, the boss had extemporised. 'I see the way you treat people, Scott: everyone gets the benefit of the doubt. Be careful – ugly fuckers lurk all around, whose kind of self-harm is to harm others. A taker will take; it's all they can think of to do. And every time they take, they're telling the world how much they hate themselves. But they're not your problem, Scott, and you shouldn't make them so.'

But he had. And yet Berenson's latest letter was surprisingly complimentary about this fact.

'I might have teased you about your so-strong moral compass, *about your po-faced gloom – lighten up, I always wanted to say! – but I knew you had the most exceptional ethics and the highest-grade integrity. What respect I had for you! I don't make things easy for people to pick up on. I am the true confessor in that respect: I take it in and give nothing away. It's impossible to do what I do, Scottie, if your clients know too much about you. They don't take note of your disapproval if they think you're no better than they are. So I was not at all surprised when you failed to grasp how disappointed I was when you quit on me, seeing as you had no idea how much respect I had for you. I saw the way you behaved with other people. Sure, you were quiet, but who gives a damn about flash? Not me! Those morons who think that if they're shouting they must be saying something? You fall over them three deep on the street. These egocentrics are confident for no good cause! So many talentless schmucks – they parrot what they see on TV, as if success comes merely by saying you're amazing. Well, the world is waiting for few people, and those who fit the bill almost always don't know it. Like you. I loved your grace, your understanding. Goddammit, Scottie, I loved having you around! I was spending so much time with the most despicable beings on earth, listening to their sordid tales, that I soothed myself by talking to you! I saw your potential, but you didn't bite. I found something for you in the end, though! And it is the most important role of all.*

In this world, if you have anything pure or beautiful, you must protect it. And to do so takes strength of body, of mind, of will and yes, a moral compass. I know all about that Machiavellian shit – I was accused of it often enough – but it only works if you do *know right from wrong. Otherwise you end up hated in a world of demons that you can't escape, and how can you protect what's precious then? The world consumes us all in the end. The fight we have to protect the things we love is constant, even when death closes the magic window on us. That's why people like you are put on this earth. I just wish there were more of you. What a world it would be if you were the common man, Scott Roth. We wouldn't be looking over our shoulders all the time to make sure we were not being raped by those who say 'It's only business'. Business is never only business. Not when someone is lying on the floor in tears and someone else is running off with all of their money. If one person causes another pain, be it through business or assault, it's still personal: it's always personal.*

You seemed so lost out there, in your years of helping those who did not want to be helped. I thought about emerging from the shadows and offering you your job back. I thought about asking you to dinner, but you wouldn't have come. I could imagine you thinking, why does my old boss want to see me? I haven't worked for him for years and we were not friends in the first place, and how does he even know where to find me? So I did not get in touch, though I should have, for both of our sakes. And now I am dead and there is nothing I can do about it. How stupid of me.

Stupid. Yes, I admit to being stupid at long last. I bet you never thought you'd hear me say that! I have been stupid, for I did not get in touch with you sooner, when we could have spoken, when we could have hashed things out. In my defence, I must always be on guard, for what I have to protect is far too important for me to be anything less than rigorous. I have set up a fail-safe process in the event of my death, by natural means or otherwise. Either is possible. So I have called on my unfaithful retainer! So much lost time; it breaks my heart. After my life, I have had few regrets. But one is that I did not spend more time in the presence of your pure soul, with no trace of pollution.

And there ended the letter. Roth read it through several more times before his plane touched down in Paris, on one occasion wiping a small gathering of moisture from the corner of his eye. It wasn't a tear, though. It must have been something to do with the descent . . .

He looked at himself in the mirror: a dandy. He called for a cab. He heard in the lobby, '*Monsieur!*' He got into his taxi; the driver did not give off the whiff of being a Mulcahy goon.

They drove through a Paris alien to him, even though it was only a few days since he'd been here. His mood was starting to curdle. He was so caught up in the romantic sweep it hadn't occurred to him until now that Mia might not be home, or that she and Becky may have gone out for the night or popped to a local bar. Or that she may have moved on, found herself someone new, a man (or woman) who did not up and leave in the middle of the night without trace or explanation. An attractive French artisan, a glamorous American businessman . . . If she *was* there, Becky may play unwanted defender, interventionist, best friend affronted on Mia's behalf, furious with all the male gender. Accusations, epithets, eye-gouging . . . He was starting to feel *le sick*. He opened the window to get some air, to cool his anxiety.

Before he knew it, the cab came to a halt outside Becky's building. He told the driver to wait – he may need a fast getaway. The street was silent, nobody coming this way or that. No unwanted interlopers.

He stepped out of the taxi and walked towards the entrance. Before he could ring the buzzer, he saw the door was ajar. He pressed his hand against it; the door swung open. He could hear a voice coming from beyond the top of the staircase, from inside the apartment. A *male* voice. Speaking in French.

'Hey!' Roth called up.

The Francophone stopped. A long, suspicious silence.

'Mia?' Roth called. 'It's Scott!'

The apartment door opened, revealing an angry-looking man staring down at him, who said, in heavily accented English, 'Who the fuck are you and why are you trying to break into my home?'

'What?'

'Go! Or I call the police!'

Roth stared up at him. Was he Mia's new boyfriend?

'GO!' the Frenchman shouted.

'Mia! Becky!'

'Who are you calling for?'

'What are you doing here?' Roth yelled at the man.

'*Quoi*? This is my home!'

'MIAAAAA!'

The Frenchman frowned with contempt. 'You are crazy!'

Roth rushed up the stairs and pushed past the man into Becky's flat before the purported tenant could do anything to stop him.

Only when he came to a halt did Roth realise that the furniture, pictures and mess he expected to see from his last visit here were gone. The empty bottles of wine, the prints on the walls, the rugs, the cushions, even the women themselves were nowhere to be seen. Instead, Roth was standing in a very male apartment, the furnishings and vast-screen TV the hallmarks of a bachelor pad: stark pictures, starker furniture . . . He explored the vista, as if he might find a trace of the scene of the night Mia gave in and they came back to an unexpectedly Becky-inhabited apartment. The wallpaper, layout and carpet were the same but everything else had changed. Roth gasped, 'Where are they?'

'Where are who?' the Frenchman replied, bristling with anger.

'Mia and Becky.'

'Who are they?'

'They lived here.'

'When?'

'Last week . . .'

'*C'est impossible,*' the Frenchman said. 'This place had been empty for months before I move in.'

Roth's head swivelled, his brain too. 'What?'

The Frenchman glared at him as if to say, *you heard*.

'When did . . .?' Roth asked, starting to feel somewhat strange.

'Two days ago.'

'What?'

'*Oui*, I move in this week, no one else here.'

Roth kept on staring round the apartment, searching for a trace of the night he'd spent here, out of body, a little out of his mind. He felt increasingly light-headed as he tried to compute, forgetting that he'd just broken into someone's property.

The Frenchman had had enough. He seized Roth and pushed him towards the door, too fast for him to do anything other than go flying down the staircase if he did not—

'Wait!' Roth gasped.

The Frenchman paused, a moment away from sending the intruder head first down the gaping mouth of the gloomy stairs. He glared at his unwelcome visitor.

'It's okay,' Roth mumbled. 'I'm going.'

Chapter 17

He took the cab back to his hotel, feeling as if he'd shatter if they drove over a stone. The sense of that apartment: empty of her; empty of the both of them and the lie they were supposed to be. It gave him no satisfaction whatsoever that his suspicions had finally been proved correct: Becky and Mia *were* in that apartment only for show, and to perform their part in the sting to lure him into the web Mulcahy had spun on behalf of his faceless, soulless superiors. Yes, now it all made sense: Mia and Becky were a part of Mulcahy's team, a conspiracy with a sizeable staff, which made sense if billions were at stake. The big American had chosen his cast well: Mia and Becky had made the requisite impression: two young, attractive women at the start of their big adventure in life – but how closely had Roth looked at the walls of 'their apartment' in the brief time he was there? He'd been disorientated by the sight of Becky, and the ominous growl of Mia's foul mood. When Roth had called their bluff, they had called his – and they never gave him the chance to look too closely at the joins, chucking together this so-called home in an afternoon, making sure he couldn't get close enough to see the fringes of the illusion. But still it hadn't worked. Still Roth had walked out in the middle of the night, driven by an instinct that *something* was amiss. That must have shocked them all: their honeytrap failing, the industry required to set up a fake flat in such a short space of time still amounting to insufficient trickery, a change of tack required: Mulcahy's emergence from the shadows to grab the key in a far more hands-on fashion. Standing in that room, trying to take it all in, the Frenchman desperate to throw Roth down the stairs . . . Flashes of the team in action: the pictures quickly nailed to the wall; the bottles of wine hastily bought and half drunk or poured down the sink; the pictures by Picasso in Mia's room – *she hadn't gone to the exhibition, some bod must have rushed to a shop to get fake mementoes* – dragging him through the lounge so fast he didn't have the chance to see through the illusion, to see the seams – but it hadn't mattered, for his gut had been dead right all along.

Back at Hôtel George V, Roth asked reception to arrange a flight to Tokyo, leaving as soon as possible. It was too late to depart that night but he could fly first thing in the morning.

Alone in his luxury hotel room, supposedly the site of his great achievement – the return of Mia – its dimensions expanded to the size of a gladiatorial arena; he despaired at having to stay in Paris for another fourteen hours. He could do battle with himself or wander into the night. If he was being followed, so what? His pursuers could do something useful for a change: they could keep him company.

On the streets, Mia's face in his mind, he was in a vast sea of suspicion, despair, disbelief. How could he have been so stupid? To have come here with the crazy idea that she loved him, that she wasn't some glorified hooker working for greedy, brutal thugs? *Jesus, Scottie, you were supposed to have learned by now!*

He saw the Arc de Triomphe, ran across the road until he reached the island on which it stood, backlit by the moon. A few people looked at him, wondering who this frantic man was, his arms stretched and twirling around through 360 degrees.

'HERE I AM!' he screamed. 'COME AND GET ME! TAKE ME WHEREVER YOU WANT TO GO! YOU CAN HAVE IT ALL, I DON'T CARE ANY MORE!'

He was possessed of a deranged energy that could harm passers-by if they got too close; they gave him a wide berth. He went running into a grid of streets, and kept going until his nervous energy was burned off. It left him weary. It was late now; he realised just how hungry he was.

The desire for a frenzy of careless consumption in a place of fine dining led him to a Left Bank café. He saw beautiful women, single, with boyfriends, husbands, lovers . . . They were all out tonight. He took on board caffeine enough to fly to Tokyo without need of a plane. Waiters recognised *femme*-related heartache, circled the wagons, made sure he had the best seat in the house, as comfortable as any man could be while nursing wounds inflicted by female hard-heartedness. He thanked his posse with a massive tip. He walked into the night with no one to warm his shoulder, nuzzle his neck. No sign of dear old Everett. Even his loneliness didn't want to spend time with him tonight.

The Arc de Triomphe appeared again; he was close to his hotel. At the apex of the grand boulevard, he felt no triumph, possessed no armies to parade the streets, no countries to invade. He stood at the edge of the Champs Élysées, an Amazon to cross. His head empty, all-over-body exhaustion; a breeze could lift him across the city and up into the sky, from where he, the Professor of Weariness, could look down and see the people who'd used him over the years, and what they'd got up to after he departed their disastrous lives. With glee he could note new lines on their faces from crises unresolved, which he could have helped avoid if only they hadn't bled him dry of whatever they could, financially, emotionally, spiritually . . . Perhaps their suffering would make him happy now; perhaps not. Either way, they'd shiver as he hissed their colossal selfishness back down their necks.

He fell on a bench with gratitude. His journey to Paris was supposed to have been about redemption. Instead, it was turning into the grand twist of the knife, the trapdoor that opens when you've hit rock bottom only to then realise how much further there is still to fall. The peril Berenson had warned him of: *there is no rock bottom*. Once you start falling, you keep on dropping until you run out of days; Roth could see that he was many years yet from the base of the bottomless pit. A chill flashback to the Frenchman's grip, his keenness to send him down the stairs, whatever injury may befall Roth by the time he hit the floor. An intruder in someone else's home – not Becky's, not Mia's – so what could he have claimed in his defence? The police would have thought him stupid, a cuckold fleeced by a woman much younger than he.

He started to shiver, the night's cold an additional insult. The wooden slats of the bench stayed firm beneath him. He cast his eyes along the Champs Élysées, looking for those still looking for him. Were they disguised tonight as lamp posts or letter boxes? Were they still watching him being sent on a bizarre, pointless errand when he should have known better? *Should have should have should have!* The ache-song of so many, not least the man who thought he was everyone's saviour.

Mia was supposed to have been *his* redemption, the last person he tried to help, the gateway to his future, revealed when Rickard Hay winkled from him the acknowledgement that *it was time to move on*. She was supposed to have been the saviour of the saviour.

What a fool he'd been.

He saw little of the sky between Paris and Tokyo, little of the cabin crew too. He woke towards the end of the flight, and quickly made the fateful decision: he'd had enough of the bullshit, as Rickard Hay might say. His grand, decade-long scheme had been a total bust. Yes, it really was time to move on. So let the world know, let it be registered by one and all: this do-gooder was officially retired.

Chapter 18

He chucked down his bags in the Hotel Hamishi and with no ceremony whatsoever dialled the tortuous number, navigating the digits carefully, his mood as dark as he'd had for years.

The phone started to ring. His mind returned to Mia. Where she was. What she was doing. *Who* she was doing. The bed was soft beneath him, the Tokyo hotel room his fourth or fifth or sixth . . .

'Who that?' came a staccato voice when the line connected.

Roth jolted at the sound of the voice: he had been certain no one would pick up. He wavered for a moment, caught unawares. 'Who – who is this?'

'You call me, who you?'

'Roth.'

There was a long pause. 'Wait,' the voice ordered, and the line went dead.

The echo of the downed phone was loud in the room. 'Hello? Hello?' But there was no point repeating it: the voice had gone.

Wait? He'd flown seven thousand miles for *wait*? For how long? For what? For who? He slammed the phone down, his instinct to get the hell out of the hotel, out of Tokyo, all the way out of this ridiculous quest right now. But . . . the gruff, harsh man must have been connected to this somehow, for he was there at the end of an instruction Berenson had given him.

'Wait . . .' he grumbled. 'All right then, I'll wait. I'll wait in Sydney shall I? Or how about the Arctic Circle? *Wait, for fuck's sake . . .*'

He wandered over to the window and gazed at the seductive skyline. But he couldn't go and explore the city – he had to *wait.*

To pass the time, he read *Winter Journal,* his next Paul Auster. He devoured the book in a couple of hours, but there was still no sign of what he was supposed to be waiting for. He sat up, his bones creaking, and called down to room service for tea. He felt sleepy from jetlag, his body clock confused. He lay on the bed, letting his eyes close. He could write sonnets to the problem-solving powers of sleep. When you're poor and live among the poorer, entertainment and healthcare you don't have to pay for are gifts from the heavens. Sleep afforded ample amounts of both. *What joy a good night's sleep!* Soon he was dozing, happy at last no longer to be 'waiting'.

And she lay on the bed, facing him. Her hair shimmered, backlit, bunched up. Her accent parlez-ed *about banking, that recurring surrealist touch. He delighted in the sound of her voice, in this enchanted capsule of calm. Close enough to kiss, secure from the world and its troubles, the sun fading, her deep blue eyes coming into view—*

The sun shone brightly. He could see the corona of her hair, heard the sound of her speaking in French . . . She placed a hand on his chest, leant in to kiss him. And now her lips on his, he began to lie back—

He laid himself all the way out of his reverie, waking abruptly and in a bad mood. Feeling distant, oddly so, he stared at the ceiling, the sense of the woman's touch upon his skin evaporating. The feel of her lips, the ache of his body in need, those gorgeous blue eyes—

Wait a minute: *blue* eyes?

But Mia had *brown* eyes.

A knock at the door roused him. He sat up quickly, got up quicker and walked towards it, feeling skittish. When he opened up, he saw a waiter standing there with his tea. Roth thanked him and tipped the man, took the beverage to the window, sat on the sill and sipped while staring at the maniac sprawl of the city. There was nothing running through his mind apart from memories of Berenson bubbling up from his subconscious. Soon he was thinking about a fragment of a conversation that had taken place during his confession, which truly had rambled far and wide.

'You don't talk about girlfriends,' Berenson had said.

'Nor do you,' Roth had replied.

'*Touché,*' the boss had grinned.

'Either there's nothing to say, or nothing that should be said.'

'People get jealous.'

'I don't know about that.'

'It's not about money, Scottie. I was asking you about girlfriends.'

'And I told you.'

'Yes – you told me nothing!'

Roth did not reply.

'This teenager—' the boss persisted.

'I thought we were talking about girlfriends.'

'Calm down, Casanova, I *am* making a point here. If you had more people in your life, people you loved, it would have placed that business in context—'

'Yes – it would have made me feel even worse.'

'I'm not sure that's possible. But for the people who'd love you – if only you'd let them – *they'd* understand. That's right, Scottie boy, *they* wouldn't have wanted him to carve you up.'

'You're talking from experience?'

'We're not talking about me. This is not my confession.'

'Are you sure about that?'

Berenson frowned. 'What do you mean?'

A knock at the door. Roth jumped out of his skin again; he hadn't ordered anything more from room service, so it couldn't be a waiter.

Another knock.

He stood up, seized up. It must be the man he'd spoken to on the phone. He had no idea who he might be, this dude from whom there was now no escape – unless he wanted to climb out of a thirty-third-storey window and take his risks with the ledge. Who cared about instructions, it was still his skin at stake.

A third knock; anger in its tone. Staccato, like the voice on the phone. Another loud bang and Roth ran to the door before it was smashed in. 'Who is it?' he called out.

'You phone me?' came the voice from the other side.

'Y . . . yes.'

'Then open door!'

'Tell me what's going on.'

'Open door now!'

'Not til you say what you want.'

'Not want! Have to give.'

'What?'

'Open or I break down!'

'You're going to break down?'

'Door! I break down door!'

'I don't think the hotel will like that.'

'Hotel can sue me!'

Roth fell silent. But this was all a part of Berenson's diffuse plan ... So he took a deep breath and opened the door – ready to shut it again super-fast if need be.

A fierce Japanese man was standing outside his room, stout and breathless, his eyebrows curled in anger. He looked testy, carried a doctor's bag. 'What took so long?' he said, pushing into the room past Roth, who quickly glanced outside and saw that no one else was prowling along the corridor.

Inside, Roth found the man already sitting down on his bed, the doctor's bag plonked down next to him. He was searching through it.

'What is this?' Roth asked, hovering near the hall in case he needed to make a quick getaway.

'Shut up your questions!' the man spat. 'Where you get number?'

Roth looked at him, uncertain what to say.

'Where you get number? Tell me or I get sumo angry!'

'From Berenson.'

'Berenson dead!'

'I know.'

'So where you get number?!'

'It was in a private box in a bank that ... he left me in his will.'

This seemed to calm the man; he even gave a little nod. He turned to the doctor's case and opened it, fished out a smallish wooden box and, with a ceremonial flourish, handed it to his host.

Roth was perplexed. The staccato man's arms remained outstretched in presentation. Eventually, he took it.

'Open box!' Staccato ordered.

Roth did so. Inside, he found two items: a small device that looked like a USB stick with a button on the side, and a larger item that was clearly a charger.

Roth looked at Staccato, utterly confused.

The Japanese man nodded, by way of explanation.

Roth shook his head.

Staccato hissed as if he were in the company of the dumbest fool in the world. *'Use when need.'*

'But . . . what *is* it?'

'Speak English?'

'Yes.'

'So use! When need!'

'But what *for?*'

'Ugh!' Staccato shook his head. 'What you do about girl?'

'Huh?'

'You sure you speak English? Girl! What you do?'

'Mia?'

'I mean girl!'

Roth looked at him, clueless.

Staccato huffed and stood up. 'I drive hours, get here, talk to shit block! That what I talk to when I get here: shit block!'

He pushed past Roth to leave.

'Wait! Don't you have anything else for me?'

'Like what?'

'Like – a key? A letter? Envelopes with *something* in them?'

Staccato gazed at Roth as if he were truly dense. He shook his head and walked out of the room.

Roth wondered if he should go after him, but guessed not. In truth, he was glad the oppressive man had gone.

He sat on the bed and opened the wooden box. He took out the small USB-like device inside, and ran his thumb over the button but did not push it down.

He stared at the ceiling and screamed.

He wandered through the Hotel Hamishi, his eyes jazzed by its retro funky style. In the computer room, all manner of gadgets lay ready for use by guests. He sat in front of a PC, logged in, plugged the USB stick into the appropriate orifice and waited.

The computer couldn't detect the device.

He scowled, pulled it out of the computer, pushed it in again, this time slightly harder. Again, the USB stick failed to register as an accessible drive. He removed it for a second time and stared at it.

He put the USB stick back into the computer a third time, and now pressed the button. Still nothing happened.

Okay, it may *look* like a memory stick, but it clearly wasn't; so what was it? He went back to his room, feeling head-scratchy. On his bed, he studied the charger the USB had been supplied with. It looked like it could plug it into virtually any mains socket in the world. Nice – and as useless as the item it served.

He felt impatient, unwilling to play Berenson's game. After to-ing and fro-ing, he called the long number again. If he'd given Roth the device for a reason, the man in whose possession Berenson had left it must know what it was for, and when to use it.

'Not supposed to call!' Staccato barked at him, horrified to hear Roth's voice. 'Unsafe to call more than once!'

'But I don't know what it's for! And if you won't give me an answer, I've come to a dead end. What would Berenson think of that?'

'He think you moron!'

'You have to tell me what you know.'

'Instructions are give you box. No more! No explanation! You know what to do! Man not know what to do not right man!'

'But Berenson was counting on me to remember something that happened ten years ago and I haven't a clue what that is!'

The line cut dead.

'Oh for fuck's sake!' Roth slammed the phone down so violently that the bedside table shook. He grabbed one of the pillows and threw it,

watched it float across the room before falling lightly against the floor. Far more satisfying to have smashed something – but then he'd only have felt guilty afterwards.

He dashed through the streets of Tokyo to burn off the tension. Despite the ever-present threat of pursuant goons, he had no plan but to keep on walking until he was done, pounding the streets so hard his feet would bleed. His mind churned. He thought about his conversation with Rickard Hay, and the uncertainty over the cause of Dieter's death.

Back in his hotel room, he called Berenson's lawyer.

'How's it going?' the older man asked, with a tinge of care in his voice that took the caller a little by surprise, yet was not unwelcome.

'It didn't occur to me to ask when I came to see you – there was a lot to take in at the time – but how did Dieter die?'

There was a pause at the other end of the line. Finally, a low voice: 'Do you know what lawyers hate most of all, Scott?

'Even more than unpaid bills?'

'We hate being asked a question we don't have the answer to.' There was another long pause, the sound of deep thoughts being had. Finally the lawyer said, a heavy dubiousness in his voice, 'Dieter – we are told – died of a heart attack.'

'What do you mean "we are told"?'

'I mean just that,' the lawyer said, his dubiousness even more pronounced. '"*We are told.*"'

'But you don't believe that?'

'Why would I not believe it?'

'You're – you're losing me . . .'

'I saw his body, his death certificate; the post-mortem said it was a heart attack. Why would I have reason to disbelieve it?'

'So it *was* a heart attack. Or no?'

And now the lawyer's voice sounded human, wistful. 'That Dieter Berenson should *cease to exist,* just like that? That such a man keels over from nowhere? He was fit as a fiddle – he had a medical three weeks before he died that gave him the all-clear. *There was nothing wrong with his heart.*'

'But medicals are no guarantee.'

'That's right.'

'And the stress, the travel, the bad hours, the rich food—'

'So maybe I'm just a friend in mourning,' the lawyer replied. 'But he had enemies with lots of money and even more connections. We'd been pals for eight years, I worked with him on deals . . . He knew too much, you see? Especially with that stupid confessions gig of his. By the time he died, he was *Murder on the Orient Express*: there were so many people who might have wanted to silence him that too many fingers pointed in too many directions at once.'

'But it still might have been a heart attack,' Roth insisted. 'Natural causes, nothing more than that.'

'Like I say,' the lawyer replied coolly, 'I don't have the answer to your question.'

Staccato, the lawyer . . . *Zero for two.*

No onward clues. No constellation by which to chart his next step. No new key. No sudden recollection. The fast-approaching buffers smashed into his face. It was over, and he knew it.

On his way to the airport, he checked his email.

A message from Mia.

His heart almost stopped. He took a deep breath and opened it.

'Scott,' the email began – no affectionate salutation, but at least it didn't start 'Dear Bastard' – *Scott, I don't know what I did to upset you, but I need your help. A couple of days after you vanished, I had to leave Paris quickly – Becky and I had a terrible falling-out. I thought I knew her well, but it turned out I was wrong. She went crazy, I've never seen her like that. She was possessed, frightening. She said she couldn't stand Paris any more and was leaving. She'd packed up all of her stuff and chucked mine on the streets!! I couldn't believe it. I'd been out the whole day. When I came back, my stuff had been ditched. I asked her why and she went completely insane. She said that she couldn't leave quickly enough, she never wanted to set foot in Paris again. She screamed that she never wanted to see me again either. I couldn't believe it. I was so depressed because of what you'd done – which I still don't understand – that I'd been walking the streets, sobbing and looking like some cliché of a damsel in distress.* You *did that to me. But when I came back and found Becky having a breakdown, I thought it must have been a bad joke. But it wasn't. She was getting in a van to go back to London. If I'd been there ten minutes later I would have missed her. She was crying half the time. I told her I had nowhere to stay but that didn't make a difference. I tried to calm her down, to stop her, but then she started to get violent, so I let her go. I couldn't stay in Paris – Becky was the only person I knew – so I went back to London, spending what little money I had left on the ticket. I don't have family I can turn to, and the friends I was hoping would put me up refused – they turned out not to be friends after all. I've tried to find work but I don't have any experience in anything, and now things are getting bleak. The only other person I could think of was you. Cos, let's face it, you owe me. You hurt me so much, Scott. I thought we were cool and then you were gone. I loved you and still do, although I'm not sure why now. You're a good and decent man. If you had your reasons for doing what you did that night then, whatever they were, I'm sure you have the grace to feel bad about it. I really could do with a friend. And I could do with that friend being you. I hope you're in London, and a tiny part of you still wants to see me. It was so wonderful when the lights went off and it was just you and me and the dark. Mia*

He read the email several times over, and then came to the only possible conclusion: he had to kill himself.

Chapter 19

Checking into the Hotel Salon felt like coming home, which only proved the extent to which, at the age of forty, he had no home of his own. Greeted warmly by the concierge, he was ushered to his old room, happily available.

He closed the door, staggered to the bed and let himself fall, landing with a light bounce before sinking into a mattress that seemed composed of silken comfort. He was back in London, in a peaceful room, the twisting and bucking of an intercontinental flight becalmed. His body had no idea what time it was; he'd been flying this way and that as if riding a bike. But it didn't matter any more. He was getting off the rollercoaster. With room service, books and films, he planned to stay hidden from the world for some time.

He woke, and called for breakfast, lunch . . . By dinnertime he was starting to feel human again. After devouring steak and chips in front of a film, he nodded off. He woke at midnight with the tray still on the bed. He shuffled around, his mind empty. He called for room service to bring some tea. He sat by the window looking out across the street in front of the hotel. Six storeys down, all was quiet.

The hotel's facilities supported all of his needs. They may still be following him, but he had no leads to pass on. He could say to Mulcahy and his goons, *sure, follow me if you want, all the way to the newsagents, because I'm not going anywhere else.* Eventually they'd tire, and he'd be a free man with a million in the bank. Yet he was haunted by the thought of Berenson scowling, saying *'I'm so disappointed in you: it turned out I couldn't even trust you.'*

'You didn't tell me anything,' Roth said in imaginary response.

'I shouldn't have had *to tell you! That was the plan!'*

'The plan you didn't tell me anything about! The plan I'm supposed to piece together from faded, mistaken memories! And this time you didn't even give me a key! This shit about relevant information – didn't you think it might backfire?'

'I had total faith in you! But even you've let me down.'

'You don't want anyone to find your treasure, Dieter, that's the truth about this quest. So well done, yes: you always did get your way in the end.'

* * *

Maybe killing himself was an over-exaggeration, but on the flight back to London, he had started to write Mia an email. He tried several versions but each time he stopped dead, caught in pincers between two thoughts, the first a deep concern, the second the squeeze of the jaws.

The first thought, about the Frenchman's comment: *'I move in this week, no one else here.'*

The second, arising from Mia's email, which had made his flight from Tokyo to London interminable. The great torment, the question only he could answer: did he mean what he'd said about 'retiring'?

He slept little (and re-dreamt his reverie – again starring a blue-eyed Mia) but that did not help; it only made it harder, as if that were possible. One could go mad, lurching back and forth with these big thoughts. His worry distilled, he bit down hard on the back of his hand. His mood on the flight from Paris to Tokyo had been grim; giving up the do-gooding had seemed so *obvious* – but that was before he'd received her email . . .

So the second reason, the squeeze of the jaws, the post-decision decision reached. He'd stick with it, with retirement. Mia had left it a couple of days too late – his angel days really were behind him.

Also on the flight back from Tokyo, it had struck Roth who Staccato might have meant when he barked, *'What you do about girl?'*

From his bedroom in the Hotel Salon, he put in another call to the lawyer. 'Listen,' he started, 'Berenson's trail has gone cold.'

Silence at the other end of the line. Roth could tell it was unaccusatory and rather, as with Rickard Hay, a sigh at the intractable nature of a very good friend.

'But there's one loose end I need to tie up,' Roth continued. 'Do you know where I could find a detective?'

* * *

'It's pretty big business,' Hayden MacDermott said, as Roth expressed surprise at the swankiness of his premises. 'There's a lot of suspicious people out there – with good reason. But I'm not complaining! How can I help?'

'It's going to sound a little strange.'

'It always does,' replied MacDermott.

'I was given a telephone number. I tried it a hundred times but it connected only once and when it did, well, I think I heard this young girl, probably no more than eight or nine, and she *may* have said . . .'

It took only thirty seconds to provide MacDermott with all of the information he had. There was not much more to say.

'Are you staying in town?' the detective asked.

'For now,' Roth said, the implication in his tone being: *not for long.*

On his way 'home' he stopped at a travel agency, the kind that offered unique experiences, globetrotting for those keen on adventure but not so much on danger. He leafed through brochures extolling the wonders of orang-utans in Borneo, the delights of the Siberian steppe, casinos in Vegas, Nepalese mountains and everything in between. Or perhaps a better trip would be to fly to Vienna and get a train to wherever took his fancy – journey with the breeze and see where he ended up, and who he met on the way. In other words travel light, and for the rest of his life.

By the time the afternoon had come, he had settled on a simple method to enable him to decide where he should start his travels. He sat by his hotel window, from which he could see down and along the street outside. He put on some music; room service had brought him a pot of fine coffee, through which he was making his way. Utterly comfortable, he watched the world pass by outside. Every time he saw a car driving east to west, he'd put a tick on the right-hand side of the sheet of paper he had placed on the windowsill in front of him. Every time he saw a car driving west to east, he'd put a tick on the left-hand side. He was going out for dinner, planned to shower at seven, at which point he'd stop counting cars. If he had more ticks on the left-hand side of the page, he'd fly to Bangkok. If he had more on the right, he'd go to Rio. And from there he would travel onwards, and keep on going until he found the place that truly felt like home. A plan of beautiful simplicity and – best of all – no thinking required.

MacDermott called at 6pm. 'The number you gave me *is* live, though I've never seen anything like it before.'

'Okay . . .'

'There are so many filters protecting the source that tracking it through the global network is like trying to find an ice cube in a glacier. Still, we've made considerable progress. It might not sound like much, but we've narrowed down the location of the number to somewhere in Europe.'

'That sounds . . . interesting.'

'I'm glad you think so – it's a big world.'

'It sure is.'

'That's all for now. I'll keep you posted.'

'Appreciate it.'

The detective rang off. Roth wandered around his room, resentful. The answer he was hoping for – *we haven't been able to find anything at all* – hadn't fluttered into his holiday-longing ears. Instead, upon his shoulders had been lain the hint of further obligation. He managed to hold this line of self-righteous selfishness until he started to think about his parents. *They* would want him to pursue this appendix to the quest. They'd want him to be clear as to whether or not the girl existed at all, so that he could flush away the spiritual drag arising from thoughts that he may have been hallucinating, recently and in the past. His parents had been quite old when they took him in, this little boy without provenance. He was so full of admiration at the risk they ran, the great start they gave this orphan. A happy blend of personalities, he an effortless child, they adept. He wished they were still around, but they'd died long ago, within a short space of each other, his mother first then his father six months later. Roth was twenty-three, heartbroken at being alone again. At least they'd passed away before the terrible incident with the teen. He couldn't have looked his parents in the face knowing that they knew that he had been responsible for the death of a young boy, that the child they'd raised so well had turned out to be a killer.

He checked his email, found a second message from Mia.

'*Dear Scott*', it said ('dear' this time, he noticed),

I hope you got my last email. I sent it a couple of days ago. I really do need to speak to you, things are getting worse and I can't think of anyone else who could help. Please get in touch. Scott: I need help. I need you. Please say you're in London. Please help me. Love Mia.

She'd used the magic words, 'I need help.' *The urge of the do-gooder to do good*. He *was* retired; he had meant what he'd said. Only, when he'd said it, there had been no one else around to hear.

Chapter 20

Dear Mia, I'm so sorry I left you that night . . .

Dear Mia, I can see right through you, trying to use me in this way . . .

Dear Mia, I love you . . .

Dear Mia, I came back to Paris but you'd gone . . .

Dear Mia, there was this French guy who said you'd never been there . . .

Dear Mia, I know who you're working for . . .

Dear Mia, I know what you're after . . .

Dear Mia, I love you . . .

Dear Mia, right now I wish we'd never met . . .

A dozen drafts unsent, he passed out on his bed.

He woke the next morning to find a text from Hayden, timed at 4.12am, asking him to come to the office as soon as he got the message.

The detective was pleased to see him, bleary-eyed and running on adrenalin alone. 'Come in!' he said, already well-caffeinated at 7.30am.

'Good news? Or bad?'

'*Odd* news,' MacDermott replied. He noted his client's wonky expression. 'Don't worry, my job is to get to the bottom of things. Unfortunately, at the bottom of things you often find the top of something else.'

Roth *really* didn't like the sound of this.

McDermott explained, 'At about 2am, we were sure we'd found the other end of the line. Whoever enabled the call was using very sneaky methods: covering tracks like I've never seen before, in private circles at least – among the military, yes, but not elsewhere. Extremely expensive to do – you can't just go onto eBay and buy it; you have to be exceptionally well-connected to get this sort of tech for civilian purposes. Layers of secrecy that are virtually impenetrable. To tell the truth, I was getting suspicious. I mean, I have *never* seen a result like this, where we had to trace a call back through so many layers. We've checked the last part of the search many many times. But it kept coming back with the same answer. So at four this morning, me and the guys had a celebratory cup of black coffee and I sent you the text.'

'Hayden,' Roth gasped, 'Just tell me what the fuck is at the other end of this phone line.'

'Moersen Bank,' the detective said, 'Based twenty-five miles outside of Geneva.'

He walked along Great Eastern Street to Bishopsgate, surrounded by people going to work, in a daze. A Swiss bank. Moersen – a name he'd never heard, a bank he'd never seen on any of his trips with Berenson nor any of the lists provided by Gordon. So who the hell had he spoken to that night? The East End merged into the City and he kept on walking, thinking, but couldn't get a handle on this latest fact.

He noticed the low-slung Audi with blacked-out windows. At the same time, the car sped up and rushed past him. He saw the number plate, tried to make a note, but it turned out of view and was already decaying in his memory. Soon there was nothing left but an overwhelming sense of stupidity, and the unsettling reminder of his pursuers. But it was clear now what he needed to do.

Although it was his confession, it had seemed to Roth at times that Berenson was reaching down into his own pit of disgust and dismay. Or was he remembering incorrectly? Much of those five hours had come back to him, yet there was no certifying the truth of any of it; of the parts he could recall, any of them could have been embroidered by his imagination. At one point, he was sure they were talking about excess, that subject so common to confessions. The boss said, 'I wonder if I've gone too far, Scottie. You know me. I can be too well prepared. I know it sounds impossible but . . . I think maybe it is.'

At this point, Roth was in no mood to offer his tormentor comfort or sympathy. Berenson, who seemed to require neither, continued. 'The world is a complicated place. Sometimes I think only complicated people understand how it works, and can do what needs to be done.'

'That sounds like an excuse to me,' Roth had replied tartly.

'All these things I'm trying to protect, from a world I know will ruin them.'

'But what if you're the one who's ruining them by trying to protect them so much?'

Berenson looked at him in disbelief. His face darkened; Roth wondered if he might have just talked himself out of a job. 'Scottie, I have three Picassos, a Titian, a Renoir, Magritte, Van Gogh . . . Did you know that?'

Roth shook his head.

'Hoppers, Rembrandts, Frank Lloyd Wright designs, Chippendale furniture, Greek and Roman sculptures thousands of years old. I've been collecting since I started making money, a long, long time now. But … I never look at it.'

'Why not?'

'My favourite piece is a marble sculpture. Dates back to Julius Caesar. I'm not talking about to his time – it's verified as having *belonged* to Caesar himself. Scottie: I put my hand on it and I'm breaking bread with the man. It's five million dollars, but no one will ever see it.'

'Why not?'

'In case it gets stolen, or damaged.'

Roth looked at him with a fresh category of surprise. 'So where *do* you keep it? Where does old Julius live? I'd love to see those pictures. Are they at your house? Because they're not at the office.'

'I don't have them at home.'

'So where are they?'

'Somewhere safe.'

'The Picassos, the Magrittes, the Van Goghs . . .?'

'Sketches. I only have a few of Van Gogh's sketches.'

'Then I'm not interested!' Roth exclaimed, a rare laugh amid the gloom. Berenson threw him a thunderous look. 'So,' he went on, less excitable now. 'When *do* you get to see all of this art?'

'I don't.'

'Are they in deep storage? Do you have them as investments?'

'I buy them because I love them.'

'But you don't ever look at them?'

'No.'

'You've got great security at your apartment,' Roth said, 'Take some of the pieces and put them on your walls!'

'Bring them out? Put them on display? Jesus Christ, you're a moron, Scottie. How did I come to employ you in the first place?'

'I'd love to meet Caesar, I'd love to break bread with the man.'

'No one gets to break bread with Caesar but me.'

'Are you serious?'

'Do I look like I'm joking?'

No, he did not, at which point Berenson seemed to remember whose confession it was and moved on to ask about Roth's childhood, a hackneyed piece of psychology if ever there was one. Roth played along, amused at Berenson struggling to get back on track by any means necessary and away from the subject of his hidden art. But it was too late for the boss to pretend he was flawless. Dieter's neuroses had shown themselves, flickering a hint of what else may lay beneath the surface.

He made his arrangements, such as they were: a flight, a word with his friends at the Hotel Salon to say he was checking out but would they mind if he left luggage with them for safe keeping? The hotel couldn't be happier to assist such a popular, valuable customer. So, all sorted but for the sorting.

He looked at his watch. There wasn't much time.

She was waiting for him, reading a book – no longer *Germinal*; a piece of junk instead. He stopped at the door, dazed by the sight of her. She hadn't noticed him, and continued to read. A miserable expression on her face, a haunted, troubled aura, someone for whom life was not going well. And yet, at the same time, she looked no different from when he'd last seen her, asleep in a Parisian apartment, astonishingly pretty and full of hope. She sat at a corner table of the café, away from everyone else, as if on a desert island, a prison island. And then she glanced up and saw him. In her eyes, a smile of bravery, a moment of sadness. He started to walk towards her, through ambient noise loud enough to keep the content of their conversation private. Their eyes held the whole way.

Mia stood as he approached, hugged him, *squeezed* him. 'Thank you,' she said. 'I didn't think you'd come.'

'I can't stay long. I'm catching a plane.'

'Where to?'

'I've only got twenty minutes.'

They sat. She ordered coffee.

They both waited for the other to start talking. No words came, only the drinks.

'It's great to see you,' she said at last. 'You look well.'

'Thank you,' he said. 'You too.'

'I look like shit.'

'No,' he replied. 'You look amazing.'

'So how come you look so good? Are you . . . seeing someone?'

'No.'

'So what's your secret?'

'I've retired.'

'From the business you were up to in Paris?'

'From a little more than that.'

A few more moments of awkwardness, and then he said: 'You better tell me what's wrong.'

She pulled a face, *everything*. 'It's all fucked up. The situation with Becky. She's a nutcase. I didn't realise, she's like no one I've ever known. What came out of her mouth, Scott, the cruellest, ugliest . . . I could see she was hurting, she'd been ripped apart, fired by her company. They told her it wasn't working out, that she wasn't a great architect after all. Thanks to you I was in such a funk I hadn't even noticed. I'd been wandering around Paris like a teenage nightmare, bursting into tears, wondering what the fuck I'd done to upset you. She packed up the entire apartment. When I got back, this van was outside, some French dude was going to drive her shit back to the UK for a couple of hundred euros. All my things, in a few black sacks: she just left it right there on the street. Anyone could have taken what little stuff I had. I was stunned, I felt like my world was ending. That's what embarrassment can do. Scott: I went out in the morning and everything was still in the flat, I come back that night and it's gone. Can you believe that?'

He didn't say but, no, actually, he couldn't believe that.

'Becky told me she was giving up the apartment and going back to London that night. She said she didn't care what I did. I could go wherever I liked, but the one place I couldn't stay was at that flat.'

There was a corner of her soul she was guarding. She paused, withering beneath his expression. 'What's wrong?'

He wanted to say her story absolutely stank but the words remained in his mouth.

'Have you come to tell *me* something?' she asked. 'Are you . . . are you *married*?'

He shook his head.

'But there *is* another woman.'

'Do you need money?' he asked. 'Because I can give you enough for a few weeks, to tide you over, until you get—'

'What?'

'I don't want you to end up on the street, I have cash if that's –'

'I don't want *money*.'

'So what *do* you want?'

'Why are you being so tough with me?' she said. 'I woke up and you were *gone*. You didn't even leave a note. You just fucking *disappeared*. What kind of behaviour is that? What kind of fucking weirdo are you?'

'I didn't come for this conversation.'

'So what did you come for?'

'You said you needed help.'

'I said I wanted to see you.'

'You said you needed help.'

'I fucking *do* need help. *I want you*.'

'For what?'

'I love you, that's for what.'

'You only got in touch after Becky ditched you,' he said. His head was starting to throb with tension.

'I was furious with you! I couldn't think of anything else for days apart from how angry I was and what I might have done wrong. I was waiting for an explanation, Scott, and too fucking angry to get in touch. And then I had this shit with Becky. I ended up flat on my face, in a matter of *days*.'

'You expect me to believe that?'

She stared at him. 'Why would I lie about something so pathetic?'

'I don't know, Mia – you can tell me if you want.'

'Tell you what?'

He caught his breath; he didn't want to be so angry with her. 'Listen,' he said, 'I have to go.'

'So why did you come?'

'I'm heading overseas.'

'Are you in trouble?'

Jesus, he thought: *you're good*.

'Is *that* why you disappeared?'

'Mia—'

'Because . . . it's okay. If something's wrong. I'd love to help, Scott. Let me help. Let me *in*.' She reached out, took his hands in hers, squeezed them tight. *Ohhhh,* he screamed inside, *you are soooooo good.*

'You and I can be great together,' she said. 'Just *think*.'

That amazing face . . .

Those clear brown eyes . . .

He pulled his hands away, took an envelope from his pocket and gave it to her. 'There's two thousand pounds cash.'

'*What*?'

'It'll keep you fine for long enough. But it's not me. I'm not the one who can help you right now.'

'Where are you going? Why won't you tell me?'

'Because it doesn't make any difference.'

'When are you coming back?'

'I don't know.'

'Take me with you!'

'Will you just *stop*?' he said. 'I went to Becky's apartment and the guy told me you were never there.'

A look of horror passed across her face. '*What*?'

'That the flat had been empty for months!'

She looked at him as if he were having a mental breakdown. 'But . . . you were there, Scott. Don't you remember?'

'I remember. Don't look at me like that, I know what I'm saying.'

'Are you sure?'

'Yes, I'm sure.'

Her brown eyes flashed at him. 'How do you know *he* wasn't lying? This fucking stranger?'

'The break-in, Mia – it's not just Becky's apartment.'

'What break-in? *I don't know what you're talking about.*'

He pushed away from the table and stood, his face aflame. 'Take the money,' he said, 'And for Christ's sake stay out of harm's way.'

'Don't go, Scott, take me with you!'

'These people are dangerous. Mulcahy and his guys - they are using you.'

'Who? Scott, who the fuck are you talking about?'

'Maybe next time we see each other, things will be better.'

'Don't leave me, Scott, please! I need you!'

But he was already walking away.

Geneva

Chapter 21

In the taxi to the hotel, over his shoulder through the rear windscreen, a stolid vehicle that had been following him all the way from the airport.

Mulcahy and his goons were back.

A flicker of how it must be to live under a totalitarian regime. But this was Geneva, not the Eastern Bloc. He was a free man, pursued by people who had nothing to do with the state, and everything to do with Berenson's billions. Not that you'd know from the surroundings. The grey buildings, the greyer sky; he may as well have been in the depths of Yugoslavia. The lake sucked the energy from the air, its chill overwhelming the slender warmth of this modest settlement. Impossible to escape the Alps, the lakes – nature's dominance.

His taxi stopped at the hotel. The car tailing him pulled into a berth on the other side of the road. Roth got out. Two men emerged from the other car at the same time. He recognised neither. They watched him as he went inside.

On this occasion, he couldn't care less about the accommodation. His hotel was, like others in this town of business, anonymously comfortable. *Perfect.* He dropped off his luggage and set out again.

Roth saw that the two men were still waiting for him outside his hotel. If they were going to be so blatant, if Mulcahy wanted to spook him so bluntly, he'd show them. He started walking, opening up his map to find his way to Moersen Bank. The two men crossed the road, their eyes hidden deep in their blank, bleak faces. They followed him.

Roth looked at his map as he walked, his pulse quickening as he felt the men getting closer. He came to a busy junction, thought about darting across the road, but paused a moment too long. The men caught up with him. They stood one on each side. Starkly different from the movie star Mulcahy, they were dressed well but had awful skin. Roth didn't meet their gaze. The crossing light turned green.

'Excuse me,' one of the men said, just as Roth was about to start walking. 'It is a little cold. Can we take you for a warm coffee? There's a lovely café nearby. We would greatly like for you to see it, Mr Kornenberg and I.'

Roth looked at the other man, who possessed a grave, unhappy expression. He decided that he didn't care much for good old Mr Kornenberg.

'It's a sweet little place,' the first man said. 'No one should visit Geneva without seeing it.'

'I'm not here for the sights,' he replied, glaring at their weather-worn faces. The crossing light turned red again.

'We'd like to make you an offer, Mr Roth,' the first man said.

Of course they knew his name; but they couldn't scare him so easily. He knew they were keen to do him harm, their sinister intent unmistakeable. 'I'm not interested.'

'But you do not know what the offer is.'

'I'm in a hurry. I'm here on business.'

'This is Geneva – who is not here on business?'

'Mr . . .?'

'Volck,' the first man said.

Roth's eyes flicked to Kornenberg – this slice of rock was moving a little too close. Cold air rushed from the lake. The city was freezing.

'You won't regret it,' Volck said, in a way that left Roth wondering what on earth they had in mind.

The red light changed to green. Everyone else moved but them.

'You've got ten minutes,' Roth said.

* * *

Ten minutes later, they still seemed to be nowhere near this sweet little café. As he'd suspected: Volck and Kornenberg were leading him to a quieter part of town where there'd be no witnesses.

'Listen,' Roth said. 'You're taking too long. I've got things to do. We can stop there.' He pointed to a busy plasticky affair adjoined to the train station. 'If you want to make me an offer, do it now.'

Kornenberg looked at Volck with irritation, but the latter was cooler. With a cordial nod of his head, Volck agreed.

The three men sat on rigid chairs amid a howl of tourists. The coffee tasted like it had suffered extraordinary rendition, but they were not here for gourmet tang.

Volck said, above the din, 'The quest you are on is of great interest to some very powerful people.'

'Quest?' Roth replied. 'You missed the boat, guys. Quest is over.'

Volck smiled. 'I don't think so. What ... business do you have here in Geneva?'

'Hold your horses, sunshine, you're giving the answers, I'm asking the questions. Why has Mulcahy sent you? Why isn't he here?'

Volck looked confused. 'Who?'

'You know very well who. Everett Mulcahy. Exeter Services Inc. Big American.'

Kornenberg stared at Roth as if he wanted to get on with ripping him apart completely.

'Has he had his rabies shot?' Roth asked, gesturing at Kornenberg.

Volck smiled thinly. 'This. . . Mulcahy is ... nothing to do with us.'

'So who *do* you work for?'

'An interested party.'

'Interested in what?'

'In the affairs of Dieter Berenson. Now you are close, Mr Roth, we offer you a simple bargain.'

'*Close*? The only thing I'm close to is my underpants.'

'Please,' Volck said. 'Mr Kornenberg has a bad temper and a sugar problem. I combine the two only when forced. Now, when you were in Tokyo, you stayed at the Hotel Hamishi where you were given a key.'

A flicker passed across Roth's face, visible enough for his new friends to see that he'd realised something he should have worked out sooner and without the help of these two frosted henchmen.

'It seems you have cause to thank us,' Volck said. 'Mr Berenson covered his tracks well, but when you have been looking for something as valuable as we have for *such* a long time, diligence leads to success. Would you not agree?'

'I have no idea what you're talking about.'

'I think you do,' Volck said. 'Berenson relied on his face, not a key. But when he died, he took his face with him. You have followed his instructions, and now you are here. So why do we not do a deal?'

'Why would I want to do a deal?'

'So that we do not do to you what we did to Berenson.'

Roth felt his blood chill. Volck's malevolence infused the threat, hanging in the air. Rabid aggression rose from him. 'And what did you – do to Berenson?' Roth asked.

'Well, you see, we went to his house, in the middle of the night, when all was silent and we went up behind him and – very loudly – we . . . shouted "BOO!".' Volck was smiling now. 'We knew your old boss well, just as we know you left him when you realised what kind of a man he was. The kind that one such as you would not want to associate with.'

'I don't like your tone,' Roth said.

'I just want to find an arrangement that is beneficial to everyone.'

'Such as?'

'Such as that we take you to the bank. And then we—'

Roth leapt off his chair, dashed out of the café. A few surprised moments later, Kornenberg and Volck rushed after him.

Cold air struck his face, tiny nodules of pain. He dived between pedestrians, struggled to avoid trams, to keep his mind on the route back to the hotel. Blurry faces skipped out of the way. Volck and Kornenberg were sure to be armed. A roar of engines. A car veered across his path. The doors swung open. Two massive men jumped out, wide as they were tall, human roadblocks impossible to pass.

Roth came to a halt a few inches before he'd have crashed into them. 'Okay!' he yelled, holding up his hands.

Volck arrived behind him, out of breath. *'I hate fucking running,'* he hissed, in a bad, sweaty temper; Kornenberg looked as if he could sprint another ten miles. Volck disappeared into the car blocking their way. Roth was then shoved in by Kornenberg, and sandwiched between the two on the back seat. The vast guys got in front, their heads squishing into the ceiling. They drove off quickly.

The sedated streets of Geneva passed by outside. There were no more attempts at bonhomie; Kornenberg's malevolence had in fact amplified. Roth couldn't see ahead with the two Alpine shoulders in the way. He didn't need to: he knew they were taking him back to his hotel, for he knew now what they wanted.

He knew now what he had.

* * *

The car stopped outside his hotel. Volck stepped out. Roth was shoved by Kornenberg into the street. The two giants stayed inside.

In the lobby, the three men crossed the hall and called for a lift. Shorn of the behemoths, they formed an unremarkable sight. Roth stared at the concierge until the lift door opened. Volck and Kornenberg ushered him in and stepped on board.

The lift was too small for the three of them. The carriage shook. Roth's mouth was dry, his heart beating fast. Volck smiled a thin grin.

The doors opened onto a small, discreet hall serving several rooms. His new friends stepped out. Roth stayed put. 'Come on,' growled Kornenberg, almost pulling Roth's arm from its socket as he dragged him from the lift.

Roth was flung at the door of his room. Kornenberg pressed the barrel of a gun into his back to persuade him further. 'We haven't got all fucking day,' he growled.

'Okay,' Roth said, fumbling with the key, his fingers trembling.

Volck said, 'We have no intention of killing you - as long as you cooperate with us.'

'Yeah, that's what you all say.'

The door unlocked. Kornenberg shoved the gun deeper into Roth's back, driving him inside.

His room seemed alien now, a conspirator against him. His luggage remained in the pile he'd left it in: there for all to see.

'Fucking come on!' Kortenberg yelled, the veins on his forehead pulsing with impatience, furious at this fool for wasting their time. *'Just give us the key.'*

'Wh– what key?'

Volck was also tiring of delays, as he walked into the room. 'You will be the third person Mr Kornenberg has killed this month. If you hope to get sympathy from him, you will be disappointed.'

Roth walked to the case, unzipped it and flung back the lid, revealing the box containing the USB stick. He could sense an almost metabolic change in the make-up of his associates.

'You see,' Volck said, his eyes alight. 'That was not so hard.'

There was a knock at the door.

Volck and Kornenberg looked at each other.

'Mr Roth?' came a voice from the hall.

Kornenberg looked at Roth with murderous intent.

Volck put his finger to his lips: *ssssshhhhhh.*

The three men stood in silence, the case open on the bed, the USB stick in full view.

'Mr Roth?' came the voice again.

Roth turned to walk towards the door.

Volck coughed.

Roth looked at him.

Volck shook his head, then whispered a few words in German to his associate.

Kornenberg put his gun away and started towards Roth.

The hotel door crashed open.

The concierge rushed in with two security guards. They smashed into Kornenberg and Roth, sending them tumbling.

'*Scheiss*!' Volck yelped, as he was also shoved across the room.

The concierge grabbed Roth and pulled him towards the exit.

'Wait!' Roth said, flying for the USB stick box before Volck could grab it. As the box fell within his grip, he saw Kornenberg vanish beneath the guards. He dashed towards the door, the USB box gripped in his hands.

The concierge led Roth out into the hall, hit the button for the service lift half a dozen times. From inside the room, the yelling signalled an ugly melee between the guards, Volck and Kornenberg. Roth and the concierge jumped into the lift as soon as the doors opened. As the doors were closing, they heard gunshots from his room. They looked at each other in horror. The lift began to descend.

'Thank you so much,' Roth gasped.

The concierge said, 'I have never seen a face as afraid as yours, when you crossed the lobby. Who are they?'

'I have no idea.'

They continued in silence, the spectre of the gunshots following them. Roth knew that any injuries suffered by the security guards would be his responsibility, him having brought these homicidal scumbags into the hotel. He felt sick, but determined to do whatever he could to help.

The lift halted, the doors opened, the concierge and Roth dashed through the bowels of the hotel to service doors that opened on to a quiet street behind the building. Vans were arriving and departing, feeding the hotel with supplies. Fresh air filled his lungs.

'It's not safe for you here,' the concierge said.

'I need to go to Moersen Bank.'

The concierge spotted a driver he recognised, ran to the van and tapped on the side. The driver smiled when he saw who it was, frowned at the state he was in, frowned even harder at the sight of Roth. The concierge spoke in flustered French. The driver listened. Finally, grim-faced, he nodded.

The concierge said to Roth, 'Get in the other side, and keep your head down.'

Roth ran to the passenger door and jumped into the van, shouting over his shoulder, 'You'll get the best review from me on Trip Advisor.'

The vehicle lurched off. The concierge rushed to the toilet where he puked up his breakfast and the remains of last night's dinner.

'Slowly,' Roth said. 'I don't want anyone to notice us.'

The driver pushed the accelerator. The vehicle lunged. The engine roar made them number one attraction on the street.

Roth looked at the driver, angry and afraid.

'Je ne parle pas Anglais,' the Genevan replied with a shrug.

They tore into the main road in front of the hotel. In the rearview mirror, Roth saw Volck and Kornenberg come out of the hotel and watch the van screech away. Their car's engine was running, the two behemoths lodged in the front. Volck and Kornenberg crammed into the seats behind them. The car lurched from zero to a fast pursuit in a few moments.

'Allez, allez!' Roth screeched.

The driver hit the gearstick to find extra juice. The van rumbled, picking up speed until it was hurtling along.

The vehicles pummelled the streets as if racing through a Hollywood film. Passers-by watched them tear past, blurs of speed amidst clouds of noise and danger. Birds flew away, stricken with fear.

Inside the van, it felt no safer than it must have looked from outside. Rocketing along at eighty miles an hour, Roth was delighted that they were getting away but terrified that this vehicle was being driven by a lunatic. The driver had taken whatever the concierge had said seriously, and was making the best of a tough job. But Roth felt a shaking in his gut at the thought that, after all he'd been through, his life might end by being slammed into a wall after an uncontrollable skid. Corners were taken with a disregard for the edge of the road and pavement; the vehicle shook, the driver possessed by an automotive devil, swerving to avoid people crossing the street with only millimetres to spare. Roth almost went flying out the window at one point, the van slammed left and then right, a heavy ballet. He scowled angrily at the driver, then cast a glance in the rearview mirror. At least it was all to good effect: his pursuers were slipping further behind. He settled a little, sighed a hopeful wisp of relief.

The van screeched to a halt. Roth was jolted forward and out of his relief. *'What the fuck?'* he yelled.

'Nous y sommes presque,' the driver muttered, wrestling with the gearstick. There was a solid crunch and a mechanistic wail from the bottom of the vehicle's guts. The van leapt forward and within a few hairy seconds was eating tarmac again at a ravenous rate. Roth looked in the rearview mirror. 'SHIT!' he yelled. Volck and Co were much closer. But his driver remained far more composed than he.

The van hit ninety on a straight road. The buildings were thinning out. Roth had lost his bearings, he had no idea where they were. The chill of danger accosted him; the van seemed ready to fall apart. They found every bump and pothole in the road, the axle bucked with the impact, the side panels shook, every loose item in the cabin flew this way and that.

The van swung into a kerb, braking hard. Roth ricocheted. The driver pointed with authority. *'Banque Moersen,'* he said.

Roth turned and saw the name glowing through the low-lit gloom of the day, written in discreet font across the front of a classy, designed building. Quiet – a Wednesday afternoon – though about to get somewhat louder.

Roth shoved the van door open, lobbed a double-edged *merci* at the driver and ran as fast as he could towards the front doors of the bank. He scaled the luscious verge separating the building from the street. His fingers were white from gripping the USB box, clutched in his hands as if he were delivering a vital organ to an operation. The air bit as the bank came close.

An engine's roar and a screech behind him. Volck, Kornenberg and the man mountains had arrived.

Roth ran through the front doors of the bank, gasping and white with fear. A woman and two men were sitting at the front desk. They looked up as he yelled, 'Lock your doors!'

Before they had a chance to react, Roth's pursuers came crashing in, a wall of meat, a tsunami.

Kornenberg slammed Roth across the back of the head; he collapsed to the floor, the box in his hands flew open, the USB went sliding in one direction, the charger the other. The front-desk staff leapt up in shock. One of them reached for a phone but was shoved so hard by a behemoth that he tumbled into a wall. Roth scrabbled along the marble floor and grabbed the USB stick before Volck could. He stumbled to his feet. Kornenberg seized him in a cobra's grasp. He felt the breath leave his body. Volck was in his face, trying to pull the USB away. Only Roth's finger and thumb offered any resistance – he grasped it so tightly the two digits were going white. Kornenberg had him imprisoned. Roth's thumb slid to the edge of the USB. It landed on the button, which depressed beneath his clasp.

Kornenberg stumbled back, let go of his prisoner, started to screech in pain. Roth was shocked by the sound coming out of the man who'd been dying to kill him a moment earlier. Kornenberg gripped his own neck and stared at Roth through terror-stricken eyes before seemingly running out of air; his scream fell silent. And then his skin began to ripple, to *bubble*. Volck was screaming too, a chilling sound; his skin was suffering the same plague. Like his colleague, he had a look of extreme panic in his eyes. Kornenberg and Volck fell to their knees, the floor, holding their ears, *ripping off their own skins*. The behemoths were screeching too, in the same unearthly tone as howled out of Kornenberg and Volck. Roth was suddenly surrounded by four crumbling men who, a few moments ago, had been trying to beat him from the face of the planet. Now they were being pummelled by what looked like invisible baseball bats wielded by unseen ghostly legends. The man mountains started to shake like mad – to *vibrate*. They tore at their skin, to stop the pain inflicted by *nothing at all visible*. Volck squealed at the highest pitch; Kornenberg gurgled. The four villains fell to the ground. They rolled, gasped for breath, smouldered, their clothes caught fire – *from the inside.*

Roth realised that the three Moersen bankers, their classy reception invaded by this bizarre nightmare, were watching in horror.

Volck fell towards Roth. *'Pleeeeaasasssse,'* he gasped. *'Sssssttoooooooppp.'*

'Stop . . . what?'

'Pppllleeeasssssseeee. Jjjjjuuuuuuuuusssssttttt sssstttoooppppppp—'.

Roth pushed him away. A moment later, Kornenberg lurched at him. Out of desperate fear, Roth punched the villain hard. Under the impact, Kornenberg exploded in a cloud of dust. The three Moersen bankers screamed; Roth spun away in horror, covered by the debris of what a moment before had been a killer.

The behemoths also evaporated: *voom, voom!* Their epic size meant they sent even larger clouds of dust swirling around the room, with an accompanying stench that made Roth want to vomit.

Volck continued to scream, his skin a landscape of pox, hard red flesh. His eyes were yellow, his voice shattered. *'Ssssssstop . . . pppppppppleeeeeaaaaase.'*

Roth suddenly realised he was still gripping the USB stick, his finger and thumb squeezing the button as if his digits had rigor mortis. A message went from his brain to his thumb: *let go!*

Volck exploded in a cloud of dust. In the next instant, Roth moved his thumb away from the button, which gave a light click as it switched off.

A silence fell across the room. Powdered remains shimmered to the ground, a new layer of dust on top of that belonging to the other perished men. Roth stared at the sandy floor. The stench of baked death, the squalid, pulverised skin; he coughed them up, desperate to get their demise out of his gullet. And then he looked at the bank staff, wondered what on earth they were going to say to him, this harbinger of mayhem.

'Julie,' said the man, 'Go get the box. Alphonse: the dustpan.'

* * *

The man who had spoken – Vincent – now led Roth to the kind of private room he was more than familiar with nowadays. As he unlocked the door, Roth could see Vincent's hands were shaking. After considerable concentration, the lock clicked and the door opened. They went inside.

A quiet room of tasteful discretion. A table in the middle and chairs at each side.

'Is there anything I can get you?' Vincent asked.

'A whisky?'

'*Monsieur* may prefer a bottle rather than a glass.'

'*Monsieur* is not the only one.'

Vincent nodded, pale. 'This is not what one expects from a Wednesday afternoon.'

'You knew I was coming?'

'*Non*, but . . . I know when I see it, *n'est-ce pas*?'

'Well, *I* don't know what that was, so maybe you can tell me.'

'*Monsieur* Berenson was our most important customer. We were briefed weeks ago to expect a man arriving with a key in unusual circumstances. Today I think qualifies as unusual circumstances. But we did not know when, or if – and we certainly did not expect that "unusual circumstances" would mean this.'

'Briefed by who?'

'The director.'

'And who briefed him?'

'That I do not know. It is like trying to find out what the Pope told the Queen of England.'

There was a knock at the door. Vincent stood up and let Julie in. She was carrying a small, rectangular steel box, which she placed on the table.

'Now,' Vincent said, 'We shall give you some privacy.'

Roth looked at them blankly, but the two Moersen bankers were already leaving. The door closed and he was alone with the box. He stared at it for several minutes. It didn't even *have* a lock.

He tried to open the lid. No movement whatsoever.

He spun it round, but could see no entry where a key may finagle to undo the latch.

He was beaten. He sighed. The container held within its dimensions – what? A sketch by Picasso? A very small statue of Julius Caesar? Another letter from his post-mortem penpal? He'd never know, because Dieter hadn't given him a key.

He sat there, despondent.

And then his brain ticked into action. He took the USB stick from his pocket, brought it to beside the box. Gritting his teeth and half-shutting his eyes, he pressed the button that atomised his pursuers.

With a light click, it opened.

Chapter 22

He was still for a few moments. Once again Berenson had confused the hell out of him; yet, by a stranger path than he dared contemplate, he was in possession of the next haul in the chase. Forcing his hands to move, he lifted the lid and looked inside the box.

He saw two envelopes, one A4, the other smaller.

He took out the A4 one first. It had a thickness. Written across the front in large letters: 'Scott Roth'. He opened it. From inside there came a sheaf of papers, which he put on the table. The words written on the top piece of paper rushed towards him as they had in Paris.

Bearer Bond

In the sum of

One million euros

But now he started to feel faint all over again, for this was not just one sheet of thick paper. This was a sheaf that stood a centimetre high off the table. He ran his hand across the bond on the top. He curled its edge back and saw what was written on the next sheet of paper:

Bearer Bond

In the sum of

One million euros

Two bearer bonds to add to the one Berenson had already given him! £800,000 times two equals *one-point-six million.* Plus £850,000 already in the bank equals . . . equals . . . *almost two-and-a-half million pounds!* And still he was nowhere near the bottom of the pile!

He flicked on through. Each sheet that passed beneath his fingers was another bearer bond worth a million euros. *Worth £800,000.*

Three!

Five!

Nine!

Ten!

Eleven!

Twelve bearer bonds in all!!

He counted them again and again, kept getting the maths wrong. His heart was racing; he was unable to contain his excitement. Finally he managed to get a grip of—

Nine point six million pounds!

Nine point six fucking million pounds!!

An insane amount of money, unimaginable. Yet there it was, right on the table in front of him. And he knew now how easy the bearer bonds were to cash – no doubt Moersen Bank would do it as had *le Banque de Louis Quatorze.* He could have ten million pounds in his account in the next couple of days.

He was speechless. *It didn't seem possible.* But it was. Just like the sixty thousand, just like the eight hundred thousand . . . On each occasion Roth had felt richer than ever – and all thanks to Dieter. Tears peppered his eyes and he felt, more than any other emotion, a sense of genuine mourning. Berenson had bestowed upon his vanished boy *true* retirement money, no-holds-barred retirement money, do-anything-you-want-for-the-rest-of-your-life retirement money. With a million, he'd given him a future. With ten, he anointed his protégé a titan, elevated the man he called his angel in the most primal of ways. He'd lifted Roth high on his shoulders. *A wave of sadness, how strange the curve*; for Berenson, this peculiar man who'd secretly kept his eye on his errant hope for subsequent years, *purposes;* the warmth of the man as vivid as the grip of his strangeness. And then he realised why he was crying. How nice it would be if they *could* have spoken again, if Dieter hadn't come back into his life a handful of days after he had left the planet.

The second envelope contained a handwritten letter, a card and another long number. But once again, no key.

'My dear Scottie,' the note began. *If you're reading this, then you have done as well as I always knew you would. There is one more step to take – if you want to. I am hoping that you will. In fact, I've been counting on it all along. But, in life, the last step is always the hardest, for the leap into the unknown asks that you accept what comes without knowing what that is. My legacy depends on you taking this leap. Every deal I ever made, every risk I ever took, every hope I ever had, every confession I ever heard now depends on you. So, all I am saying is: no pressure!*

Listen, Scottie: do you remember when we spoke about the art I had hidden away, because I was so terrified of what might happen to it? Still there. All of it. Every last piece Providence said should come to me, that I was tasked with saving from this world.

Picassos . . . Titians . . . Van Goghs . . . Magrittes . . . And, of course, Julius Caesar himself.

I understand the burden of being the guardian of a beauty so precious that you cannot bear the thought of it coming into contact with the rest of the world. Sartre was right when he said hell is other people. I know, Scottie: I've heard so many repulsive confessions that I couldn't do anything but keep my valuables locked away behind a very big door. And so I give you one last chance to take the money and run. By now you will have picked up enough to have what you deserve: a nice life, free of pain and stress. But the money is not my gift to you – as far as I'm concerned, you've earned it, doing what you've been doing this last decade unthanked, unappreciated, trying to make a difference . . . That is the lot of angels. Well, I *appreciated it, even if no one else did. So you deserve the money. Ten million pounds in total, one for each year you were striving to make the world a better place. See? It wasn't such bad business after all.*

No, my real gift to you is that you can walk away from all of this with your head held high. You can forget about my treasure as if you'd never heard of Dieter Berenson. But if you do decide to take this final step, if you do want to complete the quest I have left for you, then all you need to do is show the card in this envelope to the kind and wise people at the front desk of Moersen Bank. They will take you the rest of the way.

And so, my dear Scottie, this is the end of my long, fragmented letter. You may not have realised it, but you brought me peace of mind when no one else did. When I felt as if my life was spent among the ugliest beings in the universe. You gave me hope, though you never knew it. You made me optimistic that maybe things wouldn't be so horrible after all. What more can one man ask of another? Yours, in deepest gratitude and, yes, with love, Dieter.

He looked at the card Berenson's letter spoke of, which came from the envelope along with the message.

It said, *let me in.*

Roth stood at the front desk of Moersen Bank. Vincent and Julie inspected the card he'd taken from the private box while, nearby, Alphonse was still cleaning the lobby of dust. It took them all of three seconds to agree that this was the note the director had spoken of.

Vincent said, '*Monsieur*, please wait five minutes while I call a car.'

'Where are we going?' Roth asked.

'Underneath a mountain,' he replied.

Geneva gave way to the Swiss hinterland between the Alps and the lake. Vincent, Julie and Roth were silent as the car drove on. The sight of the four men exploding into dust had left its disturbing sediment upon them all.

Finally, Roth asked, 'Do you have *any* idea what happened back there? Did Berenson leave you any instructions about that?'

'*Monsieur* . . .' Vincent said, 'If someone asked me to describe it, I could not begin to find the words.'

Roth said, 'How about you, Julie?'

'*Monsieur*,' she replied. 'For a woman to see a man vanish in a cloud of dust? This is not so strange . . .'

They slipped further from humanity, into the frozen mountains. Geneva became a distant outcrop in the night, a hub of warmth and light growing ever smaller. The past lurked in the dark corners of the road they travelled, as they snaked their way towards Moersen Bank's deep vaults. Berenson lurked here too.

The boss had said to him, after five hours: 'So that's it, Scottie? That's your confession?'

Roth was numb from the experience. He'd been raked across the coals to no visible purpose. 'Yes,' he'd replied, exhausted.

'Well, fine. But what are you going to *do*?'

All he'd wanted to do at that moment was go home and hide beneath the sheets. The confession had taken so much longer than he'd expected, gone so much deeper. He could see why Berenson had won this role in the lives of others. He felt sick to his soul. But only now, as they drove through the mountains, a decade later, did he grasp why his old boss had been so quick to see a symmetry between Roth and the dead teen: Berenson saw the same symmetry between himself and Roth, between this young, promising talent who'd buried himself and the worldly-wise titan who tried to set him free. As far as Berenson was concerned, he'd be a surrogate father to the orphan Scott, and they a family, fractured and born in the wrong place to qualify automatically, but a family all the same, brought together for the purpose of essential family business, for fulfilling in each other's lives the void both had been unwilling, unable to admit. And when Roth had destroyed that notion by running off, by having his own ideas about how he wanted to live, he'd wounded Berenson deeply, as only a child can. Unintentionally, unknowingly; but deeply nonetheless. He'd torn the family apart. Yet the big boss, the hard, brutal businessman, had never lost his faith in his surrogate, in the vision of the life that could be, if only he'd had children of his own. This hearer of confessions had followed Roth wherever he went, to keep a watchful eye. And then died without achieving what he'd craved above all.

A sharp, hair-raising corner and the road finally surrendered its secret: the entrance to a private bank's clandestine vaults, hidden away from the rest of the world. Vast access doors loomed out of the side of the mountain onto this frightening road as if they, like it, were a part of nature – and just as solid and impregnable. In front of these doors, which were large enough to drive a truck through, military-looking security men fixed their eyes on the car as it drew closer.

'Is this where we're going?' Roth asked.

'No,' Julie replied. 'A little further.'

They drove past the colossal access doors and continued along the narrow road. A few minutes later, they arrived at a rather more stylish entrance: human-sized glass doors – bulletproof, no doubt; eclectic design visible from outside: far more like the bank's HQ in Geneva, albeit buried in the mountains.

The car stopped. Roth, Julie and Vincent stepped out into the cold, high-altitude air. The driver parked up, turned the engine off.

'We should have brought coats,' Roth said, his eyes casting around the Alpine vista. The mountains were grand - and freezing.

Vincent pressed his thumb against a panel by the entrance to the bank. A camera scanned his eyes to check his identity. A moment later, the doors unlocked – *approved*.

They walked in to the lobby. Plain-clothes security guards manned the front desk. They recognised Vincent and Julie, but were clearly surprised to see them at this unplanned time.

'*Bonsoir*,' Vincent said. '*Monsieur* Roth has provided us with the access codes for Storm 1 and Storm 2.'

The guards looked at Roth with amazement.

'There will be no more customers today,' Vincent continued. 'Please seal the front doors while we go down to the vaults.'

The guards nodded.

Vincent, Julie and Roth walked over to the super-smart lifts. They stepped into one, and began to descend into the foundations of time.

He couldn't tell how fast they were going, or how deep. The lift glided to a halt. The doors opened. Vincent and Julie stepped out into a subterranean hall, a large, plush cube leading . . . nowhere. Roth stared at the blank space, full of sheen but a dead end, a floor with no purpose. The bankers strode towards the opposite side of the hall. He could feel his brow crumple at the sight of the two heading for a wall behind which lay only mountain rock.

He gasped when they vanished through it.

He stood, gawping, suddenly alone in this subterranean lobby. The bankers were gone, invested into the granite.

'But . . .' Roth faltered.

Julie's face popped back through the wall. '*Monsieur*!' she said, her disembodied head floating in mid-air. 'What are you waiting for?'

'I don't—'

'Just walk!' she said. 'Do not mind the wall.'

She nodded reassuringly. He stepped out of the lift, felt the hall open up around him, above him, a vast area with minimal light. Julie waved him in her direction, her hand emerging from the wall as if attached to nothing else. As he got closer, she took his hand and pulled him through: *a holographic wall.*

On the other side, wowed and disorientated, he saw two vault doors, so sturdy even a glacier would not be able to breach them. He looked over his shoulder at the open lift; no sign of the wall he'd just walked through. He turned to Julie in amazement. She grinned. 'You like our little trick of the eyes?' she asked. '*Monsieur* Berenson's idea.'

'Keeping secrets even from the mountain, huh?'

'We have never been told what is inside these vaults, but we do know that their contents meant a huge amount to him.'

They arrived at the vault doors.

'Storm 1 and 2,' Vincent said. He gestured towards the keypad by the side of the entry door to Storm 1. 'Now *monsieur*: if you will.'

'If I will what?'

'Enter the code that will open the vaults.'

Roth flushed. 'What code?'

Vincent and Julie looked at each other.

'But I already gave you the card,' Roth said. '"*let me in—*"'

'Ah, *non,*' Julie explained. 'That was to prove you were the person to whom access should be given. Mr Berenson also left an entry code.'

No, he didn't, thought Roth, *he didn't give me another bloody—*

And then he realised. And started to laugh.

He turned to the keypad and was about to get busy.

'Monsieur,' said Vincent.

Roth looked at him with finger poised. 'Yes?'

'You have only one attempt. If you get it wrong, then the vault will ... be sealed.'

'For how long?'

'For ever.'

Roth paled. But it *had* to be this number, there was nothing else it could be. With haste, he keyed in the long series of digits he'd memorised, having entered them more than a hundred times in phones in hotels across the world. When his fingers were finished, he stood back, looking at Vincent and Julie with a relaxation that curdled into a sense that perhaps he'd missed a bank that held a different code from the one he'd just entered, the *correct* code, and that he may have just made a terrible mistake.

But then with a mountainous rumble, the vast doors to Storm 1 started to open. With a squall of relief he realised that he hadn't made such a howler after all, that he had tuned in to Berenson's untraceable frequency at long last.

Chapter 23

Roth gazed inside, Julie and Vincent too, unable to stop themselves. But there was nothing to see. Through the doors of Storm 1 there stood a solid wall from floor to ceiling, impassable. Roth gave a desperate yelp, his shoulders sagging, his eyebrows crumpling. But, a few steps closer, he realised that to the left of the wall sat a narrow opening through which a human could walk. *Yet another layer of secrecy.*

This opening led to a corridor that zigged and zagged every few paces. As he passed along it, Roth quickly lost all sense of the direction he was moving in, sucked into the marrow of Berenson's paranoia. There were no lights, no warnings; he was walking further into the dark, expecting at any point to hit a wall and have to turn back. The corridor seemed to grow narrower with each zig, each zag. His headspace reduced with the physical environment, to the echo of Berenson's laugh: *fooled ya!* Darker and narrower, the stuff of nightmares.

And then a crushing burst of light as a massive area opened up around him. It clashed so hard with the gloom of the corridor that he had to shield his eyes from the brightness.

He took his hand away and saw the entirety of Storm 1 stretching out ahead, a vault so large he could feel its elastic rebound against the confines of the zigzag. High ceilings and distant walls made it hard to believe that they were beneath a mountain. The more he looked, the more peculiar he found the vista to be. All the times he'd visualised Berenson's treasure trove, he'd never imagined it would look like this.

Julie and Vincent appeared behind him, equally wowed by the vastness of the subterranean cavern hot on the heels of the strange corridor. They picked up on the weirdness of the massive space too, its otherworldly nature. They couldn't see the far side of the vault: it slithered away beneath the Alps. But they could sense an atmosphere barren despite the fruitfulness of the riches it contained.

Immediately they noticed a fake living room that sat between the entrance of Storm 1 and the treasure that lay beyond. It appeared to have been put together by someone who had no idea what a home should be: carpet on the floor, a dinner table, a library; an area to crash in, plush sofas, a huge TV and a cabinet of DVDs, a fridge, rugs, throws; striving to be as cosy and comfortable as a lovers' flat in Paris. Yet there were no ceilings or walls, no fittings; no lamps to bounce or soften the light. This mocked-up room was a small bubble, otherwise lost in the vastness of the vault. Homely, yet nothing like a home. Inert, frozen, full of items that appeared to have been abandoned a few moments ago. They had crossed the border into Berenson's insanity.

Past the strange, exposed living room was the end of the quest: a seemingly infinite number of boxes, trunks and dressers, containers stacked high, labelled with precision, cupboards, bureaux – the final few moments of *Raiders of the Lost Ark. Berenson's treasure.* So damn much of it. As far as the eye could see. Way beyond the subterranean horizon, storage units of all kinds, piled up, arranged, catalogued, neat, organised, systematic. The base of a mountain filled with unidentified goodies, which so many people in the world seemed to want get their hands on, but only Roth had been able to find, only Roth had been led to by the dead man.

'How many do you think?' he asked, his slackened jaw barely recovering its ability to move.

'Many,' Vincent gasped, his eyes scanning the piles and piles of boxes, the rows and rows of cabinets, the orderly, gigantic cornucopia, the voracious appetite of all the varied containers eating up this vast space. 'So many. *Monsieur* Roth, I would say . . . hundreds.'

'How did it even get in here?' Roth asked.

Vincent looked at Julie. Julie looked at Vincent. They didn't have the faintest idea.

Roth walked to the nearest storage unit, a massive cabinet, which had a typed record fixed to its front, although he couldn't register what it said. He pulled the door open. His eyes fell upon a painting in wrapping transparent enough to let the artwork be seen.

'Zut alors!' Vincent exclaimed. *'Regardez la signature!'*

Roth zoomed in on the bottom right-hand side of the picture. 'Jesus Christ,' he exclaimed. 'A Picasso!'

And so it was. A piece of late cubism, eighteen inches by twenty-four. Covered in a clear sheet of protective plastic as it was, its vivid nature still couldn't be contained. There were more paintings behind it: four in this cabinet alone. Roth glanced at the hundreds of storage units lined up next to this. Numbers reeled through his mind. Hundreds of millions of pounds. *Billions of pounds.* 'Is there . . . Is there a toilet in here? I think I'm going to—'

He lurched towards an array of closed doors nearby, a race against vomit, hoping that behind one he would find a toilet he could throw up in.

Vincent shouted, *'Monsieur, une Magritte!'*

The delight in the Frenchman's voice diverted Roth's attention enough for the sickness to pass. Handy, for the portals he now stood in front of presented a mystery of their own. Four normal doors, the kind you'd see running off a corridor in a large office building. Nothing remotely peculiar about them other than that they were buried beneath the Alps along with everything else in this maniac place.

Julie appeared by his shoulder.

'Any idea what's in these rooms?' he asked.

'None at all,' she replied.

Roth pressed his hand against the first door.

It opened.

Julie looked at Roth.

Roth looked at Julie.

They walked on through.

A man's bedroom. A tiny space, compared to the proportions of the rest of Storm 1. A single bed centre right, against the wall, untouched for some time: inertia showed in the creases of the quilt. Several wardrobes, a TV, a coffee machine and phone so sophisticated it looked as if you could run a corporation from here. Pairs of shoes in a neat pile, reading glasses on the bedside cabinet, fine art on the walls.

Roth gasped when he saw the picture above the bed.

'*Quoi*?' Julie said.

'That painting,' he replied. 'It used to hang in Berenson's office.'

Roth rushed out of the room to the next door along. On the way, Julie grabbed Vincent, who was still standing there in bliss at the sight of so much art. His professionalism had flown; he was utterly alive with excitement.

'Allez,' she said.

'C'est magnifique!' he mumbled, almost with tears in his eyes.

Roth vanished into the next room.

'Allez!' Julie said again, before going after Roth.

Vincent realised something was happening, and went dashing after Julie. He saw her come to a peculiar halt in the doorway of the room Roth had run into.

He stopped next to her. From this angle, they could only see Roth, who was further in, standing still, staring into a section of the room they couldn't see from where they were. All expression had been wiped from his face but the starkest gaze. It was impossible to determine what had planted that look on him.

They walked forward until they too could see what had frozen him to the subterranean ground.

A young girl lay sleeping on the bed.

The child's back was to them, the only sound in this otherworldly place her soft, subtle breathing. Her long dark hair lay in a nest behind her head, shoulder perched high, the slope of her torso declining from it. She was dressed, lying on top of a mussed-up duvet. The bedroom was decorated in a lush, pretty colour palette; there were books, DVDs; two laptops and an iPad; clothes of all kinds hanging up, on the floor and every other place in between; shoes and socks and trainers and slippers. A much larger bedroom than the one next door. The walls decorated with valuable pictures; the air as clean as a desert island in the South Pacific; there was an intercom system, which led—

The child moved suddenly and sat up.

The adults leapt as if snapped at by a crocodile.

The girl spun to face them, her eyes wide and furious, ready to attack. Julie and Vincent looked to Roth as if they were about to go into cardiac arrest. The girl glared at them, a hunted animal, her breathing intense, anxious. Slight of frame yet healthy, pale of skin but bright, well looked-after but dressed in a strange assortment of clothes that didn't quite work, she stared at them as a cornered huntress, a female Kasper Hauser.

A piercing gaze – until she turned her focus on Roth. Almost instantly, her anger dissolved into a morass of pain. She began to cry, a haunted wail: *'Why did you take so long?'*

She could *talk*, albeit in a strange, unknowable accent.

'I . . . I didn't know where to . . . find you,' Roth said in disbelief. 'I . . . I couldn't be . . . sure you were real.'

But the girl's eyes were full of abandonment. 'I *spoke* to you,' she said. *'How could you not think I was real?'*

He had no answer, other than that he'd thought he'd been going bonkers before just as he thought he was going bonkers now.

'Who are you?' Julie said.

'I'm Ruby,' the little girl replied.

'Ruby who?' Vincent asked.

She looked at him as if he were dense. 'Ruby *Berenson*.'

Chapter 24

Roth had known, really, the moment he'd set eyes on her; there was no mistaking the child for anyone but Dieter's. And – like father like daughter – he could sense the struggle awaiting him if he tried to resist. As far as the little girl was concerned, he was here for a reason. A new life solidified around him as they stood there, whether he'd chosen it or not. 'Your father told me nothing about you,' he said, trying to defuse her wild look.

'Of course not,' she replied. 'He'd never be so stupid as that.'

'You – you do know about . . . Dieter, don't you?'

The child nodded, her face curling with pain obviously still fresh from the news.

'Ruby,' Julie said. 'What are you doing in this vault?'

'I live here' she replied.

The adults looked at each other all over again.

'For – for how long?'

'For ever.'

And why not? Her name was a piece of treasure, a possession stored by a man Roth knew now had turned quite, quite mad towards the end of his life. He could visualise Dieter pretending they were a real family, living a normal life, by having their bizarre make-believe nights in front of the TV in that mock-up of a den they had passed on the way in. He wondered what his old boss had told Ruby that he hadn't told Roth, including the obviously minor fact that *she* would form part of the treasure.

'How old are you?' Julie asked.

'Eight,' the child replied.

'Who stayed in the room next to yours?'

'My father.'

In his mind, Roth ran through all the letters his old boss had sent him. He hadn't missed any reference to a matter as colossal as this, surely – he'd have remembered had the old bastard said, *oh yeah, among my treasure you'll find my eight-year-old daughter*.

Every time Roth looked at the girl, she glared back, angry, or glad to see him, or fragile . . . He had no idea. All he knew was that—

Someone else was coming into the room.

A dozen versions of doom ran through Roth's mind in the moment it took them all to see who was about to attack them; instinctively Roth reached for the USB stick.

A small, shy-looking middle-aged woman walked into Ruby's bedroom, and shuffled past the disbelieving adults with a composed disdain at their presence. She stood in front of Ruby with the defiant caution of a reluctant guardian. Her expression spoke of the stonewall, the last person in the world you'd feel threatened by. A caregiver, a care*taker*. Yet she glowered at Roth with a fierce protectiveness, taking the measure of visitors whom she clearly did not want here.

'You are Scott?' she said to Roth with a middle-European accent.

'Yes,' he replied. 'And who the *fuck* are you?'

She scowled at the bad language. 'I don't know if you noticed, but there is a young child present.' Ruby continued to gaze at Roth from behind her.

'*Oui madame,*' Julie said, 'I think we had taken that much in.'

'I am Juliana,' the woman said. 'And you are Scott, no?'

'Yes.'

'Mr [illegible] talked about you.'

'What did he say? That I'm the biggest mug who ever lived?'

'He said—' she began, but stumbled on her words. Her mask of defence fell, revealing an embarrassed look. 'He said that … you were … an angel.'

Roth could sense Vincent and Julie exchanging glances. All the while, the child's gaze was upon him.

'Yes,' Juliana continued. 'He said you would come to save Ruby.'

'Dieter didn't send me,' Roth replied. 'I came here of my own volition, and how I managed to do that I'll never know.'

At the same time, the expressions of Ruby and Juliana softened in the same way: the thought that the man had failed to grasp the reality.

But they were wrong about that. He could tell what was going through their minds, and had to stamp down that kind of thinking right now. 'Don't even – That's . . . You're just plain *wrong*.'

But they were silent, letting him reach the conclusion himself.

'Sent me?' Roth exclaimed. 'What the fuck for?'

The child replied with a stern tone, as if it needed no reply, 'To look after me, of course.'

Obvious – now it had been pointed out by an eight-year-old.

He tried to stay calm. They waited for him to respond, but the child's glare kept him silent and still; and yet at the same time a sense of fury rose within him.

Juliana spoke. 'Mr Berenson knew it would be difficult for you, that the change would come as a surprise. But he said you were strong, that you would not shirk your responsibilities. He said that once upon a time a bad thing happened to you, and although you should not have blamed yourself, you did. He said that you took it very much to heart, to the point where you gave up your job to go and help strangers in need, without worrying who they were or what it might cost you.'

Her bland insistence was becoming oppressive, her voice grating; whatever she may say about him, she was reading him wrong. As for the child, who possessed a spiky, pugnacious glare, far more self-possessed than he, he couldn't stand the suggestion in her expression: that he was trapped now, that it was a done deal. A nightmare, a sensory distortion that didn't go away on waking. Yeah, nice guy; yeah, angel; pffffff. It was getting too much. He had to leave the child's bedroom before his head went kaboom.

In the vast open space of Storm 1, he tried to clear his mind. Yet all he managed to do was steer himself back to the endless pile of assets that formed Berenson's billions. He stumbled on, through cabinets and units containing every valuable artefact in the world, a collection greater than Charlie Kane's. He wandered along, his head banging, the child's eyes boring holes into his own. He stopped, leant against a cabinet and stared at the vault's high ceiling. There was no getting away from how big Storm 1 was, and how much it contained.

He spluttered a painful laugh: but what *was* he doing with his life? *Nothing.* When the lawyer had called him he was about to starve to death! And his old boss *knew* this; he also knew Roth couldn't abandon a person in need. Berenson's cunning had reached for him from beyond the grave, had grabbed him by the neck and squeezed so hard there was no slipping free.

He looked up and saw a door he hadn't noticed before, grander than the others, with an elaborate entry/exit mechanism of its own.

Vincent and Juliana arrived behind him, looking concerned about his state of mind. He was happy to see neither.

'Was Mr Berenson . . . wrong?' Juliana asked.

He didn't like the tone of her voice. 'What's through there?' he asked, pointing at the unmarked door.

'Storm 2.'

Vincent exclaimed, *'Quoi?'*

'The two vaults are joined inside,' Juliana said. 'The deliveries are made to Storm 2. My sons move the contents to wherever in the two vaults they should go. It has been a full-time job. Mr Berenson was good to my boys. He gave them work when no one else would.'

'Did he hear their confessions too?'

Juliana looked at him darkly. 'Mr Berenson has been good to you as well as my family. You should show him more respect.'

'And where are they now?' Roth asked. 'Your sons?'

'Looking for work in Geneva. Unless ... you are willing to keep them on, doing the same job?'

He ignored the plea, was in no mood to be accommodating. 'How do we get in there?'

Juliana walked over to the impregnable-looking portal. Roth and Vincent watched as the small, homely woman entered a lengthy code and Roth rolled his eyes: *more codes*. Juliana stood away, though little seemed to be happening. And then the door slid open. It was a metre thick. Roth said nothing as he walked through the open frame of dense steel layered onto rock cut out of the mountain. He felt ready for more or less anything. Storm 2 loomed as had Storm 1, but the similarity ended there. Storm 1 looked like a gigantic Aladdin's cave; Storm 2 was a global distribution network. It housed items and provisions to cater for any demand at any time when stuck beneath a mountain. It was large enough for trucks to drive into and out of – they must emerge, Roth realised, from the huge doors they'd passed on the approach road before they'd reached the Alpine face of Moersen Bank. Cupboard after cupboard, fridge after fridge – he stared at the array of facilities, the varieties of food, so much and so many that any whim could be catered for. Colossal thought had gone into this supply – colossal funding too. Dieter may have been keeping the girl away from the world, but he'd tried to bring as much of the world to her as humanly possible.

Juliana said, 'Whatever Ruby wants, she gets. We have most things here. But she is an eight-year-old girl. Her tastes are simple.'

'And what about you?'

'I have a room in Storm 1 but I do not live here. My home is Geneva – I come here in the morning and stay until six at night.'

'Is it true what Ruby told us? Has she lived here all her life?'

Juliana nodded.

'And what about you?'

'I worked for Mr Berenson for seven years, the last five looking after Ruby.'

'Here?'

'Yes.'

Roth was struggling. 'I just don't get what this *is*.'

'It is the best stocked kitchen in the world,' she replied. 'For Ruby, and for Mr Berenson while he was alive.'

'You must have had some wild parties in here, that's all I can say.'

'Mr Berenson did not come here often.

'*What?!*'

She looked surprised at his angry reaction. 'He was worried that people may find the vaults if they were following him.'

'How often did he come?'

'Two or three times a year.'

Roth could not believe what he was hearing.

Juliana added, 'He wanted no one to find his daughter.'

'Will you tell me the fuck why?'

She grimaced again at the swearing. 'He never told me. And I never asked.'

'So all of this and Dieter never even fucking came here? But I'm supposed to move in without a second thought?'

'He knew what he was asking of you, Mr Roth. He took great steps to ensure that you would be comfortable, that you would have everything you would need to escape the world. You *have* seen the contents of Storm 1?'

'*Contents?* There's a fucking *child* in there.'

'And four billion dollars worth of art, and many other things, which now belong to you.'

'And the child? She is my possession too? I mean, if I own all of the stuff in Storm 1?'

Juliana nodded.

'But, ah . . . no,' Roth exclaimed as the stickiness of his situation sank in. 'For if the child can never leave, I must be stuck here as well.'

'That is correct.'

Roth looked at Juliana as if she were mad, the vault was mad, the whole scene was mad. She looked back at him, letting him have his tantrum, natural in the circumstances, after which, he thought, she assumed he'd calm down and they could proceed with the plan. She, like them all, was in Berenson's eternal employ. He was undergoing a test, he realised, and failing miserably, the man who'd discovered the vault and the way in; now he was here, the lid had closed on him. If he wanted to escape, someone else would have to come along to free him. He didn't know whether to laugh or cry.

There flashed through his mind a recollection of a trip he'd taken with Berenson in days long past, a journey to Milan. His boss would often say, *we're flying in a couple of hours;* Roth had to be ready to zip anywhere in the world without notice. On this occasion, as they were driving to the meeting, Berenson had said, 'How are you feeling since our little chat?'

'Better,' Roth had replied, thinking of the agony of the confession to which Berenson referred, although he still felt massively bruised. The boss nodded, understanding he didn't want to talk about it now. So he immersed himself in work for the rest of the drive, leaving his assistant to brood.

The meeting took place at a bank near the convent of Santa Maria della Grazie. Berenson needed no assistance so, as Roth waited for the boss to spin his webs, he went to see Da Vinci's *The Last Supper*. Wowed by the fresco's beauty, preserved as he'd imagined Berenson's paintings to be, he noted the one stark difference: *The Last Supper* was open to the public.

Afterwards, standing by the limo, Roth had seen Berenson emerge from the building with an expression best termed *inexpressive*. In this memory, Roth could recall the name '*Banco di Venucci*' displayed in huge letters behind the boss, the institution from which he'd just emerged stated proudly on its facade. Berenson's expression had changed ever so slightly when he saw his trusty assistant. The boss had started to smile, a peculiar grin – a good meeting. A smile Roth would see many more times, of glee hidden until it was safe to unleash, at which point Berenson could laugh and laugh, another occasion when he'd bent others to his will at great profit to himself and greater cost to them.

Within this memory, the unpalatable truth of his quest became clear – just as Berenson had bent others in the past, so had he done now to Roth.

Juliana looked at him with suspicion. She must be questioning his motives. 'You didn't know about this?' she said. 'But you kept calling.'

Roth looked at her, blindsided yet again. 'What?'

'You rang and rang.'

She seemed determined to amplify his anger every time she spoke. 'Are – are you . . .?'

'Come with me.'

Juliana led him through what seemed like miles and miles of Storm 2, past ever more varieties of insanity. Shelves full of spices, rolls of wallpaper, flat packs of cabinets that could be assembled to house every new set of four or five paintings the nutty collector had bought. His eyes struggled to take in the vastness of Berenson's industry: the huge energy units; canned essentials numerous enough to survive a decade-long siege. Each twist of his head revealed another sign of excess. Each sight accrued to Berenson's maniacal determination to keep Ruby away from the world.

Finally they reached a tiny room sealed off by a door that seemed as far from Storm 1 as the earth was from the sun. There were scratches across the metal portal. Juliana unlocked it and pulled it open with solemnity.

Roth gazed into the room.

He saw a table, on which sat a telephone.

Juliana said, 'After you visited the banker in London, Mr Berenson had wanted you to call this number. I was supposed to answer, so I could confirm that it was you who had been given the first clues. If it was, I was to tell you to go to Paris. Nothing more than that. But I knew that if I gave you that clue, it would improve your chances of finding Ruby. And if you found her . . . I knew what you would want to do with the child.'

'And what,' growled Roth, 'was that?'

'Take her away from here.'

He glared but did not respond.

Juliana continued. 'I thought about disconnecting the phone, smashing it. But I had never disobeyed Mr Berenson in the past and I was not about to start. So two days after he died I moved the telephone, put it somewhere Ruby could never get to. And when you called the first few times, and Ruby had no idea, I was glad about that. But you kept on calling, at all times of the day, including when I was not around. Ruby is her father's daughter: she knew this door was locked for a reason. And there was only ever one reason here: *Ruby*. So, one night, when I was gone and she was here alone, the phone started to ring again. Ruby found a hammer and smashed the door open. She answered and spoke to you. She never would have told me but I found the door broken. It was not for me to punish her, but I made sure that she could never get in here again. She knew you were coming, Mr Roth. But ... she could not understand what was taking you so long.'

'I worked it out,' Roth said. 'I went to Paris. I didn't even need the fucking clue.'

Juliana did not reply.

'And where is Ruby's mother in all of this?' he asked.

'She is dead.'

'How?'

'I do not know. She died before I worked for Mr Berenson. He never told me what happened.'

Roth was silent for a moment. He stared at the space around him, the home within a safe within a mountain. This catacomb of insanity, where Berenson had squirrelled away his valuables: his art, his investments – *his daughter*. A place he came to no more than three times but would be happy for Roth to spend the rest of his life cooped up in.

He arrived at the first certainty he'd felt since he'd stopped feeling certain about anything. 'Well, you are right about one thing, Juliana. There is no fucking way I am leaving the child here.'

Roth looked at the eight-year-old; Julie, Vincent and Juliana watched him. 'Ruby,' he said. 'This has all come as a big shock to me. Your father never told me about you.'

The child had a gaze that could split you open. 'If he had,' she replied, 'Would you have come?'

They both knew the answer to that.

'He gave you enough money to walk away, Scott. That's right, isn't it.' A statement, not a question. 'But you came anyway.'

'Your father sent me here to do the one thing he couldn't. I'm not leaving without you.'

'What makes you think you're leaving?' she asked.

'*Excuse* me?' he exclaimed.

'Do you think this is all for *my* benefit?' Ruby pointed to Storm 2. 'Dad built this for *you*. Didn't you want to escape from the world?'

He stared at her, his skin crawling.

'He told me your life had gone to shit and you didn't want to be in the world – if you ever had.'

'Your father thought I'd live in this underground vault for the rest of my life just to keep you company?'

'To keep me *safe*. Because he knew he wouldn't be around to protect me himself.'

'Keep you safe from who? From the whole world? But it was okay for him, right? He only came here two or three times a year!'

'Scott . . .' said Julie.

'He couldn't come any more often than that,' Ruby said, 'Or else they'd have found me.'

'Who?'

'I don't know,' the child said. 'He never told me.'

'Well, isn't that just convenient for everyone but me.'

'He did it for you.'

'Didn't he think of asking *me?'*

'He said you'd help because—'

'I'm a fucking angel?'

'Because you were that rarest kind of being, who helped people in need. And I was in need.'

Roth could barely speak, he was getting so angry.

Vincent piped up. '*Monsieur,* I could think of many worse ways to spend a life than down here with all of this magnificent art.'

'Well you can take my fucking place.'

'I spoke to Dad on Skype all the time,' Ruby said.

'Good for you!'

'Scott—' said Julie.

'You can't take me away from here!' Ruby screamed. 'They'll destroy me!'

'Your father told you all of that stuff to keep you so scared that you'd *want* to stay in this fucking prison. All *they* want is the money. They don't even know you're here.'

'They do,' Juliana said, with authority.

'And how do *you* know that?' Roth spat. 'You've been stuck down here for years yourself, you're as mad as Dieter and the girl.'

'It *is* Ruby they want,' the caretaker insisted.

'And you believed him?'

'Of course. Never once did he lie to me. And it seems, Mr Roth, you have no reason to think that he lied to you.'

'You are all fucking INSANE!' Roth roared. 'Pack her things.'

The girl shrieked in terror. Juliana tried to calm her but the child's gaze was fixed on Roth as she continued to scream. But his mind was set on going.

Chapter 25

Julie sat on the bed with the eight-year-old girl, talking to her in a whisper, soothing, subtle. 'Your hair is so lovely. I cannot remember seeing such hair on such a beautiful little girl before. You must take good care of it.'

The child did not reply.

'Then it is even lovelier than it first seems,' the Frenchwoman continued warmly. 'I am a good judge of character, I see people all the time who are nervous, and weak, trying to hide something. I see your father has made you strong. So you have nothing to fear by leaving this place, nothing at all.'

But the words made no difference to the child's anxiety. She knew her fate was being decided elsewhere.

'Why are you so sure it's Ruby they want?' Roth said.

'Does it matter?' Juliana replied. 'You already know that there are many people who are trying to find her. You will play into their hands if you take her from here, back into the world.'

'It's Berenson's money they want.'

Juliana shook her head with the pain of trying to explain things to this fool. 'What do you think Ruby is?'

He glowered. 'A *child*.'

'She is *special*.'

'Because she's some billionaire's kid?'

'Because Mr Berenson told me so.'

'He really did brainwash you, didn't he. I'll bet he made it easy. I bet he heard your confession too.'

Juliana's gaze lowered. No shame in the recollection of that long afternoon in itself, but perhaps some at the nature of its contents.

'The party trick,' Roth said, 'For your benefit of course. Just like it was for mine. And then he has you, right? And your sons too. I'll bet he heard their secrets, all of the stuff they didn't want *you* to know. But *he* knows, like he knows your boys are terrified that one day he might decide to spill the things they've kept from you. All part of the family business of keeping things hidden underground. Those confessions gave good old Dieter the ammunition he needed to keep his staff in check, don't you think?'

'Are you talking from experience?'

'I didn't want to tell him anything. But he got it out of me all the same, and he never let me forget it. He's been using it ever since. I'll bet the same goes for you.'

'No, Mr Roth. My confession set me free. And I bet yours did too, if only you could admit this to yourself.'

'None of this tells me why Ruby is so special.'

'You will be spending a lot of time with her now,' Juliana said. 'You will find out.'

'I can't do this by myself.'

'Then stay,' she replied, with faultless logic, the reasoning of the paid up cult member.

'I need you to come with me.'

'No.'

'I can't do this by myself.'

'Then don't do it.'

'I'm not leaving her here.'

'Then good luck to you.'

'Don't you care enough about her to help me?'

'Mr Roth, you know nothing about Ruby, yet you are changing her life without a second thought.'

'She needs you.'

'If you take her from this place, you are disobeying Mr Berenson's wishes. I cannot be a part of that.'

'At least help me get her back to Britain.'

'Do you have children?' Juliana asked.

'No.'

'Then how do you know you can't look after her?'

'What? But . . . How do you know I *can*?'

'Are you doing anything better with your life?'

'That's neither here nor there! I do not want to do this, I do not want to take on other people's problems any more. I just want to be left in peace.'

'Mr Berenson gave you that option, and you did not take it.' Juliana had all the answers ready. Dieter had briefed her well, and she'd worked hard to master the moment, if and when it came. The more Roth let her possess it, the harder it would be for him to escape the tractor beam of this underground vault. Even now, it was starting to feel almost impossible. Dieter would have been proud of her.

In Ruby's room, the Frenchwoman was talking to the child with such care, such instant affection, that she was getting through to her in a way no one else seemed able to, least of all Roth. As he stood there, in dire straits, watching Julie engage with Ruby as if she'd known the child for years and loved her, he realised he'd been thrown a lifebelt.

'*Monsieur*?' Julie said, her eyebrows rising high on her forehead. This was the most unusual request from a client she'd ever received.

'That is some proposal,' Vincent said, nodding as if he wished Roth had asked him. 'Moersen Bank would be happy to give you special leave, Julie, if it would help one of our most valuable clients.'

Roth watched her, hope that she'd agree pouring out of him.

'But it is just—'

'A hundred thousand euros,' Roth repeated.

'For six weeks?'

He nodded.

'And all I do is help you with Ruby?'

'That is all.'

Her face showed the dilemma contained within the choice. 'But what about … those guys who . . . ?'

Roth looked at her for a few moments. '*Two* hundred thousand,' he replied.

Everything Ruby might possibly need for the next few weeks was chucked into a couple of the suitcases they'd found among the shelves of Storm 2. But the young girl's terror at the thought of leaving the vaults couldn't be contained in anything. Her fear was clearly driving her a bit mad. Julie's outstanding success in pacifying the child was already winning her fans, but even she couldn't stop Ruby from screaming at the prospect of leaving the vault. Goodness flowed from the Frenchwoman, her bearing calm and sleek. Dark brown hair, deep blue eyes; she guided the girl wisely, despite having been in the role for just a handful of minutes; used to dealing with the male ego, she was well versed in the art of handling the childish. Meanwhile, Juliana stood glum and adrift, obviously filled with terror at the removal of a child who'd become the daughter she'd never had.

Vincent came rushing back from a further review of the contents of Storm 1. '*Monsieur* Roth, I have looked through a dozen cabinets and I have seen art worth two hundred and fifty million euros.'

'It's Ruby's money,' Roth said.

'*Non,*' Vincent replied, 'The terms are clear: the contents of Storm 1 and 2 belong to the person whose name the vaults are held in.'

'Which is Ruby,' Roth insisted.

'*Non!* After *Monsieur* Berenson's death, the vault passed into the hands of the person who presented the information you did, and had the code to open the vault, as you had.'

Roth stared at him. 'But what if it had been someone else?'

'But it was not someone else.'

'*Oui, monsieur,*' Julie said. 'Vincent is correct.'

Roth stood still for a few moments.

The contents of Storm 1 and 2 were his.

The *billions* contained within the vaults were his.

'You're all fucking nuts,' he said. 'Okay, it's time to go.'

Ruby threw her arms round Juliana and screamed yet again, *'Don't let them take me away.'*

'Darling,' Juliana said, hugging the child tightly but speaking in a firm tone of voice. 'Now listen to me. Your father chose Mr Roth, and trusted him like no one else. For as long as your father was alive, it was never my business to say, but there *is* a whole world beyond this vault, a world made for you just as it is made for everyone else. Yes, full of danger, but packed with people, places and things. For as long as your father was alive, and you were a child, you were to remain here. But I did wonder what would happen when you were older, and you realised the things you saw on TV you could have for yourself.'

'But I'm so scared,' Ruby replied.

'I know. But your father decided Mr Roth was the best person to look after you when he was no longer around. If this is his decision, then trust that that is what your father would have wanted for you.'

The long silence between them left Roth wondering if either the woman or the child actually believed this. But the stoic moment was upon them.

'Go with him,' Juliana said. 'He will let no harm come to you.'

In Ruby's eyes, the reality children have to face all the time: that adults make the decisions regarding their lives, and there is nothing they can do but go along with it. Roth was surprised and thankful for Juliana's words – but then she turned to him with a glare that sent a shiver down his spine. A stark condemnation of what he was about to do, a grave warning, a reminder that he was meddling with forces he did not understand. And in so doing, he was placing at risk the only treasure from his vault that Berenson had truly wanted him to protect.

They zigzagged back to the exit of Storm 1, Roth leading this most peculiar-looking squad. Juliana was behind him, then Julie, who carried Ruby, and finally Vincent, with the child's cases.

Ruby had seen her father come and go through the zigzagging corridor many times but had never passed beyond its threshold herself. When she'd reached the incessant phone and implored Roth to come, so frightened was she of being alone, she'd had no idea that it would lead to *this*. The zigzag corridor opened wider as they spun left, spun right; the illusion was not quite the same when approached from this angle, the sense of confusion replaced by irritation.

Roth took the USB stick from his pocket. That bane of modern life, the charger – even these things ran out of juice, and probably at the worst possible time. While they'd been inside the Bank, had the forces pursuing them collected outside? Perhaps they'd already broken in and overcome the guards, had taken the lift down and were waiting outside these very vault doors to ambush them. Or maybe they'd come as far as the bottom of the mountain, blocking the only exit. Juliana was right: Roth had *no* idea who he was dealing with. Mulcahy never let on, while his dealings with Volck and Kornenberg had added a dimension to this business that left him feeling deranged.

Light, the end of the corridor – and the vast door to Storm 1. The bizarre crew halted and Julie ran to the keypad and entered the code that would open the vault from the inside. Roth held the USB stick aloft. He felt Juliana's gaze upon him; he daren't meet her eyes. Julie entered the final digit and stepped back.

The door began to move. There was an intake of breath, the sense of the presence of dozens of Volcks and Kornenbergs overwhelming.

The door slid open.

There was nobody outside.

Roth sighed in massive relief. He looked at Ruby, who was staring into the great unknown – the hall outside Storm 1 – with wide, terror-filled eyes. He then looked at Julie, could see that she had the situation in hand.

They crossed the lobby quickly, ran through the holographic wall, reached the other side. All the while, the child remained astonished by everything she was seeing, an eight-year-old astronaut on a multi-million mile voyage to Mars.

They called the lift. The silent slide. Without speaking, they rushed inside. The doors closed and they went up to ground level. Vincent's face grew strained. Juliana remained mute. Ruby started to cry. *Now* the onslaught cometh. The lobby, awash with Berenson's enemies, the hordes assembled . . . If he did need to use the USB stick, what would Ruby think of *that*? A mass evaporation would be one hell of an introduction to the outside world.

The lift came to a halt.

'Okay,' said their unwilling leader. 'Get behind me.'

They shuffled around within the limited space. Roth stood closest to the doors, Vincent to his right. Behind them were the women.

Juliana began to pray, a soft mumble they all could hear, the ushering in of the end of the world.

Once again, the doors began to open.

The security guards sat quietly; one read the paper, the other played on his phone. The only jeopardy usually to be faced here was from the coffee machine breaking down. Roth, Julie, Ruby, Vincent and Juliana emerged from the lift with trepidation, then sighed in obvious and immense relief at the lack of assembled hordes. The security guards seemed to be shocked not by the new, previously unseen girl, but by the acutely nervous condition of those returned from the bowels of the mountains.

Roth and Vincent both nodded at the guards to acknowledge the strangeness of their situation, before running to the exit doors and looking through the windows. There was no sign of doom.

Outside, with his thumb ready to descend on the button of the USB, Roth looked in every direction for a hundred Volcks, a thousand

Kornenbergs. Vincent stood beside him at this, by far the most dangerous moment of his front-desk career. But there were no ambushers here either, not outside the bank or along the road as far as they could see. Vincent and Roth exchanged glances – *thank the Lord.* But their troubles were still not over: they had a mountain to negotiate yet. Their driver was asleep. Vincent woke him with a tap on the window as Roth went back inside to get his passengers.

In the lobby, an oppressive gloom tried to push its way in. Ruby could see the entrance to the rest of the world. This thin membrane of door, after the heavy portals of Storm 1 and 2, appeared pathetic. The vast curl of a dark sky stretched beyond it across the mountains, a gloomy, unending hood covering the world in every direction, like the nightmares she'd experienced in her long, lonely sleeps, so heavy there was no way through. 'I don't want to go out there!' she screamed.

'Don't worry, *cherie*,' Julie soothed. 'We will protect you.'

'You can't, they are so much stronger.'

'It will be fine,' Roth barked, his patience worn thin by the stress.

'They want to kill me,' the child shrieked.

'You don't know what is out there,' Juliana said. 'But still it scares you half to death.'

'There's nothing out there,' Roth replied, before running through the open front doors again.

Now it was Ruby's turn to step out into the night, into fresh air for the first time in her life. Her eyes grew wide at the sight of the city in the distance, the mountains around them, the crescent moon above. She shook with fear; she was not the only one.

Roth looked at the child, a small, petrified creature with an otherworldly gaze. Suddenly he felt as if he'd made a colossal mistake. Julie, however, radiated confidence. The power of her certainty helped carry him through this terrifying moment, and he was soon able to focus again on the task ahead of them.

The driver turned the car round. They were ready to head back along the only road that led down from the mountain.

Ruby and Juliana said their goodbyes, the young and the older woman both awash with tears, hugging each other tightly, wishing this moment had never been forced upon them. They didn't want to let each other go, but practicality finally parted them: they couldn't stay outdoors in the mountains for long or else they'd freeze to death. The old caregiver allowed her new temporary guardian to take the child. The pain of separation was clearly immense.

But her work here was not yet over. Juliana had agreed to remain as keeper of the vaults until Roth had decided what to do with the treasure; a decision made with great reluctance on her part, but Roth had offered to pay her handsomely, her sons too. She had no more fight in her, today at least. She couldn't keep her eyes off the child, her custodian, her proxy daughter these last five years.

And so, with no ceremony whatsoever, three adults and one eight-year-old bundled into the large car and set off for Geneva. Through the rear windscreen, Ruby watched the woman who'd looked after her for the last five years grow smaller and smaller and then vanish, at which point she sobbed so hard that she cried herself to sleep.

She didn't wake for the entirety of the journey. The lulling motion of the car, the shock, the kicking in of the self-preservation instinct for the first time in her life totally overcame her.

They made two brief stops in Geneva: at Julie's apartment so she could grab some things; and at Roth's hotel to pick up his belongings and thank the concierge, who confirmed his fears about the security guards. Both had been felled by Kornenberg's bullets. Roth felt sick at the news, but had no time to assimilate it; he'd take care of that later. They dropped Vincent at his apartment and then carried on by road, in order to avoid airports and those lurking in them. There was much to discuss on the way.

'You *are* going to stick with us, aren't you?' Roth asked, the fear palpable in his voice that the Frenchwoman may decide it was not worth the risk after all.

'*Monsieur*,' she replied, 'I come not for the money but because I cannot believe the institution I work for allowed a child to be treated in this way.'

'But she's not your responsibility.'

'Is she yours?'

'I don't think so, yet she seems to be.'

'Then we agree.'

Roth made his appreciation plain, tried his best to reassure. 'The hotel will be quiet and away from as much danger as possible. But I cannot guarantee you anything – I certainly can't promise you'll be safe. All I can say for sure is that, by the end of your time, if we are still alive, I'll give you a very large chunk of money. Enough for you to open your own account at Moersen Bank.'

She smiled at him. 'You need help. *That* is why I come.'

He tried to smile back, but his worn-out face couldn't pull the expression together. A shame, for he was so thankful that he did not to have to do this alone.

They arrived in London amid a brisk breeze. It was possibly early morning, though none of them could really tell any more. Roth walked into the lobby of the Hotel Salon with Julie, carrying the still-sleeping Ruby, the three of them the remnants of a hidden war. The driver took a room in which he'd rest and then return to Geneva with the car. Two more rooms were booked for six weeks: one for him and one for Julie and Ruby to share. Roth asked that the two be connected by a door.

'When she wakes,' he said, 'Let me know.'

Julie nodded, her eyes bloodshot, in need of closing. She vanished into the other room .

Alone, Roth sat on the bed. He had lost track of how long he'd been awake; had forgotten what sleep was like. The tectonic plates of his life had shifted beyond his abilities to reverse the change, a singeing, ugly prospect. As for Ruby, he wondered how she'd feel when she woke and found herself in the real world.

London

Chapter 26

His eyelids flickered, his head was heavy as hell; it was dark outside. Hours had passed, he didn't know how many.

He jumped out of bed, alarmed. *He had to check they were okay.*

He knocked on the adjoining door and a few moments later, it opened from the other side. Julie emerged, her head tilted slightly. '*Bonsoir, Monsieur* Scott,' she said.

'Are you okay?'

'*Oui.*'

'And Ruby?'

She took his hand and led him into the room. The child lay awake, her eyes surrounded by dark circles as if she'd been crying in her sleep. Ruby looked at Roth with foreboding, flickers of fire emanating from within. She didn't seem afraid any longer: she looked *furious*.

'How . . . how are you feeling?' he asked.

She stared at him.

'Is your bed comfortable?'

The child glared with frosty anger.

'Ruby, you need to—'

'Why did you bring me here?' she said, in a low, shadowy voice that sent a shiver down his spine.

He was slow to respond. 'Because it would have been . . . *insane* to leave you in that vault.'

'You don't know what you're doing.'

'I don't know what your father was thinking.'

'*They will kill me,* that's what he was thinking.'

'Who will, Ruby?'

She fell silent.

'You know,' Roth said, 'I've almost been killed on this quest. Maybe the best place for me *is* in that vault. But I couldn't leave you there, and I was not going to stay. So it looks like we'll have to take our chances. It'll help if you can tell me who these people are that you're so worried about.'

Her expression was starting to break, the frustration, the strain. 'I don't know,' she gasped, sounding even younger than her years. 'But I'm so frightened. You have to take me back.'

'Smoke and mirrors and holographic walls. Your father put up so many barriers he could no longer tell what was safe and what was not. He filled your mind with dangerous stuff, but that's no surprise, considering all the horrible things he must have heard.'

'He knew what he was dealing with. *You don't*. Take me back now, Scott – I want to go home to the vault.'

He shook his head, which only set her off in a hail of despair. She screamed – her voice ripped the room apart.

'*Cherie,*' Julie said, putting her arms round the weeping girl, 'It will be okay.' But the child was crumbling like the child she was. Ruby melted to nothing, a hunted creature, those sent to protect her as bad as the doom deterred by Dieter – even worse, for Roth had *chosen* this insanity. Julie caressed her hair, her cheeks, dismantling the bomb. The Frenchwoman motioned that Roth should leave, which he did with more relief than he'd like to admit.

Half an hour passed.

An hour.

Finally Julie appeared. 'She is sleeping.'

'Thank you,' he replied.

She came into the room, closed the door, weary. Twenty-four hours earlier, her life had been its normal, high-flying banking executive self. Since then, she too had undergone changes that were hard to process.

She sat on the bed next to him, moved in close and hugged him for all she was worth. She could feel him trembling. He was surprised by the impact of her touch; his jolt made it clear how surprised. Within moments, he was hugging her back desperately. From his grip, Julie must have been able to tell that he needed looking after too. She whispered, in super-serene timbre: 'I do not envy you, *cheri* . . .'

Ruby sucked in her breath to hold in the panic, which built inside her like a formless shadow. The room was in darkness, the curtains drawn – Julie had tried to open them but Ruby had started to cry, so she left them closed. Ruby shut her eyes. She wanted to scratch the fright from her body, tear at her skin, but that wouldn't be enough; the dread would be present for as long as she was. The only place she felt remotely safe was on the duvet with Julie beside her, telling her stories, playing with her hair, explaining in that lovely accent how it was all going to be okay. Ruby liked her – but then it hadn't been the Frenchwoman's decision to take her from the safety of Storm 1.

Right now, with the adults next door, she was alone. She sat on her bed in this strange place in the dark, imagining the floor creeping with crawlies. She daren't look over the edge in case she saw spiders, centipedes, beetles, ants. She could hear the tap-tap-tapping of their many thousands of feet, too many to count. The insects would climb the walls. Up they'd go, across the ceiling, and drop onto her head, her hair, her face, crawl into her mouth . . . She had no idea when this hideous rain might start to fall, only that it would. Yet she couldn't open the curtains for fear of the world outside, even scarier than the floor churning with the ugliest of bugs. She couldn't switch on the lamp: she'd have to lean so far from the bed that she may tumble off it, and fall to the carpet where she'd be overrun by horrible beasties.

In the darkness, as the floor crawled, there was nowhere safe.

* * *

Roth was unable to relax either, despite the precautions taken. Their sixth-floor windows were not anywhere near close enough overlooked for would-be captors to spy, the rooms were large and the adjoining door created a liveable space, for now at least. The front doors were locked and barricaded by heavy chairs. A fortress in the sky, with endless supplies; they need not leave until it was safe. But when he heard the child scream, she brought doom closer to them. Julie would run into the bedroom to calm the girl, assure her, boost her, answer all of her questions, shower her with patience, but it didn't seem to matter. Juliana hadn't been so crazy after all – if nothing else, Ruby was a danger to herself, the anxiety generating too much pressure for her eight-year-old to take.

Did she know something she wasn't telling? Was that why she was so scared? The more Ruby knew, the more she could tell Roth; the more Roth knew, the better he could defend them all. It was impossible to imagine that Ruby would hold back details if she were so scared of something known. But her father had clearly frightened her into silence. Had Dieter trained her in his pursuit as well as he'd controlled the rest of them?

He berated himself all over again. How stupid he'd been to get cornered into helping someone. Post-Bradley; post-Andrea; post all of the leeching, scumbag, decade's-worth of bastards. It wasn't the child's fault, yet this was by far the worst situation he'd found himself in: there was no moving on to another shared house, and no wiping the slate clean—

The adjoining door opened. Julie came in, looking drained, a doctor emerging from another stressful operation.

'How is she?' he asked.

'Sleeping again.'

'She's sleeping a lot.'

'She is like a newborn baby. So much to take in, get used to. But she is sane, oh yes – there is nothing nuts about her. Berenson handled that side of things remarkably well, at least. Do not worry, Scott, it will not last. She will adjust.'

'How can you be so sure?'

'Because she is a woman,' Julie smiled. 'She is tough.'

'She is Berenson's daughter, so you can double that.'

'She is so *clever*. Seeing everything for the first time, able to process it better than adults with decades of practice. The world must look so strange to her; can you imagine? Can you even begin to think how you would cope if you were dropped onto this planet anew?'

'I took her from a comfortable vault and put her in another room she'll never be able to escape for the rest of her life. How could I? I was so *sure*.'

'You see that word you used?'

'What word?'

'"Vault".'

He sighed.

'Her name is Ruby,' she said, 'That is where the similarity ends. She is not an object, a precious jewel, despite what her father may have thought. She is a human, she needs to breathe air, she needs to be among people.'

'Berenson *always* knew what he was doing.'

'*Non*,' she scoffed. 'I do not agree.' She sat down on the bed beside him. 'He was a crazy man, that much is clear. You are worrying too much. Ruby is doing well, much better than you had reason to expect.'

He shook his head. 'It's a disaster. She won't even come into *this* room, let alone leave the hotel.'

'It is bound to take time. But that girl is *strong*. She is incredible! I have never seen anything like her. Not even I at that age!'

He sighed. 'What must you make of this?'

She shrugged. 'I make nothing. Banks are full of secrets.'

'But not like this.'

'*Non*, that is true: not quite like this . . .'

Ruby stayed glued to the bed, staring at everything, unable to move. Her eyes darted this way and that, at items that had grown invisible to the adults with the familiarity of years. Her mind ran through any number of interpretations, peculiar impressions of what she was seeing, and what may lie beyond the paper-thin walls separating her from the outside world. Even all she knew from her life in the vault now seemed unrecognisable, so far removed from the existence she was used to. All was alien, just as she must appear to everyone else. Apart from Roth and Julie, no one came into contact with her. She hoped they never would.

The adults entered the room. They sat down on the bed with her. He was talking, but Ruby wasn't listening. His lips were moving, his eyes, his hands; Julie was encouraging, supportive, but the child couldn't hear what he was saying, though she knew from his expression that he was trying to persuade her, sweet-talk her, win her over to his way of thinking. It didn't come naturally to him: he was no salesman. A laboured attempt that kept droning on. All the time she only thought about how she wanted to be back where she was safe, with her creature comforts, her room, her toys, Juliana— The child glared at the man. So what if Dieter had said wonderful things about him? Now she was making up her own mind, and it was very much not in his favour.

She said, 'You're a fucking fool.'

Roth halted mid-speech, his jaw slackening, stopped, stunned. The words had the desired impact, the girl awash with grim satisfaction.

'That is so rude!' Julie exclaimed. 'Apologise.'

But the child would not. She had more to say, and out it came with a sting. 'What makes you think you can help me when you don't know anything?' she demanded, her voice taking on that same cruel edge her father had been able to assume so quickly. 'What makes you think you're so much greater than everyone else, that you know what's right for someone better than they know themselves?'

'Ruby!' chided Julie. 'This is not helping!'

'They're coming after me!' Ruby continued. 'Is this how you'll help me, by handing me over to the people who want me dead?'

Roth was aghast, unready for this blowtorch of condescension. And still she hadn't finished.

'Juliana told you all you needed to know. You didn't listen, because you know what's best for everyone in the universe! Dad told me how you wasted years thinking you knew right when everyone else was wrong, how only you could save the world, but you messed it up, and now we're going to—'

'Your father didn't tell me anything,' Roth said, finding his voice.

'There is nothing he didn't give you that you wouldn't have needed if you were not the stupidest—'

'ENOUGH!'

His shout cut through the tension, but unfortunately through the child as well. Ruby paused, her eyes wide. She staggered for a moment, gawping, then broke into tears. A rainstorm of emotion, a squall; her anger converted into grief. The atmosphere curdled, a mini-meltdown, with only Julie maintaining her composure. The child crumbled into a tumult, her crying elemental, painfully acute. Roth felt helpless, his emotions bruised from the turbulence. Julie indicated that he should go next door, leave them while she comforted the child. He did so with a sickness in his gut and his mouth.

With Roth gone, Julie sat with Ruby in the darkened room, comforting her, but also angry at her outburst. 'Now, *mademoiselle*, what is all this rage?'

'The longer we're here, the more danger I'm in.'

'But, Ruby, I would not have left you in the vault either, if it had been my choice.'

'You don't know who you're dealing with.'

'None of us do.'

'*My dad knew*. And there's no way he'd have gone to such lengths if he didn't know the dangers were real.'

'*Cherie*, your father was wrong. He was so frightened of his little girl growing up that he put her into captivity. *This* is the world for you to live in, Ruby – yes it is. The worst danger is to let life pass you by.'

'Like it's passing *you* by?'

The punch landed hard. The Frenchwoman stared at the child for a few moments, had to remind herself that Ruby had much social learning yet to do. 'Yes, I work too hard, for now at least.'

'But your life is not what you want it to be, is it?'

The child possessed a conflicted expression, at once adoring and struggling to break free. Strange weather. 'We live in a world that is not so perfect,' the Frenchwoman said. 'We all have pictures in our heads of what an ideal life looks like; at times we are closer than at others. It is hard to . . . It can be hard to get things right. I have a nice life, but there are things I wish I – I wish I could click my fingers and, poof!, they would be as I'd like them. Yes, I am happy, my job is a good one, I get opportunities to travel and meet interesting people but . . . Yes, I am happy. But, who knows what waits around the corner? Who knows who will turn up in your bank one day? Did I expect this? How could I? But that is life: the unexpected as well as the expected, danger as well as safety.'

Maybe, but the confessor had taught his daughter much about human nature deep beneath the mountains. 'He's going to make you rich, isn't he.'

The ugly implication hovered in the air.

'Ruby, that is—'

'Why you're really here?'

Was this going to be a contest after all? Julie's resolve stiffened. 'I sincerely believe you are better off in the real world than the fake one your father tried to create for you. So go a little easier on Scott, no?'

Chapter 27

Days passed. Food was delivered and eaten. Films watched. Books read. Roth kept an eye on the goings-on of the world beyond their window. Julie sat with Ruby and held the girl, who was crying once more. They were waiting for the emotional clouds to clear, though no one knew what they'd see when the atmosphere broke – if it ever did. After she'd finished crying, the child slept. Julie walked next door to attend to her other charge, the faltering saviour. Trying to keep Roth on the straight and narrow as well as the eight-year-old was like trying to keep two canoes floating in the same direction. Endless talk, with the child, with the man; with the man about the child and the child about the man. Relentless, angry, calmer, polite, enraged, furious, meek, caring, ebullient. Talk, food, films, talk, music, tea, more talk, talk, and more and more talk, hair-caressing, whispering in ears, closed doors and hour-long discussions, deep in the darker places of the child's psyche, where angels fear to go, for the blowback was rough, the girl at times unbelievably nasty. Perhaps she had reason to be, perhaps not. But Julie remained amateur child therapist, amateur grown-man shrink, in two rooms, day after day. By this haphazard means, their abnormal existence slowly became their normality.

The child edged off the bed onto the terrifying floor, the home of zillions of insects. Now she'd landed, she could see they did not exist, were only a figment of her skewed sense of the world. Standing on carpet was so unlike standing on the floor of Storm 1, this building entirely different to the mountain. She made her way round the bed, inspecting up close items she'd hitherto seen only from afar. The desk, the hotel stationery, the TV, the carpet; the Bible in the drawer, the towels, the free soap and shampoo, the contents of the minibar (*they* were cute), the room service menu, the space beneath the bed, inside the wardrobes, the curves of the chairs, the air conditioning unit, the floor plan of the hotel on the back of the room door.

And then she stopped.

'What is it, *cherie*?' Julie asked.

Ruby pointed at the window: the curtains were still drawn.

'You want me to open them?'

She nodded.

The Frenchwoman did so. Daylight filled the room with a gasp of freshness. Ruby covered her eyes. Julie watched, as nervous as the child. One step forward, two steps in the dark. She was right: Ruby was strong – but far from impervious; a shame, for then they wouldn't have had to worry about her. It was clear that a large part of the girl wanted desperately to be normal, to experience the world the adults had told her about.

Ruby forced herself to look out of the window at the wide-open sky as it appeared from behind her lowering palms. Instantly the outside world filled her brain with overwhelming amounts of data. The imagery of her better dreams made real, the world she'd seen only through a screen, in depictions that came nowhere near. Such *brightness*, the glare of the sun illuminating the immense variety of life on Planet Earth.

The child said, pale as a ghost, staring at the sky, 'That's where they'll come from.'

Julie asked, 'Did your father tell you that?'

'I dreamt it.'

'Was that because of something he said?'

'I . . . I can't remember,' Ruby replied.

'The sky is so big,' Julie explained, 'It is everywhere above us. Even when you were in the vault, it was outside, covering all. Let's look out of the window together.'

The child shook her head vigorously.

'You do not have to worry, *cherie,* I will keep you safe.'

Ruby stared at Julie as if she did not trust the Frenchwoman just as she did not trust the man. But finally, she reached out her hand. Julie took it and led her over to the window, though it could have been a furnace, so firmly did the child steel herself. She gave a whimper, a sigh. Julie squeezed her hand reassuringly.

They stood for some minutes in this way, looking through the glass at the sky above London, which ran in every direction until the horizon ate it up. A mass absorption was taking place, the child consuming the world with every cell in her body, each of the many billions she possessed working overtime. The vision scared the living hell out of her, yet she did not turn away. Instead, she kept gazing through the magic window that brought the world to her. She looked at the heavens, at the clouds passing over London. She stared at the blue skies emerging from the gloom – it didn't stop changing! Every time she thought she'd seen it all, another feature appeared, darkness and brightness side by side. If you wanted to catch up on a lifetime of sky, Britain was the place to be: no LA summer blandness, no eastern Europe murk: it rained, it shone, splurges of gold and scarlet and grey sprayed across the heavens alongside one another.

'What is up there?' the child asked. 'Past the sky?'

'Space,' Julie replied. 'Lots of it.'

Ruby gazed at the heavens, amazed by the concept. Then she looked down at the comings and goings of unknown, random people in front of the hotel, who had no idea that she was up there watching them. She gazed at these people with the same intensity as she had stared at the sky.

'Julie!' she said. 'Look at that woman!'

'Ah yes! She must have dressed in the dark this morning.'

The child was consumed by such a gasp of laughter that Julie looked at her in shock. She hadn't so far heard so much as a titter from the little girl; she'd been wondering if the eight-year-old was even capable of humorous expression. But now Ruby couldn't stop. Her howls liberated the room. Soon she was laughing so hard, Julie started too. Tears were rolling down their cheeks. Against all the odds, they were actually sharing a moment of fun.

Roth came into the room. He too was shocked as, from the child, there came the laughter of someone who sounded as if she'd never really laughed before, who was only now finding out how much she enjoyed it, how good it made her feel. He looked at Julie, a smile of utter relief climbing onto his face. In this room now filled with daylight, a vast advance. He couldn't bear to think how badly he'd have coped on his own, had the Frenchwoman not agreed to help him. He decided to up her bonus to half a million.

Ruby watched with wonder the ebb and flow of nature and mankind, of the sky and the street outside. Julie sat next to her and together they observed people, what they were wearing, how they walked, what they might be talking about. Or they'd watch a plane cross the sky, sliding in and out of the clouds. When she grew tired, the child would lay her head against Julie's shoulder and, if she fell asleep, the Frenchwoman would put her to bed. Sometimes Ruby napped during the day and woke in the middle of the night. Julie would sense her stirring and wake from her own slumber. Sometimes she'd find the little girl crying uncontrollably; on other occasions she'd be sad and motionless, or staring out of the window at the night sky. On still other occasions Julie would be woken by the sound of Ruby screaming in her sleep, sweating, shaking, moaning in the grip of a nightmare. The Frenchwoman would wake her carefully; the child would jump from the dream into the arms of her waiting guardian, who would hold her until the trembling eased. They could be there for quite some time.

And then, one morning, the child poked her nose through the adjoining door into Roth's room. He was so surprised to see her large intense eyes staring back at him that he leapt from the bed and sent his cup of tea flying. Ruby suffered the quiet rumbling of one who can't keep a laugh in. It built and built, her face cracking bit by bit, until she was snorting and Roth was beaming and Julie was chuckling at the sound of her peals of delight. And then she started to wander around his room with the same curiosity that she'd shown when examining everything else.

Soon Ruby decided that she liked his room more than the one she shared with Julie. So she settled by Roth's window, which had a slightly clearer view of the street below. She consumed this new detail with greed, monastic in her devotion to the sight of people free to do whatever they wanted, and the ever-changing vista of the sky. Meanwhile, the adults watched her, saying nothing, doing nothing, just letting her be an eight-year-old child for the first time in her life.

When evening came, they ordered food and ate together. Juliana's cooking had sustained Ruby for a long time, but choice put a grin on the child's face. She looked through the menu, selected what she wanted and, with great anticipation, watched the room service trolley arrive with the order. Roth guarded the door to make sure no unwanted fiends could rush in behind the waiter. They asked for the same staff member to deliver their food each night, to minimise the risk of an unrecognised interloper trying to seize the girl. The hotel accommodated Roth's paranoia without question, like any organisation so exposed to the dark side of human nature that they were no longer surprised by it.

Ruby showed flickers of enjoyment, in spite of herself and her determination to be gloomy. The impact of the world, the introduction of so much. Inspecting the plates of food when they arrived, translating the aromas into tastes, the tastes into new sensations. Leaps of experience, the simplest, safest kind: the culinary. Mealtimes became an occasion for excitement, for informality as the atmosphere became less stiff. Food relaxed them all, the chat between the adults without purpose. They'd ramble on about anything as long as it wasn't business. Ruby would sit silently, listening or not; it was hard to tell much of the time.

Roth tried to talk about Dieter as much as possible, as ever more memories returned to him. About the man. About moments with the man. He tried to think of the personal, yet so many of his tales were work-related. Still, they were crackers. 'There were six of us: Dieter, his four opponents and myself. The business was done – Dieter had the deal, terms that were amazing for him and awful for the other guys – and now he was going to have some fun; I'd never seen anything like it in my life! The best kind of poker, no one could beat him at this. All of those confessions had left him with an unerring eye for the human lie; the other guys didn't have a chance. Well, he gave me one of those looks that you just don't forget. And then he proceeded to take them all apart, one by one. He swore to me afterwards that he hadn't heard their confessions; he was working from instinct and perception, not inside information. Sure, he knew a little bit about them, but not in the kind of detail he went into that night. One by one, he faced them all down, pulled apart their personalities and lay them revealed for what they were. These were not weak men; they were tough competitors, not afraid of Dieter. But they should have been! Oh yes, they should have been. After a fifteen-minute "character consultation", the first guy looked like he was about to cry. Dieter had pulled him apart with such accuracy that there was nothing the guy could do but take it. He was *shocked*. And then, finished with him, Dieter turned on guy number two, did the exact same thing to him, only this one couldn't quite stop himself –he tried to hide a tear, but of course we saw it. Savaged. Now, guys numbers three and four were starting to look *very* uncomfortable. They knew what was coming, and did not want to go through that humiliation. Dieter turned to them both with a grin. *Who's next?* he asked. Both volunteered the other. Dieter laughed – it proved what he already knew: that they were not honourable men. So Dieter attacked them both at the same time, going back and forth, turning the screw until they each called it quits, got up and left. Well, now there were just four of us: Dieter, me and his first two unwilling subjects. There was a silence. Finally it was broken when one of the men, trying to regain a little dignity, called the waiter over, paid the bill for us all, got up and left. The final dude scurried off more or less at the same time. And then it was just Dieter and me. He turned and said, "That's how you deal with the scum of the earth." So what I learned at school that night was, your lessons can appear from nowhere.'

'You really did like him,' said Julie.

'I've never met anyone else like him in my life,' he replied. 'How can that not be appealing?'

In the middle of dinner on their tenth night at the hotel, despite having a mouthful of cheeseburger, Ruby began to talk, about nothing, about everything, about the first thing that came into her head. 'It's incredible,' she said, 'How clear things look in the sunlight. When the sun comes out and starts to shine, everything looks so *amazing*.'

'Yes, it does,' said Julie, hiding her surprise that the child had uttered something more than a snapped, purposeful direction.

'And when I shower, the water feels so different from back home. But I suppose that's what happens when you're no longer living under a mountain.'

'Yes I couldn't agree more.'

Ruby mused on. 'I was looking at the waiter when he brought in our food. He can't be old.'

'Probably in his twenties,' Roth said.

'How do you get a job like that?' the child wondered.

'Do you want to work in a hotel?' Julie asked.

'No. But he must see a lot of people. If you're like me, and you haven't seen anyone at all, that could be a good way to catch up.'

'Catch up on the human race?'

The child smiled. 'Why not?'

'Why not indeed!' Roth said.

'It might take some time,' Julie said. 'There are a great many people in the world.'

'But he goes into everyone's rooms, says hi to interesting guests. He always smiles when he comes in here.'

'That's his job.'

'To smile?' Ruby exclaimed. 'He gets paid to do that?'

'That's not quite what I meant,' said Roth, tickled by the notion. 'Although it might as well be. I'm sure there's many times where he has to be pleasant to guests he wants to scream at for being so rude.'

'We're not rude,' Ruby said.

'That's right!' Julie chimed. 'We do not like rude people!'

'Think about all those who've stayed in this room since the hotel was built,' Ruby said. 'The book in the room said this place was opened fifteen years ago. So if there was a new person staying here every day, that's fifteen times 365 days. That's 5,475 different people staying in just this one room!'

Julie was thoroughly enjoying the child's wild thoughts. 'But some people would have stayed here for more than one night, like us.'

'The hotel has more than a hundred rooms! That's tens of thousands of people, all coming here!'

'A small city's worth!' Roth agreed.

'Every kind of person under the sun! Old, young, boys, girls . . .' She was thinking and talking, talking and thinking, all of the input finally having an output. Notes, comments and reviews on all she'd seen and read and heard Roth and Julie discuss. Her conversation had so far retained a Teutonic gravity; now she wanted to *chat*. 'I watched this plane cross the sky,' she said. 'It flew in and out of the clouds, like it was weaving a thread. It vanished and a few moments later it appeared again from the other side. What was it like for the people on board? They must have felt as if the clouds were swimming around them like dolphins!'

'Yes,' Julie said, enchanted. 'It is a strange experience. You will do it one day.'

The child looked terrified and delighted by the prospect. 'Flying seems so scary, although Dad did it all the time.' She leapt subjects yet again. 'I saw a man and woman walking along outside the hotel, so well dressed! She had an amazing suit, light grey, was holding the man's hand; squeezing tight – I think she loved him! He was smart, not handsome; a bit wonky, but had a big smile on his face, super-happy. Awesome shoes, so well polished. You could see the plane in his shoes, the plane that was flying in and out of the clouds!'

'Yes, Ruby,' Roth nodded, thrilled. He looked at Julie, who was equally besotted by the progress they seemed at last to be making.

Inevitably, the child found great fun in the scatological. 'And there was this big guy walking along, he was seven feet tall! Holding on to a kid's hand on one side and a balloon the other. I thought how funny it would be if the balloon lifted them all the way up into the sky and they floated to the moon! And . . . and if they had fallen, from all that way up, they'd have made *such* a mess on the floor! They might have landed on the woman with the hat that looked like a bird had taken a huge poo on her head! It was soooo funny! And this woman had no idea! But all I could think of was this bird flying around that had taken a gigantic poo on her head! And then this man and his son fall down from the sky and land on this woman's head – right in the poo!'

Ruby was crying with laughter. Roth and Julie gazed at her in delight, the sound of her joy filling the room previously so mournful, so tense. Suddenly it seemed possible, the plan the adults had been cooking up, the plan they thought may not see the light of day for a long time, if at all.

'Scott and I have been having a chat,' Julie said, apprehensive yes, but hopeful. The morning had been pleasant, the child was in good spirits. 'We want you to come with us to a clothes shop.'

Ruby's jaws ground to a halt. Her lips tightened. Roth thought: *damn, too soon.*

But their intention had been revealed, and the girl was too smart to think that if they stopped mentioning it now, it wouldn't come up again soon.

'Just a few streets away,' Roth said.

'We will be with you,' added Julie.

'We won't let anyone get near you.'

'Because you're a gorgeous young lady.'

'And it's a lovely day outside.'

'A beauty needs to have the best clothes, *tres chic*!'

'You'll be the belle of the town.'

'Of the world!'

They came to a halt, having run out of air. Their hope was grappled to the floor by the dismay on the girl's face, her sheer abundant horror at the prospect.

But then she got up from the bed and walked across the room to the full-length mirror on the wall, and stood in front of it. Ruby inspected the child in the reflection, dressed in clothes that had never seen the light of day, chosen by her father or Juliana, neither knowing much about fashion. The adults watched in silence, wondering what was passing through her mind.

Quietly, she turned to them and said, 'Okay.'

So tightly did Ruby grip Julie's hand as they emerged from the hotel, the Frenchwoman thought she might pass out from being over-squeezed. Ruby took each step as if recovering from a serious illness. Her feet shuffled and stammered along the pavement. Roth stood so close on her other side they appeared to be conjoined. His eyes darted all over the place, searching for anyone too interested – or too carefully disinterested. The warm sun was a tonic, but the sounds and movements of others were different now that Ruby was no longer protected by a glass window and six floors: her brain was taxed by the torrents of information, the feel of the breeze, the texture of *everything*, the sights and sounds of a real dog passing by, the motion of cars and buses, the smell of strangers up close. Such variety – how could you process it all? She squeezed the adults' hands even tighter, trembling as she tried to absorb all of this *new* newness. The Frenchwoman explained everything, assured Ruby that there was nothing to be afraid of, saying how well she was doing, how wonderful she'd look in her new clothes. But for the eight-year-old, direct experience of the outside world was like being thrown into a sea of eels.

Her head tilted upwards.

She stopped dead.

Roth's heart skipped – was this the attack?

But there was nothing to be afraid of – unless you'd never seen the naked sky before. Ruby's face filled with wonder at the endless landscape that stretched across the heavens, a crossroads for the world, access to all no longer blocked by a ceiling, a mountain – not even a window.

'Come on, *cherie*,' said Julie, keen not to stand still for too long.

They got moving again, but the child's gaze kept flipping up to the sky, slowing her pace to a halt. Their destination was a five-minute walk from the hotel, but it took twenty minutes and felt like an hour. They arrived at the exclusive children's label looking like they'd just hiked over a volcano mid-eruption. This swanky London outlet was used to catering for billionaires and celebrities and Julie had called ahead to book, to insist on the utmost privacy.

Ruby might be a strange creature, but her personal shopper, Sophie, had had many clients far weirder, and engaged with the child with relaxed charm. She brought items she hoped Ruby might like and, with Julie advising, they shopped until the girl had forgotten all of her troubles. Meanwhile, Roth guarded the entrance with unease. His eyes darted this way and that; he kept a tight grip on the USB stick, although he doubted that vaporising more Volcks and Kornenbergs would be a great idea while standing in the middle of a children's fashion house.

Thankfully, the USB stick stayed nestled in his pocket; he had no need for it today. A taxi back to the hotel returned them to safe familiarity. Ruby put her bags of clothes in a row by the bed, onto which she then dropped and fell asleep, exhausted by the trip. The adults sat in the lounge next door, taking afternoon tea, somewhat pooped themselves.

'You were wonderful,' Roth said. 'I really couldn't have done it without you.'

'*Monsieur*, for five hundred thousand euros, you have the right to expect good service.'

He nodded, but then smiled in a faded, helpless fashion.

'You are unhappy?' she asked.

'A little, yes.'

'*Pourquoi?*'

'I . . . have no idea.'

'You are tired. You shared the strain with Ruby today.'

'She was terrified. If I were her, I don't think I could do this.'

'But you are not her.'

'It embarrasses me how glad I am about that.'

Julie smiled. 'Her father was truly an odd man. I thought my dad was protective but . . .'

'Is she going to be okay?'

'Why not? She has you to help her.'

Roth pulled a face as if to say, *it couldn't be any worse*.

'*Non*,' she protested. 'You are good.'

'I'd be totally lost without you.'

'I am here because of you. You have put our little team together. Mr Berenson knew what he was doing putting you in charge. Maybe he thought some day you could run one of his companies.'

Roth stared into the distance. 'She needs more than a caretaker.'

'What is bothering you?'

After a long anxious gap, he said, '*I've missed something*. There was a bank I was supposed to go to, I'm sure. I haven't gone there because

I've forgotten something Dieter wanted me to remember. I followed the markers he left, but what if there's a bank still waiting for me to appear, where the staff have crucial information that explains what nothing else can? Am I supposed to go to every bank in the world and say "I'm Scott Roth, did Dieter Berenson leave something for me?"? I can't! But if I don't, I might not know all I need, to protect Ruby.'

'Well, I think you are doing a super job. And as I am the only observer, that makes my opinion conclusive, *n'est-ce pas?*'

'I don't want to be responsible for her death, Julie. I don't want to look down at another dead kid. I've spent too much of my life doing that. What if Ruby's right to be so scared? Because when it comes down to it, she'll be the one who's dead.'

'So what is the answer? Put her back in the bank?'

'The thought has occurred to me.'

'Pah!' she replied, summoning all of her Gallic disdain. 'That is mad talk!'

'No one in their right mind could have done what Dieter did without good reason. You saw how much effort had gone into Storm 1 and 2. But I can't work it out. So I keep on coming back to the conclusion: I *must* have missed something.'

'You have found what Berenson left for you at the end of the hunt. What use is any other clue if it only points to where you have already arrived?'

'But *why*, Julie? That's what I still don't know. If I did, perhaps I'd have a better sense of the dangers facing us, if they're real or not. The dangers scaring the shit out of Ruby.'

'What difference does "why" make? There are no more dangers facing her than anyone else out there in the real world.'

'But what if they *are* biding their time? What if Mulcahy or any other lunatic appears just when we think it's safe?'

'What on earth would they be waiting for?'

'I don't know, that's the problem.'

'You are being scrupulous, Scott. But you are worrying too much. Just like any decent parent.'

His expression blanked out. His mind was elsewhere; he was thinking. And then he said, 'Juliana believes she's special.'

'That could mean anything.'

'But what if it means *something?*'

'It may mean nothing! You are not going to search every bank in the world for this *missing* clue. Anyway, why are you so sure that Ruby is the special one?'

'What?'

'This is not something you have thought of?'

He didn't have a clue what she was talking about.

She shook her head and smiled. The poor boy was blind.

The child awoke, screaming. Julie jumped at the shriek. Ruby trembled with anxiety, her eyes wide, her mouth a grimace.

Roth appeared at the connecting door, as white as a sheet. 'What's going on?'

Julie shook her head: no idea. The girl had pushed herself backwards to the end of the bed and flattened herself against the wall, trying to hammer her way through it. Sobbing, she shrieked, a primal wail of mortal fear. She stared into the distance at something that only she could see, something that wasn't there.

'Ruby, what is wrong?'

But the child was insensible with fright, her gaze trance-like, the invisible made visible in the form of emotion. Her screeching pierced Roth's own fragile shell. Julie hugged the girl tighter than ever, muffling the animal sounds coming from the back of her throat. But she kept on trying to push back through the wall, burrowing into a hole where she'd be safe from the unknown terror her father had inculcated deep within her bones. Roth felt helpless all over again as he watched the Frenchwoman grapple with this broken child's emotional chaos, a simple fear of everything, the good as well as the bad, the exciting as well as the harmful. He realised they had the whole distance yet to run.

It was late. He lay on his bed, utterly drained. He had no idea what he was doing here. Just a couple of months earlier his life had been miserable, but in its familiar way. Now he may as well have been on the moon. Having found the vaults and Berenson's treasure, he had every reason to assume the quest would have been over by now, and he'd be taking off for the rest of his life and travelling on his merry yacht on his merry way around the merry world. But with Berenson there were always secrets – but never a confession of his own.

Roth had wondered soon after his own spilling what Berenson might have to say in his. In the next moment he realised that his old boss would never endure his own poison and open up to an ear, sympathetic or otherwise. A confession required the will to confess or the will to resist being forced to confess. Roth couldn't think of anyone strong enough to shoehorn Berenson into an ample *mea culpa*, warranted or not; meanwhile, his old boss never appeared to feel that he had anything *to* confess. Yet in the eight months Roth worked for him, he saw enough dirty dancing committed by Dieter for him to have accumulated a career's worth of voodoo blowback. He saw elbows in the ribcage, knives in the back, bombs thrown from afar, asymmetric warfare, guerrilla warfare, the use of the neutron bomb, a man with a pivoting morality and a wicked sense of the proportionate, lies, damned lies and *outrageous* lies. To have asked Berenson if he'd undertaken his own medicine would have been to bring in your direction Orson Welles' grin as he emerged from the doorway in *The Third Man*. You could hear the zither play, and Berenson's hysterics at the notion that he – the great confessor – should ever be so stupid as to succumb to his own cheap party trick.

The handle of the door turned. Julie came in, looking as tired as he felt. She closed the door. 'Even Zola would have to admit that these are hard times.'

Roth said, 'I'm going to hand her over to Social Services.'

She sat down next to him on the bed. 'You cannot do that.'

'It's one step forward, three steps back. She needs a shrink, not a loser like me. I smuggled her across the border—'

'Get some lawyers.'

'I could go to jail!'

'Get *good* lawyers. You have billions.'

'*Ruby* has billions.'

'Whoever has the billions, use them!'

He looked at her for a few moments. 'What did you mean before?'

She grinned. 'I wondered how long it would take you to ask. *Monsieur* Berenson chose *you* for this task. It was not to find Ruby, nor to free her from the vault. It was not even to be her surrogate father.'

'So what was it?'

'Have you thought about what happened when you arrived at Moersen Bank? About those men who went vwooom?'

'I've been trying *not* to think about them.'

'Why did *we* not evaporate?' Julie asked. 'What is different between us and them?'

Roth had no answer.

'I do not know what Berenson wants you to do with Ruby,' she continued, 'But I can tell you this. There is something special about the child, Scott, yes – but there is also something special about *you*.'

'Like what?'

'*Monsieur*,' she replied. 'I only work here.'

It was time to put a call in to his fixer.

'Scott!' said Gordon Weston. 'How's my favourite customer?'

'Always glad to speak to you.'

'You're such a liar!'

'It's been an interesting couple of weeks . . .'

'Are you okay?' the Mikhail banker asked. 'You sound a little tense. New York didn't agree with you, huh? So tell me, what can I do? Not another one of your wretched lists, I hope?'

'I'm past that.'

'Thank the Lord!'

'It's an immigration issue.'

'Have you been deported?'

'Not me. Can you recommend a lawyer?'

'Don't you have one?'

'He's Berenson's guy. It's time I got one of my own.'

'I know plenty. You sure you don't want another long list?'

'I'm sure. You choose one for me.'

'Are you back in town, or is it just your money?'

'Me too.'

'Good! In that case I think we should have that dinner.'

Roth was about to say no: Ruby was nowhere near ready to attend such an occasion and he couldn't leave her unprotected. But they remained in a race against time, not just against the hordes who may or may not be collecting but also against the pressure they were under stuck in two hotel rooms. The emergence from the chrysalis was under way; they had to keep going, for his and Julie's sakes as well as Ruby's. Weston would be the perfect host for what could turn out to be a difficult experience all round: if Ruby was going to freak, Gordon could be relied on to bite his tongue for the sake of their business as well as their increasingly warm friendship. 'You know what? That sounds like a great idea. But I might have extra guests.'

Weston roared with laughter. 'Spoken like a true rich man! Of course, as long as we're not talking about a football squad.'

'Just two more.'

'That's fine. Have a think about when, my friend – the sooner the better. And in the meantime, I'll get those details for you!'

He checked his email.

To: Scott Roth

From: Mia Fletcher

A mass of text – no paragraphs or spacing: an email splurged rather than written. Its mere layout screamed trouble. He considered it for a moment. And then he pressed delete.

Chapter 28

He thought – forty times a day – *I could not do this without Julie*. A mantra of the obvious; he knew he was leaning on her as much as was the child. The mental health of the so-called angel and the living buried treasure were reliant on the good offices, good vibes and good nature of the Frenchwoman. He thanked the Lord that Juliana had rejected his offer, as he surely would have failed by now had the caregiver – the *caretaker* – had her corrosive input. Ruby would be back in the vault, the status quo resumed – if that's what failure looked like. Equally, he praised the unknown forces that had led Berenson to choose Moersen Bank, and Moersen Bank to choose Julie. He may have offered her a life-changing amount of money, but this was still a task like no other. He hadn't made her his partner in this venture; she'd assumed that responsibility herself, without needing to be asked. She'd led them through this dangerous landscape singlehandedly; he knew he'd always be in her debt, however much he paid her. Along with her silken presence, she brought an assumption of success.

The day after the clothes shop excursion, Roth, Ruby and Julie took a walk round the block. The day after that, a cab ride that lasted a whole thirty minutes. Roth felt he'd made the right decision accepting Weston's offer, though he knew that Julie would again be the linchpin for that event's success. He admired her patience, the composure required to keep the child (and her guardian) on an even keel. She exerted these pressures invisibly: he barely noticed when and how she was keeping him in check, stopping him from dying from a cardiac arrest.

Today, they were heading out for lunch again, just the three of them. Roth thought that maybe they'd lunch with Weston in a week or two. For now, they were keeping progress steady. Their current lunching venue was modest – the fewer people around the better – and private, almost exclusively so. The taxi driver was under strict instructions where to go. Roth carried the USB stick, having made sure it was charged. Maybe their pursuers stayed away because they knew he had this persuasive device. *Care given, care taken.*

But in the middle of the subtle, expensive restaurant, the proximity of strangers was taking its toll on the little girl. Her face grew overcast as the presence and chatter of the other diners had its impact on her, a vertigo sufferer taken higher and higher in a rollercoaster car.

'I don't feel well,' Ruby said.

'What is wrong, *cherie*?'

'I feel . . . sick.'

Roth said, 'We can go back to the hotel any time you want.'

The child was getting paler.

'D'you need the bathroom?' Julie asked.

Ruby didn't answer. Her eyes focused on nothing in the middle distance; she looked as if she'd been seized by despair. The adults had no idea what was going on inside her mind, or what she'd say next.

Tears appeared in her eyes.

'Ruby,' Julie asked, taking her hand. 'What's wrong?'

The child looked at the adults, with hollowed-out eyes. 'They're coming for me,' she said, a tremble in her voice.

'Do not worry. You are safe, *cherie*. We will not let anything bad happen to you.'

'They're coming,' the child repeated, so pale she looked almost a blank. 'They've been waiting, but they're coming now. They know where we are. They'll be here soon.'

'What makes you think so?' Roth asked.

The girl couldn't hold her composure any longer, burst into tears. Julie hugged her, tried to comfort her, soothe her, but the fear was real and the outpouring unwilling to be staunched. Roth watched the girl, the tight, torn expression on her face. Her imagination – her dreams – were abundant, but her grasp of the world still so tenuous. She was getting from somewhere blips of suggestions that her life would soon be over. There was no mistaking the power of her grief, how frightening it was. Worse: the child's anxiety was contagious.

Ruby now looked at Roth, wiped away some of the tears and with determination said, 'Can we go to the zoo?'

'L – London Zoo?' Roth said, taken aback.

The girl nodded. 'I want to see a giraffe. You know how I adore giraffes, Julie.'

'Oui mademoiselle,' the Frenchwoman replied, sadly. 'I know.'

'Dad promised me I'd see real giraffes one day. I want to see one before they kill me.'

'You're going to be okay,' Roth insisted.

'You don't believe that,' she replied. 'Why should I?'

She waited for him to respond, but he had no answer. Her fear had infected him too, and now he didn't know what to do for the best.

They went early in the morning, arriving at London Zoo as it opened, transported there by rapid cab paid to stay and wait. Julie, Roth and Ruby started off walking quickly towards the giraffes, but then slowed their pace; it was impossible to pass big cats and small mammals, exotic birds and penguins without stopping to look at them. But the zoo got busier as more people arrived. They were still nowhere near their destination but already they'd stayed longer than intended. Longer than felt safe.

'Come on,' said Roth, ushering his party in the direction they needed to go.

'That way!' Ruby exclaimed, leaping forward in her excitement, as if nothing else mattered in the world.

'Wait! he said, losing sight of her as she turned a corner. His anxiety levels burst through the roof. *'Ruby!'* he yelled, rushing as fast he could go, knocking people out of the way in his haste.

'Ohhhhhhhhhhhhhhhhhhh!' the child shrieked.

Fear thudded terror in his heart as he pushed himself faster than ever, feeling sick. He turned the corner, desperate.

Ruby stood with her face pressed against the railings of the giraffe house. He arrived behind her, scooped her up into his arms. At the same time, his eyes were filled with the most magnificent sight, the same as had made her shriek – *with delight*: the giraffe family having its breakfast. The largest – the father – munched on the top branches of a tall tree, tipping onto his back legs to get to the highest leaves. Smaller adults and impossibly cute calves skipped around the enclosure, unaffected by the attention poured on them by doting humans, and by Ruby – for whom all thought of danger had flown away.

Julie arrived behind them, her own face pale with fright. But now she could see what was going on: Ruby watching the giraffes, Roth watching Ruby. She took Roth's arm, felt her heartbeat calm from its hurtling pace.

Roth let Ruby go. The child pressed her face against the railings to get as close as she could. A baby giraffe wandered in her direction until they were nose to nose on either side of the fence. The giraffe stared into her eyes – and then stuck out its tongue and gave her a massive lick across the face. Ruby burst out laughing. The baby giraffe wandered on, to its family and breakfast.

The child looked at Roth with the biggest grin, gurgling with pleasure, radiant, charmed, *happy*.

A woman remarked what a lovely family they were. Roth thought she meant the giraffes, but when she went on to say how proud he and Julie must be of their beautiful daughter, all three were struck dumb – and then burst out laughing. Their mirth was so good-natured the woman didn't take offence, but they didn't hang around long enough to explain why they found her compliment so funny.

'I couldn't believe how friendly they were!' Ruby exclaimed.

'And so dignified,' Julie said, 'Despite that daffy neck. I mean: what on earth is that for?'

'They must have grown in a world with very tall trees and very little bits of food only at the top! They must have had to stretch and stretch to get it, and one day realised that their necks had grown to the height of a house!'

'They must chew their food well, to make sure it goes all the way down! Take very big gulps!'

They were laughing hard. The strain of recent anxiety had vanished from the eight-year-old's face. Her shoulders were no longer hunched, her excitement boundless: *this* was how childhood should be.

Ruby turned to him, her eyes wide with excitement. 'Can we get a giraffe to come and live with us?'

'I don't know about that,' he replied, gently.

'They can have a room in this hotel, we can be best friends! It doesn't have to be a big one, Scott, it can be one the young giraffes.'

'But it would grow big,' Julie said. 'It would need its own room!'

'Can you imagine how big its poo would be?' Ruby said. 'We'd need another room! A roomful of poo would smell so bad!'

Julie was laughing, Roth too. The Frenchwoman glanced at him with a gleeful, cheeky grin. He looked back at her, caught in the glow of the moment. A peal of happiness washed through his body, of a kind that had seemed unthinkable just a short time before.

Ruby was so excited, she didn't settle for her afternoon nap for a long time. But finally, as if someone had flicked a switch, her eyes closed and she fell into a deep sleep. When she was snoring, Julie ambled next door. Roth was lying on the bed. She settled next to him, put her hand on his side. Sunlight came in through the window, forming a glow around her hair as it bunched up on the pillow. Her large blue eyes looked into his. He felt bliss. And déjà vu.

He'd been confused as to why, in his reverie, Mia was talking about banks in French. As she lay here now, looking at him, Roth realised that Julie, not Mia, was the woman in his dream. He'd told himself a little white lie: that Julie was essential in helping with the child, and no more than that.

'What are you thinking?' the Frenchwoman asked.

'I . . . ' He trailed off, awkward.

But she'd picked up on his expression – that his thought may have something to do with her. She smiled. 'That is fine, *cheri*. You do not need to tell me.'

'I think I might be going mad.'

'There is much to be said for madness. Otherwise it would have gone out of fashion long ago.'

They sat in silence, lying next to each other, resting.

Felt good.

Felt damn good.

They couldn't stay in the Hotel Salon for ever. Julie was right: regardless of exactly whose money it was, Roth and Ruby were possessed of a fortune. They could go anywhere, do anything, at least once they'd normalised the child's status – a couple of large lawyer invoices would no doubt land at some point in respect of that. The question would then be: where should they go? Maybe to a quiet, beautiful corner of England? Or Rio, Bangkok, retire from the front line of the human race? The child required stimulation, so perhaps a city, but one smaller than London. He felt burnt by the quantity of people in this great place, though he'd have better spent the last ten years in pursuit of every cultural event it offered rather than every down-and-out. They could travel the world in comfort. A tough decision of the nicest kind, and one which they need not take just yet.

There was a little café near to the hotel, which he'd discovered during his first stay. Thirty seconds away, they could be there and back within forty-five minutes, a refreshing, simple sojourn, and an effective way to add to Ruby's understanding of the outside world.

'This was one of my favourite books at college,' Julie said, as they walked in the bright, fresh air. 'Such scope, and beauty. I realised how wonderful literature could be; I have never stopped loving it since.'

'Spoken like a true banker,' Roth said.

The Frenchwoman grinned. 'I was not always in banking! I have enjoyed my time in Geneva, but I knew that I would be leaving soon, if not the bank then the city. I can ski on weekends. You cannot do that in London or New York, but now I am getting on a bit, my weekend skiing days are behind me, and it is time to—'

A man leant out of the low-slung Audi, grabbed Ruby by the arm and pulled her in. The door closed, the car screamed away.

The child was gone.

Roth heard Julie shriek as he grabbed the USB stick from his pocket, held it high. He stabbed his thumb hard on the button.

'Scott, do someth—'

Her voice was drowned out by the sound of tyres screeching. The Audi lost control, swung across the road, veered and smashed into a lamp post.

Other people were moving nearby. *A wider attack?* He covered the distance to the vehicle in seconds. His fingers grasped the handle, pulled the door so hard it almost came off in his hand. The child shaken, dazed but unhurt, stared up at him.

There was nobody else in the car.

'They just vanished in a cloud of dust,' Ruby said, stunned.

Chapter 29

Inside the Audi, a thick layer of vaporised remains: the men who'd tried to abduct the child had come off badly thanks to Roth's USB stick. He shoved the device into his pocket and pulled Ruby from the car. They went rushing from the vehicle, caught a hold of Julie too. The three left behind questions and no one to answer them. He didn't care – they had to get to safety. A cab passed by. They stopped it and jumped in. They were back at the hotel in moments.

Roth had a freak-out on his hands, but it was neither Ruby nor himself screaming this time – it was Julie. 'What are these people trying to do?' the Frenchwoman exploded, her eyes bloodshot, her nerves shredded. 'They are monsters, they are despicable, why cannot they just leave us alone? They try to steal Ruby off the street? Why cannot we take care of our own business? What business is our business of theirs?'

'What happened?' Roth asked Ruby, in a much calmer tone.

'They were driving,' the child recounted, still trembling but remarkably composed. 'Then they started to squeal and the car began to swerve because the driver let go of the wheel. He put his hands to his ears and – and was shrieking and the man holding me let go and – screamed as if he was in pain and – *they all just vanished into dust*.'

The Gallic hurricane continued to swirl around the room. 'They are the worst kind of people! I have seen many sick bastards in my life but these are detestable!'

'Ruby,' Roth asked. 'What did they say?'

'Nothing,' she replied. 'Scott – why did they explode?'

He took the USB stick from his pocket and showed it to her. 'Your father arranged for me to have it,' he said. 'Do you know what it is?'

The child stared at it, then looked at him blankly. Slowly, she shook her head.

Julie swooped in and embraced Ruby in a huge hug. 'Oh, my dear, I am so sorry, I am supposed to be looking after you.'

'It's okay,' the child said.

'I should have been watching.'

'It just happened –'

'It is my fault, a shocking failure!

'Julie, you don't need to –'

'This is totally unacceptable!'

'But you –'

'What kind of account manager am I?!'

She realised the coldness of her words the moment they'd come out of her mouth. She looked at Ruby, appalled at herself.

The child stared back at her. 'What kind of account am I?' she said, with hard-headed brutality.

The Frenchwoman was motionless for a moment. And then she melted into tears. Ruby looked at Roth. He didn't know what to say. The sight of the child in the vault of her bank had been as much of a shock to Julie as it had been to him. But he could see that, behind Ruby's eyes, she was trying to find her way through all of the sadness, the pain. Her guardian was crying so hard, she was crying enough for them both. And now their little life felt as if it was packed to the overflow with stress and grief yet again.

Roth settled Ruby into bed, a first. Julie was too distressed, too ashamed. The child was calm at least. She realised the Frenchwoman had acted as their lightning conductor today. Poor Julie was frazzled by the strike, a misstep alien to her, a perfectionist in her life as well as her work; perhaps the borders had grown blurry over this strange episode. Ruby didn't want her to suffer, but the look on her face had been shaming. The Frenchwoman continued to berate herself, while Roth and Ruby were far more relaxed. Even so, as they sat quietly in Ruby's room, it was inevitable that the subject of the day would arise.

'I told you, Scott.'

'Yes, Ruby, you did. I'm sorry I didn't listen.'

'Well . . . Now you know I'm not bonkers.'

He nodded. They'd have to rearrange how they lived their lives – and where. Plenty to think about all over again. She settled comfortably, less agitated than she'd been. 'Dad would always say, "I never believed in angels until I met Scott Roth, this nutty guy who left a well-paid job zipping around the world mixing it with big shots to go running off to save a planet that didn't want to be saved."'

Roth chuckled. 'Sounds like Dieter . . .'

'He never spoke about anyone the way he spoke about you. And we chatted all the time on the phone, by Skype; he told me about people he knew over the years, giving me lessons in life, trying to keep my head in order.'

'Ruby, you're the most well-balanced person I have met for a very long time.'

'He felt it was safe to come and see me only two or three times a year, and even then only for a couple of days. He was so busy but it was always so dangerous out there.'

'And he really never told you why?'

She shook her head. 'When he had to leave, we'd be crying . . .'

'I'm sure.' He gave a little sigh for her. 'It must have been tough.'

'Dad thought more of you than anyone else he ever met.' Ruby nodded. 'Julie and Vincent are right. He wanted you to have everything in the vaults.'

'No, I don't deserve it. And the truth is, I don't want it. Dieter has already given me more money than I'll ever need, and far more than I expected to have. I wouldn't know what to do with the rest.'

'You would,' she insisted. 'He told me about the teenager.'

Roth's face dimmed a little. 'He did, huh?'

'He spoke about it often; he couldn't get over it. He was amazed that this guy tried to rob and kill you, and though you were only defending yourself, you still said *"I stole all of his time"*.'

'Oh, Dieter, is there no one you didn't tell?!'

'It impressed him. Not much did.'

'And that's why he thought I was such an angel?'

'No,' she replied. 'He said he *knew* you were an angel within five seconds of meeting you. He wanted to keep you safe in his organisation, give you a life you deserved but wouldn't know how to come by yourself. And then, when you left, he accepted that you were going into a world that wouldn't appreciate you but that's how you were made. Because that's what you were put on this earth to do. If he couldn't change your mind, he wanted to keep an eye on you after you'd quit, to make sure you didn't get in trouble. So he hired a detective. A woman.'

'Are you fucking *kidding* me?'

'That's not very angelic language,' Ruby said, smiling. 'She was one of the best detectives in the country. She was beautiful. She was my mother.'

'What?'

'At first, she met with my dad every couple of months, to tell him how you were getting on. She said you were being used and abused like crazy, but that you kept on trying to help people. It wasn't that Dad wanted you to stop – he realised you had to have your way. But he said that if you ever got into real trouble, he had to know. So he asked my mother to follow you, to keep an eye on you. And then he realised that he was starting to fall in love with her. They'd talk about business – about *you* – then go on to other things, until the meeting had run hours longer than planned and even Dad – who always returned phone calls quickly – had a pile of messages waiting for him. One day, he asked her out on a proper date. She agreed, they got married three months later, and had me the following year.' Ruby paused. This was the first time she'd ever told anyone this: the first time she'd ever had anyone to tell. But it didn't end there. 'That's the nice part,' the child explained, 'The part my dad never tired of telling me. But there was the other part, which he told me only once. When I was six months old, my mother was murdered.'

'Oh, *Ruby* . . .'

'She returned to work after having me. He begged her not to, but she ran towards danger. After three days back, she got caught in a bad situation and— Well, Dad never told me what happened, only that she was never coming back.' Once again, the little girl looked like the small, frail child Berenson must have always seen her to be. 'He decided the world was too dangerous for me. When he visited Storm 1, he'd say "It hasn't got any nicer out there".'

'I'm so sorry. I had no idea.'

She was silent a few moments. She looked tired. She lay back and her eyes started to close. 'He loved me so much, Scott. He couldn't . . . he couldn't . . .'

'Ruby?'

'He couldn't bear the thought that I'd be out there alone in. . . '

'In the world, sweetie? Out there alone in the world?'

But she was already breathing the soft hush of slumber. 'Yeah,' he said. 'I know how that feels.'

He stood up and walked into the next room.

Julie was scrolling through emails on her phone with a distant expression. She looked at Roth, drained, still appalled with herself.

He sat next to her. 'You didn't mean for it to come out that way.'

'*Non* . . . but that is how it came out.'

Now it was his turn to give her a healing hug, put his arms round her and squeeze her tight in an embrace of care and affection. Slowly, as he spoke, she put her arms round him. 'You're here to do a job,' he said, 'And you're doing it so well that it doesn't even feel like you're doing it any more. We've all been under terrific strain, and you've handled it better than Ruby and me by miles. So you said something a little off *once*. At no other time have you put a foot wrong. We're both so thankful for that. Ruby is fine. You know she'd make it clear to you if she was not. So come on, don't take it to heart. We still have so much to do. You're not getting away from us yet.'

She looked grateful for the sentiment, but sad nonetheless. 'Scott . . . How could I have said that?'

'Listen: she's fine. She went off to sleep with no problems at all.'

'Ah . . . that is a good sign.'

'You need to relax too. So, tonight, consider yourself *en vacances*.'

She tried to smile, but it didn't quite work.

He looked at her with affection. Her glorious blue prophecy-fulfilling eyes returned his gaze. In devastation comes renewal; in stress, release. He felt her forehead rest against his; their faces were close enough for their lips to touch. A moment later he realised she was kissing him back.

Chapter 30

They were still in bed when a call came through on the hotel phone. He looked at the clock. 7.04am. Julie was asleep next to him.

He answered, mumbled, 'Hi—'

'Mr Roth, this is reception. A package has just arrived for you, marked for your immediate attention. Shall I send it up?'

He thought for a moment. 'No,' he said, 'I'll come down.'

Julie was stirring from her sleep. 'What is it?'

'Don't worry, I need to go and grab something from downstairs, I'll be ten seconds.'

She murmured and drifted off. He pulled on jeans and a T-shirt, checked Ruby to make sure she was okay: the child was snoring like a long-distance lorry driver. He went back into his room and out into the hall. Heading down, he moved quickly.

At reception, he saw the package waiting for him at the front desk. A large oblong, eighteen inches by twenty-four by twenty, covered in efficient brown wrapping. A note attached said: 'To Scott Roth, Hotel Salon, London – For His Immediate Attention'.

He looked at the concierge. 'This came by post?'

'By courier.'

'Just now?'

'Yes, Mr Roth, a minute ago.'

'Has he left?'

'He went straight away.'

Roth thought for a few moments. 'Was he Japanese?'

'He had a helmet on, sir. I couldn't see.'

There was something about the box that made him reluctant to take it up to their rooms. 'Do you have somewhere I can open it?'

He was led to a small meeting room on the ground floor of the hotel. 'Take as long as you need,' the concierge said, and left him alone.

The package sat on the table. Roth found scissors and cut away the wrapping. Underneath, a sturdy steel construction, airtight. The appearance: a picnic cool box-alike, though far more sophisticated. Sizeable, inexplicable – bigger than any other container he'd opened on this quest. A serious-looking mechanism on top with a button covered by clear plastic. A note was affixed to it, which contained only a phone number. He'd spent long enough in New York to recognise the dial code along with the international prefix for calling from London. He put the note down, looked at the box.

'What now, Dieter? Is this where I've been going wrong?' he said.

He flicked up the plastic cover and pressed the button. An impregnable mechanism unlocked audibly. The box lid slid open.

An awful smell struck him. He began to gag. *'What the fuck . . .?'*

He looked inside the box. His guts curdled at the sight.

Mia's severed head stared back up at him.

* * *

He reeled, turned, was fulsomely sick into a wastepaper basket. The stink of the remains of last night's food was nowhere near as bad as the smell coming from the box. He slammed it shut. The mechanism whirred to locked. He sat on the floor, dizzy. *Mia's dead face – her eyes open – gazing up at him. The serration at the base, the blood dry, discoloured. The freshness of her beauty wasted.*

A fury rose within him. He grabbed the note, rushed to the table, dialled the number so hard the phone travelled across the wood. His breathing was rapid. The line connected.

'Who the fuck are—'

'Scottie!' said Everett Mulcahy.

His rage died in his mouth.

The big American continued, in his best talkshow voice, 'Shall I take it from your silence that you do not approve of our gift?

'You fucking monster.'

'It wasn't me personally but . . . you're not grateful?' There was a pause at the end of the line, then a chuckle. 'Well,' he said, 'So long as you get the point. Forget about her, she's not important. Do you know who is? The girl.'

'What the fuck are you talking about?'

'Berenson couldn't *quite* stay away from her. New York was the most likely place, he was there so often. We also tracked him to Paris and Geneva. He was a tricky bastard. He gave you a nasty little device, didn't he? Some sneaky piece of shit that gets demons but leaves humans safe.'

Roth's mind reeled. 'What do you want with Ruby?'

'None of your business.'

'How could you do this to Mia?'

'*I* didn't do it.'

'But your people did.'

'They're not "my" people, Scottie.'

'You bastards, I'll get you for this.'

'Easy, angel – you're not the avenging kind.'

'So what kind am I?'

Mulcahy's voice glowed with pleasure. 'Who knows who you're talking to when you meet someone new? It's a tough break. You get the shit, you live your life this way. D'you know how high the suicide rate is among angels?' He laughed. 'But it makes sense: those who give everything one day find they have nothing left to give. Berenson warned you about *that*, right? Or was he *so* selfish? Have you felt on edge? After years of being so strong, so weak? You know what I'm talking about. That money will bring you no satisfaction, Scottie, because folk like you are not satisfied by money. You get me now?'

Roth remained silent.

'I'll take that as a yes.'

'You're full of shit.'

'And you're swimming in the wrong sea, buddy. You've got a fortune now, the extent of Berenson's earthly wealth. Take it, run away. This is good advice: the best you're going to get.'

'I don't want your fucking advice.'

'I know what I'm talking about – which is more than you do.'

'And what do *you* get out of this?'

'That's no concern of yours,' Mulcahy replied, a distant timbre to his voice. 'Certainly not now.'

The line went dead.

'Mulcahy?' said Roth. 'Mulcahy?!'

The American was gone.

The room fell silent, dominated by that ghastly box.

He put the phone down, lost.

And then he realised. *'FUCK,'* he yelled, and went running from the room.

He rushed to the door, pounding through the passageways of the hotel until he reached the lobby and the reception desk.

'Don't let anybody touch that box.'

The concierge started to speak, but Roth was already running off.

Three stairs at a time, faster than the lift; his mind filled with grisly images. His fear merged with the air, his fright as large as the hotel.

After what seemed like a thousand leaps, he pushed through the doors onto the sixth-floor hall. Light was shining from the open door to his room – the door he'd left closed.

'NO NO NO NO NO!' he yelled.

He rushed along the corridor, a ghastly struggle within. His heart racing; he couldn't believe he'd been so stupid, not now, after all they'd been through. The corridor reeled out ahead of him, took for ever to cross, elongated the closer he came to the end until there was even more of it, and he could no longer keep on running and would never reach where he desperately needed to be.

Finally he was skidding through the open door and running into his hotel room. In a short moment he could see that the bed in which he'd left Julie asleep ten minutes ago was now empty, the duvet a pile on the floor. She was nowhere to be seen. He ran through the adjoining door into the room the two had shared. Again, he consumed the facts: nobody here, not Ruby, not Julie, though the child's bedclothes had also been thrown around.

He ran back into his room, called Julie's number, his heart racing, *if she could just tell him where they were . . .* He heard ringing, a familiar tone. He looked in the direction of the sound, saw Julie's phone lying on the desk by the window, chiming away with a call from him.

He wanted to vomit all over again.

He ran from the room, down the stairs, through reception and out to the front of the hotel. On the street, no sign of anyone. He wanted to run, but to where? Berenson's enemies had made off with the one thing his boss had wanted him to protect. A ticking clock boomed inside his head.

He ran back into the hotel. The concierge could see he was distressed and offered to help, but Roth ignored him and rushed towards the stairs.

At the last moment, he remembered the box.

He veered through the halls until he found the meeting room, where he grabbed the package and note, took them upstairs with him.

Back in his room he opened the note, dialled Mulcahy's New York number, but nothing. The line on which they'd spoken just a few minutes earlier had been disconnected.

Nowhere

Chapter 31

Somewhere in London, Ruby and Julie were being kidnapped – or worse. And he was nowhere, standing in the middle of a crisis without a clue what to do. A band of tension tightened round his head, haunted by the thought that they might be dead already, murdered in the hotel rooms when their attackers arrived. There was no blood, no trace of a struggle – but the killers were no doubt professionals; they'd leave no trace but for the absence of the people supposed to be there. His brain felt as if it would crush beneath the pressure. He was right, he was wrong, they were dead, still alive . . . All he knew was that he didn't know. All the while, time ticked past.

A curdling of life so quickly. Not only Ruby and Julie but Mia too. The thought of her face staring up at him, Mia the Innocent, Mia the Guilty – either way, she hadn't deserved *that*. How could people like Mulcahy persuade themselves they were not composed of base material? How could they give themselves the benefit of the doubt?

Someone was coming into the room.

He jumped as a man of medium height approached, his skin grey, a suit once smart now tending to shabby. Unperturbed; businesslike. Meanwhile, Roth felt as if he were unravelling.

The man looked at Roth with a blank expression. He took two envelopes from his inside pocket and held them out. Roth could see his name written on the top envelope. He looked up at the man, who waited for him to take the envelopes.

'What have you done with them?' he demanded.

No reply.

'Who do you work for?'

The man continued to stare at him as he held out the envelopes.

'And if I were to kill *you*?' Roth said.

'Then that would be bad news for me,' the stranger replied, without any trace of an accent, without any fear.

Roth snatched the letters.

The man turned to leave.

'Wait!'

'You have all you need from me,' the stranger said, without stopping.

'Wait – or you're dead.'

The man paused, turned and looked at Roth.

'Where are they?' he demanded.

'If I knew that, do you think they would have sent me?'

He had no reply. The man turned and continued towards the door. This time Roth let him go.

He looked at the letters in his hands. The envelope underneath also had his name on it. Twenty-five minutes had passed since he'd last seen Ruby and Julie.

He sat at the desk by the window, opened the first letter. He let loose a wild laugh: it contained a small key, which looked like it might unlock a private box in a bank somewhere in the known universe.

He opened the second letter. It contained a business card, the name of a banker and bank in London. He knew the institution from his earlier searches: five minutes away. He turned the card over. A long number was printed on the back.

He grabbed the key and went running from the room.

He had no idea what he'd find. The same as Mia? Is *that* what he'd see when he opened his latest box, two more masks of death?

He stopped running, dropped to the pavement, was sick into the gutter. A deep drilling in his chest, agonising. Before passers-by could help or protest, he launched himself onwards.

He arrived at the bank looking terrible, ran through the doors and rushed to the front desk. The staff well dressed and composed, the dishevelled man an ugly contrast. He took the card from his pocket. 'Robert Lancaster?' he said, reading the name. 'I need to see him now.'

'He's a very busy—'

'NOW!' Roth shrieked.

Awkwardly, a front-desker reached for a phone and dialled. Ages seemed to pass. 'Yes,' the man said. 'We have someone here for you, he looks like . . .' He glanced at Roth, unable to describe how he looked. In the end he didn't have to. 'Okay, I'll tell him to wait.' He put the phone down, said to Roth, 'Mr Lancaster will be here in a moment. He said you're not to leave under any circumstances.'

Roth stepped away from the desk, his head pounding.

An excruciating minute later, a harried man appeared from a lift. His eyes scanned the reception and fixed on the only person it could be. 'Mr Roth,' he said. 'I'm Lancaster. Do you have the number?'

Roth handed him the card he'd been given by the stranger in the hotel. Lancaster surveyed it, then looked up. 'This way.'

Roth followed him along a series of corridors and through a sequence of doors that were unlocked by codes Lancaster punched in with finger-blurring speed. Finally they arrived at a meeting room. Another code and in they went.

Discreet, classy, identical to the rest. Just how many rooms were there like this in the world?

Roth could see a box on the table.

Large.

Too large to contain just envelopes.

He wanted to throw up again.

Lancaster said, frazzled, 'I'm told you will have the key.'

Roth took it from his pocket and handed it to the banker, increasingly terrified as to what may be waiting in that box.

'Can I get you anything?'

'A fucking Uzi.'

Lancaster didn't laugh. 'Even for our business, these are exceptional circumstances. I'll be outside if you need me.'

He left the room.

Roth pulled the box to him, inserted the key, twisted the lock.

Click.

The lid opened.

He looked inside, his heart pounding.

No decapitated heads.

His heartbeat slowed a little. He picked out the one item in there: an iPod, with 'play me' written across it in a neat hand.

He pressed the wheel in the centre. The device woke up, showed the music stored on its memory: a total of one track, with the title '*listen to me*'.

Attached to the device was a set of headphones, unopened. He broke the cover, plugged the phones into his ears and the socket into the iPod. He pressed play.

At first, silence. Then a voice, scrambled for security, sounding like an alien. 'Mr Roth,' the bizarre, disjointed tone said. 'Our business is concluded. The child is mine, and the French girl – she is dead.'

His eyes flooded; he felt the worst pains of stress and sadness motor through his body, his head. He missed the next few sentences. It was difficult to hear. *This world, it defeats me every time. Just when I thought my life was finally worth living.* But he had to listen to the message. He spun the track back, let it play. 'She is dead,' the alien, mangled voice said again. 'So you can thank me for saving you the trouble of saving her. Your friend Dieter Berenson has led you a dance. I wonder what he told you – or rather what he did not. I'll bet the old fraudster never made any of this clear. He said what you wanted to hear and strung you along like a puppet. A hypocrite as well as a charlatan; he wouldn't have known the truth if it leapt out at him from a box of chocolates. The great confessor? What a load of rubbish. He'd never tell you the truth because he *couldn't* tell you the truth. He'd never confess because he didn't have it in him to confess. Dieter paid for you, no doubt. How much? Five million? Ten? Enough to free you from work for the rest of your life. Well, Mr Roth, listen to me: *take the money and run.*'

Roth wiped his eyes. The alien human voice punched further into him, turned him inside out.

'The child. You must be wondering why so much fuss over the child. Well, let me be the gentleman your sponsor never was – let me tell you what this is all about. The reason I have pursued this child for years is simple: she is owed to me. Your friend became obliged to me in a way he could never come to terms with. His fault, of course – your old boss was a deeply flawed man. I have been looking for that little girl for years. I'd have been much happier to take her while Dieter was still alive: then his debt would have truly been repaid. Still, it is satisfying all the same to know that I have the one thing he wanted me never to possess. Only those who have been robbed can truly understand how I feel. Stolen from, by one of the worst crooks in the world. A deeply criminal man, who had no shame whatsoever. The self-confessed confessor, a huckster. I wonder how many people he conned with that ridiculous party trick of his. But he knew he was storing up trouble for himself. He looked after the girl too well, you see? *He acknowledged the extent of his debt.* And you did what any angel would do, the one thing her father could not. You set her free. And in doing so made it possible for me to grab her. For which I can only thank you.'

It was early, but already the day seemed to Roth to have lasted for a thousand years.

'I'd say you've done well out of this adventure,' the mangled voice continued. 'Millions of pounds for a couple of months' work. You have no business being involved in this, whatever pangs you may experience, whatever good intentions you feel gripped by. Let me remind you, in case it is not yet perfectly clear: you are out of your league. Hear me on this point, and do not let any vestige of duty drive you on. I wouldn't want any harm to come to you. Keep in mind that angels die in this world all the time. And so, Mr Roth, that is all I have to say. I am a busy man, and I have already spent far too much time on this business. I suggest you take out the earphones when this track comes to an end.'

At which point the track came to an end. Roth looked at the iPod in time to see it start to burn from the inside. Flickers of flames leapt from its body, setting alight the earphones too. Roth pulled them free, threw them onto the table and watched as the device disintegrated into a pile of ash.

Chapter 32

He was still. He couldn't move. He felt ill all over; he felt disbelief at the world's method. They couldn't have disabled him any more effectively had they cut off his legs. The words were cacophonous.

She is owed to me.

She is dead.

He left the room, the vanished iPod, the sweaty, overstressed banker. He rushed back to his hotel, hoping beyond reason that Ruby and Julie would be there. But they were not.

He sat alone in the room so recently filled with a woman and a child and even a little love. The words rushed around his head:

She is owed to me.

She is dead.

She is owed to me.

She is dead.

Unlike the iPod, the words did not dissolve once they'd been heard. They repeated continually, each time just as hard to believe.

She is owed to me.

She is dead.

Ruby – *she is owed to me.*

Julie – *she is dead.*

In the mud of disaster, he recognised his mistake: to have started to think of them as part of his life. Julie, no mere account manager; Ruby, his to protect. He'd paid for his hubris, innocent though it was. He'd paid for the hubris of others too, a far more terrible burden. The alien mangled voice had been correct: Berenson had dragged him into something beyond his powers. His impenetrable plan – for which Roth's consent to involvement had *not* been sought – was an appalling mistake – an overestimation – from the beginning. And for what?

After all that, it was no more than a property dispute.

He gazed at the window from which he, Ruby and Julie had watched the world go by. The light was profane, normality a taunt. He could think of nothing, his brain was empty. He stood, and having done so realised there was nowhere else to go. No one else to care for.

He walked into the bathroom, but on arriving had no idea why. And then the reason presented itself. He dropped to his knees at the toilet bowl as the upsurge burst from him. He vomited so hard it hurt, a guttural-sounding mix of shame, despair and stomach acid; there was nothing else in him to throw up. His chest aflame, he leant back against the bath, gazing upwards at the harsh light shining down at him without mercy.

She is owed to me.

She is dead.

She is owed to me.

She is dead.

They were six storeys up. The pavement below was concrete. Five seconds, ten at most – and it would be over.

He stood, wobbly on his legs. Steadied himself against the bath, the light harsh. He walked to the bedroom, opened the window, the cool air refreshing. No noise from the street below. He looked down; no one around.

He stepped on to the ledge and jumped.

* * *

What goes through the mind when you're tumbling to your death? There was little time to think of anything; a few seconds at most.

He realised he'd fallen in love with Julie, wished achingly that he'd met her ten years ago.

What an amazing woman Ruby would have grown up to be, had her life not been so distorted from the start.

He thought about how much time and energy he'd wasted, helping people who didn't deserve it.

He thought about the teen he'd killed. About Mia.

He thought to himself: *from the earliest age, I knew it wouldn't be easy. But I had no idea it would be this hard.*

And then the rush of the pavement beneath him as it arrived.

* * *

How does it feel the moment you hit the ground after jumping from a window six storeys up?

How does it feel when all of your troubles are over?

* * *

What goes through the mind when you open your eyes and realise that you're still alive, even though you've fallen six storeys – and hit solid concrete – and look around and see cracks several feet long from the impact of where you've just landed and it's clear your bones should have been pulverised and your internal organs should have collapsed and your skull should have shattered and your brain should be glooping across the pavement and you should be very dead?

Moving ought to be impossible, his body destroyed. Yet as he tried to sit up, he sat up. As he tried to look around, he looked around. As he tried to stand, he stood. He felt no pain at all.

He scanned the scene for anyone who'd witnessed his falling, his hitting the ground and his getting up. There were no bystanders, no shocked witnesses. He started to run before any appeared, but couldn't help a quick glance back at the crater he'd made, and from which he should not have been able to emerge alive, let alone unhurt.

* * *

He was back in the hotel room. He walked over to the window from which he'd launched himself a couple of minutes earlier, looked down and saw the impact marks he'd made in the pavement. Passers-by were staring at them, probably wondering why the local authority hadn't sent someone to fix the damage. He pulled the window closed, as if he could shut out what he'd just tried to do.

He thought, *I should be dead*.

He walked to the bathroom. Took off his shirt, inspected his back, the part of his body that had hit the ground first. No injuries – no cuts, bruises, no shattered shoulder blade. No pain at all. He put his shirt back on. He turned to the sink and washed his face. He cleaned his teeth to excise the foul taste that lingered from his series of vomits.

Angel.

He looked up at the mirror, at the face reflecting back at him. It clouded over. And there again, the word:

Angel.

He felt his stomach and mind both churn, thought again of the death of the teen for which he couldn't forgive himself . . . He'd given up the corporate world and its material comforts to help those who others had written off as helpless, and persisted in the face of resistance. He'd handed out his money even though it left him impoverished and, in the days before the call from the lawyer, starving . . . He'd never lost faith in the human race (that is, until the end, the Bradley incident and his cleaning-out by Anthea). And here the crazy thoughts should stop – but it was true: he'd started life with a blank where his biological parents should be. He'd never asked anyone for information about them, had never *wanted* to know, so had learned nothing. No one encouraged him to be curious about his birth parents – no one referred to them. He thought people were simply being ultra-sensitive around him, daring not to breathe a word about the subject. It hadn't occurred to him that there might be nothing *to* know. That rather than being born, he might have . . . arrived.

He could feel the edges of madness grind close. He shook his head to break the spell Mulcahy had managed to spin. How easy it was to dismiss the notion out of hand – had he not seen men blown to dust by a USB stick. A strange device provided by a strange man further to Berenson's opaque instructions. Psychotic words swirled around his head, but the evidence, *the survival after the plunge* . . . Yes – perhaps people do fall six storeys, hit concrete and live, but without bones shattered by the impact, internal organs mashed?

She is owed to me.

She is dead.

Angel.

A thought flickered into his mind. He ran into the lounge, searched through his bags for the note that had told him to go to the Hotel Hamishi. He found it among his pile of letters from Berenson, sat down by the phone and dialled. His heart sank – the number might have worked in the Tokyo hotel but it sure didn't sound like it was going anywhere now. But then:

'Who this?' came the staccato voice.

'Oh, thank the Lord!' Roth exclaimed.

Staccato growled, 'You?! Why you use number?!'

'I'm in London.'

'Should not call this again!'

'I need your help.'

'You find girl?'

'What's the stick? What does it do?'

'Bath getting cold! You find girl?'

'What does the USB stick do?'

'Answer, shit block: *you find girl?*'

'You mean Ruby?'

'Yes, of course.'

'They got her; I don't know where she is.'

'What?' Staccato exclaimed. *'Find* her!'

'How?'

'Find girl or else.'

'What's so important about her?'

'You have two jobs, find girl, protect girl!'

'Who are these people, what do they want?'

'You not read letter in box?'

'What letter?'

'What you mean "what letter?"'

'There was no letter.'

'You find stick in box?'

'Yes.'

'And charger?'

'Yes.'

'And letter?'

'There was no letter in the box.'

'Ahhhhhhh!!! Moron! Berenson make big mistake choosing you!'

'He didn't tell me anything!'

'Too dangerous to say! Why you think Berenson go so much trouble?!'

'You have to tell me what you know.'

'You dumb pricky, that what me know!'

'What's so special about her?'

'Go find girl, or all is lost.'

'You *have* to help me.'

'I do all I can. No more I can do.'

'But you know more and you're not saying.'

'All Berenson tell me I tell you. Girl of importance, must be protected at all costs. You lose girl, schmucky? Find her, find her! How much more you need know?'

'But for crissake *how*?'

'I drip enough!'

The line went dead.

'ARRRGGGCHHHHH!!!!' Roth screamed.

His head spun. He rushed to the bag where he kept the box containing the USB stick. He looked, but there was nothing. He *knew* this – he'd have seen it already if there was.

But . . .

Now that he looked at it again, he realised that the inlay on one side of the box didn't quite fit into the frame. He pressed it, felt it sink beneath his thumb. When it stopped moving, he let go. The inlay sprang open to reveal a secret cavity – with a note inside.

He gazed at it for a few moments, appalled at having missed it. Weeks had passed since he'd been given this box – the note had lain unread for all that time.

He took it from the cavity, opened it, saw the same scrawl as had plastered the previous dispatches from Berenson. He unfolded it quickly. This one even had a title: *'The Confessor's Confession.'*

'Dearest Scott,' the note said.

I don't know when you will come upon this letter. I do hope sooner. If it turns out to be later then, well . . . we always knew it was not a perfect world.

I haven't been strictly honest with you. I hope you'll understand why. But now I'm going to tell you everything. I have called this part of the letter the Confessor's Confession. In doing so, I make you my confessor, a privilege I granted no one else in my life. Who could be as lucky as you?!

First, let me apologise for my method; I suspect it's been its own kind of insanity. But the greater the trail I left, the more likely it was that the wrong people would find my treasure. Layers of secrecy were not enough, for what I have entrusted to you is of the greatest value to me. Within this box, you'll have found a little handykins to use when the time is right. Trust me, you'll know when that is. And equally, you do not want me to give you an explanation of how I came to be in possession of this device. You know that I am a man of contacts and – most of all – confessions. Let's just leave it at that.

What I do feel it's appropriate to share now is how I came to have my sideline as a confessor. You never asked me. Just like you never asked me how I made my money. Well, the two are connected.

I started with nothing. I came from nowhere. Not a bean to my name, like you. We were both subject to the forces of a fickle, frightening world. You got picked up by loving, adoptive parents. I got hurt, time and again. But the pain I suffered bred intense ambition, Scottie, as fierce and driving as that of anyone I've ever met. I did what I had to in order to get ahead. I clawed my way up the ladder of success. I have nothing to apologise for.

So I'm twenty-five. Things are finally moving. I'm offered a share in a deal that's my chance to break into the big time – I won't pass it up for anything. Four of us are involved, a bunch of pirates – well, I've never raped but I sure have pillaged. The deal is going well, the joy unimaginable! To have dreamt of this kind of success for fifteen years and for it finally to be happening? Nothing on earth can spoil the moment for me.

One of the guys I'm working with comes to me and says he wants to talk about a matter that has nothing to do with the deal. He says he has something he needs to get off his chest and for some inexplicable reason has decided that I'm the man to listen. He says he's been waiting for ten years to find someone he feels able to confess to – and that person is me.

Now, all this is coming as a rather unforeseen development – I have no idea what I should make of it, or why he should think this in the first place. All I know is that he's decided this is how it is. He's older than me and very well-connected. I want to keep him on my side, so there's nothing I can say but 'sure'. We go to a restaurant, sit with some wine and I decide to be as sycophantic as possible. I'm gonna crawl so far up his backside he can tell me anything he wants and I'll say it's fine. But as he's confessing, a truly awful story comes out of his mouth, about a terrible deed he's done. Disgusting, Scottie – I mean truly abhorrent. Now I see why he's kept it quiet for all these years, and why he feels the need to get it out of his system, to tell someone. And as I hear it, instead of sitting quietly and saying nothing, I realise that I do have a stance to take and I end up giving him a really hard time. Afterwards, I'm sure the guy's gonna hate me and never want to work with me again. I'm sure I've just made the biggest mistake of my career. But I also know that I couldn't keep it in, what I said to him. It came out, and there was nothing I could do to stop it – you know me, Scottie, I've always been a self-righteous bastard. So I'm thinking, goodbye success! This guy's going to make sure I can never show my face in this town again. But his reaction is the opposite. He tells me he feels so good at being able to get that off his chest. He says for the first time in an unapologetic life he can understand why people go to confession. I tell him it's not a problem, though of course I think he's the biggest piece of shit I've ever met because of what he's just told me; how little I knew of the world then! This, by the way, was when the first of my grey hairs appeared.

To say thanks for listening to his sordid shit, the guy writes me a cheque. I look at it and feel this warmth go through my body. It's a huge amount. I didn't do it for money, only to save face and stay in the guy's good books, but now I'm staring at enough to live on for a year. The last thing I was expecting. And it comes at a very handy time, as I had built up a lot of debt on the way to this deal. Needless to say, I cash the cheque and assume that's that.

Well, I assume wrong. Turns out this guy is so pleased at being able to confess this awful deed to someone he trusts not to spill the beans that he refers me to a friend of his. So I get a call out of the blue from guy number two, who asks me if I wouldn't mind performing the function again. I'm still so keen to make my way up the ladder of success that I say yes. So I hear the second man's confession. He looks like a regular kind of chap, a businessman on the up, no Brad Pitt. I do it the same way I did it the first time – we go somewhere expensive and private for lunch. We have some good wine. He's paying – obviously. He starts to talk and I listen. He also has foul stuff to admit – there come a few more grey hairs. Now, the first guy looked like a dodgy character – it wasn't a *surprise that he'd behaved so ugly in the past – but this one looks like a choirboy. You never can tell: the unlikeliest dude on the train fucks beagles two at a time. Forgive me for being coarse, but that's what this is: the trade of depravity; you need to call it true. I didn't realise I was learning the ways of my second vocation, but as we all discover sooner or later in life, anything can happen to anyone at any time. To this day I still don't know why these guys chose me; I was good at keeping a straight face while listening to crazy shit, but that doesn't explain it. I suppose they had good judgement. They saw in me what I hadn't seen in myself: that I was the greatest confessor never to wear a dog collar.*

After our lunch, this second man also feels so relieved that he too wants to thank me. Now I see it clearly: the possibility of another happy payment. But this guy doesn't want to do that – my heart is broken! Instead, he cuts me in on a deal. Scottie, I earn more off this than I do my own.

Word gets out. Suddenly I have a sideline feeding into my main business, and it's proving as successful! I get more referrals, people call me out of the blue, and the moment I pick up the phone, I know what they want. So, once a month, then once a week, then twice a week I'm hearing confessions. By this point I'm also doing pretty damn good as a businessman. It's all happening, I'm working eighteen hours a day, seven days a week. As a result of my success, I'm not hearing the confessions of your average pleb, oh no! My practice is the opposite of yours: I deal with rich, powerful, well-connected people. I listen to the darkest secrets of entrepreneurs, bankers and players. All kinds of characters, Scottie. Some are savage competitors, others are visionaries with insight as sinister as it is effective. A few are breathless talents, others lucky bastards. Their lust for victory leads them down paths that grow ever grimmer, until they look over their shoulder and see their woeful, misbegotten history behind them. All of their life they have taken what they wanted but failed to understand that what they take also takes from them. They come to realise this only years later when, contaminated by their deeds, they see they're so far beyond redemption that there's nothing they can do but plead forgiveness from me, their proxy priest.

Sometimes the lunches go on for ages. I book out four hours as a maximum and when time's up, that's it – unless of course I like them or what they're telling me is so juicy I don't want it to end. Sometimes, as they confess, they start to laugh, because there's so much of it. They realise how shameless they've been – they're embarrassed by how much they have to be embarrassed about. They laugh about the most godforsaken deeds as if they've told me their favourite anecdote. I nail them, Scottie – I get them to acknowledge what they've done, so they feel like they've actually confessed. Amazing . . . People lose count. They know they're doing wrong but they see the act in isolation. They don't think about how shit builds up, how bad deeds make a bad person. At times I know they confess simply so they can make room for more misdeeds. They're polluted in their cells. They don't want salvation – they make their peace with God by shooting at the sky. They are blasphemers, heretics, apostates. Yet now and then, they still need to unburden themselves of the weight of their evil.

And then there are the others, the dark light to the beauty of angels such as your good self. They look like humans, sound like humans, feel like humans – but they're not humans. They're the devil's businesspeople. They're not responsible for all of the evil on earth; mankind is perfectly capable of doing bad by itself. But their work could not have been this successful had they not had so many willing associates. Millions are dedicated to this cause to this day, interacting with humans while advancing the demonic agenda of their boss. But others have proved to be rather more independent: they've seen what they can possess for themselves, how rich they can become if they do not work to a higher agenda, how much fun they can have satisfying their own cravings. Many have forsaken their demonic paymaster to go into business for their own gain and have done well indeed. They have settled down, raised families with humans, creating generations of people descended from the demonic source. I met many such demons and their descendants in the highest echelons of society, and in my confessions. There are plenty in the lower reaches too: you met many in your decade-long pursuit. So we are the same, like always. Only this is the point where my story gets a little more complicated.

A few years into my practice as a confessor, I receive a call from someone I know by reputation as a businessman – a thug, but a very successful thug indeed. By this stage, my terms are settled: hearing some of these confessions takes too much of a toll not to charge these guys a hell of a lot. (You saw how dispirited I could be after one of my ugly lunches. I always agreed the fee in advance and they always ponied up the money before I heard their confession; like all providers of professional services, I wanted funds on account.) It doesn't have to be money – this guy offers me a piece of market-sensitive information about a deal he's involved with. A super deal, Scottie, one that's so tempting I can't resist. He's gonna tell me how to invest five million dollars to make twenty-five million in a year. I know his reputation, that he's good for it. This is one of those rare chances to make all the money with none of the effort. So he comes and we go to lunch.

Scottie, let me tell you this: I think I've heard it all, but five minutes in, I can't take any more of it. I realise I'm listening to the confession of the modern-day Marquis de Sade. Tales of the most disgusting perversion, and on and on he *goes, it just keeps on getting worse. I realise this guy is a monster, right out here in the world, getting away with it. And he's chosen to unburden himself to me. After twenty minutes I can't listen to him any more. It's filthy, sordid – it makes* all *of my hair turn white. I stop him, say it's the end of the confession. He's furious, tells me that he's only just getting started and has so much more to say, so much more that he has to get rid of and I'm the only person who can do it. But I know I'll be dead from shock if I listen to him any longer. So no, I insist, that's the end, the confession is over whether he likes it or not. Well, he does* not *like it, not one bit. He's boiling with temper, and he's not going anywhere. So I get up and leave. I even pay the bill on my way out, that's how keen I am to get away. Frankly, I'm glad to see the back of him.*

But here lies my *confession, Scottie, the source of the dispute – and the reason for all of this secrecy. As far as I'm concerned, I've heard enough of his horror stories to warrant using the information he's given me; this fucker's got twenty hideous minutes out of me, though it was more like four hours' worth. He's unloaded on me plenty, to the tune of a full confession. So I go ahead and make the investment with the information he gave me. It turns out to be even better than he said it would be. I put in all I have at the time – fifteen million. A year later, I have more than a hundred million. Astonishing – it sets me up for good. But, well . . . this guy, he's not so happy about it, he doesn't quite share my view. The way he sees it, I've only listened to a tiny part of his confession so I'm not entitled to use the information he's given me. He says I've made a fortune off of his back without keeping my side of the bargain, so I'm in breach of our agreement. He says that money is no compensation for such a grievance – he's too rich already. So he tells me he's going to take what's most important to me, and in such fashion shall his claim be settled.*

Well, I know from hearing this bastard confess that there's only one thing that can mean. It's a threat against my family. I don't even have a family at the time, which makes it even worse. He's telling me I'll never *have a family, and if I try, he'll make sure I fail. He has form. I know: he's told me in his confession. So I have no choice but to take him seriously.*

Roth paused in his reading. He sat there, trying to picture what on earth this appalling monster could look like, what terrible misdeeds he must have confessed and what he may still have had yet to divulge. After a moment of unhappy contemplation, he realised that he couldn't even begin to visualise it, so he read on through to the end of the note.

I have no choice but to believe he means what he says. And I realise this most salient fact from the start: he is a demon, a kind of evil I cannot fight. So I have to take matters into my own hands, be as cautious as a man can be. Which brings me to your good self. All of the treasure waiting for you at the end of this search is yours and yours alone. I want you to take it and vanish to a place where no such hideous fiend can find you. You'll be surprised by some of the things I have placed in my chest, but you must protect all I have left you. Scottie: I am trusting you on this point: not one piece of treasure can you leave. I know you'll do the right thing: you can't help yourself.

'One last point. No doubt you're wondering how to avoid this wretched individual who has brought such tension into my life. His name is Larry Hector, his company is Marshland, based in Milan. So now you know the identity of my nemesis, you can stay the hell away from him. He is pure toxic waste.

Chapter 33

Not even the broadest search terms could flush out an address for Marshland in Milan on the Internet – Hector clearly didn't want to be found. Roth could go to the city and work his way through lists of banks again, but there was a much faster way.

'Scott!' said Hayden MacDermott. 'How the hell are you?'

'I couldn't even begin to explain.'

'I'm used to that.'

'I need you to find me an address for a company the Internet doesn't know exists.'

'Simple!'

He waited. He couldn't concentrate on anything else. He thought about coffee, whisky, food, but had an appetite only for the address.

Ten minutes later, his phone rang. It was Hayden, who said, 'Got it! I'll text it to you. And Scott, next time – please make it a little harder than that.'

* * *

It was the late afternoon of his longest, hardest day. He was in Milan, riding in a taxi from the airport to Marshland's offices. No luggage. He'd simply left the Hotel Salon, hailed a cab to Heathrow and taken the first available flight as if he were catching a bus. He didn't notice take-off, turbulence – he didn't even notice the landing. All he could think of was getting to the offices of Marshland before the end of the working day and standing face to face with Larry Hector. When the ping pinged and the cabin light went off, he leapt out of his seat and rushed from the plane.

The taxi pulled up outside of Marshland's offices in central Milan at 4.20pm. He had a sense of its corruption from the determined nature of its cleanliness on a street called La Via Dante. He paid the driver with euros from an airport cashpoint. He gasped when he saw the building next door.

Banco di Venucci.

In the depths of Storm 1, feeling grim, he'd recalled Berenson walking towards him with a smile on his face and this very bank in the background. But in that recollection, he'd not taken into account the *angle* of Berenson's march. As he stood before the two buildings, he realised that Berenson had been walking towards him not from *Banco di Venucci*, but from the Marshland building next door – about which he'd had no recollection whatsoever. He couldn't even remember coming to Milan with Berenson in the first place. But he also knew far more than Dieter had wanted him to, thanks to the message on the exploding iPod. The control his old boss had exerted over this process was slipping away, as was bound to happen when you tried to steer a ship from beyond the grave. He shivered at the sight of the bank, a shiver at the sight of the stone not yet overturned, and now it was too late. A design, yes. A quest for hidden treasure . . . or had he been misled all this time, sent only to transact a piece of unfinished business between two men who functioned at the highest level? *It didn't matter.* Regardless of the thoughts rushing through his head, Ruby and Julie were missing, and he had no other leads. The warmth of the sun was fading. He walked into Marshland's offices.

The lobby was a gloomy, barren room: high ceilings, a cold decor, almost medieval. Roth felt it close in around him as he stepped towards the only person present: a receptionist hunched over the desk in front of him. Little sound came from anywhere else in the building, a large office on a weekday afternoon silenced by the compression of time within its walls.

There was a flicker of attention from the receptionist, who looked up at Roth with dark eyes. '*Signor*?'

'I'm here to see Larry Hector,' he replied.

The man glowered with disdain. 'Who?'

'You know who.'

The receptionist shook his head a little, mumbled under his breath and looked back down at his desk.

Roth loudly cleared his throat.

The receptionist looked up.

Roth was now leaning against the desk with the USB stick in his hand and his fingers on the button, plain to see. 'I'm gonna melt you, my friend, if you don't tell Mr Hector I'm here.'

The receptionist reached beneath the desk. Roth leapt back, held the USB high. The receptionist froze, his eyes staring at the stick.

'Why don't we try that again?' Roth said. 'I asked—'

He was cut off by the sound of an elevator opening. Roth turned in its direction. A large figure emerged from it, walking towards him, soaking up the horror on Roth's face.

Everett Mulcahy.

The big American came towards him as if he were on his way to collect an Academy Award. Roth turned to the receptionist, who glared back at him with an expression that said yes, he *did* know who Larry Hector was and, yes, he *had* pressed the button to call him as soon as he'd seen Roth walk in: this was no team of amateurs.

Mulcahy put an arm round Roth's shoulder, revelling in the glory of a sporting victory as he moved in close in the oppressive lobby. 'Scottie, so good to see you!!Why don't we go for a little drive?'

Roth looked at him, terrified.

'C'mon,' Mulcahy said. 'We're only gonna take you to the airport.'

'I just got here,' he replied.

'Then I hope you enjoyed your brief stay in Milan.'

Roth tried to hold firm. 'I want to see Hector,' he said.

Mulcahy replied, 'He's not here.'

'When will he be back?'

'Why don't we take that drive?'

'I'm not getting in a car with you.'

'You don't understand, buddy. You're already in it.'

The lobby was empty apart from the big American, the receptionist and Roth. There was no one else to prove he'd ever set foot in here, so no one to notice if he vanished. Mulcahy was right: it didn't matter if Roth stood in the lobby or sat in the back of the car. There was no way he could prevent what was about to happen – it was already too late to get away, and he hadn't even noticed. He looked at the receptionist, who glowered back with superior satisfaction. Yes, Roth truly was an amateur. Mulcahy pushed him towards the door. Roth felt too weary to resist any longer.

He walked onto the Via Dante, fear crawling all over him. A sleek, discreet limo awaited them, which hadn't been there when Roth had arrived. Mulcahy opened the back door, pushed him in and climbed in after him.

It was just the two of them inside. Mulcahy tapped the separating window. The driver glanced over his shoulder, his expression blank. He saw his passengers, then returned to the wheel, moved them off at a swift pace.

'So we're going to the airport?' Roth said.

'Yup.'

'Where are we really going?'

'Stop trembling, Scottie, you have nothing to fear. I am *personally* going to put you on the plane back to London. From there, with Berenson's billions, you can go anywhere in the world. Really, you should be paying us.' The big American turned and looked out of the window at the streets passing by outside. 'This city is so beautiful . . . I don't know why it gets such a bad press. As for *The Last Supper* ...'

'Where are you taking me?' Roth asked.

'I told you: the airport.'

'And then what happens?'

'And then you'll do what you were supposed to do this morning: walk away.'

'Dieter Berenson didn't want me to do that.'

'Dieter Berenson is dead.'

Roth's terror was such that he could barely feel his legs. Mulcahy seemed as relaxed as if he were watching a ball game, but to Roth the glare of the situation seemed to rise from the road.

'You're not going to take me to the airport, are you?' Roth asked.

'You've had a hard day,' Mulcahy replied. 'You're feeling strung out. It's understandable.'

'You're going to kill me, aren't you.'

'Why would I want to do that?'

'You've wanted to get rid of me from the beginning.'

'Don't take it so personally, Scottie - it really has nothing to do with you.'

'You're going to kill me because you're the kind of people who kill people.'

'Now that's not a very nice thing to say.'

'You killed Mia.'

'You're not Mia.'

'She—'

'Forget about her, Scottie.'

'Everett, what have you done with them?'

'Walk away.'

'Where are they?'

'Get on that plane and fly the hell out of this business.'

'Tell me, Everett.'

'It's no concern of yours.'

'I can't walk away.'

'Yes you can. It'll be easy. You have no idea how easy it will be.'

'I can't walk away. Hector knows that, and so do you.'

Mulcahy gave a heartfelt sigh as if to recognise that, after all of his efforts, Roth still wouldn't let it go.

'So where are we really heading to?' he asked again. 'Would you truly let me get on a plane and fly away with all of that money?'

'Scott, did you ever think that you could?'

'Never. That's why Dieter chose me.'

There was a long pause. A sigh. 'You're not going to get her.'

'I have to see Hector. We have to talk.'

'No fucking way are you getting in to see Larry Hector.'

Roth looked out of the window. They were no longer following the route to the airport. 'So it *is* my turn now?'

'All you have to do is say the word, Scottie, and you can be back in London tonight and living like a billionaire tomorrow. It would be my fucking pleasure to end this horrible day on a good note.'

'And that would be a good note?'

'*Yes!* Dieter did you the worst turn of your life getting you involved with this business. I want you out of here – yes I do! It's old shit between Larry and Berenson. You're too good for it. Take the money, go make the world a better place and stay the fuck away from Hector and the girl.'

'Where is she?'

Mulcahy did not reply.

'Where's Ruby?'

Again, no response.

The drone of the limo was drilling through his brain. 'Are you going to cut off my head too?'

'Not unless you make us.'

'Is that what you said to Mia?'

'Mia had nothing to do with me.'

Roth wasn't convinced. He could easily imagine Mulcahy recruiting her into his gang, bending her to do whatever it took to seduce Roth and dropping her like a shot when she'd failed in her allotted task.

Milan thinned out. They were heading towards an *autostrade* that, according to the massive sign, was going nowhere near the airport.

'Everett,' Roth said. 'If you get me in to see Hector, I'll give you ten million pounds.'

He heard Mulcahy gasp. He tried hard not to look at him, wanted the American to stew. He could feel that seductive gaze turn upon him, but Roth did not gaze back. Gradually, Mulcahy turned to face forward again. Roth was sure he could feel from that side of the limo a sense of conflict. For the first time, he'd lost his cocky air, the certainty that came from never having to make a hard decision.

Roth said, 'You know I'm good for it.'

They continued in silence. So he'd found Mulcahy's weak spot after all: the same as pretty much everyone else's. Yes, and Roth had a trick or two up his own sleeve, such as noticing how Mulcahy's clothes spoke of a man well paid but far from rich, in a field of graft that kept him a long way from retirement. Perhaps there was a chance of a big kill at some point, but when you're dealing with the likes of Larry Hector, you know they keep all of the riches for themselves and deny everyone else, despite being fabulously wealthy already. Under the offer of enough money to free himself from work for the rest of his life, Mulcahy seemed about to explode – for reasons not remotely connected to the USB stick.

'All right then,' Roth said. 'I'll throw in a couple of Picassos.'

The big American *spun* towards him now, at the prospect of *so much fucking money* that he could spend the rest of his life as the playboy everyone had always thought he should be.

'I can wire you the cash first thing in the morning,' Roth said, 'You'll have to trust me on the rest. Twenty million or so in total. How old are you, Everett? Thirty-five? Forty?'

'Thirty-seven.'

'How much longer can you carry on doing this kind of work?'

The big American did not reply.

Roth persisted: 'With this kind of money you could stop working tomorrow. You'd love that, right?'

'Do you know how angry he'd be with me?'

'That's why it's twenty million.'

'Hector is a dangerous man —'

'That's why it's twenty million.'

Mulcahy shifted uncomfortably. Did not reply.

Roth continued. 'He won't hurt you. He can't. You're *gifted*, Everett, one of the beautiful people. No harm will come to you in this world. Trust me. After all, *I'm an angel*.'

Mulcahy looked at him with an empty, frozen glaze. Roth almost felt sorry for him and yet . . . how satisfying it was.

After what felt like years, Mulcahy leant forward and switched on the mic. He said, 'Take us back to the office.'

The driver looked at him in the mirror with surprise. Greatly annoyed, Mulcahy nodded repeatedly. A moment later, Roth felt the limo start to turn. They were heading back to Milan.

'Give me your phone,' Mulcahy said.

Roth unlocked it, handed it over. The big American opened the notepad, typed in his account number and sort code, gave the phone back with aggressive irritation. 'You know what you just did?' he said.

'Yeah,' Roth replied. 'I think I do. How – bad would it have been?'

'The only way to kill an angel is to cut off its head.'

Roth fell silent.

'There are times when I hate this fucking business,' the American said. 'I should have gone to Hollywood like everyone said.'

'Was . . . Mia an angel?'

'Are you fucking kidding me?'

'How did you get her involved?'

Mulcahy looked at Roth as if he were going crazy. '*Involved*? She was never involved with us.'

'What?'

'She just sat down next to you on the train and started talking. She blew into the picture like a leaf.'

'I don't . . .'

'Yeah, we had someone on the Eurostar that day; we'd been trailing you from the moment you arrived at Berenson's lawyer's. The day he died we put a guy there to see who turned up looking like . . . well, frankly as bad as you. But he was watching you from three rows away. You didn't even notice our guy on the train because you were so besotted with Mia.'

Intense pain started shooting through Roth's brain. The worst day of his life was getting even worse. 'You mean you – you didn't tell Mia to sit down by me?'

'No.'

'Or start talking to me?'

'No.'

'Or . . . flirt with me?'

'Kiddo, she did that all by herself. She must have thought you were something.'

'Mia wasn't a part of your team?'

'Christ, Scottie, what have you been smoking?'

'She had nothing to do with this?'

'Nothing at all.'

'So . . . so . . . so why did you cut off her fucking head?'

Mulcahy looked at him, cast in a deep shadow. 'To show you that we would.'

They drove on in silence.

A coincidence. No more, no less. A set of circumstances that ran alongside each other but were never connected – except in his mind.

The break-in at the Hotel Foucault had nothing to do with her.

She really *had* been kicked out by Becky, who really *had* had to leave the apartment fast, in a foul mood, and jobless.

She really *had* been contacting him since then because she really *did* need his help.

She really *had* sat down to talk with him on the Eurostar because she really *did* like him.

She really *had* told him she loved him because she *did* love him.

And now she was dead.

To show him that they would.

They were back in Milan; the sun had excused itself for the day.

Mulcahy said to Roth, 'So, there'll be ten million pounds in my account first thing in the morning?'

Roth nodded, listless.

'And two Picassos? Worth ten million? When do I get those?'

'Within the next couple of weeks. They're in the vaults in Geneva.'

Mulcahy sighed a deep breath, took out his phone and pressed a couple of buttons. When the line connected, he said: 'Larry? It's Everett. Listen, I'm with Roth . . . We were on our way to the airport but he said a couple of things that made me think you should ... talk to him before we—' He paused. 'I know. I wouldn't recommend it if I didn't think it worthwhile. Talk to him for five minutes and—' Another pause, then a stricken expression. 'Yes, Larry – but he said Berenson had told him something dynamite that he wants you to know.' Mulcahy looked at Roth to make sure he'd registered the fine print of the lie. Roth nodded to show that he'd taken it in. They both awaited the conclusion of the thought process at the other end of the line. A look of relief finally passed across Mulcahy's face. 'Good! We'll drop him off in a few minutes. When you're done, I'll take him to the airport. Okay? Bye.'

Mulcahy switched off the phone and looked at Roth. 'Hector will see you,' he said. 'We're going back to his office, you'll have five minutes. He wants me to wait with the driver and, when you're done, we really will take you to the airport this time. Understand?'

Roth nodded.

'Ten million in my account by tomorrow morning, Scott, okay? Ten million tomorrow and two Picassos within a week. Or else I'll track you down and cut your fucking head off myself.'

Chapter 34

Darkness now. Roth and Mulcahy waited in the reception. It was almost ten o'clock at night. Both could feel the weight of their weariness, a day spent struggling against the forces of the world. The receptionist remained a hostile presence in the company of those supposed to have long gone away.

They heard the front door open. Their eyes ran to it. Three suits came into the reception: a corpulent man in his fifties and his two outrider flunkeys.

Mulcahy said, 'Larry.'

The corpulent man turned at the calling of his name.

Roth's eyes zoomed in. So *this* was the fiend, the devil from whom Berenson had been trying to protect Ruby all these years by burying her beneath a mountain. *This* was the man his old boss had referred to as a demon, and not with a flourish but a sense of reportage, having mixed with them often enough to know. But Hector looked so *human* – how on earth could he be anything but? A fat, disgusting, ugly, greedy leech, yes, a grotesque pervert, but a card-carrying member of the species Homo sapiens all the same. He was scowling, clean-shaven, his eyes turning glassy. His expression was one of deep dissatisfaction, as if he was stuck in this world for the duration and he knew nothing would ever truly please him. His skin was pallid in the artificial light, sweaty from a day that had drained him, but in which he still had work to do. Bleak, sour-faced, sharp-eyed, a narrow glance, his focus settled on Roth. At which point his expression emptied.

The two men looked at each other across the fragile horizon of the events that had brought them to this point. Roth tried hard to maintain his cool, but proximity to Hector was causing his fury to boil. The corpulent man barked at the two flunkeys, who departed with gloomy expressions. He then cast Mulcahy an empty look and headed towards an elevator, which opened as if obeying an invisible command from the boss. He stepped inside.

Mulcahy coughed. Roth looked at him. The movie star nodded that he should follow Hector in.

'I'll be waiting outside,' Mulcahy said.

Roth walked into the lift as the doors were closing, and turned round in time to see just how pale Mulcahy had become.

They journeyed upwards in silence, an unhealthy distaste brewing. This man who'd sent goons chasing him across the globe; who'd sought revenge against Berenson; who may have been responsible for the death of Ruby's mother; whose minions undoubtedly *had* murdered Mia; who may have been liable for the death of Berenson himself; the *demon* who had stolen Ruby and Julie from him.

Over the lift's noise, he could hear Hector wheezing. No . . . The idea that he could be anything but human was utterly implausible.

* * *

His eyes were drawn to the panoramic view as they walked into the top floor, the penthouse, the command HQ. From the window of Hector's office, Milan appeared washed of light and colour. Hector headed towards a coffee machine and started brewing a pot. Roth looked at him: no, it was the man who was tired, not the suit, which had probably cost more than most people earned in months. A tie was discarded in a crumple on the desk. Roth looked at Hector's shoes: polished this morning but dusty now. His eyes cast their way up the man as he continued to make the coffee. Roth decided he was glossy from the fat of the land, incapable of doing anything but abusing others. His mind boggled as he tried to imagine what Hector had told Berenson in those appalling twenty minutes, and what other deviancies he never got to confess. Suddenly it was all too conceivable that Hector *was* a demon. Roth wondered how he must appear to him, after the day *he'd* had. But then Hector knew all about his day.

The corpulent man walked towards him, holding two cups of coffee. He hadn't asked Roth if he'd wanted any, or how he liked it. He simply handed him the cup. The scent was strong, the liquid hot. No milk, cream or sugar: straight black. Hector looked at him with aggressive impassivity. It was impossible to know what was going on behind those sour eyes.

'You got my message,' Hector said.

'You mean the iPod?' Roth replied.

The corpulent man downed his coffee in one go. 'It's late,' he said. 'Everett thought you had something I should hear, so say it and go.'

Roth couldn't help but glare at the man. 'I came to listen to the rest of your confession.'

Hector stared at Roth for a long moment. He held the empty coffee cup loose in his hand, didn't take his eyes off of the visitor. 'I see someone's been telling tales,' he said eventually. 'But I wonder if you got the whole story or just the parts that flatter your old boss, as big a liar as any man I ever met.'

Roth held firm, though he was scared to death. 'I'm offering you a chance to let Berenson clear what you perceive to be his debt—'

'"*What I perceive to be . . .*"' Hector exclaimed, an acid, charmless grin. '"What I perceive to be his debt!" Yes, Dieter really has told you some *whoppers*.'

'You never got to finish your confession. Now's your chance. I don't have anything else to do. We can take all night if need be.'

'Why don't you get to the point, Mr Roth. You're here to do two things: find the girl and kill me.'

'If you believe that, why did you let me in?'

'Because I have nothing to fear from you. Dieter was a vindictive man. Sending an angel to kill me in the event of his own death? Ironic *and* vindictive – yes, *very* Dieter. And to keep *you* in the dark, to tell you enough to bring you this far but not so much that you could decide for yourself whether or not to go all the way . . . If I were you, Mr Roth, I'd feel hard done by, however much money your former employer has stuffed down your throat. But he made two mistakes. First, angels don't murder humans. And second, Dieter must have known there was something in your past to show that you were at least *capable* of killing—'

Roth found it impossible not to let the briefest of reactions cross his face. Hector picked up on the flicker.

The corpulent man nodded, satisfied that he was right. 'But he's miscalculated.'

Roth pretended to ignore him. 'Where's the girl?'

'I have no intention of spending a second longer with you, as you clearly have nothing to say that I would want to hear. I will call you a car and you can go.'

'What about—'

What about Mulcahy, he was going to say. *Mulcahy, who was waiting for him downstairs, as he'd arranged with you, Mr Hector, not ten minutes ago.*

But then Roth stopped, for he knew from that one comment of Hector's that Mulcahy would not be waiting downstairs to take him to the airport. That Mulcahy was already paying the price for his extremely recent disloyalty.

'I am not what you think I am,' Hector said. 'I am not what Berenson told you. But I have worked among demons for so long that I no longer fear the extremities of their behaviour – or my own.' His gaze rose to meet Roth's eyes. 'But I am curious about one thing. What *did* Dieter tell you about my confession?'

Roth glared at him for a long moment. 'He said it was the worst he ever heard. That it was so bad, he had to stop after twenty minutes.'

Hector's eyes narrowed, as if he were thinking about a past insult. His cold gaze focused again on Roth. 'You find it hard to accept what you are, because you're so used to thinking you're one of us. It's the same with them. With the demons. They lose track. I am sure Dieter heard many confessions from dark angels who had no idea that that's what they were. However much of a shock it must have been when they found out – when he told them – I'm sure they were also relieved: at last they understood why they felt and behaved as they did. There's much work to be done in this world by the dark angels, Mr Roth; the devil trained them well. I wouldn't expect you to agree – but what it means for people such as I, who have no qualms about dealing with them, is that we can get very rich indeed. They are prepared to do anything, Mr Roth, as am I. They crush the good and pulverise the weak in the pursuit of the dollar, and for some there is a higher agenda, but for others, it's all about themselves. Ever wondered how the CEO can sleep at night having made twenty thousand people jobless that day? Do you know what social cost that causes? Dieter had no qualms about dealing with them. None at all. He took whatever they were offering and heard the worst of their confessions. You know what I'm talking about, Mr Roth. You've already had dealings with some of our nefarious partners, the people who go puff! If you like, you can take out your little USB stick and prove I'm not one of them.'

'I don't need to bother,' Roth replied. 'I know what you are.'

'Yes. I'm a man who's been repaid on a long-standing debt, no more, no less. Your precious former boss made his billions the same way I did: by trading with demons. Which is why he prized the company of angels. For who does the confessor have to confess to? And believe me, Dieter had much to confess.'

'Did you murder him?'

'He died from a heart attack.'

'Did you have him killed?'

'By natural causes . . . ?'

'It's a simple question, and if you're not afraid of me—'

'That's right,' said Hector. 'Not one bit.'

'All right then,' Roth said, his voice flickering with anger. 'I'll ask you again, and this time I want the truth. Did you kill Dieter Berenson?'

'No. I. Did. Not. Nor did I have anyone do it for me. There are many others who I'm sure are only too happy that Dieter is dead. The man had much to trouble his conscience and make his heart seize up in the small hours of the night without anyone putting acid in his tea.'

'I came here to make a deal,' Roth said. 'If you let me have the child, I'll hear the rest of your confession. I'll clear Dieter's debt.'

'What makes you think I need to confess?'

'The same thing that made you do it the first time.'

'And what was that?'

'Vanity.'

Hector snorted. 'You think *you* could hear *my* confession? You think *you* could last longer than Dieter? You think *you* could last that long? Your angel ears couldn't cope. Twenty minutes, and *he* could take no more. But that didn't stop him from making his fortune off my back. Do you think Berenson would have been a hotshot without the financial boost he got from me? *Not on your life.* And now he's screwed you like he screwed me. Thanks to good old Dieter, you're standing in front of the one human demons fear. He sent you to kill me, knowing that you could not. You're not going to clear his debt by listening to my confession, by promising me redemption or by giving me a full performance of *Apocalypse Now*. Our business is done, Mr Roth. It's time for you to go.'

Hector walked to his desk, picked up the phone. 'Hello?' he barked. 'Yes. I want you to send a car, to be here in five minutes. For a Mr Scott Roth.'

He put the phone down, looked up in time to see a fire extinguisher swing towards him. It hit him full in the face. His head spun, the crack of his neck loud and clear. His body dropped to the floor. He lived a few seconds more: just enough to look into the eyes of the man who'd killed him.

The angel.

Chapter 35

Roth stared at Hector until he was sure the venal man was dead. The last flicker of life, the shock on his face that this angel *had* smashed him hard enough with a fire extinguisher to force the life from his body. And now Roth was alone, the only living being in the billionaire's penthouse, a room in which no doubt many incidents had occurred that would have formed part of the confession he was ready to hear, had Hector taken him up on the offer.

The telephone rang. Roth jumped out of his skin. He saw on the screen that the call was coming from reception. He was about to pick it up but then paused. He put the fire extinguisher down, took a handkerchief from his pocket and used it to keep his fingerprints off the receiver as he answered with a cough, 'Yes?'

'Mr Roth's car is here,' the receptionist said.

He put the phone down, looked across Hector's desk, which was covered with all kinds of letters, papers, contracts. He couldn't see a clue as to where Ruby may be. His eyes settled back on the phone; he noticed the button that would bring up Hector's contacts. He pressed it and the massive list, alphabetised by name, opened. It took a few minutes to scrawl through to Mulcahy's mobile number, but finally he found it and made the call.

'Larry,' Mulcahy exclaimed, the moment he answered, terror in his voice, 'What the fuck's going on? Why are you doing this to me?'

'It's Roth. Where is she?'

'Scott? Jesus— What have you – Scottie, you . . . you have to help, they've thrown me into the back of a truck, they're going to take me somewhere out of the way and they're going to fucking kill me.'

'Where is she?'

'Let me talk to Hector.'

'Where is she?'

'Scottie, tell Larry to come to the phone—'

'Tell me where she is.'

'They're going to kill me!' Mulcahy wailed, his voice full of dread and self-pity. 'This is not how it's supposed to be.'

'EVERETT: TELL ME WHERE SHE IS.'

There was a long, anxiety-inducing silence. Finally Mulcahy spoke, sounding zombified by the turn of events that had befallen him in the last thirty minutes. 'There's a . . . a town near Como. It's called Binago. Hector has – some property nearby, a street of houses in the middle of – of – nowhere. He calls it "the storage".'

'The storage?' Roth said.

'Scottie,' Mulcahy sounded weak. 'I can't die. I'm too . . . *special*.'

'Listen Everett, get the fuck out of that truck, okay? Do whatever it takes and then come to London. The twenty million will still be yours. You know where to find me. *Good luck*.'

He put the phone down before Mulcahy could say any more. He rubbed the fire extinguisher clean of prints with his handkerchief; the coffee cup too. As for the rest of his DNA, well, maybe angels didn't have any, so maybe they wouldn't find out that it was he who'd beaten Larry Hector to death. He paused to look down at the hideous man, this mixer with demons, this fetid barrel of shite. Suddenly he wanted the world to know that he *had* been the one to vanquish this repulsive creature. After all, if experience had taught him anything, it was that he only had to claim self-defence to get away with a killing.

The elevator travelled fast. He stepped out quickly when it reached the ground floor and walked through the lobby with his head down. He strode past the receptionist, still crouched over his books, without being noticed.

Outside, the car Hector had ordered was waiting for him. He tapped on the window; the driver looked his way.

'*Signor* Roth?'

He nodded. The door unlocked, he got in.

'The storage,' Roth said.

The driver looked at him with surprise.

'Get a fucking move on,' Roth barked.

The driver put the car into motion. They left La Via Dante behind.

Hurtling along the *autostrade*, he shivered at the notion of the human race having passed into coexistence with angels and demons; that these guardians and wrongdoers had settled on earth, forgotten their roots, engaged and traded with humans as if they *were* humans. Became friends with humans. Became *lovers* of humans. Had kids with humans? Failed along with humans? Found themselves in dosshouses with humans?

Yes, Dieter and Hector had been correct. These demons were not so unfamiliar to the angel, who had exhausted himself trying to help *people, people, people.* How many of those into whom he'd poured his heart and soul during his lost decade were demons living up to their nature, squandering the good of the cosmos, including his unquestioning help? Scott Roth, smashing his head against devils in dives across London; a joke, yes, and one he told at his own expense, over and over again for ten long years . . .

The car turned off the *autostrade*. The tone of the road altered, the drone louder, gravelly. Como sank away as they scavenged along a narrower, smaller route. Roth stared at the surroundings, at the gradual returning to the primitive. The car meandered along a dusty road. Civilisation fell ever more behind. The signs said Binago was 300 metres ahead.

The last stretch: a dirt track. Wherever they were going offered little pretension. A profound darkness, sinister, unending. Dust rose around them.

Roth could feel the car slow. There was a small offshoot of road, barely noticeable. The driver looked at him in the rearview mirror. The distant city lights swung to the right as they turned in a new direction.

Soon they came to a tiny village, composed of no more than a row of houses spread along a single road. Flat, low, hard constructs, possibly hundreds of years old, their bricks compressed by time, weathered by many summers of sunshine, and many frosty winters too. An array of vehicles parked one after the other along the road, impressive for a one-goat village, an outpost lagging several hundred years behind civilisation. Pretty, picturesque – and invisible to the rest of the world.

The car drew to a halt outside of the first house. One storey high, it seemed to have no rear, just a stern, squat facade, not so much built as carved from rock. Impregnable. *Storage indeed.*

'Ecco, Signor,' said the driver.

'Wait for me,' Roth commanded.

He got out of the car. Now the night was his enemy, the town surrounded by nothingness, the void of the depth of darkness. Behind the row of houses the world no longer existed, the isolation disturbing; he felt sick at the nature of this squalid little place: a village unlived in for years, used – for what purpose?

He heard revving. The car he'd arrived in swung around and hurtled off the way they'd come.

'Wait!' yelled Roth, although he knew there was no point.

A silence befell him, the one-street town deserted but for him. He walked over to the first parked car, saw the keys were in the ignition.

The front door of the first house opened. Roth turned to see a man with a gun slung over his shoulder staring back at him, aggressive in a faintly stupid way. He called out in Italian. Roth looked at him blankly. The man spoke again, this time in heavily accented English. 'Who are you?'

'Hector sent me,' Roth replied.

'For what?'

'To move the girl.'

The man stared at him.

Gripped the gun a little tighter.

Glared at Roth with ageing eyes.

'You are early,' he said.

Roth walked towards the rustic house, his heart pounding.

He passed through the heavy front door into a small, unfurnished room. A villager once used this space to live, no doubt with his goats and chickens as well as his table and chairs. Two more goons stood around inside, younger than the grizzled guy who'd met Roth at the door. All three had loaded guns and empty expressions. They were tired, cramped, irritated it was late, and they were still at work. One, barely out of his teens, looked like he hadn't washed in weeks.

Roth noticed a hallway at the back of the room. He could see two doors leading off it, to rooms at the rear of the property. No sound or movement came from either; they had no visible markings. To his right, he saw a table with a long knife.

'You have something for me?' the older man said.

Roth looked at him, a little disorientated.

'You have . . . note?' he repeated.

Roth noticed that one of the younger goons had a bunch of keys attached to a clip on his belt. 'Yes,' he said, 'I have the authorisation.'

The grizzled older guy gestured that he should give it to him.

Roth reached into his pocket, but there was nothing in there that he could pass off as such. 'Where did I . . . ?' he mumbled. 'Ah, here it is.' He pulled the USB stick out and held it high for them all to see, to fear. 'Open the doors,' he barked, pointing to the rooms at the back of the property.

The men all raised their guns.

Roth pressed the button on the USB stick.

Nothing happened.

He leapt for the keys on the younger goon's belt.

The guns all erupted at once.

The heat of the scorched air, the scraping of hot nails across his body, the splintering of stone walls, the febrile screaming of his killers. A mist haze rising from the smoke of the barrels. The gunfire going on for what seemed like years.

And then it stopped.

The air cooled. Roth looked up. The three guards were a few feet away. Smoke wheezed from their rifles and disbelief from their faces. They had layered eighty rounds into him in the space of twenty seconds, yet he stood untouched. The two younger guys were filled with terror at the sight of a man who should be dead, drew signs of the cross upon themselves. They couldn't believe the report of their eyes.

Roth realised that he had the bunch of keys in his hand – he'd grabbed them from the younger goon in the melee.

A flicker in the older man's eyes; he dashed towards the table.

Roth yanked a gun from one of the younger men, and screamed as loudly as he could, *'STOP!'*

Another second and the grizzled older man would have had the knife – and that would have been the end of *this* angel, for he knew what they were dealing with even if his younger associates did not. On another occasion he may have risked that leap, certain the angel would not kill him. But as the grizzled old guy turned to Roth, pale and with no knife in hand, he knew that if he'd taken that last leap, *this* angel would have shot the shit out of him.

The younger men bolted, their voices clattering in fear. In an instant they were gone. It was just the two of them.

The grizzled older man stared at Roth.

And then he too lowered his gaze, took a breath and walked from the room, following his accomplices out of the small, dense house.

Roth stood with the gun trained on an empty space. He let out a loud gasp of relief, then turned and rushed into the small, humid hallway and the two doors he'd noticed when he came into the house. He could hear the sound of the cars outside driving away.

He turned to the door on the left and tried several of the keys. At last, one fit. He twisted it. Heard the lock inside click.

He was about to turn the handle, when he felt the cold, hard gaze of Dieter Berenson glowering down at him from high above.

Was I right about you, Scottie, after all? Was I right to entrust you with the only treasure that has ever meant anything to me?

He gripped the handle, turned it.

The door swung open.

* * *

Her eyes were red and moist and wide as her gaze fell upon him. Ruby burst into tears at the sight of him.

He ran to her, enclosed her in a massive hug, his own eyes filling with water. 'I'm so sorry, I'm so sorry,' he exclaimed. 'Are you okay?'

'Yes,' came her muffled response. 'But what about Julie?'

'You don't know?'

Ruby shook her head. 'I haven't seen her since we got taken from the hotel.'

He stepped back. Away from her.

Ruby didn't like the look in his eyes. 'What is it?'

'I'm just . . .' He was almost back at the door.

'Where are you going?' she said, starting to panic.

He ran out into the hall. As he pulled the door to a close behind him, he heard the child scream *'Scott!'*

Her voice was silenced by its slam.

He rushed to the door to the right, had no idea what he was going to find. This place, this storage of the dead as well as the living.

He fumbled; his hands were trembling too much, his mouth dry, his bones heavy. Julie's face kept flashing through his mind: *she is dead, she is dead, she is dead*. None of the keys worked. His fingers kept scrambling; Julie in his reverie, looking at him, making him smile.

She is owed to me.

She is dead.

A key fit. He turned it, heard the lock click.

He put his forehead against the door, utterly exhausted, unable to take this last step, this last risk with his sanity.

He took a deep breath, turned the handle.

The door opened before him

* * *

Julie began to weep when she saw him. She was traumatised and dishevelled but she was alive, unbeaten, unharmed.

Roth walked towards her with dull, heavy legs.

When he was close enough, he put his arms round her trembling body and squeezed her tight. She clung on to him, emotion, strain, relief gushing out. They cried together for a long time.

* * *

Roth ran along the street, trying cars until he found one unlocked and with the keys in the ignition. He opened the back door, Ruby climbed in, slumped on the seat and was asleep as soon as he closed it. Roth and Julie got into the front. He set the car running, hit the accelerator hard. Within a few moments they'd left this hateful place behind. The satnav would guide them back to Milan.

The grimy roads were hard to negotiate; they kept their eyes peeled for any of Roth's departed gunmen friends. But the guards were nowhere to be seen, had freaked and fled. The night echoed; they were alone in an uninhabited world. He couldn't stop looking at Julie, at Ruby in the back, to make sure they were still really there and that he wasn't having another one of his 'episodes'. Julie gazed back at him. Her exhaustion offered no resistance to her feelings any longer; they were seared together by this unworldly experience. Both, he thought, must have aged a decade in this one day. She put her hand on his thigh, and then she too fell asleep.

They reached the *autostrade*. He kept a steady check on his mirrors, but it was clear they were not being followed – for now, at least. In Milan they'd rest for the night, travel back to London in the morning. After that, who knew? He set the car to cruise and sat back.

They were returning from the face of the eternal furnace; from the storage, the container of threatened life, the transit point to where? He shuddered at the thought of what would have become of them if Hector had had his way, if Roth had arrived tomorrow and Ruby and Julie had been moved on to whatever destiny the corpulent man had in store for them. He reflected upon the second human life he'd taken – the feel of the fire extinguisher smashing into his enemy's face; the sound of his neck twisting so far it broke. *And he didn't feel the slightest bit bad.* This was no repeat of the teen – this was angelic justice, and the least he could do for Mia. As for Mulcahy, he felt no anger towards the big American, strangely. He'd wait to see if he emerged and claimed his twenty million, which Roth would give him gladly, although Mulcahy may by then be rather diminished, in confidence, physically – probably both.

And finally, he thought of the man himself, of the puppetmaster, of good old Dieter Berenson. He had the right to be furious about this whole experience, of being driven this way and that, of having the responsibility of second-guessing the dead. And, of course, of the immense danger he'd been placed in from the moment he'd set foot in the lawyer's office. And yet, he found himself longing for Dieter to be in the car with them, telling him the truth, or another kind of story. He wanted the old charlatan – for that brickbat *was* true – raising his eyebrows and giving a little shrug, emanating his unassailable calm. And then Roth realised that he was smiling at the thought of his old boss, listening to the sins of demons as they mixed with the righteous and good; of the mocking glance Berenson would throw when detecting a falsehood; and of the sheer warmth of the man, whose depth of feeling for those he loved could never be doubted. This genius who'd left him billions of dollars and the daughter he was sure only he in this world was capable of looking after. Of the tease who'd sent him back and forth across the world on a chase without clues. And of the confessor who'd confessed it all to him, even if he'd had to die first in order to do it.

They walked into the lobby of Milan's finest hotel, Roth's arm round Julie, the child asleep in the Frenchwoman's embrace.

The concierge welcomed these late-arriving guests, who looked as if they'd just emerged from the harsh desert. '*Buona notte,*' he said. 'A family room?'

A look of surprise passed across Scott Roth's face. And then he gave a little nod. 'Yes,' he said. 'A family room.'

Printed in Great Britain
by Amazon